THE THIRD GHOST STORY
MEGAPACK®

THE THIRD GHOST STORY MEGAPACK®

Edited by John Gregory Betancourt

WILDSIDE PRESS

NOTE

Language has not been updated for "political correctness" and some stories may contain language which some might find offensive. Please note that languages change and evolve, and what was acceptable in the time of original publication may prove offensive to some today.

CONTENTS

A NOTE FROM THE PUBLISHER

Over the last two years, our MEGAPACK® series of ebook anthologies has proved to be one of our most popular endeavors. (Maybe it helps that we sometimes offer them as free premiums to our email list!) One question we keep getting asked is, "Who's the editor?"

The MEGAPACK®s (except where specifically credited) are a group effort. Everyone at Wildside works on them. This includes John Betancourt, Carla Coupe, Steve Coupe, Sam Cooper, Bonner Menking, Colin Azariah-Kribbs, A.E. Warren, and many of Wildside's authors…who often suggest stories to include (and not just their own!).

RECOMMEND A FAVORITE STORY?

Do you know a great classic science fiction story, or have a favorite author whom you believe is perfect for the MEGAPACK® series? We'd love your suggestions! You can contact the publisher at wildsidepress@yahoo.com.

Note: *we only consider stories that have already been professionally published.* This is not a market for new works.

—John Betancourt
Publisher, Wildside Press LLC
wildsidepress.com | bcmystery.com

THE DEAD AND THE COUNTESS,
by Gertrude Atherton

It was an old cemetery, and they had been long dead. Those who died nowadays were put in the new burying-place on the hill, close to the Bois d'Amour and within sound of the bells that called the living to mass. But the little church where the mass was celebrated stood faithfully beside the older dead; a new church, indeed, had not been built in that forgotten corner of Finisterre for centuries, not since the calvary on its pile of stones had been raised in the tiny square, surrounded then, as now, perhaps, by gray naked cottages; not since the castle with its round tower, down on the river, had been erected for the Counts of Croisac. But the stone walls enclosing that ancient cemetery had been kept in good repair, and there were no weeds within, nor toppling headstones. It looked cold and gray and desolate, like all the cemeteries of Brittany, but it was made hideous neither by tawdry gew-gaws nor the license of time.

And sometimes it was close to a picture of early beauty. When the village celebrated its yearly *pardon*, a great procession came out of the church—priests in glittering robes, young men in their gala costume of black and silver, holding flashing standards aloft, and many maidens in flapping white head-dress and collar, black frocks and aprons flaunting with ribbons and lace. They marched, chanting, down the road beside the wall of the cemetery, where lay the generations that in their day had held the banners and chanted the service of the *pardon*. For the dead were peasants and priests—the Croisacs had their burying-place in a hollow of the hills behind the castle—old men and women who had wept and died for the fishermen that had gone to the *grande pêche* and returned no more, and now and again a child, slept there. Those who walked past the dead at the *pardon*, or after the marriage ceremony, or took part in any one of the minor religious festivals with which the Catholic village enlivens its existence—all, young and old, looked grave and sad. For the women from childhood know that their lot is to wait and dread and weep, and the men that the ocean is treacherous and cruel, but that bread can be wrung from no other master.

Therefore the living have little sympathy for the dead who have laid down their crushing burden; and the dead under their stones slumber contentedly enough. There is no envy among them for the young who wander at evening and pledge their troth in the Bois d'Amour, only pity for the groups of women who wash their linen in the creek that flows to the river. They look like pictures in the green quiet book of nature, these women, in their glistening white head-gear and deep collars; but the dead know better than to envy them, and the women—and the lovers—know better than to pity the dead.

The dead lay at rest in their boxes and thanked God they were quiet and had found everlasting peace.

And one day even this, for which they had patiently endured life, was taken from them.

The village was picturesque and there was none quite like it, even in Finisterre. Artists discovered it and made it famous. After the artists followed the tourists, and the old creaking *diligence* became an absurdity. Brittany was the fashion for three months of the year, and wherever there is fashion there is at least one railway. The one built to satisfy the thousands who wished to visit the wild, sad beauties of the west of France was laid along the road beside the little cemetery of this tale.

It takes a long while to awaken the dead. These heard neither the voluble working-men nor even the first snort of the engine. And, of course, they neither heard nor knew of the pleadings of the old priest that the line should be laid elsewhere. One night he came out into the old cemetery and sat on a grave and wept. For he loved his dead and felt it to be a tragic pity that the greed of money, and the fever of travel, and the petty ambitions of men whose place was in the great cities where such ambitions were born, should shatter forever the holy calm of those who had suffered so much on earth. He had known many of them in life, for he was very old; and although he believed, like all good Catholics, in heaven and purgatory and hell, yet he always saw his friends as he had buried them, peacefully asleep in their coffins, the souls lying with folded hands like the bodies that held them, patiently awaiting the final call. He would never have told you, this good old priest, that he believed heaven to be a great echoing palace in which God and the archangels dwelt alone waiting for that great day when the elected dead should rise and enter the Presence together, for he was a simple old man who had read and thought little; but he had a zigzag of fancy in his humble mind, and he saw his friends and his ancestors' friends as I have related to you, soul and body in the deep undreaming sleep of death, but sleep, not a rotted body deserted by its affrighted mate; and to all who sleep there comes, sooner or later, the time of awakening.

He knew that they had slept through the wild storms that rage on the coast of Finisterre, when ships are flung on the rocks and trees crash down in the Bois d'Amour. He knew that the soft, slow chantings of the *pardon* never struck a chord in those frozen memories, meagre and monotonous as their store had been; nor the bagpipes down in the open village hall—a mere roof on poles—when the bride and her friends danced for three days without a smile on their sad brown faces.

All this the dead had known in life and it could not disturb nor interest them now. But that hideous intruder from modern civilization, a train of cars with a screeching engine, that would shake the earth which held them and rend the peaceful air with such discordant sounds that neither dead nor living could sleep! His life had been one long unbroken sacrifice, and he sought in vain to imagine one greater, which he would cheerfully assume could this disaster be spared his dead.

But the railway was built, and the first night the train went screaming by, shaking the earth and rattling the windows of the church, he went out and out and sprinkled every grave with holy water.

And thereafter twice a day, at dawn and at night, as the train tore a tunnel in the quiet air, like the plebian upstart it was, he sprinkled every grave, rising sometimes from a bed of pain, at other times defying wind and rain and hail. And for a while he believed that his holy device had deepened the sleep of his dead, locked them beyond the power of man to awake. But one night he heard them muttering.

It was late. There were but a few stars on a black sky. Not a breath of wind came over the lonely plains beyond, or from the sea. There would be no wrecks to-night , and all the world seemed at peace. The lights were out in the village. One burned in the tower of Croisac, where the young wife of the count lay ill. The priest had been with her when the train thundered by, and she had whispered to him:

"Would that I were on it! Oh, this lonely lonely land! this cold echoing château, with no one to speak to day after day! If it kills me, *mon père*, make him lay me in the cemetery by the road, that twice a day I may hear the train go by— the train that goes to Paris! If they put me down there over the hill, I will shriek in my coffin every night."

The priest had ministered as best he could to the ailing soul of the young no-blewoman, with whose like he seldom dealt, and hastened back to his dead. He mused, as he toiled along the dark road with rheumatic legs, on the fact that the woman should have the same fancy as himself.

"If she is really sincere, poor young thing," he thought aloud, "I will forbear to sprinkle holy-water on her grave. For those who suffer while alive should have all they desire after death, and I am afraid the count neglects her. But I pray God that my dead have not heard that monster to-night." And he tucked his gown under his arm and hurriedly told his rosary.

But when he went about among the graves with the holy-water he heard the dead muttering.

"Jean-Marie," said a voice, fumbling among its unused tones for forgotten notes, "art thou ready? Surely that is the last call."

"Nay, nay," rumnbled another voice, "that is not the sound of a trumpet, François. That will be sudden and loud and sharp, like the great blasts of the north when they come plunging over the sea from out the awful gorges of Ice-land. Dost thou remember them, François? Thank the good God they spared us to die in our beds with our grandchildren about us and only the little wind sigh-ing in the Bois d'Amour. Ah, the poor comrades that died in their manhood, that went to the *grande pêche* once too often! Dost thou remember when the great wave curled round Ignace like his poor wife's arms, and we saw him no more? We clasped each other's hands, for we believed that we should follow, but we lived and went again and again to the *grande pêche,* and died in our beds. *Grâce à Dieu!*"

"Why dost thou think of that now—here in the grave where it matters not, even to the living?"

"I know not; but it was of that night when Ignace went down that I thought as the living breath went out of me. Of what didst thou think as thou layest dying?"

"Of the money I owed to Dominique and could not pay. I sought to ask my son to pay it, but death had come suddenly and I could not speak. God knows how they treat my name to-day in the village of St. Hilaire."

"Thou art forgotten," murmured another voice. I died forty years after thee and men remember not so long in Finisterre. But thy son was my friend and I re-member that he paid the money."

"And my son, what of him? Is he, too, here?"

"Nay; he lies deep in the northern sea. It was his second voyage, and he had returned with a purse for the young wife, the first time. But he returned no more, and she washed in the river for the dames of Croisac, and by-and-by she died. I would have married her but she said it was enough to lose one husband. I married another, and she grew ten years in every three that I went to the *grande pêche*. Alas for Brittany, she has no youth!"

"And thou? Wert thou an old man when thou camest here?"

"Sixty. My wife came first, like many wives. She lies here. Jeanne!"

"Is't thy voice, my husband? Not the Lord Jesus Christ's? What miracle is this? I thought that terrible sound was the trumpet of doom."

"It could not be, old Jeanne, for we are still in our graves. When the trump sounds we shall have wings and robes of light, and fly straight up to heaven. Hast thou slept well?"

"Ay! But why are we awakened? Is it time for purgatory? Or have we been there?"

"The good God knows. I remember nothing. Art frightened? Would that I could hold thy hand, as when thou didst slip from life into that long sleep thou didst fear, yet welcome."

"I am frightened, my husband. But it is sweet to hear thy voice, hoarse and hollow as it is from the mould of the grave. Thank the good God thou didst bury me with the rosary in my hands," and she began telling the beads rapidly.

"If God is good," cried François, harshly, and his voice came plainly to the priest's ears, as if the lid of the coffin had rotted, "why are we awakened before our time? What foul fiend was it that thundered and screamed through the frozen avenues of my brain? Has God, perchance, been vanquished and does the Evil One reign in His stead?"

"Tut, tut! Thou blasphemest! God reigns, now and always. It is but a punishment He has laid upon us for the sins of earth."

"Truly, we were punished enough before we descended to the peace of this narrow house. Ah, but it is dark and cold! Shall we lie like this for an eternity, perhaps? On earth we longed for death, but feared the grave. I would that I were alive again, poor and old and alone and in pain. It were better than this. Curse the foul fiend that woke us!"

"Curse not, my son," said a soft voice, and the priest stood up and uncovered and crossed himself, for it was the voice of his aged predecessor. "I cannot tell thee what this is that has rudely shaken us in our graves and freed our spirits of their blessed thraldom, and I like not the consciousness of this narrow house, this load of earth on my tired heart. But it is right, it must be right, or it would not be at all—ah, me!"

For a baby cried softly, hopelessly, and from a grave beyond came a mother's anguished attempt to still it.

"Ah, the good God!" she cried. "I, too, thought it was the great call, and that in a moment I should rise and find my child and go to my Ignace, my Ignace whose bones lie white on the floor of the sea. Will he find them, my father, when the dead shall rise again? To lie here and doubt!—that were worse than life."

"Yes, yes," said the priest; "all will be well, my daughter."

"But all is not well, my father, for my baby cries and is alone in a little box in the ground. If I could claw my way to her with my hands—but my old mother lies between us."

"Tell your beads!" commanded the priest, sternly—" tell your beads, all of you. All ye that have not your beads, say the 'Hail Mary!' one hundred times."

Immediately a rapid, monotonous muttering arose from every lonely chamber of that desecrated ground. All obeyed but the baby, who still moaned with the hopeless grief of deserted children. The living priest knew that they would talk no more that night, and went into the church to pray till dawn. He was sick with horror and terror, but not for himself. When the sky was pink and the air full of the sweet scents of morning, and a piercing scream tore a rent in the early silences, he hastened out and sprinkled his graves with a double allowance of holy-water. The train rattled by with two short derisive shrieks, and before the earth had ceased to tremble the priest laid his ear to the ground. Alas, they were still awake!

"The fiend is on the wing again," said Jean-Marie; "but as he passed I felt as if the finger of God touched my brow. It can do us no harm."

"I, too, felt that heavenly caress!" exclaimed the old priest.

"And I!" "And I!" "And I!" came from every grave but the baby's.

The priest of earth, deeply thankful that his simple device had comforted them, went rapidly down the road to the castle. He forgot that he had not broken his fast nor slept. The count was one of the directors of the railroad, and to him he would make a final appeal.

It was early, but no one slept at Croisac. The young countess was dead. A great bishop had arrived in the night and administered extreme unction. The priest hopefully asked if he might venture into the presence of the bishop. After a long wait in the kitchen, he was told that he could speak with *Monsieur l' Évêque*. He followed the servant up the wide spiral stair of the tower, and from its twenty-eighth step entered a room hung with purple cloth stamped with golden fleurs-de-lis. The bishop lay six feet above the floor on one of the splendid carved cabinet beds that are built against the walls in Brittany. Heavy curtains shaded his cold white face. The priest, who was small and bowed, felt immeasurably below that august presence, and sought for words.

"What is it, my son?" asked the bishop, in his cold weary voice. "Is the matter so pressing? I am very tired."

Brokenly, nervously, the priest told his story, and as he strove to convey the tragedy of the tormented dead he not only felt the poverty of his expression—for was little used to narrative— but the torturing thought assailed him that what he said sounded wild and unnatural, real as it was to him. But he was not prepared for its effect on the bishop. He was standing in the middle of the room, whose gloom was softened and gilded by the waxen lights of a huge candelabra; his eyes, which had wandered unseeingly from one massive piece of carved furniture to another, suddenly lit on the bed, and he stopped abruptly, his tongue rolling out. The bishop was sitting up, livid with wrath.

"And this was thy matter of life and death, thou prating madman!" he thundered. "For this string of foolish lies I am kept from my rest, as if I were another old lunatic like thyself! Thou art not fit to be a priest and have the care of souls. To-morrow—"

But the priest had fled, wringing his hands.

As he stumbled down the winding stair he ran straight into the arms of the count. Monsieur de Croisac had just closed a door behind him. He opened it, and, leading the priest into the room, pointed to his dead countess, who lay high

13

up against the wall, her hands clasped, unmindful for evermore of the six feet of carved cupids and lilies that upheld her. On high pedestals at head and foot of her magnificent couch the pale flames rose from tarnished golden candlesticks. The blue hangings of the room, with their white fleurs-de-lis, were faded, like the rugs on the old dim floor; for the splendor of the Croisacs had departed with the Bourbons. The count lived in the old château because he must; but he reflected bitterly to-night that if he had made the mistake of bringing a young girl to it, there were several things he might have done to save her from despair and death.

"Pray for her," he said to the priest. "And you will bury her in the old cemetery. It was her last request."

He went out, and the priest sank on his knees and mumbled his prayers for the dead. But his eyes wandered to the high narrow windows through which the countess had stared for hours and days, stared at the fishermen sailing north for the *grande pêche*, followed along the shore of the river by wives and mothers, until their boats were caught in the great waves of the ocean beyond; often at naught more animate than the dark flood, the wooded banks, the ruins, the rain driving like needles through the water. The priest had eaten nothing since his meagre breakfast at twelve the day before, and his imagination was active. He wondered if the soul up there rejoiced in the death of the beautiful restless body, the passionate brooding mind. He could not see her face from where he knelt, only the waxen hands clasping a crucifix. He wondered if the face were peaceful in death, or peevish and angry as when he had seen it last. If the great change had smoothed and sealed it, then perhaps the soul would sink deep under the dark waters, grateful for oblivion, and that cursed train could not awaken it for years to come. Curiosity succeeded wonder. He cut his prayers short, got to his weary swollen feet and pushed a chair to the bed. He mounted it andhis face was close to the dead woman's. Alas! it was not peaceful. It was stamped with the tragedy of a bitter renunciation. After all, she had been young, and at the last had died unwillingly. There was still a fierce tenseness about the nostrils, and her upper lip was curled as if her last word had been an imprecation. But she was very beautiful, despite the emaciation of her features. Her black hair nearly covered the bed, and her lashes looked too heavy for the sunken cheeks.

"*Pauvre petite!*" thought the priest. "No, she will not rest, nor would she wish to. I will not sprinkle holy-water on her grave. It is wondrous that monster can give comfort to any one, but if he can, so be it."

He went into the little oratory adjoining the bedroom and prayed more fervently. But when the watchers came an hour later they found him in a stupor, huddled at the foot of the altar.

* * * *

When he awoke he was in his own bed in his little house beside the church. But it was four days before they would let him rise to go about his duties, and by that time the countess was in her grave.

The old housekeeper left him to take care of himself. He waited eagerly for the night. It was raining thinly, a gray quiet rain that blurred the landscape and soaked the ground in the Bois d'Amour. It was wet about the graves, too; but the priest had given little heed to the elements in his long life of crucified self, and as he heard the remote echo of the evening train he hastened out with his holy-water and had sprinkled every grave but one when the train sped by.

Then he knelt and listened eagerly. It was five days since he had knelt there last. Perhaps they had sunk again to rest. In a moment he wrung his hands and raised them to heaven. All the earth beneath him was filled with lamentation. They wailed for mercy, for peace, for rest; they cursed the foul fiend who had shattered the locks of death; and among the voices of men and children the priest distinguished the quavering notes of his aged predecessor; not cursing, but praying with bitter entreaty. The baby was screaming with the accents of mortal terror and its mother was too frantic to care.

"Alas," cried the voice of Jean-Marie, "that they never told us what purgatory was like! What do the priests know? When we were threatened with punishment of our sins not a hint did we have of this. To sleep for a few hours, haunted with the moment of awakening! Then a cruel insult from the earth that is tired of us, and the orchestra of hell. Again! and again! and again! Oh God! How long? How long?"

The priest stumbled to his feet and ran over graves and paths to the mound above the countess. There he would hear a voice praising the monster of night and dawn, a note of content in this terrible chorus of despair which he believed would drive him mad. He vowed that on the morrow he would move his dead, if he had to unbury them with his own hands and carry them up the hill to graves of his own making.

For a moment he heard no sound. He knelt and laid his ear to the grave, then pressed it more closely and held his breath. A long rumbling moan reached it, then another and another. But there were no words.

"Is she moaning in sympathy with my poor friends?" he thought; "or have they terrified her? Why does she not speak to them? Perhaps they would forget their plight were she to tell them of the world they have left so long. But it was not their world. Perhaps that it is which distresses her, for she will be lonelier here than on earth. Ah!"

A sharp horrified cry pierced to his ears, then a gasping shriek, and another; all dying away in a dreadful smothered rumble.

The priest rose and wrung his hands, looking to the wet skies for inspiration.

"Alas!" he sobbed, "she is not content. She has made a terrible mistake. She would rest in the deep sweet peace of death, and that monster of iron and fire and the frantic dead about her are tormenting a soul so tormented in life. There may be rest for her in the vault behind the castle, but not here. I know, and I shall do my duty—now, at once."

He gathered his robes about him and ran as fast as his old legs and rheumatic feet would take him towards the château, whose lights gleamed through the rain. On the bank of the river he met a fisherman and begged to be taken by boat. The fisherman wondered, but picked the priest up in his strong arms, lowered him into the boat, and rowed swiftly towards the château. When they landed he made fast.

"I will wait for you in the kitchen, my father," he said; and the priest blessed him and hurried up to the castle.

Once more he entered through the door of the great kitchen, with its blue tiles, its glittering brass and bronze warming-pans which had comforted nobles and monarchs in the days of Croisac splendor. He sank into a chair beside the stove while a maid hastened to the count. She returned while the priest was still shivering, and announced that her master would see his holy visitor in the library.

It was a dreary room where the count sat waiting, for the priest, and it smelled of musty calf, for the books on the shelves were old. A few novels and newspapers lay on the heavy table, a fire burned on the andirons, but the paper on the wall was very dark and the fleurs-de-lis were tarnished and dull. The count, when at home, divided his time between this library and the water, when he could not chase the boar or the stag in the forests. But he often went to Paris, where he could afford the life of a bachelor in a wing of his great hotel; he had known too much of the extravagance of women to give hiswife the key of the faded salons. He had loved the beautiful girl when he married her, but her repinings and bitter discontent had alienated him, and during the past year he had held himself aloof from her in sullen resentment. Too late he understood, and dreamed passionately of atonement. She had been a high-spirited brilliant eager creature, and her unsatisfied mind had dwelt constantly on the world she had vividly enjoyed for one year. And he had given her so little in return!

He rose as the priest entered, and bowed low. The visit bored him, but the good old priest commanded his respect; moreover, he had performed many offices and rites in his family. He moved a chair towards his guest, but the old man shook his head and nervously twisted his hands together.

"Alas, *monsieur le comte*," he said, "it may be that you, too, will tell me that I am an old lunatic, as did *Monsieur l' Évêque*. Yet I must speak, even if you tell your servants to fling me out of the château."

The count had started slightly. He recalled certain acid comments of the bishop, followed by a statement that a young *curé* should be sent, gently to supersede the old priest, who was in his dotage. But he replied suavely:

"You know, my father, that no one in this castle will ever show you disrespect. Say what you wish; have no fear. But will you not sit down? I am very tired."

The priest took the chair and fixed his eyes appealingly on the count.

"It is this, monsieur." He spoke rapidly, lest his courage should go. "That terrible train, with its brute of iron and live coals and foul smoke and screeching throat, has awakened my dead. I guarded them with holy-water and they heard it not, until one night when I missed—I was with madam as the train shrieked by shaking the nail out of the coffins. I hurried back, but the mischief was done, the dead were awake, the dear sleep of eternity was shattered. They thought it was the last trump and wondered why they still were in their graves. But they talked together and it was not so bad at the first. But now they are frantic. They are in hell, and I have come to beseech you to see that they are moved far up on the hill. Ah, think, think, monsieur, what it is to have the last long sleep of the grave so rudely disturbed—the sleep for which we live and endure so patiently!"

He stopped abruptly and caught his breath. The count had listened without change of countenance, convinced that he was facing a madman. But the farce wearied him, and involuntarily his hand had moved towards a bell on the table.

"Ah, monsieur, not yet! not yet!" panted the priest. "It is of the countess I came to speak. I had forgotten. She told me she wished to lie there and listen to the train go by to Paris, so I sprinkled no holy-water on her grave. But she, too, is wretched and horror-stricken, monsieur. She moans and screams. Her coffin is new and strong, and I cannot hear her words, but I have heard those frightful sounds from her grave to-night, monsieur; I swear it on the cross. Ah, monsieur, thou dost believe me at last!"

For the count, as white as the woman had been in her coffin, and shaking from head to foot, had staggered from his chair and was staring at the priest as if he saw the ghost of his countess. "You heard—?" he gasped.

"She is not at peace, monsieur. She moans and shrieks in a terrible, smothered way, as if a hand were on her mouth—"

But he had uttered the last of his words. The count had suddenly recovered himself and dashed from the room. The priest passed his hand across his forehead and sank slowly to the floor.

"He will see that I spoke the truth," he thought, as he fell asleep, "and to-morrow he will intercede for my poor friends."

* * * *

The priest lies high on the hill where no train will ever disturb him, and his old comrades of the violated cemetery are close about him. For the Count and Countess of Croisac, who adore his memory, hastened to give him in death what he most had desired in the last of his life. And with them all things are well, for a man, too, may be born again, and without descending into the grave.

THE CEDAR CLOSET,
by Lafcadio Hearn

It happened ten years ago, and it stands out, and ever will stand out, in my memory like some dark, awful barrier dividing the happy, gleeful years of girl-hood, with their foolish, petulant sorrows and eager, innocent joys, and the bright, lovely life which has been mine since. In looking back, that time seems to me shadowed by a dark and terrible brooding cloud, bearing in its lurid gloom what, but for love and patience the tenderest and most untiring, might have been the bolt of death, or, worse a thousand times, of madness. As it was, for months after "life crept on a broken wing," if not "through cells of madness," yet verily "through haunts of horror and fear." O, the weary, weary days and months when I longed piteously for rest! when sunshine was torture, and every shadow filled with horror unspeakable; when my soul's craving was for death; to be allowed to creep away from the terror which lurked in the softest murmur of the summer breeze, the flicker of the shadow of the tiniest leaf on the sunny grass, in every corner and curtain-fold in my dear old home. But love conquered all, and I can tell my story now, with awe and wonder, it is true, but quietly and calmly.

Ten years ago I was living with my only brother in one of the quaint, ivy-grown, red-gabled rectories which are so picturesquely scattered over the fair breadth of England. We were orphans, Archibald and I; and I had been the busy, happy mistress of his pretty home for only one year after leaving school, when Robert Draye asked me to be his wife. Robert and Archie were old friends, and my new home, Draye's Court, was only separated from the parsonage by an old gray wall, a low iron-studded door in which admitted us from the sunny parson-age dawn to the old, old park which had belonged to the Drayes for centuries. Robert was lord of the manor; and it was he who had given Archie the living of Draye in the Wold.

It was the night before my wedding day, and our pretty home was crowded with the wedding guests. We were all gathered in the large old-fashioned draw-ing-room after dinner. When Robert left us late in the evening, I walked with him, as usual, to the little gate for what he called our last parting; we lingered awhile under the great walnut-tree, through the heavy, somber branches of which the September moon poured its soft pure light. With his last good-night kiss on my lips and my heart full of him and the love which warmed and glorified the whole world for me, I did not care to go back to share in the fun and frolic in the drawing-room, but went softly upstairs to my own room. I say "my own room," but I was to occupy it as a bedroom to-night for the first time. It was a pleasant south room, wainscoted in richly-carved cedar, which gave the atmosphere a spicy fragrance. I had chosen it as my morning room on my arrival in our home; here I had read and sang and painted, and spent long, sunny hours while Archibald was busy in his study after breakfast. I had had a bed arranged there as I preferred being alone to sharing my own larger bedroom with two of my bridesmaids. It looked bright and cozy as I came in; my favorite low chair was drawn before the fire, whose rosy light glanced and flickered on the glossy dark walls, which gave the room its name, "The Cedar Closet." My maid was busy preparing my toilet table, I sent her away, and sat down to wait for my brother, who I knew would come to bid me good-night. He came; we had our last fireside talk in my girlhood's home; and when he left me there was an incursion of all my bridesmaids for a "dressing-gown reception."

When at last I was alone I drew back the curtain and curled myself up on the low wide window-seat. The moon was at its brightest; the little church and quiet churchyard beyond the lawn looked fair and calm beneath its rays; the gleam of the white headstones here and there between the trees might have reminded me that life is not all peace and joy—that tears and pain, fear and parting, have their share in its story—but it did not. The tranquil happiness with which my heart was full overflowed in some soft tears which had no tinge of bitterness, and when at last I did lie down, peace, deep and perfect, still seemed to flow in on me with the moonbeams which filled the room, shimmering on the folds of my bridal dress, which was laid ready for the morning. I am thus minute in describing my last waking moments, that it may be understood that what followed was not creation of a morbid fancy.

I do not know how long I had been asleep, when I was suddenly, as it were, wrenched back to consciousness. The moon had set, the room was quite dark; I could just distinguish the glimmer of a clouded, starless sky through the open window. I could not see or hear anything unusual, but not the less was I conscious of an unwonted, a baleful presence near; an indescribable horror cramped the very beatings of my heart; with every instant the certainty grew that my room was shared by some evil being. I could not cry for help, though Archie's room was so close, and I knew that one call through the death-like stillness would bring him to me; all I could do was to gaze, gaze, gaze into the darkness. Suddenly—and a throb stung through every nerve—I heard distinctly from behind the wainscot against which the head of my bed was placed a low, hollow moan, followed on the instant by a cackling, malignant laugh from the other side of the room. If I had been one of the monumental figures in the little churchyard on which I had seen the quiet moonbeams shine a few hours before I could not have been more utterly unable to move or speak; every other faculty seemed to be lost in the one intent strain of eye and ear. There came at last the sound of a halting step, the tapping of a crutch upon the floor, then stillness, and slowly, gradually the room filled with light—a pale, cold, steady light. Everything around was exactly as I had last seen it in the mingled shine of the moon and fire, and though I heard at intervals the harsh laugh, the curtain at the foot of the bed hid from me whatever uttered it. Again, low but distinct, the piteous moan broke forth, followed by some words in a foreign tongue, and with the sound a figure started from behind the curtain—a dwarfed, deformed woman, dressed in a loose robe of black, sprinkled with golden stars, which gave forth a dull, fiery gleam, in the mysterious light; one lean, yellow hand clutched the curtain of my bed; it glittered with jeweled rings;—long black hair fell in heavy masses from a golden circlet over the stunted form. I saw it all clearly as I now see the pen which writes these words and the hand which guides it. The face was turned from me, bent aside, as if greedily drinking in those astonished moans; I noted even the streaks of gray in the long tresses, as I lay helpless in dumb, bewildered horror.

"Again!" she said hoarsely, as the sounds died away into indistinct murmurs, and advancing a step she tapped sharply with a crutch on the cedar wainscot; then again louder and more purposeful rose the wild beseeching voice; this time the words were English.

"Mercy, have mercy! not on me, but on my child, my little one; she never harmed you. She is dying—she is dying here in darkness; let me but see her face once more. Death is very near, nothing can save her now; but grant one ray of light, and I will pray that you may be forgiven, if forgiveness there be for such as you."

"What, you kneel at last! Kneel to Gerda, and kneel in vain. A ray of light; Not if you could pay for it in diamonds. You are mine! Shriek and call as you will, no other ears can hear. Die together. You are mine to torture as I will; mine, mine, mine!" and again an awful laugh rang through the room. At the instant she turned. O the face of malign horror that met my gaze! The green eyes flamed, and with something like the snarl of a savage beast she sprang toward me; that hideous face almost touched mine; the grasp of the skinny jeweled hand was all but on me; then—I suppose I fainted.

For weeks I lay in brain fever, in mental horror and weariness so intent, that even now I do not like to let my mind dwell on it. Even when the crisis was safely past I was slow to rally; my mind was utterly unstrung. I lived in a world of shadows. And so winter wore by, and brought us to the fair spring morning when at last I stood by Robert's side in the old church, a cold, passive, almost unwilling bride. I cared neither to refuse nor consent to anything that was suggested; so Robert and Archie decided for me, and I allowed them to do with me as they would, while I brooded silently and ceaselessly on the memory of that terrible night. To my husband I told all one morning in a sunny Bavarian valley, and my weak, frightened mind drew strength and peace from his; by degrees the haunting horror wore away, and when we came home for a happy reason nearly two years afterward, I was as strong and blithe as in my girlhood. I had learned to believe that it had all been, not the cause, but the commencement of my fever. I was to be undeceived.

Our little daughter had come to us in the time of roses; and now Christmas was with us, our first Christmas at home, and the house was full of guests. It was a delicious old-fashioned Yule; plenty of skating and outdoor fun, and no lack of brightness indoors. Toward New Year a heavy fall of snow set in which kept us all prisoners; but even then the days flew merrily, and somebody suggested tableaux for the evenings. Robert was elected manager; there was a debate and selection of subjects, and then came the puzzle of where, at such short notice, we could procure the dresses required. My husband advised a raid on some mysterious oaken chests which he knew had been for years stowed away in a turret-room. He remembered having, when a boy, seen the housekeeper inspecting them, and their contents had left a hazy impression of old stand-alone brocades, gold tissues, sacques, hoops, and hoods, the very mention of which put us in a state of wild excitement. Mrs. Moultrie was summoned, looked duly horrified at the desecration of what to her were relics most sacred; but seeing it was inevitable, she marshaled the way, a protest in every rustle and fold of her stiff silk dress.

"What a charming old place," was the exclamation with variations as we entered the long oak-joisted room, at the further end of which stood in goodly array the chests whose contents we coveted. Bristling with unspoken disapproval, poor Mrs. Moultrie unlocked one after another, and then asked permission to retire, leaving us unchecked to "cry havoc." In a moment the floor was covered with piles of silks and velvets.

"Meg," cried little Janet Crawford, dancing up to me, "isn't it a good thing to live in the age of tulle and summer silks? Fancy being imprisoned for life in a fortress like this!" holding up a thick crimson and gold brocade, whale-boned and buckramed at all points. It was thrown aside, and she half lost herself in another chest and was silent. Then—"Look, Major Fraudel This is the very thing for you—a true astrologer's robe, all black velvet and golden stars. If it were but long enough; it just fits me."

I turned and saw—the pretty slight figure, the innocent girlish face dressed in the robe of black and gold, identical in shape, pattern and material with what I too well remembered. With a wild cry I hid my face and cowered away.

"Take it off! O, Janet—Robert—take it from her!"

Every one turned wondering. In an instant my husband saw, and catching up the cause of my terror, flung it hastily into the chest again, and lowered the lid. Janet looked half offended, but the cloud passed in an instant when I kissed her, apologizing as well as I could. Rob laughed at us both, and voted an adjournment to a warmer room, where we could have the chests brought to us to ransack at leisure. Before going down, Janet and I went into a small anteroom to examine some old pictures which leaned against the wall.

"This is just the thing, Jennie, to frame the tableaux," I said, pointing to an immense frame, at least twelve feet square. "There is a picture in it," I added, pulling back the dusty folds of a heavy curtain which fell before it.

"That can be easily removed," said my husband, who had followed us.

With his assistance we drew the curtain quite away, and in the now fast waning light could just discern the figure of a girl in white against a dark background. Robert rang for a lamp, and when it came we turned with much curiosity to examine the painting, as to the subject of which we had been making odd merry guesses while we waited. The girl was young, almost childish—very lovely, but, oh, how sad! Great tears stood in the innocent eyes and on the round young cheeks, and her hands were clasped tenderly around the arms of a man who was bending toward her, and, did I dream?—no, there in hateful distinctness was the hideous woman of the Cedar Closet—the same in every distorted line, even to the starred dress and golden circlet. The swarthy hues of the dress and face had at first caused us to overlook her. The same wicked eyes seemed to glare into mine. After one wild bound my heart seemed to stop its beating, and I knew no more. When I recovered from a long, deep swoon, great lassitude and intense nervous excitement followed; my illness broke up the party, and for months I was an invalid. When again Robert's love and patience had won me back to my old health and happiness, he told me all the truth, so far as it had been preserved in old records of the family.

It was in the sixteenth century that the reigning lady of Draye Court was a weird, deformed woman, whose stunted body, hideous face, and a temper which taught her to hate and vilify everything good and beautiful for the contrast offered to herself, made her universally feared and disliked. One talent only she possessed; it was for music; but so wild and strange were the strains she drew from the many instruments of which she was mistress, that the gift only intensified the dread with which she was regarded. Her father had died before her birth; her mother did not survive it; near relatives she had none; she had lived her lonely, loveless life from youth to middle age. When a young girl came to the Court, no one knew more than that she was a poor relation. The dark woman seemed to look more kindly on this young cousin than on any one that had hitherto crossed her somber path, and indeed so great was the charm which Marian's goodness, beauty and innocent gayety exercised on every one that the servants ceased to marvel at her having gained the favor of their gloomy mistress. The girl seemed to feel a kind of wondering, pitying affection for the unhappy woman; she looked on her through an atmosphere created by her own sunny nature, and for a time all went well. When Marian had been at the Court for a year, a foreign musician appeared on the scene. He was a Spaniard, and had been engaged by Lady Draye to build for her an organ said to be of fabulous power and sweetness. Through long bright summer days he and his employer were shut up together in the music-room—he busy in the construction of the wonderful instrument, she aiding and watching his work. These days were spent by Marian in various ways—pleasant idleness and pleasant work, long canters on her chestnut pony, dreamy mornings by the brook with rod and line, or in the village near, where she found a welcome everywhere. She played with the children, nursed the babies, helped the mothers in a thousand pretty ways, gossiped with old people, brightening the day for everybody with whom she came in contact. Then in the evening she sat with Lady Draye and the Spaniard in the saloon talking in that soft foreign tongue which they generally used. But this was but the music between the acts; the terrible drama was coming. The motive was of course the same as that of every life drama which has been played out from the old, old days when the curtain rose upon the garden scene of Paradise. Philip and Marian loved each other, and having told their happy secret to each other, they, as in duty bound, took it to their patroness. They found her in the music room. Whether the glimpses she caught of a beautiful world from which she was shut out maddened her, or whether she, too, loved the foreigner, was never certainly known; but through the closed door passionate words were heard, and very soon Philip came out alone, and left the house without a farewell to any in it. When the servants did at last venture to enter, they found Marian lifeless on the floor, Lady Draye standing over her with crutch uplifted, and blood flowing from a wound in the girl's forehead. They carried her away and nursed her tenderly; their mistress locked the door as they left, and all night long remained alone in darkness. The music which came out without pause on the still night air was weird and wicked beyond any strains which had ever before flowed even from beneath her fingers; it ceased with morning light; and as the day wore on it was found that Marian had fled during the night, and that Philip's organ had sounded its last strain—Lady Draye had shattered and silenced it forever. She never seemed to notice Marian's absence and no one dared to mention her name. Nothing was ever known certainly of her fate; it was supposed that she had joined her lover.

Years passed, and with each Lady Draye's temper grew fiercer and more malevolent. She never quitted her room unless on the anniversary of that day and night, when the tapping of her crutch and high-heeled shoes was heard for hours as she walked up and down the music-room, which was never entered save for this yearly vigil. The tenth anniversary came round, and this time the vigil was not unshared. The servants distinctly heard the sound of a man's voice mingling in earnest conversation with her shrill tones; they listened long, and at last one of the boldest ventured to look in, himself unseen. He saw a worn, traveled-stained man; dusty, foot-sore, poorly dressed, he still at once recognized the handsome, gay Philip of ten years ago. He held in his arms a little sleeping girl; her long curls, so like poor Marian's, strayed over his shoulder. He seemed to be pleading in that strange musical tongue for the little one; for as he spoke he lifted, O, so tenderly, the cloak which partly concealed her, and showed the little face, which he doubtless thought might plead for itself. The woman, with a furious gesture, raised her crutch to strike the child; he stepped quickly backward, stooped to kiss the little girl, then, without a word, turned to go. Lady Draye called on him to return with an imperious gesture, spoke a few words, to which he seemed to listen gratefully, and together they left the house by the window which opened on the terrace. The servants followed them, and found she led the way to the parsonage, which was at the time unoccupied. It was said that he was in some political danger as well as in deep poverty, and that she had hidden him here until she could help him to a better asylum. It was certain that for many nights she went to the parsonage and returned before dawn, thinking herself unseen. But one morning she did not come home; her people consulted together; her relenting toward Philip had made them feel more kindly toward her than ever before; they sought her at the parsonage and found her lying across its threshold dead, a vial clasped in her rigid fingers. There was no sign of the late presence of Philip and his child; it was believed she had sped them on their way before she killed herself. They laid her in a suicide's grave. For more than fifty years after the parsonage was shut up. Though it had been again inhabited no one had ever been terrified by the specter I had seen; probably the Cedar Closet had never before been used as a bedroom.

Robert decided on having the wing containing the haunted room pulled down and rebuilt, and in doing so the truth of my story gained a horrible confirmation. When the wainscot of the Cedar Closet was removed a recess was discovered in the massive old wall, and in this lay moldering fragments of the skeletons of a man and child!

There could be but one conclusion drawn, the wicked woman had imprisoned them there under pretense of hiding and helping them; and once they were completely at her mercy, had come night after night with unimaginable cruelty to gloat over their agony, and, when that long anguish was ended, ended her odious life by a suicide's death. We could learn nothing of the mysterious painting. Philip was an artist, and it may have been his work. We had it destroyed, so that no record of the terrible story might remain. I have no more to add, save that but for those dark days left by Lady Draye as a legacy of fear and horror, I should never have known so well the treasure I hold in the tender, unwearying, faithful love of my husband—known the blessing that every sorrow carries in its heart, that

"Every cloud that spreads above
And veileth love, itself is love."

THE WRAITH OF BARNJUM,
by F. Anstey

I frankly admit, whatever may be the consequences of doing so, that I was not fond of Barnjum; in fact, I detested him. Everything that fellow said and did jarred upon me to an absolutely indescribable extent, although I did not discover for some time that he regarded me with a strange and unreasonable aversion.

We were so essentially unlike in almost every particular—I, with my innate refinement and high culture, my over-fastidious exclusiveness in the choice of associates; and he, a big, red, coarse brute, with neither sweetness nor light, who knew himself a Philistine, and seemed to like it—we were so unlike, that I often asked him, with a genuine desire for information, *what* had I in common with him?

And yet it will scarcely be believed, perhaps, that with such good reasons for keeping apart, we were continually seeking one another's company with a zest that knew no satiety. The only explanation I can offer for such a phenomenon is, that our mutual antipathy had become so much a part of ourselves, that we could not let it perish for lack of nourishment.

Perhaps we were not conscious of this at the time, and when we agreed to go on a walking tour together in North Wales, I think it was chiefly because we knew that we could devise no surer means of annoying one another; but, however that may be, in an ill-starred day for my own peace of mind, we started upon a journey from which but one of us was fated to return.

I pass by the painful experiences of the first few days of that unhappy tour. I will say nothing of Barnjum's grovelling animalism, of his consummate selfishness, his more than bucolic indifference to the charms of Nature, nor even of the mean and sordid way in which he contrived to let me in for railway tickets and hotel bills.

I wish to tell my melancholy story with perfect impartiality, and I am sure that I am not reduced to exciting any prejudice to secure the sympathies of all readers.

I shall pass, then, to the memorable day when my disgust, so long pent up, so imperfectly concealed, culminated in one grand outburst of a not ignoble indignation, to the hour when I summoned up moral courage to sever the bonds which linked us so unequally.

I remember it so well, that brilliant morning in June when we left the Temperance Hotel, Doldwyddlm, and scaled in sulky silence the craggy heights of Cader Idris, which, I presume, still overhang that picturesque village, while, as we ascended, an ever-changing and ever-improving panorama unrolled itself before my delighted eyes.

The air up there was keen and bracing, and I recollect that I could not repress an aesthetic shudder at the crude and primitive tone which Barnjum's nose had assumed under atmospheric influences. I mentioned this (for we still maintained the outward forms of friendship), when he retorted, with the brutal personality which formed so strong an ingredient of his character, that if I could only see myself in that suit of mine, and that hat (referring to the dress I was then wearing), I should feel the propriety of letting his nose alone. To which I replied, with a sarcasm that I feel now was a little too crushing, that I had every intention of doing so, as it was quite painful enough to merely contemplate such a spectacle; and he, evidently meaning to be offensive, remarked, that no one could help his nose getting red, but that any man in my position could at least *dress* like a gentleman I took no notice of this insult; a Bunting (I don't think I mentioned before that my name is Philibert Bunting)—a Bunting can afford to pass such insinuations by; indeed, I find it actually cheaper to do so, and I flattered myself that my dress was distinguished by a sort of studied looseness, that would appeal at once to a cultivated and artistic eye, though of course Barnjum's hard and shallow organs could not be expected to appreciate it.

I overlooked it, then, and presently we found ourselves skirting the edge of a huge chasm, whose steep sides sloped sheer down into the slate-blue waters of the lake below.

How can I hope to give an idea of the magnificent view which met our eyes as we stood there—a view of which, as far as I am aware, no description has ever yet been attempted?

To our right towered the Peaks of Dolgelly, with their saw-like outline cutting the blue sky with a faint grating sound, while the shreds of white cloud lay below in drifts. At our feet were the sun-lit waters of the lake, upon which danced a fleet of brown-sailed herring-boats; beyond was the plain of Capel Curig, and there, over on the left, sparkled the falls of Y-Dydd.

As I took all this in I felt a longing to say something worthy of the occasion. Being possessed of a considerable fund of carefully-dried and selected humour, I frequently amuse myself by a species of intellectual exercise, which consists in so framing a remark that a word or more therein may bear two entirely opposite constructions; and some of the quaint names of the vicinity seemed to me just then admirably adapted for this purpose.

I was about to gauge my dull-witted companion's capacity by some such test, when he forestalled me.

"You ought to live up here, Bunting," said he; "you were made for this identical old mountain."

I was not displeased, for, Londoner as I am, I have the nerve and steadiness of a practised mountaineer.

"Perhaps I was," I said good-humouredly; "but how did *you* find it out?"

"I'll tell you," he replied, with one of his odious grins. "This is Cader Idris, ain't it? well, and you're a *cad awry dressed*, ain't you? Cader Idrissed, see?" (he was dastard enough to explain) "That's how *I* get at it!"

He must have been laboriously leading up to that for the last ten minutes!

I solemnly declare that it was not the personal outrage that roused me; I simply felt that a paltry verbal quibble of that description, emitted amidst such scenery and at that altitude, required a protest in the name of indignant Nature, and I protested accordingly, although with an impetuosity which I afterwards regretted, and of which I cannot even now entirely approve.

He happened to be standing on the brink of an abyss, and had just turned his back upon me, as, with a vigorous thrust of my right foot, I launched him into the blue aether, with the chuckle at his unhallowed jest still hovering upon his lips.

I am aware that by such an act I took a liberty which, under ordinary circumstances, even the licence of a life-long friendship would scarcely have justified; but I thought it only due to myself to let him see plainly that I desired our acquaintanceship to cease from that instant, and Barnjum was the kind of man upon whom a more delicate hint would have been distinctly thrown away.

I watched his progress with some interest as he rebounded from point to point during his descent. I waited—punctiliously, perhaps, until the echoes he had aroused had died away on the breeze, and then, slowly and thoughtfully, I retraced my steps, and left a spot which was already becoming associated for me with memories the reverse of pleasurable.

* * * *

I took the next up-train, and before I reached town had succeeded in dismissing the incident from my mind, or if I thought of it at all, it was only to indulge relief at the reflection that I had shaken off Barnjum for ever.

But when I had paid my cab, and was taking out my latch-key, a curious thing happened—the driver called me back.

"Beg pardon, sir," he said hoarsely, "but I think you've bin and left something white in my cab!"

I turned and looked in: there, grinning at me from the interior of the hansom, over the folding-doors, was the wraith of Barnjum!

I had presence of mind enough to thank the man for his honesty, and go upstairs to my rooms with as little noise as possible. Barnjum's ghost, as I expected, followed me in, and sat down coolly before the fire, in my arm-chair, thus giving me an opportunity of subjecting the apparition to a thorough examination.

It was quite the conventional ghost, filmy, transparent, and, though wanting firmness in outline, a really passable likeness of Barnjum. Before I retired to rest I had thrown both my boots and the contents of my bookcase completely through the thing, without appearing to cause it more than a temporary inconvenience— which convinced me that it was indeed a being from another world.

Its choice of garments struck me even then as decidedly unusual. I am not narrow; I cheerfully allow that, assuming the necessity for apparitions at all, it is well that they should be clothed in robes of some kind; but Barnjum's ghost delighted in a combination of costume which set the fitness of things at defiance.

It wore that evening, for instance, to the best of my recollection, striped pantaloons, a surplice, and an immense cocked hat; but on subsequent occasions its changes of costume were so rapid and eccentric, that I ceased to pay much attention to them, and could only explain them on the supposition that somewhere in space there exists a supernatural store in the nature of a theatrical wardrobe, and that Barnjum's ghost had the run of it.

I had not been in very long before my landlady came up to see if I wanted anything, and of course as soon as she came in, she saw the wraith. At first she objected to it very strongly, declaring that she would not have such nasty things in *her* house, and if I wanted to keep ghosts, I had better go somewhere else; but I pacified her at last by representing that it would give her no extra trouble, and that I was only taking care of it for a friend.

26

When she had gone, however, I sat up till late, thinking calmly over my position, and the complications which might be expected to ensue from it.

It would be very easy to harrow the reader's feelings and work upon his sympathies here by a telling description of my terror and my guilty confusion at the unforeseen consequences of what I had done. But I think, in relating an experience of this kind, the straightforward way is always the best, and I do not care to heighten the effect by attributing to myself a variety of sensations which I do not remember to have actually felt at the time.

My first impression had not unnaturally been that the spectre was merely the product of overwrought nerves or indigestion, but it seemed improbable that a cabman should be plagued by a morbid activity of imagination, and that a landlady's digestion could be delicate sufficiently to evolve a thing so far removed from the merely commonplace; and, reluctantly enough, I was forced to the conclusion that it was a real ghost, and would probably continue to haunt me to the end of my days.

Of course I was disgusted by this exhibition of petty revenge and low malice on the part of Barnjum, which might be tolerated perhaps in a Christmas annual, with a full-page illustration, but which, in real life and the height of summer, was a glaring anachronism.

Still, it was of no use to repine then; I resolved to look at the thing in a common-sense light—I told myself that I had made my ghost, and would have to live with it. And after all, I had much to be thankful for: Barnjum in the spirit was a decided improvement upon Barnjum in the flesh; and as the spirit did not appear to be gifted with speech, it was unlikely to tell tales.

Luckily for me, too, Barnjum was absolutely unknown about town: his only relative was an aunt resident at Camberwell, and so there was no danger of any suspicion being excited by chance recognition in the circles to which I belonged.

It would have been folly to shut one's eyes to the fact that it might require considerable nerve to re-enter society closely attended by an obscure and fancifully-attired apparition.

Society would sneer considerably at first and make remarks, but I was full of tact and knowledge of the world, and I knew, too, that men have overcome far more formidable obstacles to social success than any against which I should be called upon to contend.

And so, instead of weakly giving way to unreasonable panic, I took the more manly course of determining to live it down, with what success I shall have presently to show.

When I went out after breakfast the next morning, Barnjum's ghost insisted upon coming too, and followed me, to my intense annoyance, all down St. James's Street; in fact, for many weeks it was almost constantly by my side, and rendered me the innocent victim of mingled curiosity and aversion.

I thought it best to affect to be unaware of the presence of anything of a ghostly nature, and when taxed with it, ascribed it to the diseased fancy of my interlocutor; but, by-and-by, as the whole town began to ring with the story, I found it impossible to pretend ignorance any longer.

So I gave out that it was an artfully-contrived piece of spectral mechanism, of which I was the inventor, and for which I contemplated taking out a patent; and this would have earned for me a high reputation in the scientific world if Messrs. Maskelyne and Cooke had not grown envious of my fame, declaring that they had long since anticipated the secret of my machine, and could manufacture one in every way superior to it, which they presently did.

Then I was obliged to confide (in the strictest secrecy) to two members of the Peerage (both persons of irreproachable breeding, with whom I was at that time exceedingly intimate) that it was indeed a *bonâ fide* apparition, and that I rather liked such things about me. I cannot explain how it happened, but in a very short time the story had gone the round of the clubs and drawing-rooms, and I found myself launched as a lion of the largest size—if it is strictly correct to speak of launching a lion.

I received invitations everywhere, on the tacit understanding that I was to bring my ghost, and the wraith of Barnjum, as some who read this may remember, was to be seen at all the best houses in town for the remainder of the season; while in the following autumn, I was asked down for the shooting by several wealthy *parvenus*, with a secret hope, unless I am greatly mistaken, that the ghost might conceive the idea of remaining with them permanently, thereby imparting to their brand-new palaces the necessary flavour of legend and mystery; but of course it never did.

To tell the truth, whatever novelty there was about it soon wore off—too soon, in fact, for, fickle as society is, I have no hesitation in asserting that we ought to have lasted it at least a second season, if only Barnjum's ghost had not persisted in making itself so ridiculously cheap that, in little more than a fortnight, society was as sick of it as I was myself.

And then the inconveniences which attached to my situation began to assert themselves more and more emphatically.

I began to stay at home sometimes in the evening, when I observed that the phantom had an unpleasant trick of illuminating itself at the approach of darkness with a bilious green light, which, as it was not nearly strong enough to enable me to dispense with a reading lamp, merely served to depress me.

And then it began to absent itself occasionally for days together, and though at first I was rather glad not to see so much of it, I grew uneasy at last. I was always fancying that the Psychical Society, who are credited with understanding the proper treatment of spectres in health and disease, from the tomb upwards, might have got hold of it and be teaching it to talk and compromise me. I heard afterwards that one of their most prominent members did happen to come across it, but, with a scepticism which I cannot but think was somewhat wanting in discernment, rejected it as a palpable imposition.

I had to leave the rooms where I had been so comfortable, for my landlady complained that the street was blocked up by a mob of the lowest description from seven till twelve every evening, and she really could not put up with it any longer.

On inquiry I found that this was owing to Barnjum's ghost getting out upon the roof almost every night after dark, and playing the fool among the chimney-pots, causing me, as its apparent owner, to be indicted five times for committing a common nuisance by obstructing the thoroughfare, and once for collecting an unlawful assembly: I spent all my spare cash in fines.

I believe there were portraits of us both in the "Illustrated Police News," but the distinction implied in this was more than outweighed by the fact that Barnjum's wraith was slowly but surely undermining both my fortune and my reputation.

It followed me one day to one of the underground railway stations, and *would* get into a compartment with me, which led to a lawsuit that made a nine days' sensation in the legal world. I need only mention the celebrated case of "The Metropolitan District Railway *v.* Bunting," in which the important principle was once for all laid down that a railway company by the terms of its contract is entitled to refuse to carry ghosts, spectres, or any other supernatural baggage, and can moreover exact a heavy penalty from passengers who infringe its bye-laws in this respect.

This was, of course, a decision against me, and carried heavy costs, which my private fortune was just sufficient to meet.

But Barnjum's ghost was bent upon alienating me from society also, for at one of the best dances of the season, at a house where I had with infinite pains just succeeded in establishing a precarious footing, that miserable phantom disgraced me for ever by executing a shadowy but decidedly objectionable species of *cancan* between the dances!

Feeling indirectly responsible for its behaviour, I apologised profusely to my hostess, but the affair found its way into the society journals, and she never either forgave or recognised me again.

Shortly after that, the committee of my club (one of the most exclusive in London) invited me to resign, intimating that, by introducing an acquaintance of questionable antecedents and disreputable exterior into the smoking-room, I had abused the privileges of membership.

I had been afraid of this when I saw it following me into the building, arrayed in Highland costume and a tall hat; but I was quite unable to drive it away.

Up to that time I had been at the bar, where I was doing pretty well, but now no respectable firm of solicitors would employ a man who had such an unprofessional thing as a phantom about his chambers. I threw up my practice, and had no sooner changed my last sovereign than I was summoned for keeping a ghost without a licence!

Some men, no doubt, would have given up there and then in despair—but I am made of sterner stuff, and, besides, an idea had already occurred to me of turning the table upon my shadowy persecutor.

Barnjum's ghost had ruined me: why should I not endeavour to turn an honest penny out of Barnjum's ghost? It was genuine—as I well knew; it was, in some respects, original; it was eminently calculated to delight the young and instruct the old; there was even a moral or two to be got out of it, and though it had long failed to attract in town, I saw no reason why it should not make a great hit in the provinces.

I borrowed the necessary funds and had soon made all preliminary arrangements for running the wraith of Barnjum on a short tour in the provinces, deciding to open at Tenby, in South Wales.

I took every precaution, travelling by night and keeping within doors all day, lest the shade (which was deplorably destitute of the commonest professional pride) should get about and exhibit itself beforehand for nothing; and so successful was I, that when it first burst upon a Welsh audience, from the platform of the Assembly Rooms, Tenby, no ghost could have wished for a more enthusiastic reception, and—for the first and last time—I felt positively proud of it!

But the applause gradually subsided, and was succeeded by an awkward pause. It had not struck me till that moment that it would be necessary to do or say anything in particular during the exhibition, beyond showing the spectators round the phantom, and making the customary assurance that there was no deception and no concealed machinery, which I could do with a clear conscience. But a terrible conviction struck me as I stood there bowing repeatedly, that the audience had come prepared for a comic duologue, with incidental music and dances.

This was quite out of the question, even supposing that Barnjum's ghost would have helped me to entertain them, which, perhaps, I could scarcely expect. As it was, it did nothing at all, except grimace at the audience and make an idiotic fool of itself and me—an exhibition of which they soon wearied. I am perfectly certain that an ordinary magic lantern would have made a far deeper impression upon them.

Whether the wraith managed in some covert way, when my attention was diverted, to insult the national prejudices of that sensitive and hot-blooded nation, I cannot say. All I know is, that after sitting still for some time they suddenly rose as one man; chairs were hurled at me through the ghost, and the stage was completely wrecked before the audience could be induced to go away.

It was all over. I was hopelessly ruined now! My weak fancy that even a spectre would have some remnants of common decency and good-feeling hanging about it, had put the finishing touch to my misfortunes!

I paid for the smashed platform and windows with the money that had been taken at the doors, and then I travelled back to London, third class, that night, with the feeling that everything was against me.

* * * *

It was Christmas, and I was sitting gloomily in my shabby Bloomsbury lodgings, watching with a miserable, apathetic interest Barnjum's wraith as, clad in a Roman toga, topboots, and a turban, it flitted about the horsehair furniture.

I was wondering if they would admit me into any workhouse while the spectre continued my attendant; I was utterly and completely wretched, and now, for the first time, I really repented my conduct in having parted with Barnjum so abruptly by the bleak cliff side, that bright June morning.

I had heard no more of him—I knew he must have reached the bottom after his fall, because I heard the splash he made—but no tidings had come of the discovery of his body; the lake kept its dark secret well.

If I could only hope that this insidious shade, now that it had hounded me down to poverty, would consider this as a sufficient expiation of my error and go away and leave me in peace! But I felt, only too keenly, that it was one of those one-idea'd apparitions, which never know when they have had enough of a good thing—it would be sure to stay and see the very last of me!

All at once there came a sharp tap at my door, and another figure strode solemnly in. This, too, wore the semblance of Barnjum, but was cast in a more substantial mould, and possessed the power of speech, as I gathered from its addressing me instantly as a cowardly villain.

I started back, and stood behind an arm-chair, facing those two forms, the shadow and the solid, with a feeling of sick despair. "Listen to me," I said, "both of you: so long as your—your original proprietor was content with a single wraith, I put up with it; I did not enjoy myself—but I endured it. But a *brace* of apparitions is really carrying the thing too far; it's more than any one man's fair allowance, and I won't stand it. I defy the pair of you. I will find means to escape you. I will leave the world! Other people can be ghosts as well as you—it's not a monopoly! If you don't go directly, I shall blow my brains out!"

There was no firearm of any description in the house, but I was too excited for perfect accuracy.

"Blow your brains out by all means!" said the solid figure; "I don't know what all this nonsense you're talking is about. I'm not a ghost that I'm aware of; I'm alive (no thanks to you); and, to come back to the point—scoundrel!"

"Barnjum—and alive!" I cried, almost with relief. "If that is so," I added, feeling that I had been imposed upon in a very unworthy and ungentlemanly manner, "will you have the goodness to tell me what right you have to this ridiculous apparition here?"

He did not seem to have noticed it particularly till then. "Hullo!" he said, looking at it with some curiosity, "what d'ye call *that* thing?"

"I call it a beastly nuisance!" I said. "Ever since—since I last saw you, it's been following me about everywhere in a—in a very annoying manner!"

Will it be believed that the unfeeling brute only chuckled at this? "*I* don't know anything about it," he said, "but all I can say is that it serves you jolly well right, and I hope it will go on annoying you."

"This is ungenerous," I said, determined to appeal to any better feelings he might have; "we did not part on—on the best of terms perhaps—"

"Considering that you kicked me over a precipice when I wasn't looking," he retorted brutally, "we may take that as admitted."

"But, at all events," I argued, "it is ridiculous to cherish an old grudge all this time; you must see the absurdity of it yourself."

"No, I don't," he said.

I determined to make a last effort to move him. "It is Christmas Eve, Barnjum," I said earnestly, "Christmas Eve. Think of it. At this hour, thousands of throbbing human hearts are speeding the cheap but genial Christmas card to such of their relations as they consider at all likely to respond with a turkey. The costermonger, imaginative for the nonce, is investing damaged evergreens with a purely fictitious value, and the cheery publican is sending the member of his village goose-club back to his cottage home, rich in the possession of a shot-distended bird and a bottle of poisonous port. Hear my appeal. If I was hasty with you, I have been punished. That detestable thing on the hearthrug there has dogged my path to misery and ruin; you cannot be without *some* responsibility for its conduct. I ask you now, as a man—nay, as an individual—to call it off. You can do it well enough if you only choose; you know you can."

But Barnjum wouldn't; he only looked at his own wraith with a grim satisfaction as it capered in an imbecile fashion upon the rug.

"Do," I implored him; "I would do it for *you*, Barnjum. I've had it about me for six months, and I *am* so sick of it."

Still he hesitated. Some waits outside were playing one of those pathetic American melodies—I forget now whether it was "Silver Threads among the Gold," or "In the Sweet By-and-By"—but, at all events, they struck some sympathetic chord in Barnjum's rough bosom, for his face began to twitch, and presently he burst unexpectedly into tears.

"You don't deserve it," he said between his sobs, "but be it so"; then, turning to the ghost, he added: "Here, you, what's your name? avaunt! D'ye hear, hook

31

it!"

It wavered for an instant, and then, to my joy, it suddenly "gave" all over, and, shrivelling up into a sort of cobweb, was drawn by the draught into the fireplace, and carried up the chimney, and I never saw it again.

* * * *

Barnjum's escape was very simple; he had fallen upon one of the herring-boats in the lake, and the heap of freshly-caught fish lying on the deck had merely broken his fall instead of his neck. As soon as he had recovered from the effects, he was called away from this country upon urgent business, and found himself unable to return for months.

But to this day the appearance of the wraith is a mystery to me. If Barnjum had been the kind of man to be an "esoteric Buddhist," it might be accounted for as an "astral shape"; but esoteric Buddhism requires an exemplary character and years of abstract meditation—both of which conditions were far beyond Barnjum's attainment.

The shape may have been one of those subtle emanations which we are told some people are constantly shedding, like the coats of an onion, and which certain conditions of the atmosphere, and the extreme activity of Barnjum's mind under sudden excitement, possibly contributed to materialise in this particular instance.

Or, perhaps, it was merely a caprice of one of those vagrant *Poltergeists*, or supernatural buffoons, which took upon itself, very officiously, the duty of avenging my behaviour to Barnjum.

Upon one point I am clear: the whole of this system of deliberate persecution being undertaken directly on Barnjum's account, he is morally and legally bound to reimburse me for the heavy expense and damage which have resulted therefrom.

Hitherto I have been unable to impress Barnjum with this principle, and so my wrongs are still without redress.

I may be asked why I do not make them the basis of an action at law; but persons of any refinement will understand my reluctance to resort to legal proceedings against one with whom I have at least lived on a footing of friendship. I would fain persuade, and shrink from appealing to force; and, besides, I have not succeeded as yet in persuading any solicitor—even a shady one—to take up my case.

THE JOLLY CORNER,
by Henry James

CHAPTER I

"Every one asks me what I 'think' of everything," said Spencer Brydon; "and I make answer as I can—begging or dodging the question, putting them off with any nonsense. It wouldn't matter to any of them really," he went on, "for, even were it possible to meet in that stand-and-deliver way so silly a demand on so big a subject, my 'thoughts' would still be almost altogether about something that concerns only myself." He was talking to Miss Staverton, with whom for a couple of months now he had availed himself of every possible occasion to talk; this disposition and this resource, this comfort and support, as the situation in fact presented itself, having promptly enough taken the first place in the considerable array of rather unattenuated surprises attending his so strangely belated return to America. Everything was somehow a surprise; and that might be natural when one had so long and so consistently neglected everything, taken pains to give surprises so much margin for play. He had given them more than thirty years—thirty-three, to be exact; and they now seemed to him to have organised their performance quite on the scale of that licence. He had been twenty-three on leaving New York—he was fifty-six today; unless indeed he were to reckon as he had sometimes, since his repatriation, found himself feeling; in which case he would have lived longer than is often allotted to man. It would have taken a century, he repeatedly said to himself, and said also to Alice Staverton, it would have taken a longer absence and a more averted mind than those even of which he had been guilty, to pile up the differences, the newnesses, the queernesses, above all the bignesses, for the better or the worse, that at present assaulted his vision wherever he looked.

The great fact all the while, however, had been the incalculability; since he *had* supposed himself, from decade to decade, to be allowing, and in the most liberal and intelligent manner, for brilliancy of change. He actually saw that he had allowed for nothing; he missed what he would have been sure of finding, he found what he would never have imagined. Proportions and values were upside-down; the ugly things he had expected, the ugly things of his far-away youth, when he had too promptly waked up to a sense of the ugly—these uncanny phenomena placed him rather, as it happened, under the charm; whereas the "swagger" things, the modern, the monstrous, the famous things, those he had more particularly, like thousands of ingenuous enquirers every year, come over to see, were exactly his sources of dismay. They were as so many set traps for displeasure, above all for reaction, of which his restless tread was constantly pressing the spring. It was interesting, doubtless, the whole show, but it would have been too disconcerting hadn't a certain finer truth saved the situation. He had distinctly not, in this steadier light, come over *all* for the monstrosities; he had come, not only in the last analysis but quite on the face of the act, under an impulse with which they had nothing to do. He had come—putting the thing pompously—to look at his "property," which he had thus for a third of a century not been within four thousand miles of; or, expressing it less sordidly, he had yielded to the humour of seeing again his house on the jolly corner, as he usually, and quite fondly, described it—the one in which he had first seen the light, in which various members of his family had lived and had died, in which the holidays of his overschooled boyhood had been passed and the few social flowers of his chilled adolescence gathered, and which, alienated then for so long a period, had, through the successive deaths of his two brothers and the termination of old arrangements, come wholly into his hands. He was the owner of another, not quite so "good"—the jolly corner having been, from far back, superlatively extended and consecrated; and the value of the pair represented his main capital, with an income consisting, in these later years, of their respective rents which (thanks precisely to their original excellent type) had never been depressingly low. He could live in "Europe," as he had been in the habit of living, on the product of these flourishing New York leases, and all the better since, that of the second structure, the mere number in its long row, having within a twelvemonth fallen in, renovation at a high advance had proved beautifully possible.

These were items of property indeed, but he had found himself since his arrival distinguishing more than ever between them. The house within the street, two bristling blocks westward, was already in course of reconstruction as a tall mass of flats; he had acceded, some time before, to overtures for this conversion —in which, now that it was going forward, it had been not the least of his astonishments to find himself able, on the spot, and though without a previous ounce of such experience, to participate with a certain intelligence, almost with a certain authority. He had lived his life with his back so turned to such concerns and his face addressed to those of so different an order that he scarce knew what to make of this lively stir, in a compartment of his mind never yet penetrated, of a capacity for business and a sense for construction. These virtues, so common all round him now, had been dormant in his own organism—where it might be said of them perhaps that they had slept the sleep of the just. At present, in the splendid autumn weather—the autumn at least was a pure boon in the terrible place— he loafed about his "work" undeterred, secretly agitated; not in the least "minding" that the whole proposition, as they said, was vulgar and sordid, and ready to climb ladders, to walk the plank, to handle materials and look wise about them, to ask questions, in fine, and challenge explanations and really "go into" figures.

It amused, it verily quite charmed him; and, by the same stroke, it amused, and even more, Alice Staverton, though perhaps charming her perceptibly less. She wasn't, however, going to be better-off for it, as *he* was—and so astonishingly much: nothing was now likely, he knew, ever to make her better-off than she found herself, in the afternoon of life, as the delicately frugal possessor and tenant of the small house in Irving Place to which she had subtly managed to cling through her almost unbroken New York career. If he knew the way to it now better than to any other address among the dreadful multiplied numberings which seemed to him to reduce the whole place to some vast ledger-page, overgrown, fantastic, of ruled and criss-crossed lines and figures—if he had formed, for his consolation, that habit, it was really not a little because of the charm of his having encountered and recognised, in the vast wilderness of the wholesale, breaking through the mere gross generalisation of wealth and force and success, a small still scene where items and shades, all delicate things, kept the sharpness of the notes of a high voice perfectly trained, and where economy hung about like the scent of a garden. His old friend lived with one maid and herself dusted her relics and trimmed her lamps and polished her silver; she stood oft, in the awful modern crush, when she could, but she sallied forth and did battle when the challenge was really to "spirit," the spirit she after all confessed to, proudly and a little shyly, as to that of the better time, that of *their* common, their quite far-away and antediluvian social period and order. She made use of the street-cars when need be, the terrible things that people scrambled for as the panic-stricken at sea scramble for the boats; she affronted, inscrutably, under stress, all the public concussions and ordeals; and yet, with that slim mystifying grace of her appearance, which defied you to say if she were a fair young woman who looked older through trouble, or a fine smooth older one who looked young through successful indifference with her precious reference, above all, to memories and histories into which he could enter, she was as exquisite for him as some pale pressed flower (a rarity to begin with), and, failing other sweetnesses, she was a sufficient reward of his effort. They had communities of knowledge, "their" knowledge (this discriminating possessive was always on her lips) of presences of the other age, presences all overlaid, in his case, by the experience of a man and the freedom of a wanderer, overlaid by pleasure, by infidelity, by passages of life that were strange and dim to her, just by "Europe" in short, but still unobscured, still exposed and cherished, under that pious visitation of the spirit from which she had never been diverted.

She had come with him one day to see how his "apartment-house" was rising; he had helped her over gaps and explained to her plans, and while they were there had happened to have, before her, a brief but lively discussion with the man in charge, the representative of the building firm that had undertaken his work. He had found himself quite "standing up" to this personage over a failure on the latter's part to observe some detail of one of their noted conditions, and had so lucidly argued his case that, besides ever so prettily flushing, at the time, for sympathy in his triumph, she had afterwards said to him (though to a slightly greater effect of irony) that he had clearly for too many years neglected a real gift. If he had but stayed at home he would have anticipated the inventor of the sky-scraper. If he had but stayed at home he would have discovered his genius in time really to start some new variety of awful architectural hare and run it till it burrowed in a gold mine. He was to remember these words, while the weeks elapsed, for the small silver ring they had sounded over the queerest and deepest of his own lately most disguised and most muffled vibrations.

It had begun to be present to him after the first fortnight, it had broken out with the oddest abruptness, this particular wanton wonderment: it met him there —and this was the image under which he himself judged the matter, or at least, not a little, thrilled and flushed with it—very much as he might have been met by some strange figure, some unexpected occupant, at a turn of one of the dim passages of an empty house. The quaint analogy quite hauntingly remained with him, when he didn't indeed rather improve it by a still intenser form: that of his opening a door behind which he would have made sure of finding nothing, a door into a room shuttered and void, and yet so coming, with a great suppressed start, on some quite erect confronting presence, something planted in the middle of the place and facing him through the dusk. After that visit to the house in construction he walked with his companion to see the other and always so much the better one, which in the eastward direction formed one of the corners—the "jolly" one precisely, of the street now so generally dishonoured and disfigured in its westward reaches, and of the comparatively conservative Avenue. The Avenue still had pretensions, as Miss Staverton said, to decency; the old people had mostly gone, the old names were unknown, and here and there an old association seemed to stray, all vaguely, like some very aged person, out too late, whom you might meet and feel the impulse to watch or follow, in kindness, for safe restoration to shelter.

They went in together, our friends; he admitted himself with his key, as he kept no one there, he explained, preferring, for his reasons, to leave the place empty, under a simple arrangement with a good woman living in the neighbourhood and who came for a daily hour to open windows and dust and sweep. Spencer Brydon had his reasons and was growingly aware of them; they seemed to him better each time he was there, though he didn't name them all to his companion, any more than he told her as yet how often, how quite absurdly often, he himself came. He only let her see for the present, while they walked through the great blank rooms, that absolute vacancy reigned and that, from top to bottom, there was nothing but Mrs. Muldoon's broomstick, in a corner, to tempt the burglar. Mrs. Muldoon was then on the premises, and she loquaciously attended the visitors, preceding them from room to room and pushing back shutters and throwing up sashes—all to show them, as she remarked, how little there was to see. There was little indeed to see in the great gaunt shell where the main dispositions and the general apportionment of space, the style of an age of ampler allowances, had nevertheless for its master their honest pleading message, affecting him as some good old servant's, some lifelong retainer's appeal for a character, or even for a retiring-pension; yet it was also a remark of Mrs. Muldoon's that, glad as she was to oblige him by her noonday round, there was a request she greatly hoped he would never make of her. If he should wish her for any reason to come in after dark she would just tell him, if he "plased," that he must ask it of somebody else.

The fact that there was nothing to see didn't militate for the worthy woman against what one *might* see, and she put it frankly to Miss Staverton that no lady could be expected to like, could she?"craping up to thim top storeys in the ayvil hours." The gas and the electric light were off the house, and she fairly evoked a gruesome vision of her march through the great grey rooms—so many of them as there were too!—with her glimmering taper. Miss Staverton met her honest glare with a smile and the profession that she herself certainly would recoil from such an adventure. Spencer Brydon meanwhile held his peace—for the moment; the question of the "evil" hours in his old home had already become too grave for him. He had begun some time since to "crape," and he knew just why a packet of candles addressed to that pursuit had been stowed by his own hand, three weeks before, at the back of a drawer of the fine old sideboard that occupied, as a "fixture," the deep recess in the dining-room. Just now he laughed at his companions—quickly however changing the subject; for the reason that, in the first place, his laugh struck him even at that moment as starting the odd echo, the conscious human resonance (he scarce knew how to qualify it) that sounds made while he was there alone sent back to his ear or his fancy; and that, in the second, he imagined Alice Staverton for the instant on the point of asking him, with a divination, if he ever so prowled. There were divinations he was unprepared for, and he had at all events averted enquiry by the time Mrs. Muldoon had left them, passing on to other parts.

There was happily enough to say, on so consecrated a spot, that could be said freely and fairly; so that a whole train of declarations was precipitated by his friend's having herself broken out, after a yearning look round: "But I hope you don't mean they want you to pull *this* to pieces!" His answer came, promptly, with his re-awakened wrath: it was of course exactly what they wanted, and what they were "at" him for, daily, with the iteration of people who couldn't for their life understand a man's liability to decent feelings. He had found the place, just as it stood and beyond what he could express, an interest and a joy. There were values other than the beastly rent-values, and in short, in short—! But it was thus Miss Staverton took him up. "In short you're to make so good a thing of your sky-scraper that, living in luxury on *those* ill-gotten gains, you can afford for a while to be sentimental here!" Her smile had for him, with the words, the particular mild irony with which he found half her talk suffused; an irony without bitterness and that came, exactly, from her having so much imagination—not, like the cheap sarcasms with which one heard most people, about the world of "society," bid for the reputation of cleverness, from nobody's really having any. It was agreeable to him at this very moment to be sure that when he had answered, after a brief demur, "Well, yes; so, precisely, you may put it!" her imagination would still do him justice. He explained that even if never a dollar were to come to him from the other house he would nevertheless cherish this one; and he dwelt, further, while they lingered and wandered, on the fact of the stupefaction he was already exciting, the positive mystification he felt himself create.

He spoke of the value of all he read into it, into the mere sight of the walls, mere shapes of the rooms, mere sound of the floors, mere feel, in his hand, of the old silver-plated knobs of the several mahogany doors, which suggested the pressure of the palms of the dead the seventy years of the past in fine that these things represented, the annals of nearly three generations, counting his grandfather's, the one that had ended there, and the impalpable ashes of his long-extinct youth, afloat in the very air like microscopic motes. She listened to everything; she was a woman who answered intimately but who utterly didn't chatter. She scattered abroad therefore no cloud of words; she could assent, she could agree, above all she could encourage, without doing that. Only at the last she went a little further than he had done himself. "And then how do you know? You may still, after all, want to live here." It rather indeed pulled him up, for it wasn't what he had been thinking, at least in her sense of the words, "You mean I may decide to stay on for the sake of it?"

"Well, *with* such a home—!" But, quite beautifully, she had too much tact to dot so monstrous an *i*, and it was precisely an illustration of the way she didn't rattle. How could any one—of any wit—insist on any one else's "wanting" to live in New York?

"Oh," he said, "I *might* have lived here (since I had my opportunity early in life); I might have put in here all these years. Then everything would have been different enough—and, I dare say, 'funny' enough. But that's another matter. And then the beauty of it—I mean of my perversity, of my refusal to agree to a 'deal'—is just in the total absence of a reason. Don't you see that if I had a reason about the matter at all it would *have* to be the other way, and would then be

37

inevitably a reason of dollars? There are no reasons here *but* of dollars. Let us therefore have none whatever—not the ghost of one."

They were back in the hall then for departure, but from where they stood the vista was large, through an open door, into the great square main saloon, with its almost antique felicity of brave spaces between windows. Her eyes came back from that reach and met his own a moment. "Are you very sure the 'ghost' of one doesn't, much rather, serve—?"

He had a positive sense of turning pale. But it was as near as they were then to come. For he made answer, he believed, between a glare and a grin: "Oh ghosts—of course the place must swarm with them! I should be ashamed of it if it didn't. Poor Mrs. Muldoon's right, and it's why I haven't asked her to do more than look in."

Miss Staverton's gaze again lost itself, and things she didn't utter, it was clear, came and went in her mind. She might even for the minute, off there in the fine room, have imagined some element dimly gathering. Simplified like the death-mask of a handsome face, it perhaps produced for her just then an effect akin to the stir of an expression in the "set" commemorative plaster. Yet whatever her impression may have been she produced instead a vague platitude. "Well, if it were only furnished and lived in—!"

She appeared to imply that in case of its being still furnished he might have been a little less opposed to the idea of a return. But she passed straight into the vestibule, as if to leave her words behind her, and the next moment he had opened the house-door and was standing with her on the steps. He closed the door and, while he re-pocketed his key, looking up and down, they took in the comparatively harsh actuality of the Avenue, which reminded him of the assault of the outer light of the Desert on the traveller emerging from an Egyptian tomb. But he risked before they stepped into the street his gathered answer to her speech. "For me it *is* lived in. For me it is furnished." At which it was easy for her to sigh "Ah yes!" all vaguely and discreetly; since his parents and his favourite sister, to say nothing of other kin, in numbers, had run their course and met their end there. That represented, within the walls, ineffaceable life.

It was a few days after this that, during an hour passed with her again, he had expressed his impatience of the too flattering curiosity—among the people he met—about his appreciation of New York. He had arrived at none at all that was socially producible, and as for that matter of his "thinking" (thinking the better or the worse of anything there) he was wholly taken up with one subject of thought. It was mere vain egoism, and it was moreover, if she liked, a morbid ob-session. He found all things come back to the question of what he personally might have been, how he might have led his life and "turned out," if he had not so, at the outset, given it up. And confessing for the first time to the intensity within him of this absurd speculation—which but proved also, no doubt, the habit of too selfishly thinking—he affirmed the impotence there of any other source of interest, any other native appeal. "What would it have made of me, what would it have made of me? I keep for ever wondering, all idiotically; as if I could possibly know! I see what it has made of dozens of others, those I meet, and it positively aches within me, to the point of exasperation, that it would have made something of me as well. Only I can't make out what, and the worry of it, the small rage of curiosity never to be satisfied, brings back what I remember to have felt, once or twice, after judging best, for reasons, to burn some important letter unopened. I've been sorry, I've hated it—I've never known what was in the letter. You may, of course, say it's a trifle—!"

"I don't say it's a trifle," Miss Staverton gravely interrupted.

She was seated by her fire, and before her, on his feet and restless, he turned to and fro between this intensity of his idea and a fitful and unseeing inspection, through his single eye-glass, of the dear little old objects on her chimney-piece. Her interruption made him for an instant look at her harder. "I shouldn't care if you did!" he laughed, however; "and it's only a figure, at any rate, for the way I now feel. *Not* to have followed my perverse young course—and almost in the teeth of my father's curse, as I may say; not to have kept it up, so, 'over there,' from that day to this, without a doubt or a pang; not, above all, to have liked it, to have loved it, so much, loved it, no doubt, with such an abysmal conceit of my own preference; some variation from *that*, I say, must have produced some different effect for my life and for my 'form.' I should have stuck here—if it had been possible; and I was too young, at twenty-three, to judge, *pour deux sous*, whether it *were* possible. If I had waited I might have seen it was, and then I might have been, by staying here, something nearer to one of these types who have been hammered so hard and made so keen by their conditions. It isn't that I admire them so much—the question of any charm in them, or of any charm, beyond that of the rank money-passion, exerted by their conditions *for* them, has nothing to do with the matter: it's only a question of what fantastic, yet perfectly possible, development of my own nature I mayn't have missed. It comes over me that I had then a strange *alter ego* deep down somewhere within me, as the full-blown flower is in the small tight bud, and that I just took the course, I just transferred him to the climate, that blighted him for once and for ever."

"And you wonder about the flower," Miss Staverton said. "So do I, if you want to know; and so I've been wondering these several weeks. I believe in the flower," she continued, "I feel it would have been quite splendid, quite huge and monstrous."

"Monstrous above all!" her visitor echoed; "and I imagine, by the same stroke, quite hideous and offensive."

"You don't believe that," she returned; "if you did you wouldn't wonder. You'd know, and that would be enough for you. What you feel—and what I feel *for* you—is that you'd have had power."

"You'd have liked me that way?" he asked.

She barely hung fire. "How should I not have liked you?"

"I see. You'd have liked me, have preferred me, a billionaire!"

"How should I not have liked you?" she simply again asked.

He stood before her still—her question kept him motionless. He took it in, so much there was of it; and indeed his not otherwise meeting it testified to that. "I know at least what I am," he simply went on; "the other side of the medal's clear enough. I've not been edifying—I believe I'm thought in a hundred quarters to have been barely decent. I've followed strange paths and worshipped strange gods; it must have come to you again and again—in fact you've admitted to me as much—that I was leading, at any time these thirty years, a selfish frivolous scandalous life. And you see what it has made of me."

She just waited, smiling at him. "You see what it has made of *me*."

"Oh you're a person whom nothing can have altered. You were born to be what you are, anywhere, anyway: you've the perfection nothing else could have blighted. And don't you see how, without my exile, I shouldn't have been waiting till now—?" But he pulled up for the strange pang.

"The great thing to see," she presently said, "seems to me to be that it has spoiled nothing. It hasn't spoiled your being here at last. It hasn't spoiled this. It hasn't spoiled your speaking—" She also however faltered.

He wondered at everything her controlled emotion might mean. "Do you believe then—too dreadfully!—that I *am* as good as I might ever have been?"

"Oh no! Far from it!" With which she got up from her chair and was nearer to him. "But I don't care," she smiled.

"You mean I'm good enough?"

She considered a little. "Will you believe it if I say so? I mean will you let that settle your question for you?" And then as if making out in his face that he drew back from this, that he had some idea which, however absurd, he couldn't yet bargain away: "Oh you don't care either—but very differently: you don't care for anything but yourself."

Spencer Brydon recognised it—it was in fact what he had absolutely professed. Yet he importantly qualified. "*He* isn't myself. He's the just so totally other person. But I do want to see him," he added. "And I can. And I shall."

Their eyes met for a minute while he guessed from something in hers that she divined his strange sense. But neither of them otherwise expressed it, and her apparent understanding, with no protesting shock, no easy derision, touched him more deeply than anything yet, constituting for his stifled perversity, on the spot, an element that was like breatheable air. What she said however was unexpected. "Well, *I've* seen him."

"You—?"

"I've seen him in a dream."

"Oh a 'dream'—!" It let him down.

"But twice over," she continued. "I saw him as I see you now."

"You've dreamed the same dream—?"

"Twice over," she repeated. "The very same."

This did somehow a little speak to him, as it also gratified him. "You dream about me at that rate?"

"Ah about *him*!" she smiled.

His eyes again sounded her. "Then you know all about him." And as she said nothing more: "What's the wretch like?"

She hesitated, and it was as if he were pressing her so hard that, resisting for reasons of her own, she had to turn away. "I'll tell you some other time!"

CHAPTER II

It was after this that there was most of a virtue for him, most of a cultivated charm, most of a preposterous secret thrill, in the particular form of surrender to his obsession and of address to what he more and more believed to be his privilege. It was what in these weeks he was living for—since he really felt life to begin but after Mrs. Muldoon had retired from the scene and, visiting the ample house from attic to cellar, making sure he was alone, he knew himself in safe possession and, as he tacitly expressed it, let himself go. He sometimes came twice in the twenty-four hours; the moments he liked best were those of gathering dusk, of the short autumn twilight; this was the time of which, again and again, he found himself hoping most. Then he could, as seemed to him, most intimately wander and wait, linger and listen, feel his fine attention, never in his life before so fine, on the pulse of the great vague place: he preferred the lampless hour and only wished he might have prolonged each day the deep crepuscular spell. Later—rarely much before midnight, but then for a considerable vigil—he watched with his glimmering light; moving slowly, holding it high, playing it far, rejoicing above all, as much as he might, in open vistas, reaches of communication between rooms and by passages; the long straight chance or show, as he would have called it, for the revelation he pretended to invite. It was a practice he found he could perfectly "work" without exciting remark; no one was in the least the wiser for it; even Alice Staverton, who was moreover a well of discretion, didn't quite fully imagine.

He let himself in and let himself out with the assurance of calm proprietorship; and accident so far favoured him that, if a fat Avenue "officer" had happened on occasion to see him entering at eleven-thirty, he had never yet, to the best of his belief, been noticed as emerging at two. He walked there on the crisp November nights, arrived regularly at the evening's end; it was as easy to do this after dining out as to take his way to a club or to his hotel. When he left his club, if he hadn't been dining out, it was ostensibly to go to his hotel; and when he left his hotel, if he had spent a part of the evening there, it was ostensibly to go to his club. Everything was easy in fine; everything conspired and promoted: there was truly even in the strain of his experience something that glossed over, something that salved and simplified, all the rest of consciousness. He circulated, talked, renewed, loosely and pleasantly, old relations—met indeed, so far as he could, new expectations and seemed to make out on the whole that in spite of the career, of such different contacts, which he had spoken of to Miss Staverton as ministering so little, for those who might have watched it, to edification, he was positively rather liked than not. He was a dim secondary social success—and all with people who had truly not an idea of him. It was all mere surface sound, this murmur of their welcome, this popping of their corks—just as his gestures of response were the extravagant shadows, emphatic in proportion as they meant little, of some game of *ombres chinoises*. He projected himself all day, in thought, straight over the bristling line of hard unconscious heads and into the other, the real, the waiting life; the life that, as soon as he had heard behind him the click of his great house-door, began for him, on the jolly corner, as beguilingly as the slow opening bars of some rich music follows the tap of the conductor's wand.

He always caught the first effect of the steel point of his stick on the old marble of the hall pavement, large black-and-white squares that he remembered as the admiration of his childhood and that had then made in him, as he now saw, for the growth of an early conception of style. This effect was the dim reverberating tinkle as of some far-off bell hung who should say where?—in the depths of the house, of the past, of that mystical other world that might have flourished for him had he not, for weal or woe, abandoned it. On this impression he did ever the same thing; he put his stick noiselessly away in a corner—feeling the place once more in the likeness of some great glass bowl, all precious concave crystal, set delicately humming by the play of a moist finger round its edge. The concave crystal held, as it were, this mystical other world, and the indescribably fine murmur of its rim was the sigh there, the scarce audible pathetic wail to his strained ear, of all the old baffled forsworn possibilities. What he did therefore by this appeal of his hushed presence was to wake them into such measure of ghostly life as they might still enjoy. They were shy, all but unappeasably shy, but they weren't really sinister; at least they weren't as he had hitherto felt them —before they had taken the Form he so yearned to make them take, the Form he at moments saw himself in the light of fairly hunting on tiptoe, the points of his evening shoes, from room to room and from storey to storey.

That was the essence of his vision—which was all rank folly, if one would, while he was out of the house and otherwise occupied, but which took on the last verisimilitude as soon as he was placed and posted. He knew what he meant and what he wanted; it was as clear as the figure on a cheque presented in demand for cash. His *alter ego* "walked"—that was the note of his image of him, while his image of his motive for his own odd pastime was the desire to waylay him and meet him. He roamed, slowly, warily, but all restlessly, he himself did—Mrs. Muldoon had been right, absolutely, with her figure of their "craping"; and the presence he watched for would roam restlessly too. But it would be as cautious and as shifty; the conviction of its probable, in fact its already quite sensible, quite audible evasion of pursuit grew for him from night to night, laying on him finally a rigour to which nothing in his life had been comparable. It had been the theory of many superficially-judging persons, he knew, that he was wasting that life in a surrender to sensations, but he had tasted of no pleasure so fine as his actual tension, had been introduced to no sport that demanded at once the patience and the nerve of this stalking of a creature more subtle, yet at bay perhaps more formidable, than any beast of the forest. The terms, the comparisons, the very practices of the chase positively came again into play; there were even moments when passages of his occasional experience as a sportsman, stirred memories, from his younger time, of moor and mountain and desert, revived for him—and to the increase of his keenness—by the tremendous force of analogy. He found himself at moments—once he had placed his single light on some mantel-shelf or in some recess—stepping back into shelter or shade, effacing himself behind a door or in an embrasure, as he had sought of old the vantage of rock and tree; he found himself holding his breath and living in the joy of the instant, the supreme suspense created by big game alone.

He wasn't afraid (though putting himself the question as he believed gentlemen on Bengal tiger-shoots or in close quarters with the great bear of the Rockies had been known to confess to having put it); and this indeed—since here at least he might be frank!—because of the impression, so intimate and so strange, that he himself produced as yet a dread, produced certainly a strain, beyond the liveliest he was likely to feel. They fell for him into categories, they fairly became familiar, the signs, for his own perception, of the alarm his presence and his vigilance created; though leaving him always to remark, portentously, on his probably having formed a relation, his probably enjoying a consciousness, unique in the experience of man. People enough, first and last, had been in terror of apparitions, but who had ever before so turned the tables and become himself, in the apparitional world, an incalculable terror? He might have found this sublime had he quite dared to think of it; but he didn't too much insist, truly, on that side of his privilege. With habit and repetition he gained to an extraordinary degree the power to penetrate the dusk of distances and the darkness of corners, to resolve back into their innocence the treacheries of uncertain light, the evil-looking forms taken in the gloom by mere shadows, by accidents of the air, by shifting effects of perspective; putting down his dim luminary he could still wander on without it, pass into other rooms and, only knowing it was there behind him in case of need, see his way about, visually project for his purpose a comparative clearness. It made him feel, this acquired faculty, like some monstrous stealthy cat; he wondered if he would have glared at these moments with large shining yellow eyes, and what it mightn't verily be, for the poor hard-pressed *alter ego*, to be confronted with such a type.

He liked however the open shutters; he opened everywhere those Mrs. Muldoon had closed, closing them as carefully afterwards, so that she shouldn't notice: he liked—oh this he did like, and above all in the upper rooms!—the sense of the hard silver of the autumn stars through the window-panes, and scarcely less the flare of the street-lamps below, the white electric lustre which it would have taken curtains to keep out. This was human actual social; this was of the world he had lived in, and he was more at his ease certainly for the countenance, coldly general and impersonal, that all the while and in spite of his detachment it seemed to give him. He had support of course mostly in the rooms at the wide front and the prolonged side; it failed him considerably in the central shades and the parts at the back. But if he sometimes, on his rounds, was glad of his optical reach, so none the less often the rear of the house affected him as the very jungle of his prey. The place was there more subdivided; a large "extension" in particular, where small rooms for servants had been multiplied, abounded in nooks and corners, in closets and passages, in the ramifications especially of an ample back staircase over which he leaned, many a time, to look far down—not deterred from his gravity even while aware that he might, for a spectator, have figured some solemn simpleton playing at hide-and-seek. Outside in fact he might himself make that ironic *rapprochement*; but within the walls, and in spite of the clear windows, his consistency was proof against the cynical light of New York.

It had belonged to that idea of the exasperated consciousness of his victim to become a real test for him; since he had quite put it to himself from the first that, oh distinctly! he could "cultivate" his whole perception. He had felt it as above all open to cultivation—which indeed was but another name for his manner of spending his time. He was bringing it on, bringing it to perfection, by practice; in consequence of which it had grown so fine that he was now aware of impressions, attestations of his general postulate, that couldn't have broken upon him at once. This was the case more specifically with a phenomenon at last quite frequent for him in the upper rooms, the recognition—absolutely unmistakeable, and by a turn dating from a particular hour, his resumption of his campaign after a diplomatic drop, a calculated absence of three nights—of his being definitely followed, tracked at a distance carefully taken and to the express end that he should the less confidently, less arrogantly, appear to himself merely to pursue. It worried, it finally quite broke him up, for it proved, of all the conceivable impressions, the one least suited to his book. He was kept in sight while remaining himself—as regards the essence of his position—sightless, and his only recourse then was in abrupt turns, rapid recoveries of ground. He wheeled about, retracing his steps, as if he might so catch in his face at least the stirred air of some other quick revolution. It was indeed true that his fully dislocalised thought of these manoeuvres recalled to him Pantaloon, at the Christmas farce, buffeted and tricked from behind by ubiquitous Harlequin; but it left intact the influence of the conditions themselves each time he was re-exposed to them, so that in fact this association, had he suffered it to become constant, would on a certain side have but ministered to his intenser gravity. He had made, as I have said, to create on the premises the baseless sense of a reprieve, his three absences; and the result of the third was to confirm the after-effect of the second.

On his return that night—the night succeeding his last intermission—he stood in the hall and looked up the staircase with a certainty more intimate than any he had yet known. "He's *there*, at the top, and waiting—not, as in general, falling back for disappearance. He's holding his ground, and it's the first time—which is a proof, isn't it? that something has happened for him." So Brydon argued with his hand on the banister and his foot on the lowest stair; in which position he felt as never before the air chilled by his logic. He himself turned cold in it, for he seemed of a sudden to know what now was involved. "Harder pressed?—yes, he takes it in, with its thus making clear to him that I've come, as they say, 'to stay.' He finally doesn't like and can't bear it, in the sense, I mean, that his wrath, his menaced interest, now balances with his dread. I've hunted him till he has 'turned'; that, up there, is what has happened—he's the fanged or the antlered animal brought at last to bay." There came to him, as I say—but determined by an influence beyond my notation!—the acuteness of this certainty; under which however the next moment he had broken into a sweat that he would as little have consented to attribute to fear as he would have dared immediately to act upon it for enterprise. It marked none the less a prodigious thrill, a thrill that represented sudden dismay, no doubt, but also represented, and with the selfsame throb, the strangest, the most joyous, possibly the next minute almost the proudest, duplication of consciousness.

"He has been dodging, retreating, hiding, but now, worked up to anger, he'll fight!"—this intense impression made a single mouthful, as it were, of terror and applause. But what was wondrous was that the applause, for the felt fact, was so eager, since, if it was his other self he was running to earth, this ineffable identity was thus in the last resort not unworthy of him. It bristled there—somewhere near at hand, however unseen still—as the hunted thing, even as the trodden worm of the adage must at last bristle; and Brydon at this instant tasted probably of a sensation more complex than had ever before found itself consistent with sanity. It was as if it would have shamed him that a character so associated with his own should triumphantly succeed in just skulking, should to the end not risk the open; so that the drop of this danger was, on the spot, a great lift of the whole situation. Yet with another rare shift of the same subtlety he was already trying to measure by how much more he himself might now be in peril of fear; so rejoicing that he could, in another form, actively inspire that fear, and simultaneously quaking for the form in which he might passively know it.

The apprehension of knowing it must after a little have grown in him, and the strangest moment of his adventure perhaps, the most memorable or really most interesting, afterwards, of his crisis, was the lapse of certain instants of concentrated conscious *combat*, the sense of a need to hold on to something, even after the manner of a man slipping and slipping on some awful incline; the vivid impulse, above all, to move, to act, to charge, somehow and upon something—to show himself, in a word, that he wasn't afraid. The state of "holding on" was thus the state to which he was momentarily reduced; if there had been anything, in the great vacancy, to seize, he would presently have been aware of having clutched it as he might under a shock at home have clutched the nearest chairback. He had been surprised at any rate—of this he *was* aware—into something unprecedented since his original appropriation of the place; he had closed his eyes, held them tight, for a long minute, as with that instinct of dismay and that terror of vision. When he opened them the room, the other contiguous rooms, extraordinarily, seemed lighter—so light, almost, that at first he took the change for day. He stood firm, however that might be, just where he had paused; his resistance had helped him—it was as if there were something he had tided over. He knew after a little what this was—it had been in the imminent danger of flight. He had stiffened his will against going; without this he would have made for the stairs, and it seemed to him that, still with his eyes closed, he would have descended them, would have known how, straight and swiftly, to the bottom.

Well, as he had held out, here he was—still at the top, among the more intricate upper rooms and with the gauntlet of the others, of all the rest of the house, still to run when it should be his time to go. He would go at his time—only at his time: didn't he go every night very much at the same hour? He took out his watch—there was light for that: it was scarcely a quarter past one, and he had never withdrawn so soon. He reached his lodgings for the most part at two—with his walk of a quarter of an hour. He would wait for the last quarter—he wouldn't stir till then; and he kept his watch there with his eyes on it, reflecting while he held it that this deliberate wait, a wait with an effort, which he recognised, would serve perfectly for the attestation he desired to make. It would prove his courage —unless indeed the latter might most be proved by his budging at last from his place. What he mainly felt now was that, since he hadn't originally scuttled, he had his dignities—which had never in his life seemed so many—all to preserve and to carry aloft. This was before him in truth as a physical image, an image almost worthy of an age of greater romance. That remark indeed glimmered for him only to glow the next instant with a finer light; since what age of romance, after all, could have matched either the state of his mind or, "objectively," as they said, the wonder of his situation? The only difference would have been that, brandishing his dignities over his head as in a parchment scroll, he might then— that is in the heroic time—have proceeded downstairs with a drawn sword in his other grasp.

At present, really, the light he had set down on the mantel of the next room would have to figure his sword; which utensil, in the course of a minute, he had taken the requisite number of steps to possess himself of. The door between the rooms was open, and from the second another door opened to a third. These rooms, as he remembered, gave all three upon a common corridor as well, but there was a fourth, beyond them, without issue save through the preceding. To have moved, to have heard his step again, was appreciably a help; though even in recognising this he lingered once more a little by the chimney-piece on which his light had rested. When he next moved, just hesitating where to turn, he found himself considering a circumstance that, after his first and comparatively vague apprehension of it, produced in him the start that often attends some pang of recollection, the violent shock of having ceased happily to forget. He had come into sight of the door in which the brief chain of communication ended and which he now surveyed from the nearer threshold, the one not directly facing it. Placed at some distance to the left of this point, it would have admitted him to the last room of the four, the room without other approach or egress, had it not, to his intimate conviction, been closed *since* his former visitation, the matter probably of a quarter of an hour before. He stared with all his eyes at the wonder of the fact, arrested again where he stood and again holding his breath while he sounded his sense. Surely it had been *subsequently* closed—that is it had been on his previous passage indubitably open!

He took it full in the face that something had happened between—that he couldn't have noticed before (by which he meant on his original tour of all the rooms that evening) that such a barrier had exceptionally presented itself. He had indeed since that moment undergone an agitation so extraordinary that it might have muddled for him any earlier view; and he tried to convince himself that he might perhaps then have gone into the room and, inadvertently, automatically, on coming out, have drawn the door after him. The difficulty was that this exactly was what he never did; it was against his whole policy, as he might have said, the essence of which was to keep vistas clear. He had them from the first, as he was well aware, quite on the brain: the strange apparition, at the far end of one of them, of his baffled "prey"(which had become by so sharp an irony so little the term now to apply!) was the form of success his imagination had most cherished, projecting into it always a refinement of beauty. He had known fifty times the start of perception that had afterwards dropped; had fifty times gasped to himself. "There!" under some fond brief hallucination. The house, as the case stood, admirably lent itself; he might wonder at the taste, the native architecture of the particular time, which could rejoice so in the multiplication of doors—the opposite extreme to the modern, the actual almost complete proscription of them; but it had fairly contributed to provoke this obsession of the presence encountered telescopically, as he might say, focused and studied in diminishing perspective and as by a rest for the elbow.

It was with these considerations that his present attention was charged—they perfectly availed to make what he saw portentous. He *couldn't*, by any lapse, have blocked that aperture; and if he hadn't, if it was unthinkable, why what else was clear but that there had been another agent? Another agent?—he had been catching, as he felt, a moment back, the very breath of him; but when had he been so close as in this simple, this logical, this completely personal act? It was so logical, that is, that one might have *taken* it for personal; yet for what did Brydon take it, he asked himself, while, softly panting, he felt his eyes almost leave their sockets. Ah this time at last they *were*, the two, the opposed projections of him, in presence; and this time, as much as one would, the question of danger loomed. With it rose, as not before, the question of courage—for what he knew the blank face of the door to say to him was "Show us how much you have!" It stared, it glared back at him with that challenge; it put to him the two alternatives: should he just push it open or not? Oh to have this consciousness was to *think*—and to think, Brydon knew, as he stood there, was, with the lapsing moments, not to have acted! Not to have acted—that was the misery and the pang—was even still not to act; was in fact *all* to feel the thing in another, in a new and terrible way. How long did he pause and how long did he debate? There was presently nothing to measure it; for his vibration had already changed—as just by the effect of its intensity. Shut up there, at bay, defiant, and with the prodigy of the thing palpably proveably *done*, thus giving notice like some stark signboard—under that accession of accent the situation itself had turned; and Brydon at last remarkably made up his mind on what it had turned to.

It had turned altogether to a different admonition; to a supreme hint, for him, of the value of Discretion! This slowly dawned, no doubt—for it could take its time; so perfectly, on his threshold, had he been stayed, so little as yet had he either advanced or retreated. It was the strangest of all things that now when, by his taking ten steps and applying his hand to a latch, or even his shoulder and his knee, if necessary, to a panel, all the hunger of his prime need might have been met, his high curiosity crowned, his unrest assuaged—it was amazing, but it was also exquisite and rare, that insistence should have, at a touch, quite dropped from him. Discretion—he jumped at that; and yet not, verily, at such a pitch, because it saved his nerves or his skin, but because, much more valuably, it saved the situation. When I say he "jumped" at it I feel the consonance of this term with the fact that—at the end indeed of I know not how long—he did move again, he crossed straight to the door. He wouldn't touch it—it seemed now that he might if he would: he would only just wait there a little, to show, to prove, that he wouldn't. He had thus another station, close to the thin partition by which revelation was denied him; but with his eyes bent and his hands held off in a mere intensity of stillness. He listened as if there had been something to hear, but this attitude, while it lasted, was his own communication. "If you won't then— good: I spare you and I give up. You affect me as by the appeal positively for pity: you convince me that for reasons rigid and sublime—what do I know?—we both of us should have suffered. I respect them then, and, though moved and privileged as, I believe, it has never been given to man, I retire, I renounce— never, on my honour, to try again. So rest for ever—and let *me*!"

That, for Brydon, was the deep sense of this last demonstration—solemn, measured, directed, as he felt it to be. He brought it to a close, he turned away; and now verily he knew how deeply he had been stirred. He retraced his steps, taking up his candle, burnt, he observed, well-nigh to the socket, and marking again, lighten it as he would, the distinctness of his footfall; after which, in a moment, he knew himself at the other side of the house. He did here what he had not yet done at these hours—he opened half a casement, one of those in the front, and let in the air of the night; a thing he would have taken at any time previous for a sharp rupture of his spell. His spell was broken now, and it didn't matter—broken by his concession and his surrender, which made it idle henceforth that he should ever come back. The empty street—its other life so marked even by great lamp-lit vacancy—was within call, within touch; he stayed there as to be in it again, high above it though he was still perched; he watched as for some comforting common fact, some vulgar human note, the passage of a scavenger or a thief, some night-bird however base. He would have blessed that sign of life; he would have welcomed positively the slow approach of his friend the policeman, whom he had hitherto only sought to avoid, and was not sure that if the patrol had come into sight he mightn't have felt the impulse to get into relation with it, to hail it, on some pretext, from his fourth floor.

The pretext that wouldn't have been too silly or too compromising, the explanation that would have saved his dignity and kept his name, in such a case, out of the papers, was not definite to him: he was so occupied with the thought of recording his Discretion—as an effect of the vow he had just uttered to his intimate adversary—that the importance of this loomed large and something had overtaken all ironically his sense of proportion. If there had been a ladder applied to the front of the house, even one of the vertiginous perpendiculars employed by painters and roofers and sometimes left standing overnight, he would have managed somehow, astride of the window-sill, to compass by outstretched leg and arm that mode of descent. If there had been some such uncanny thing as he had found in his room at hotels, a workable fire-escape in the form of notched cable or a canvas shoot, he would have availed himself of it as a proof—well, of his present delicacy. He nursed that sentiment, as the question stood, a little in vain, and even—at the end of he scarce knew, once more, how long—found it, as by the action on his mind of the failure of response of the outer world, sinking back to vague anguish. It seemed to him he had waited an age for some stir of the great grim hush; the life of the town was itself under a spell—so unnaturally, up and down the whole prospect of known and rather ugly objects, the blankness and the silence lasted. Had they ever, he asked himself, the hard-faced houses, which had begun to look livid in the dim dawn, had they ever spoken so little to any need of his spirit? Great built voids, great crowded stillnesses put on, often, in the heart of cities, for the small hours, a sort of sinister mask, and it was of this large collective negation that Brydon presently became conscious—all the more that the break of day was, almost incredibly, now at hand, proving to him what a night he had made of it.

He looked again at his watch, saw what had become of his time-values (he had taken hours for minutes—not, as in other tense situations, minutes for hours) and the strange air of the streets was but the weak, the sullen flush of a dawn in which everything was still locked up. His choked appeal from his own open window had been the sole note of life, and he could but break off at last as for a worse despair. Yet while so deeply demoralised he was capable again of an impulse denoting—at least by his present measure—extraordinary resolution; of retracing his steps to the spot where he had turned cold with the extinction of his last pulse of doubt as to there being in the place another presence than his own. This required an effort strong enough to sicken him; but he had his reason, which over-mastered for the moment everything else. There was the whole of the rest of the house to traverse, and how should he screw himself to that if the door he had seen closed were at present open? He could hold to the idea that the closing had practically been for him an act of mercy, a chance offered him to descend, depart, get off the ground and never again profane it. This conception held together, it worked; but what it meant for him depended now clearly on the amount of forbearance his recent action, or rather his recent inaction, had engendered. The image of the "presence" whatever it was, waiting there for him to go—this image had not yet been so concrete for his nerves as when he stopped short of the point at which certainty would have come to him. For, with all his resolution, or more exactly with all his dread, he did stop short—he hung back from really seeing. The risk was too great and his fear too definite: it took at this moment an awful specific form.

He knew—yes, as he had never known anything—that, *should* he see the door open, it would all too abjectly be the end of him. It would mean that the agent of his shame—for his shame was the deep abjection—was once more at large and in general possession; and what glared him thus in the face was the act that this would determine for him. It would send him straight about to the window he had left open, and by that window, be long ladder and dangling rope as absent as they would, he saw himself uncontrollably insanely fatally take his way to the street. The hideous chance of this he at least could avert; but he could only avert it by recoiling in time from assurance. He had the whole house to deal with, this fact was still there; only he now knew that uncertainty alone could start him. He stole back from where he had checked himself—merely to do so was suddenly like safety—and, making blindly for the greater staircase, left gaping rooms and sounding passages behind. Here was the top of the stairs, with a fine large dim descent and three spacious landings to mark off. His instinct was all for mildness, but his feet were harsh on the floors, and, strangely, when he had in a couple of minutes become aware of this, it counted somehow for help. He couldn't have spoken, the tone of his voice would have scared him, and the common conceit or resource of "whistling in the dark" (whether literally or figuratively) have appeared basely vulgar; yet he liked none the less to hear himself go, and when he had reached his first landing—taking it all with no rush, but quite steadily—that stage of success drew from him a gasp of relief.

The house, withal, seemed immense, the scale of space again inordinate; the open rooms, to no one of which his eyes deflected, gloomed in their shuttered state like mouths of caverns; only the high skylight that formed the crown of the deep well created for him a medium in which he could advance, but which might have been, for queerness of colour, some watery under-world. He tried to think of something noble, as that his property was really grand, a splendid possession; but this nobleness took the form too of the clear delight with which he was finally to sacrifice it. They might come in now, the builders, the destroyers—they might come as soon as they would. At the end of two flights he had dropped to another zone, and from the middle of the third, with only one more left, he recognised the influence of the lower windows, of half-drawn blinds, of the occasional gleam of street-lamps, of the glazed spaces of the vestibule. This was the bottom of the sea, which showed an illumination of its own and which he even saw paved—when at a given moment he drew up to sink a long look over the banisters—with the marble squares of his childhood. By that time indubitably he felt, as he might have said in a commoner cause, better; it had allowed him to stop and draw breath, and the case increased with the sight of the old black-and-white slabs. But what he most felt was that now surely, with the element of impunity pulling him as by hard firm hands, the case was settled for what he might have seen above had he dared that last look. The closed door, blessedly remote now, was still closed—and he had only in short to reach that of the house.

He came down further, he crossed the passage forming the access to the last flight and if here again he stopped an instant it was almost for the sharpness of the thrill of assured escape. It made him shut his eyes—which opened again to the straight slope of the remainder of the stairs. Here was impunity still, but impunity almost excessive; inasmuch as the side-lights and the high fantracery of the entrance were glimmering straight into the hall; an appearance produced, he the next instant saw, by the fact that the vestibule gaped wide, that the hinged halves of the inner door had been thrown far back. Out of that again the *question* sprang at him, making his eyes, as he felt, half-start from his head, as they had done, at the top of the house, before the sign of the other door. If he had left that one open, hadn't he left this one closed, and wasn't he now in *most* immediate presence of some inconceivable occult activity? It was as sharp, the question, as a knife in his side, but the answer hung fire still and seemed to lose itself in the vague darkness to which the thin admitted dawn, glimmering archwise over the whole outer door, made a semicircular margin, a cold silvery nimbus that seemed to play a little as he looked—to shift and expand and contract.

49

It was as if there had been something within it, protected by indistinctness and corresponding in extent with the opaque surface behind, the painted panels of the last barrier to his escape, of which the key was in his pocket. The indistinctness mocked him even while he stared, affected him as somehow shrouding or challenging certitude, so that after faltering an instant on his step he let himself go with the sense that here *was* at last something to meet, to touch, to take, to know —something all unnatural and dreadful, but to advance upon which was the condition for him either of liberation or of supreme defeat. The penumbra, dense and dark, was the virtual screen of a figure which stood in it as still as some image erect in a niche or as some black-vizored sentinel guarding a treasure. Brydon was to know afterwards, was to recall and make out, the particular thing he had believed during the rest of his descent. He saw, in its great grey glimmering margin, the central vagueness diminish, and he felt it to be taking the very form toward which, for so many days, the passion of his curiosity had yearned. It gloomed, it loomed, it was something, it was somebody, the prodigy of a personal presence.

Rigid and conscious, spectral yet human, a man of his own substance and stature waited there to measure himself with his power to dismay. This only could it be—this only till he recognised, with his advance, that what made the face dim was the pair of raised hands that covered it and in which, so far from being offered in defiance, it was buried, as for dark deprecation. So Brydon, before him, took him in; with every fact of him now, in the higher light, hard and acute—his planted stillness, his vivid truth, his grizzled bent head and white masking hands, his queer actuality of evening-dress, of dangling double eye-glass, of gleaming silk lappet and white linen, of pearl button and gold watch-guard and polished shoe. No portrait by a great modern master could have presented him with more intensity, thrust him out of his frame with more art, as if there had been "treatment," of the consummate sort, in his every shade and salience. The revulsion, for our friend, had become, before he knew it, immense —this drop, in the act of apprehension, to the sense of his adversary's inscrutable manoeuvre. That meaning at least, while he gaped, it offered him; for he could but gape at his other self in this other anguish, gape as a proof that *he*, standing there for the achieved, the enjoyed, the triumphant life, couldn't be faced in his triumph. Wasn't the proof in the splendid covering hands, strong and completely spread?—so spread and so intentional that, in spite of a special verity that surpassed every other, the fact that one of these hands had lost two fingers, which were reduced to stumps, as if accidentally shot away, the face was effectually guarded and saved.

"Saved," though, *would* it be?—Brydon breathed his wonder till the very impunity of his attitude and the very insistence of his eyes produced, as he felt, a sudden stir which showed the next instant as a deeper portent, while the head raised itself, the betrayal of a braver purpose. The hands, as he looked, began to move, to open; then, as if deciding in a flash, dropped from the face and left it uncovered and presented. Horror, with the sight, had leaped into Brydon's throat, gasping there in a sound he couldn't utter; for the bared identity was too hideous as *his*, and his glare was the passion of his protest. The face, *that* face, Spencer Brydon's?—he searched it still, but looking away from it in dismay and denial, falling straight from his height of sublimity. It was unknown, inconceivable, awful, disconnected from any possibility!—He had been "sold," he inwardly moaned, stalking such game as this: the presence before him was a presence, the horror within him a horror, but the waste of his nights had been only grotesque and the success of his adventure an irony. Such an identity fitted his at *no* point, made its alternative monstrous. A thousand times yes, as it came upon him nearer now, the face was the face of a stranger. It came upon him nearer now, quite as one of those expanding fantastic images projected by the magic lantern of childhood; for the stranger, whoever he might be, evil, odious, blatant, vulgar, had advanced as for aggression, and he knew himself give ground. Then harder pressed still, sick with the force of his shock, and falling back as under the hot breath and the roused passion of a life larger than his own, a rage of personality before which his own collapsed, he felt the whole vision turn to darkness and his very feet give way. His head went round; he was going; he had gone.

CHAPTER III

What had next brought him back, clearly—though after how long?—was Mrs. Muldoon's voice, coming to him from quite near, from so near that he seemed presently to see her as kneeling on the ground before him while he lay looking up at her; himself not wholly on the ground, but half-raised and upheld—conscious, yes, of tenderness of support and, more particularly, of a head pillowed in extraordinary softness and faintly refreshing fragrance. He considered, he wondered, his wit but half at his service; then another face intervened, bending more directly over him, and he finally knew that Alice Staverton had made her lap an ample and perfect cushion to him, and that she had to this end seated herself on the lowest degree of the staircase, the rest of his long person remaining stretched on his old black-and-white slabs. They were cold, these marble squares of his youth; but *he* somehow was not, in this rich return of consciousness—the most wonderful hour, little by little, that he had ever known, leaving him, as it did, so gratefully, so abysmally passive, and yet as with a treasure of intelligence waiting all round him for quiet appropriation; dissolved, he might call it, in the air of the place and producing the golden glow of a late autumn afternoon. He had come back, yes—come back from further away than any man but himself had ever travelled; but it was strange how with this sense what he had come back *to* seemed really the great thing, and as if his prodigious journey had been all for the sake of it. Slowly but surely his consciousness grew, his vision of his state thus completing itself; he had been miraculously *carried* back—lifted and carefully borne as from where he had been picked up, the uttermost end of an interminable grey passage. Even with this he was suffered to rest, and what had now brought him to knowledge was the break in the long mild motion.

It had brought him to knowledge, to knowledge—yes, this was the beauty of his state; which came to resemble more and more that of a man who has gone to sleep on some news of a great inheritance, and then, after dreaming it away, after profaning it with matters strange to it, has waked up again to serenity of certitude and has only to lie and watch it grow. This was the drift of his patience—that he had only to let it shine on him. He must moreover, with intermissions, still have been lifted and borne; since why and how else should he have known himself, later on, with the afternoon glow intenser, no longer at the foot of his stairs—situated as these now seemed at that dark other end of his tunnel—but on a deep window-bench of his high saloon, over which had been spread, couch-fashion, a mantle of soft stuff lined with grey fur that was familiar to his eyes and that one of his hands kept fondly feeling as for its pledge of truth. Mrs. Muldoon's face had gone, but the other, the second he had recognised, hung over him in a way that showed how he was still propped and pillowed. He took it all in, and the more he took it the more it seemed to suffice: he was as much at peace as if he had had food and drink. It was the two women who had found him, on Mrs. Muldoon's having plied, at her usual hour, her latch-key—and on her having above all arrived while Miss Staverton still lingered near the house. She had been turning away, all anxiety, from worrying the vain bell-handle—her calculation having been of the hour of the good woman's visit; but the latter, blessedly, had come up while she was still there, and they had entered together. He had then lain, beyond the vestibule, very much as he was lying now—quite, that is, as he appeared to have fallen, but all so wondrously without bruise or gash; only in a depth of stupor. What he most took in, however, at present, with the steadier clearance, was that Alice Staverton had for a long unspeakable moment not doubted he was dead.

"It must have been that I *was*." He made it out as she held him. "Yes—I can only have died. You brought me literally to life. Only," he wondered, his eyes rising to her, "only, in the name of all the benedictions, how?"

It took her but an instant to bend her face and kiss him, and something in the manner of it, and in the way her hands clasped and locked his head while he felt the cool charity and virtue of her lips, something in all this beatitude somehow answered everything.

"And now I keep you," she said.

"Oh keep me, keep me!" he pleaded while her face still hung over him: in response to which it dropped again and stayed close, clingingly close. It was the seal of their situation—of which he tasted the impress for a long blissful moment in silence. But he came back. "Yet how did you know—?"

"I was uneasy. You were to have come, you remember—and you had sent no word."

"Yes, I remember—I was to have gone to you at one today." It caught on to their "old" life and relation—which were so near and so far. "I was still out there in my strange darkness—where was it, what was it? I must have stayed there so long." He could but wonder at the depth and the duration of his swoon.

"Since last night?" she asked with a shade of fear for her possible indiscretion.

"Since this morning—it must have been: the cold dim dawn of today. Where have I been," he vaguely wailed, "where have I been?" He felt her hold him close, and it was as if this helped him now to make in all security his mild moan. "What a long dark day!"

All in her tenderness she had waited a moment. "In the cold dim dawn?" she quavered.

But he had already gone on piecing together the parts of the whole prodigy. "As I didn't turn up you came straight—?"

She barely cast about. "I went first to your hotel—where they told me of your absence. You had dined out last evening and hadn't been back since. But they appeared to know you had been at your club."

"So you had the idea of *this*—?"

"Of what?" she asked in a moment.

"Well—of what has happened."

"I believed at least you'd have been here. I've known, all along," she said, "that you've been coming."

"'Known' it—?"

"Well, I've believed it. I said nothing to you after that talk we had a month ago—but I felt sure. I knew you *would*," she declared.

"That I'd persist, you mean?"

"That you'd see him."

"Ah but I didn't!" cried Brydon with his long wail. "There's somebody—an awful beast; whom I brought, too horribly, to bay. But it's not me."

At this she bent over him again, and her eyes were in his eyes. "No—it's not you." And it was as if, while her face hovered, he might have made out in it, hadn't it been so near, some particular meaning blurred by a smile. "No, thank heaven," she repeated, "it's not you! Of course it wasn't to have been."

"Ah but it *was*," he gently insisted. And he stared before him now as he had been staring for so many weeks. "I was to have known myself."

"You couldn't!" she returned consolingly. And then reverting, and as if to account further for what she had herself done, "But it wasn't only *that*, that you hadn't been at home," she went on. "I waited till the hour at which we had found Mrs. Muldoon that day of my going with you; and she arrived, as I've told you, while, failing to bring any one to the door, I lingered in my despair on the steps. After a little, if she hadn't come, by such a mercy, I should have found means to hunt her up. But it wasn't," said Alice Staverton, as if once more with her fine intentions—"it wasn't only that."

His eyes, as he lay, turned back to her. "What more then?"

She met it, the wonder she had stirred. "In the cold dim dawn, you say? Well, in the cold dim dawn of this morning I too saw you."

"Saw *me*—?"

"Saw *him*," said Alice Staverton. "It must have been at the same moment."

He lay an instant taking it in—as if he wished to be quite reasonable. "At the same moment?"

"Yes—in my dream again, the same one I've named to you. He came back to me. Then I knew it for a sign. He had come to you."

At this Brydon raised himself; he had to see her better. She helped him when she understood his movement, and he sat up, steadying himself beside her there on the window-bench and with his right hand grasping her left. "*He* didn't come to me."

"You came to yourself," she beautifully smiled.

"Ah I've come to myself now—thanks to you, dearest. But this brute, with his awful face—this brute's a black stranger. He's none of *me*, even as I *might* have been," Brydon sturdily declared.

But she kept the clearness that was like the breath of infallibility. "Isn't the whole point that you'd have been different?"

He almost scowled for it. "As different as *that*—?"

Her look again was more beautiful to him than the things of this world. "Haven't you exactly wanted to know *how* different? So this morning," she said, "you appeared to me."

"Like *him*?"

"A black stranger!"

"Then how did you know it was I?"

"Because, as I told you weeks ago, my mind, my imagination, has worked so over what you might, what you mightn't have been—to show you, you see, how I've thought of you. In the midst of that you came to me—that my wonder might be answered. So I knew," she went on; "and believed that, since the question held you too so fast, as you told me that day, you too would see for yourself. And when this morning I again saw I knew it would be because you had—and also then, from the first moment, because you somehow wanted me. *He* seemed to tell me of that. So why," she strangely smiled, "shouldn't I like him?"

It brought Spencer Brydon to his feet. "You 'like' that horror—?"

"I *could* have liked him. And to me," she said, "he was no horror. I had accepted him."

"'Accepted'—?" Brydon oddly sounded.

"Before, for the interest of his difference—yes. And as *I* didn't disown him, as *I* knew him—which you at last, confronted with him in his difference, so cruelly didn't, my dear—well, he must have been, you see, less dreadful to me. And it may have pleased him that I pitied him."

She was beside him on her feet, but still holding his hand—still with her arm supporting him. But though it all brought for him thus a dim light, "You 'pitied' him?" he grudgingly, resentfully asked.

"He has been unhappy, he has been ravaged," she said.

"And haven't I been unhappy? Am not I—you've only to look at me!—ravaged?"

"Ah I don't say I like him *better*," she granted after a thought. "But he's grim, he's worn—and things have happened to him. He doesn't make shift, for sight, with your charming monocle."

"No"—it struck Brydon; "I couldn't have sported mine 'down-town.' They'd have guyed me there."

"His great convex pince-nez—I saw it, I recognised the kind—is for his poor ruined sight. And his poor right hand—!"

"Ah!" Brydon winced—whether for his proved identity or for his lost fingers. Then, "He has a million a year," he lucidly added. "But he hasn't you."

"And he isn't—no, he isn't—*you*!" she murmured, as he drew her to his breast.

THE ROLL-CALL OF THE REEF,
by A. T. Quiller-Couch

"Yes, sir," said my host, the quarryman, reaching down the relics from their hook in the wall over the chimney-piece; "they've hung there all my time, and most of my father's. The women won't touch 'em; they're afraid of the story. So here they'll dangle, and gather dust and smoke, till another tenant comes and tosses 'em out o' doors for rubbish. Whew! 'tis coarse weather, surely."

He went to the door, opened it, and stood studying the gale that beat upon his cottage-front, straight from the Manacle Reef. The rain drove past him into the kitchen, aslant like threads of gold silk in the shine of the wreck-wood fire. Meanwhile, by the same firelight, I examined the relics on my knee. The metal of each was tarnished out of knowledge. But the trumpet was evidently an old cavalry trumpet, and the threads of its parti-colored sling, though fretted and dusty, still hung together. Around the side-drum, beneath its cracked brown varnish, I could hardly trace a royal coat-of-arms and a legend running, "Per Mare Per Terram"—the motto of the marines. Its parchment, though black and scented with woodsmoke, was limp and mildewed; and I began to tighten up the straps—under which the drumsticks had been loosely thrust—with the idle purpose of seeing if some music might be got out of the old drum yet.

But as I turned it on my knee, I found the drum attached to the trumpet-sling by a curious barrel-shaped padlock, and paused to examine this. The body of the lock was composed of half a dozen brass rings, set accurately edge to edge; and, rubbing the brass with my thumb, I saw that each of the six had a series of letters engraved around it.

I knew the trick of it, I thought. Here was one of those word padlocks, once so common; only to be opened by getting the rings to spell a certain word, which the dealer confides to you.

My host shut and barred the door, and came back to the hearth.

"'Twas just such a wind—east by south—that brought in what you've got between your hands. Back in the year 'nine, it was; my father has told me the tale a score o' times. You're twisting round the rings, I see. But you'll never guess the word. Parson Kendall, he made the word, and he locked down a couple o' ghosts in their graves with it; and when his time came he went to his own grave and took the word with him."

"Whose ghosts, Matthew?"

"You want the story, I see, sir. My father could tell it better than I can. He was a young man in the year 'nine, unmarried at the time, and living in this very cottage, just as I be. That's how he came to get mixed up with the tale."

He took a chair, lighted a short pipe, and went on, with his eyes fixed on the dancing violet flames:

"Yes, he'd ha' been about thirty year old in January, eighteen 'nine. The storm got up in the night o' the twenty-first o' that month. My father was dressed and out long before daylight; he never was one to bide in bed, let be that the gale by this time was pretty near lifting the thatch over his head. Besides which, he'd fenced a small 'taty-patch that winter, down by Lowland Point, and he wanted to see if it stood the night's work. He took the path across Gunner's Meadow— where they buried most of the bodies afterward. The wind was right in his teeth at the time, and once on the way (he's told me this often) a great strip of oarweed came flying through the darkness and fetched him a slap on the cheek like a cold hand. He made shift pretty well till he got to Lowland, and then had to drop upon hands and knees and crawl, digging his fingers every now and then into a shingle to hold on, for he declared to me that the stones, some of them as big as a man's head, kept rolling and driving past till it seemed the whole foreshore was moving westward under him. The fence was gone, of course; not a stick left to show where it stood; so that, when first he came to the place, he thought he must have missed his bearings. My father, sir, was a very religious man; and if he reckoned the end of the world was at hand—there in the great wind and night, among the moving stones—you may believe he was certain of it when he heard a gun fired, and, with the same, saw a flame shoot up out of the darkness to windward, mak-ing a sudden fierce light in all the place about. All he could find to think or say was, 'The Second Coming! The Second Coming! The Bridegroom cometh, and the wicked He will toss like a ball into a large country'; and being already upon his knees, he just bowed his head and 'bided, saying this over and over.

"But by'm by, between two squalls, he made bold to lift his head and look, and then by the light—a bluish color 'twas—he saw all the coast clear away to Manacle Point, and off the Manacles in the thick of the weather, a sloop-of-war with topgallants housed, driving stern foremost toward the reef. It was she, of course, that was burning the fire. My father could see the white streak and the ports of her quite plain as she rose to it, a little outside the breakers, and he guessed easy enough that her captain had just managed to wear ship and was try-ing to force her nose to the sea with the help of her small bower anchor and the scrap or two of canvas that hadn't yet been blown out of her. But while he looked, she fell off, giving her broadside to it, foot by foot, and drifting back on the breakers around Carn Du and the Varses. The rocks lie so thick thereabout that 'twas a toss up which she struck first; at any rate, my father couldn't tell at the time, for just then the flare died down and went out.

"Well, sir, he turned then in the dark and started back for Coverack to cry the dismal tidings—though well knowing ship and crew to be past any hope, and as he turned the wind lifted him and tossed him forward 'like a ball,' as he'd been saying, and homeward along the foreshore. As you know, 'tis ugly work, even by daylight, picking your way among the stones there, and my father was prettily knocked about at first in the dark. But by this 'twas nearer seven than six o'clock, and the day spreading. By the time he reached North Corner, a man could see to read print; hows'ever, he looked neither out to sea nor toward Cov-erack, but headed straight for the first cottage—the same that stands above North Corner today. A man named Billy Ede lived there then, and when my father burst into the kitchen bawling, 'Wreck! wreck!' he saw Billy Ede's wife, Ann, stand-ing there in her clogs with a shawl over her head, and her clothes wringing wet.

"'Save the chap,' says Billy Ede's wife, Ann. 'What d'ee mean by crying stale fish at that rate?'

"'But 'tis a wreck, I tell 'e,'

"'I'v a-zeed'n, too; and so has every one with an eye in his head,'

"And with that she pointed straight over my father's shoulder, and he turned; and there, close under Dolor Point, at the end of Coverack town he saw another wreck washing, and the point black with people, like emmets, running to and fro in the morning light. While he stood staring at her, he heard a trumpet sounded on board, the notes coming in little jerks, like a bird rising against the wind; but faintly, of course, because of the distance and the gale blowing—though this had dropped a little.

"'She's a transport,' said Billy Ede's wife, Ann, 'and full of horse-soldiers, fine long men. When she struck they must ha' pitched the horses over first to lighten the ship, for a score of dead horses had washed in afore I left, half an hour back. An' three or four soldiers, too—fine long corpses in white breeches and jackets of blue and gold. I held the lantern to one. Such a straight young man.'

"My father asked her about the trumpeting.

"'That's the queerest bit of all. She was burnin' a light when me an' my man joined the crowd down there. All her masts had gone; whether they carried away, or were cut away to ease her, I don't rightly know. Her keelson was broke under her and her bottom sagged and stove, and she had just settled down like a setting hen—just the leastest list to starboard; but a man could stand there easy. They had rigged up ropes across her, from bulwark to bulwark, an' beside these the men were mustered, holding on like grim death whenever the sea made a clean breach over them, an' standing up like heroes as soon as it passed. The captain an' the officers were clinging to the rail of the quarter-deck, all in their golden uniforms, waiting for the end as if 'twas King George they expected. There was no way to help, for she lay right beyond cast of line, though our folk tried it fifty times. And beside them clung a trumpeter, a whacking big man, an' between the heavy seas he would lift his trumpet with one hand, and blow a call; and every time he blew the men gave a cheer. There (she says)—hark 'ee now—there he goes agen! But you won't hear no cheering any more, for few are left to cheer, and their voices weak. Bitter cold the wind is, and I reckon it numbs their grip o' the ropes, for they were dropping off fast with every sea when my man sent me home to get his breakfast. Another wreck, you say? Well, there's no hope for the tender dears if 'tis the Manacles. You'd better run down and help yonder; though 'tis little help any man can give. Not one came in alive while I was there. The tide's flowing, an' she won't hold together another hour, they say.'

"Well, sure enough, the end was coming fast when my father got down to the Point. Six men had been cast up alive, or just breathing—a seaman and five troopers. The seaman was the only one that had breath to speak; and while they were carrying him into the town, the word went round that the ship's name was the *Despatch*, transport, homeward bound from Corunna, with a detachment of the Seventh Hussars, that had been fighting out there with Sir John Moore. The seas had rolled her further over by this time, and given her decks a pretty sharp slope; but a dozen men still held on, seven by the ropes near the ship's waist, a couple near the break of the poop, and three on the quarter-deck. Of these three my father made out one to be the skipper; close to him clung an officer in full regimentals—his name, they heard after, was Captain Duncanfield; and last came the tall trumpeter; and if you'll believe me, the fellow was making shift there, at the very last, to blow 'God Save the King.' What's more, he got to 'Send us victorious,' before an extra big sea came bursting across and washed them off the deck—every man but one of the pair beneath the poop—and he dropped his hold before the next wave; being stunned, I reckon. The others went out of sight at once, but the trumpeter—being, as I said, a powerful man as well as a tough swimmer—rose like a duck, rode out a couple of breakers, and came in on the crest of the third. The folks looked to see him broke like an egg at their very feet; but when the smother cleared, there he was, lying face downward on a ledge below them; and one of the men that happened to have a rope round him—I forget the fellow's name, if I ever heard it—jumped down and grabbed him by the ankle as he began to slip back. Before the next big sea, the pair were hauled high enough to be out of harm, and another heave brought them up to grass. Quick work, but master trumpeter wasn't quite dead; nothing worse than a cracked head and three staved ribs. In twenty minutes or so they had him in bed, with the doctor to tend him.

Now was the time—nothing being left alive upon the transport—for my father to tell of the sloop he'd seen driving upon the Manacles. And when he got a hearing, though the most were set upon salvage, and believed a wreck in the hand, so to say, to be worth half a dozen they couldn't see, a good few volunteered to start off with him and have a look. They crossed Lowland Point; no ship to be seen on the Manacles nor anywhere upon the sea. One or two was for calling my father a liar. 'Wait till we come to Dean Point,' said he. Sure enough, on the far side of Dean Point they found the sloop's mainmast washing about with half a dozen men lashed to it, men in red jackets, every mother's son drowned and staring; and a little further on, just under the Dean, three or four bodies cast up on the shore, one of them a small drummer-boy, side-drum and all; and nearby part of a ship's gig, with *H.M.S. Primrose* cut on the sternboard. From this point on the shore was littered thick with wreckage and dead bodies— the most of them marines in uniform—and in Godrevy Cove, in particular, a heap of furniture from the captain's cabin, and among it a water-tight box, not much damaged, and full of papers, by which, when it came to be examined, next day, the wreck was easily made out to be the *Primrose* of eighteen guns, outward bound from Portsmouth, with a fleet of transports for the Spanish war—thirty sail, I've heard, but I've never heard what became of them. Being handled by merchant skippers, no doubt they rode out the gale, and reached the Tagus safe and sound. Not but what the captain of the *Primrose*—Mein was his name—did quite right to try and club-haul his vessel when he found himself under the land; only he never ought to have got there, if he took proper soundings. But it's easy talking.

"The *Primrose*, sir, was a handsome vessel—for her size one of the handsomest in the King's service—and newly fitted out at Plymouth Dock. So the boys had brave pickings from her in the way of brass-work, ship's instruments, and the like, let alone some barrels of stores not much spoiled. They loaded themselves with as much as they could carry, and started for home, meaning to make a second journey before the preventive men got wind of their doings, and came to spoil the fun. 'Hullo!' says my father, and dropped his gear, 'I do believe there's a leg moving!' and running fore, he stooped over the small drummer-boy that I told you about. The poor little chap was lying there, with his face a mass of bruises, and his eyes closed; but he had shifted one leg an inch or two, and was still breathing. So my father pulled out a knife, and cut him free from his drum—that was lashed on to him with a double turn of Manila rope—and took him up and carried him along here to this very room that we're sitting in. He lost a good deal by this; for when he went back to fetch the bundle he'd dropped, the preventive men had got hold of it, and were thick as thieves along the foreshore; so that 'twas only by paying one or two to look the other way that he picked up anything worth carrying off; which you'll allow to be hard, seeing that he was the first man to give news of the wreck.

"Well, the inquiry was held, of course, and my father gave evidence, and for the rest they had to trust to the sloop's papers, for not a soul was saved besides the drummer-boy, and he was raving in a fever, brought on by the cold and the fright. And the seaman and the five troopers gave evidence about the loss of the *Despatch*. The tall trumpeter, too, whose ribs were healing, came forward and kissed the book; but somehow his head had been hurt in coming ashore, and he talked foolish-like, and 'twas easy seen he would never be a proper man again. The others were taken up to Plymouth, and so went their ways; but the trumpeter stayed on in Coverack; and King George, finding he was fit for nothing, sent him down a trifle of a pension after a while—enough to keep him in board and lodging, with a bit of tobacco over.

"Now the first time that this man—William Tallifer he called himself—met with the drummer-boy, was about a fortnight after the little chap had bettered enough to be allowed a short walk out of doors, which he took, if you please, in full regimentals. There never was a soldier so proud of his dress. His own suit had shrunk a brave bit with the salt water; but into ordinary frock an' corduroy he declared he would not get, not if he had to go naked the rest of his life; so my father—being a good-natured man, and handy with the needle—turned to and repaired damages with a piece or two of scarlet cloth cut from the jacket of one of the drowned Marines. Well, the poor little chap chanced to be standing, in this rig out, down by the gate of Gunner's Meadow, where they had buried two score and over of his comrades. The morning was a fine one, early in March month; and along came the cracked trumpeter, likewise taking a stroll.

"'Hullo!' says he; 'good mornin'! And what might you be doin' here?'

"'I was a-wishin',' says the boy, 'I had a pair o' drumsticks. Our lads were buried yonder without so much as a drum tapped or a musket fired; and that's not Christian burial for British soldiers.'

"'Phut!' says the trumpeter, and spat on the ground; 'a parcel of Marines!'

"The boy eyed him a second or so, and answered up: 'If I'd a tav of turf handy, I'd bung it at your mouth, you greasy cavalryman, and learn you to speak respectful of your betters. The Marines are the handiest body o' men in the service.'

"The trumpeter looked down on him from the height of six-foot-two, and asked: 'Did they die well?'

"'They died very well. There was a lot of running to and fro at first, and some of the men began to cry, and a few to strip off their clothes. But when the ship fell off for the last time, Captain Mein turned and said something to Major Griffiths, the commanding officer on board, and the Major called out to me to beat to quarters. It might have been for a wedding, he sang it out so cheerful. We'd had word already that 'twas to be parade order; and the men fell in as trim and decent as if they were going to church. One or two even tried to shave at the last moment. The Major wore his medals. One of the seamen, seeing I had work to keep

59

the drum steady—the sling being a bit loose for me, and the wind what you remember—lashed it tight with a piece of rope; and that saved my life afterward, a drum being as good as cork until it's stove. I kept beating away until every man was on deck—and then the Major formed them up and told them to die like British soldiers, and the chaplain was in the middle of a prayer when she struck. In ten minutes she was gone. That was how they died, cavalryman.'

"'And that was very well done, drummer of the Marines. What's your name?'

"'John Christian.'

"'Mine's William George Tallifer, trumpeter of the Seventh Light Dragoons—the Queen's Own. I played "God Save the King" while our men were drowning. Captain Duncanfield told me to sound a call or two, to put them in heart; but that matter of "God Save the King" was a notion of my own. I won't say anything to hurt the feelings of a Marine, even if he's not much over five-foot tall; but the Queen's Own Hussars is a tearin' fine regiment. As between horse and foot, 'tis a question o' which gets a chance. All the way from Sahagun to Corunna 'twas we that took and gave the knocks—at Mayorga and Rueda, and Bennyventy.'—The reason, sir, I can speak the names so pat, is that my father learnt them by heart afterward from the trumpeter, who was always talking about Mayorga and Rueda and Bennyventy—'We made the rear-guard, after General Paget; and drove the French every time; and all the infantry did was to sit about in wine-shops till we whipped 'em out, an' steal an' straggle an' play the tom-fool in general. And when it came to a stand-up fight at Corunna, 'twas we that had to stay seasick aboard the transports, an' watch the infantry in the thick o' the caper. Very well they behaved, too—'specially the Fourth Regiment, an' the Forty-Second Highlanders and the Dirty Half-Hundred. Oh, ay; they're decent regiments, all three. But the Queen's Own Hussars is a tearin' fine regiment. So you played on your drum when the ship was goin' down? Drummer John Christian, I'll have to get you a new pair of sticks.'"

The very next day the trumpeter marched into Helston, and got a carpenter there to turn him a pair of box-wood drumsticks for the boy. And this was the beginning of one of the most curious friendships you ever heard tell of. Nothing delighted the pair more than to borrow a boat off my father and pull out to the rocks where the *Primrose* and the *Despatch* had struck and sunk; and on still days 'twas pretty to hear them out there off the Manacles, the drummer playing his tattoo—for they always took their music with them—and the trumpeter practicing calls, and making his trumpet speak like an angel. But if the weather turned roughish, they'd be walking together and talking; leastwise the youngster listened while the other discoursed about Sir John's campaign in Spain and Portugal, telling how each little skirmish befell; and of Sir John himself, and General Baird, and General Paget, and Colonel Vivian, his own commanding officer, and what kind of men they were; and of the last bloody stand-up at Corunna, and so forth, as if neither could have enough.

But all this had to come to an end in the late summer, for the boy, John Christian, being now well and strong again, must go up to Plymouth to report himself. 'Twas his own wish (for I believe King George had forgotten all about him), but his friend wouldn't hold him back. As for the trumpeter, my father had made an arrangement to take him on as lodger, as soon as the boy left; and on the morning fixed for the start, he was up at the door here by five o'clock, with his trumpet slung by his side, and all the rest of his belongings in a small valise. A Monday morning it was, and after breakfast he had fixed to walk with the boy some way on the road toward Helston, where the coach started. My father left them at breakfast together, and went out to meat the pig, and do a few odd morning jobs of that sort. When he came back, the boy was still at table, and the trumpeter sat with the rings in his hands, hitched together just as they be at this moment.

"'Look at this,' he says to my father, showing him the lock. 'I picked it up off a starving brass-worker in Lisbon, and it is not one of your common locks that one word of six letters will open at any time. There's janius in this lock; for you've only to make the rings spell any six-letter word you please and snap down the lock upon that, and never a soul can open it—not the maker, even—until somebody comes along that knows the word you snapped it on. Now Johnny here's goin', and he leaves his drum behind him; for, though he can make pretty music on it, the parchment sags in wet weather, by reason of the sea-water gettin' at it; an' if he carries it to Plymouth, they'll only condemn it and give him another. And, as for me, I shan't have the heart to put lip to the trumpet any more when Johnny's gone. So we've chosen a word together, and locked 'em together upon that; and, by your leave, I'll hang 'em here together on the hook over your fireplace. Maybe Johnny'll come back; maybe not. Maybe, if he comes, I'll be dead an' gone, an' he'll take 'em apart an' try their music for old sake's sake. But if he never comes, nobody can separate 'em; for nobody beside knows the word. And if you marry and have sons, you can tell 'em that here are tied together the souls of Johnny Christian, drummer of the Marines, and William George Tallifer, once trumpeter of the Queen's Own Hussars. Amen.'

"With that he hung the two instruments 'pon the hook there; and the boy stood up and thanked my father and shook hands; and the pair went out of the door, toward Helston.

"Somewhere on the road they took leave of one another; but nobody saw the parting, nor heard what was said between them. About three in the afternoon the trumpeter came walking back over the hill; and by the time my father came home from the fishing, the cottage was tidied up, and the tea ready, and the whole place shining like a new pin. From that time for five years he lodged here with my father, looking after the house and tilling the garden. And all the time he was steadily failing; the hurt in his head spreading, in a manner, to his limbs. My father watched the feebleness growing on him, but said nothing. And from first to last neither spake a word about the drummer, John Christian; nor did any letter reach them, nor word of his doings.

"The rest of the tale you're free to believe, sir, or not, as you please. It stands upon my father's words, and he always declared he was ready to kiss the Book upon it, before judge and jury. He said, too, that he never had the wit to make up such a yarn, and he defied any one to explain about the lock, in particular, by any other tale. But you shall judge for yourself.

"My father said that about three o'clock in the morning, April fourteenth, of the year 'fourteen, he and William Tallifer were sitting here, just as you and I, sir, are sitting now. My father had put on his clothes a few minutes before, and was mending his spiller by the light of the horn lantern, meaning to set off before daylight to haul the trammel. The trumpeter hadn't been to bed at all. Toward the last he mostly spent his nights (and his days, too) dozing in the elbow-chair where you sit at this minute. He was dozing then (my father said) with his chin dropped forward on his chest, when a knock sounded upon the door, and the door opened, and in walked an upright young man in scarlet regimentals.

"He had grown a brave bit, and his face the color of wood-ashes; but it was the drummer, John Christian. Only his uniform was different from the one he used to wear, and the figures '38' shone in brass upon his collar.

"The drummer walked past my father as if he never saw him, and stood by the elbow-chair and said:

"'Trumpeter, trumpeter, are you one with me?'

"And the trumpeter just lifted the lids of his eyes, and answered: 'How should I not be one with you, drummer Johnny—Johnny boy? If you come, I count; if you march, I mark time; until the discharge comes.'

"'The discharge has come tonight,' said the drummer; 'and the word is Corunna no longer.' And stepping to the chimney-place, he unhooked the drum and trumpet, and began to twist the brass rings of the lock, spelling the word aloud, so—'C-O-R-U-N-A.' When he had fixed the last letter, the padlock opened in his hand.

"'Did you know, trumpeter, that, when I came to Plymouth, they put me into a line regiment?'

"'The 38th is a good regiment,' answered the old Hussar, still in his dull voice; 'I went back with them from Sahagun to Corunna. At Corunna they stood in General Fraser's division, on the right. They behaved well.'

"'But I'd fain see the Marines again,' says the drummer, handing him the trumpet; 'and you, you shall call once more for the Queen's Own. Matthew,' he says, suddenly, turning on my father—and when he turned, my father saw for the first time that his scarlet jacket had a round hole by the breast-bone, and that the blood was welling there—'Matthew, we shall want your boat.'

"Then my father rose on his legs like a man in a dream, while the two slung on, the one his drum, and t'other his trumpet. He took the lantern and went quaking before them down to the shore, and they breathed heavily behind him; and they stepped into his boat, and my father pushed off.

"'Row you first for Dolor Point,' says the drummer. So my father rowed them past the white houses of Coverack to Dolor Point, and there, at a word, lay on his oars. And the trumpeter, William Tallifer, put his trumpet to his mouth and sounded the reveille. The music of it was like rivers running.

"'They will follow,' said the drummer. 'Matthew, pull you now for the Manacles.'

"So my father pulled for the Manacles, and came to an easy close outside Carn Du. And the drummer took his sticks and beat a tattoo, there by the edge of the reef; and the music of it was like a rolling chariot.

"'That will do,' says he, breaking off; 'they will follow. Pull now for the shore under Gunner's Meadow.'

"Then my father pulled for the shore and ran his boat in under Gunner's Meadow. And they stepped out, all three, and walked up to the meadow. By the gate the drummer halted, and began his tattoo again, looking outward the darkness over the sea.

"And while the drum beat, and my father held his breath, there came up out of the sea and the darkness a troop of many men, horse and foot, and formed up among the graves; and others rose out of the graves and formed up—drowned Marines with bleached faces, and pale Hussars, riding their horses, all lean and shadowy. There was no clatter of hoofs or accouterments, my father said, but a soft sound all the while like the beating of a bird's wing; and a black shadow lay like a pool about the feet of all. The drummer stood upon a little knoll just inside the gate, and beside him the tall trumpeter, with hand on hip, watching them gather; and behind them both, my father, clinging to the gate. When no more came, the drummer stopped playing, and said, 'Call the roll.'

"Then the trumpeter stepped toward the end man of the rank and called, 'Troop Sergeant-Major Thomas Irons,' and the man answered in a thin voice, 'Here.'

"'Troop Sergeant-Major Thomas Irons, how is it with you?'

"The man answered, 'How should it be with me? When I was young, I betrayed a girl; and when I was grown, I betrayed a friend, and for these I must pay. But I died as a man ought. God save the King!'

"The trumpeter called to the next man, 'Trooper Henry Buckingham,' and the next man answered, 'Here.'

"'Trooper Henry Buckingham, how it is with you?'

"'How should it be with me? I was a drunkard, and I stole, and in Lugo, in a wine-shop, I killed a man. But I died as a man should. God save the King!'

"So the trumpeter went down the line; and when he had finished, the drummer took it up, hailing the dead Marines in their order. Each man answered to his name, and each man ended with 'God save the King!' When all were hailed, the drummer stepped backward to his mound, and called:

"'It is well. You are content, and we are content to join you. Wait, now, a little while.'

"With this he turned and ordered my father to pick up the lantern, and lead the way back. As my father picked it up, he heard the ranks of the dead men cheer and call, 'God save the King!' all together, and saw them waver and fade back into the dark, like a breath fading off a pane.

"But when they came back here to the kitchen, and my father set the lantern down, it seemed they'd both forgot about him. For the drummer turned in the lantern-light—and my father could see the blood still welling out of the hole in his breast—and took the trumpet-sling from around the other's neck, and locked drum and trumpet together again, choosing the letters on the lock very carefully. While he did this, he said:

"'The word is no more Corunna, but Bayonne. As you left out an "n" in Corunna, so must I leave out an "n" in Bayonne,' And before snapping the padlock, he spelt out the word slowly—'B-A-Y-O-N-E.' After that, he used no more speech; but turned and hung the two instruments back on the hook; and then took the trumpeter by the arm; and the pair walked out into the darkness, glancing neither to right nor left.

"My father was on the point of following, when he heard a sort of sigh behind him; and there, sitting in the elbow-chair, was the very trumpeter he had just seen walk out by the door! If my father's heart jumped before, you may believe it jumped quicker now. But after a bit, he went up to the man asleep in the chair and put a hand upon him. It was the trumpeter in flesh and blood that he touched; but though the flesh was warm, the trumpeter was dead.

"Well, sir, they buried him three days after; and at first my father was minded to say nothing about his dream (as he thought it). But the day after the funeral, he met Parson Kendall coming from Helston market: and the parson called out:

'Have 'ee heard the news the coach brought down this mornin'?' 'What news?' says my father. 'Why, that peace is agreed upon.' 'None too soon,' says my father. 'Not soon enough for our poor lads at Bayonne,' the parson answered. 'Bayonne!' cries my father, with a jump. 'Why, yes,' and the parson told him all about a great sally the French had made on the night of April 13th. 'Do you happen to know if the 38th Regiment was engaged?' my father asked. 'Come, now,' said Parson Kendall, 'I didn't know you was so well up in the campaign. But, as it happens, I do know that the 38th was engaged, for 'twas they that held a cottage and stopped the French advance.'

"Still my father held his tongue; and when, a week later, he walked into Helston and bought a *Mercury* off the Sherborne rider, and got the landlord of the 'Angel' to spell out the list of killed and wounded, sure enough, there among the killed was Drummer John Christian, of the 38th Foot.

"After this there was nothing for a religious man but to make a clean breast. So my father went up to Parson Kendall, and told the whole story. The parson listened, and put a question or two, and then asked:

"'Have you tried to open the lock since that night?'

"'I haven't dared to touch it,' says my father.

"'Then come along and try.' When the parson came to the cottage here, he took the things off the hook and tried the lock. 'Did he say "Bayonne"? The word has seven letters.'

"'Not if you spell it with one "n" as he did,' says my father.

"The parson spelt it out—'B-A-Y-O-N-E,' 'Whew!' says he, for the lock had fallen open in his hand.

"He stood considering it a moment, and then he says: 'I tell you what. I shouldn't blab this all round the parish, if I was you. You won't get no credit for truth-telling, and a miracle's wasted on a set of fools. But if you like, I'll shut down the lock again upon a holy word that no one but me shall know, and neither drummer nor trumpeter, dead or alive, shall frighten the secret out of me.'

"'I wish to heaven you would, parson,' said my father.

"The parson chose the holy word there and then, and shut the lock upon it, and hung the drum and trumpet back in their place. He is gone long since, taking the word with him. And till the lock is broken by force, nobody will ever separate those two."

THE BOWMEN,
by Arthur Machen

It was during the Retreat of the Eighty Thousand, and the authority of the Censorship is sufficient excuse for not being more explicit. But it was on the most awful day of that awful time, on the day when ruin and disaster came so near that their shadow fell over London far away; and, without any certain news, the hearts of men failed within them and grew faint; as if the agony of the army in the battlefield had entered into their souls.

On this dreadful day, then, when three hundred thousand men in arms with all their artillery swelled like a flood against the little English company, there was one point above all other points in our battle line that was for a time in awful danger, not merely of defeat, but of utter annihilation. With the permission of the Censorship and of the military expert, this corner may, perhaps, be described as a salient, and if this angle were crushed and broken, then the English force as a whole would be shattered, the Allied left would be turned, and Sedan would inevitably follow.

All the morning the German guns had thundered and shrieked against this corner, and against the thousand or so of men who held it. The men joked at the shells, and found funny names for them, and had bets about them, and greeted them with scraps of music-hall songs. But the shells came on and burst, and tore good Englishmen limb from limb, and tore brother from brother, and as the heat of the day increased so did the fury of that terrific cannonade. There was no help, it seemed. The English artillery was good, but there was not nearly enough of it; it was being steadily battered into scrap iron.

There comes a moment in a storm at sea when people say to one another, "It is at its worst; it can blow no harder," and then there is a blast ten times more fierce than any before it. So it was in these British trenches.

There were no stouter hearts in the whole world than the hearts of these men; but even they were appalled as this seven-times-heated hell of the German cannonade fell upon them and overwhelmed them and destroyed them. And at this very moment they saw from their trenches that a tremendous host was moving against their lines. Five hundred of the thousand remained, and as far as they could see the German infantry was pressing on against them, column upon column, a gray world of men, ten thousand of them, as it appeared afterwards.

There was no hope at all. They shook hands, some of them. One man improvised a new version of the battle-song, "Good-by, good-by to Tipperary," ending with "And we shan't get there." And they all went on firing steadily. The officer pointed out that such an opportunity for high-class fancy shooting might never occur again; the Tipperary humorist asked, "What price Sidney Street?" And the few machine guns did their best. But everybody knew it was of no use. The dead gray bodies lay in companies and battalions, as others came on and on and on, and they swarmed and stirred, and advanced from beyond and beyond.

"World without end. Amen," said one of the British soldiers with some irrelevance as he took aim and fired. And then he remembered—he says he cannot think why or wherefore—a queer vegetarian restaurant in London where he had once or twice eaten eccentric dishes of cutlets made of lentils and nuts that pretended to be steak. On all the plates in this restaurant there was printed a figure of St. George in blue, with the motto, "*Adsit Anglis Sanctus Georgius*"—"May St. George be a present help to the English." This soldier happened to know Latin and other useless things, and now, as he fired at his man in the gray advancing mass—three hundred yards away—he uttered the pious vegetarian motto. He went on firing to the end, and at last Bill on his right had to clout him cheerfully over the head to make him stop, pointing out as he did so that the King's ammunition cost money and was not lightly to be wasted in drilling funny patterns into dead Germans.

For as the Latin scholar uttered his invocation he felt something between a shudder and an electric shock pass through his body. The roar of the battle died down in his ears to a gentle murmur; instead of it, he says, he heard a great voice and a shout louder than a thunder-peal crying, "Array, array, array!"

His heart grew hot as a burning coal, it grew cold as ice within him, as it seemed to him that a tumult of voices answered to his summons. He heard, or seemed to hear, thousands shouting: "St. George! St. George!"

"Ha! Messire, ha! sweet Saint, grant us good deliverance!"

"St. George for merry England!"

"Harow! Harow! Monseigneur St. George, succor us!"

"Ha! St. George! Ha! St. George! a long bow and a strong bow."

"Heaven's Knight, aid us!"

And as the soldier heard these voices he saw before him, beyond the trench, a long line of shapes, with a shining about them. They were like men who drew the bow, and with another shout, their cloud of arrows flew singing and tingling through the air towards the German hosts.

The other men in the trench were firing all the while. They had no hope; but they aimed just as if they had been shooting at Bisley.

Suddenly one of them lifted up his voice in the plainest English.

"Gawd help us!" he bellowed to the man next to him, "but we're blooming marvels! Look at those gray…gentlemen, look at them! D'ye see them? They're not going down in dozens nor in 'undreds; it's thousands, it is. Look! look! there's a regiment gone while I'm talking to ye."

"Shut it!" the other soldier bellowed, taking aim, "what are ye gassing about?"

But he gulped with astonishment even as he spoke, for, indeed, the gray men were falling by the thousands. The English could hear the guttural scream of the German officers, the crackle of their revolvers as they shot the reluctant; and still line after line crashed to the earth.

All the while the Latin-bred soldier heard the cry:

"Harow! Harow! Monseigneur, dear Saint, quick to our aid! St. George help us!"

"High Chevalier, defend us!"

The singing arrows fled so swift and thick that they darkened the air, the heathen horde melted from before them.

"More machine guns!" Bill yelled to Tom.

"Don't hear them," Tom yelled back.

"But, thank God, anyway; they've got it in the neck."

In fact, there were ten thousand dead German soldiers left before that salient of the English army, and consequently there was no Sedan. In Germany, a country ruled by scientific principles, the Great General Staff decided that the contemptible English must have employed shells containing an unknown gas of a poisonous nature, as no wounds were discernible on the bodies of the dead German soldiers. But the man who knew what nuts tasted like when they called themselves steak knew also that St. George had brought his Agincourt Bowmen to help the English.

OMAN,
by Leopold Kompert

The uproarious merriment of a wedding-feast burst forth into the night from a brilliantly lighted house in the "gasse" (narrow street). It was one of those nights touched with the warmth of spring, but dark and full of soft mist. Most fitting it was for a celebration of the union of two yearning hearts to share the same lot, a lot that may possibly dawn in sunny brightness, but also become clouded and sullen—for a long, long time! But how merry and joyous they were over there, those people of the happy olden times! They, like us, had their troubles and trials, and when misfortune visited them it came not to them with soft cushions and tender pressures of the hand. Rough and hard, with clinched fist, it laid hold upon them. But when they gave vent to their happy feelings and sought to enjoy themselves, they were like swimmers in cooling waters. They struck out into the stream with freshness and courage, suffered themselves to be borne along by the current whithersoever it took its course. This was the cause of such a jubilee, such a thoughtlessly noisy outburst of all kinds of soul-possessing gayety from this house of nuptials.

"And if I had known," the bride's father, the rich Ruben Klattaner, had just said, "that it would take the last gulden in my pocket, then out it would have come."

In fact, it did appear as if the last groschen had really taken flight, and was fluttering about in the form of platters heaped up with geese and pastry-tarts. Since two o'clock—that is, since the marriage ceremony had been performed out in the open street—until nearly midnight, the wedding-feast had been progressing, and even yet the *sarvers*, or waiters, were hurrying from room to room. It was as if a twofold blessing had descended upon all this abundance of food and drink, for, in the first place, they did not seem to diminish; secondly, they ever found a new place for disposal. To be sure, this appetite was sharpened by the presence of a little dwarf-like, unimportant-looking man. He was esteemed, however, none the less highly by every one. They had specially written to engage the celebrated "Leb Narr," of Prague. And when was ever a mood so out of sorts, a heart so imbittered as not to thaw out and laugh if Leb Narr played one of his pranks. Ah, thou art now dead, good fool! Thy lips, once always ready with a witty reply, are closed. Thy mouth, then never still, now speaks no more! But when the hearty peals of laughter once rang forth at thy command, intercessors, as it were, in thy behalf before the very throne of God, thou hadst nothing to fear. And the joy of that "other" world was thine, that joy that has ever belonged to the most pious of country rabbis!

In the mean time the young people had assembled in one of the rooms to dance. It was strange how the sound of violins and trumpets accorded with the drolleries of the wit from Prague. In one part the outbursts of merriment were so boisterous that the very candles on the little table seemed to flicker with terror; in another an ordinary conversation was in progress, which now and then only ran over into a loud tittering, when some old lady slipped into the circle and tried her skill at a redowa, then altogether unknown to the young people. In the very midst of the tangle of dancers was to be seen the bride in a heavy silk wedding-gown. The point of her golden hood hung far down over her face. She danced continuously. She danced with every one that asked her. Had one, however, observed the actions of the young woman, they would certainly have seemed to him hurried, agitated, almost wild. She looked no one in the eye, not even her own bridegroom. He stood for the most part in the door-way, and evidently took more pleasure in the witticisms of the fool than in the dance or the lady dancers. But who ever thought for a moment why the young woman's hand burned, why her breath was so hot when one came near to her lips? Who should have noticed so strange a thing? A low whispering already passed through the company, a stealthy smile stole across many a lip. A bevy of ladies was seen to enter the room suddenly. The music dashed off into one of its loudest pieces, and, as if by enchantment, the newly made bride disappeared behind the ladies. The bridegroom, with his stupid, smiling mien, was still left standing on the threshold. But it was not long before he too vanished. One could hardly say how it happened. But people understand such skillful movements by experience, and will continue to understand them as long as there are brides and grooms in the world.

This disappearance of the chief personages, little as it seemed to be noticed, gave, however, the signal for general leave-taking. The dancing became drowsy; it stopped all at once, as if by appointment. That noisy confusion now began which always attends so merry a wedding-party. Half-drunken voices could be heard still intermingled with a last, hearty laugh over a joke of the fool from Prague echoing across the table. Here and there some one, not quite sure of his balance, was fumbling for the arm of his chair or the edge of the table. This resulted in his overturning a dish that had been forgotten, or in spilling a beer-glass. While this, in turn, set up a new hubbub, some one else, in his eagerness to betake himself from the scene, fell flat into the very débris. But all this tumult was really hushed the moment they all pressed to the door, for at that very instant shrieks, cries of pain, were heard issuing from the entrance below. In an instant the entire outpouring crowd with all possible force pushed back into the room, but it was a long time before the stream was pressed back again. Meanwhile, painful cries were again heard from below, so painful, indeed, that they restored even the most drunken to a state of consciousness.

"By the living God!" they cried to each other, "what is the matter down there? Is the house on fire?"

"She is gone! she is gone!" shrieked a woman's voice from the entry below.

"Who? who?" groaned the wedding-guests, seized, as it were, with an icy horror.

"Gone! gone!" cried the woman from the entry, and hurrying up the stairs came Selde Klattaner, the mother of the bride, pale as death, her eyes dilated with most awful fright, convulsively grasping a candle in her hand. "For God's sake, what has happened?" was heard on every side of her.

The sight of so many people about her, and the confusion of voices, seemed to release the poor woman from a kind of stupor. She glanced shyly about her then, as if overcome with a sense of shame stronger than her terror, andsaid, in a suppressed tone:

"Nothing, nothing, good people. In God's name, I ask, what was there to happen?"

Dissimulation, however, was too evident to suffice to deceive them.

"Why, then, did you shriek so, Selde," called out one of the guests to her, "if nothing happened?"

"Yes, she has gone," Selde now moaned in heart-rending tones, "and she has certainly done herself some harm!"

The cause of this strange scene was now first discovered. The bride has disappeared from the wedding-feast. Soon after that she had vanished in such a mysterious way, the bridegroom went below to the dimly-lighted room to find her, but in vain. At first thought this seemed to him to be a sort of bashful jest; but not finding her here, a mysterious foreboding seized him. He called to the mother of the bride:

"Woe to me! This woman has gone!"

Presently this party, that had so admirably controlled itself, was again thrown into commotion. "There was nothing to do," was said on all sides, "but to ransack every nook and corner. Remarkable instances of such disappearances of brides had been known. Evil spirits were wont to lurk about such nights and to inflict mankind with all sorts of sorceries." Strange as this explanation may seem, there were many who believed it at this very moment, and, most of all, Selde Klattaner herself. But it was only for a moment, for she at once exclaimed:

"No, no, my good people, she is gone; I know she is gone!"

Now for the first time many of them, especially the mothers, felt particularly uneasy, and anxiously called their daughters to them. Only a few showed courage, and urged that they must search and search, even if they had to turn aside the river Iser a hundred times. They urgently pressed on, called for torches and lanterns, and started forth. The cowardly ran after them up and down the stairs. Before any one perceived it the room was entirely forsaken.

Ruben Klattaner stood in the hall entry below, and let the people hurry past him without exchanging a word with any. Bitter disappointment and fear had almost crazed him. One of the last to stay in the room above with Selde was, strange to say, Leb Narr, of Prague. After all had departed, he approached the miserable mother, and, in a tone least becoming his general manner, inquired:

"Tell me, now, Mrs. Selde, did she not wish to have 'him'?"

"Whom? whom?" cried Selde, with renewed alarm, when she found herself alone with the fool.

"I mean," said Leb, in a most sympathetic manner, approaching still nearer to Selde, "that maybe you had to make your daughter marry him."

"Make? And have we, then, made her?" moaned Selde, staring at the fool with a look of uncertainty.

"Then nobody needs to search for her," replied the fool, with a sympathetic laugh, at the same time retreating. "It's better to leave her where she is."

Without saying thanks or good-night, he was gone.

Meanwhile the cause of all this disturbance had arrived at the end of her flight.

Close by the synagogue was situated the house of the rabbi. It was built in an angle of a very narrow street, set in a framework of tall shade-trees. Even by daylight it was dismal enough. At night it was almost impossible for a timid person to approach it, for people declared that the low supplications of the dead could be heard in the dingy house of God when at night they took the rolls of the law from the ark to summon their members by name.

Through this retired street passed, or rather ran, at this hour a shy form. Arriving at the dwelling of the rabbi, she glanced backward to see whether any one was following her. But all was silent and gloomy enough about her. A pale light issued from one of the windows of the synagogue; it came from the "eternal lamp" hanging in front of the ark of the covenant. But at this moment it seemed to her as if a supernatural eye was gazing upon her. Thoroughly affrighted, she seized the little iron knocker of the door and struck it gently. But the throb of her beating heart was even louder, more violent, than this blow. After a pause, footsteps were heard passing slowly along the hallway.

The rabbi had not occupied this lonely house a long time. His predecessor, almost a centenarian in years, had been laid to rest a few months before. The new rabbi had been called, from a distant part of the country. He was unmarried, and in the prime of life. No one had known him before his coming. But his personal nobility and the profundity of his scholarship made up for his deficiency in years. An aged mother had accompanied him from their distant home, and she took the place of wife and child.

"Who is there?" asked the rabbi, who had been busy at his desk even at this late hour and thus had not missed hearing the knocker.

"It is I," the figure without responded, almost inaudibly.

"Speak louder, if you wish me to hear you," replied the rabbi.

"It is I, Ruben Klattaner's daughter," she repeated.

The name seemed to sound strange to the rabbi. He as yet knew too few of his congregation to understand that this very day he performed the marriage ceremony of the person who had just repeated her name. Therefore he called out, after a moment's pause, "What do you wish so late at night?"

"Open the door, rabbi," she answered, pleadingly, "or I shall die at once!"

The bolt was pushed back. Something gleaming, rustling, glided past the rabbi into the dusky hall. The light of the candle in his hand was not sufficient to allow him to descry it. Before he had time to address her, she had vanished past him and had disappeared through the open door into the room. Shaking his head, the rabbi again bolted the door.

On reëntering the room he saw a woman's form sitting in the chair which he usually occupied. She had her back turned to him. Her head was bent low over her breast. Her golden wedding-hood, with its shading lace, was pulled down over her forehead. Courageous and pious as the rabbi was, he could not rid himself of a feeling of terror.

"Who are you?" he demanded, in a loud tone, as if its sound alone would banish the presence of this being that seemed to him at this moment to be the production of all the enchantments of evil spirits.

She raised herself, and cried in a voice that seemed to come from the agony of a human being:

"Do you not know me—me, whom you married a few hours since under the *chuppe* (marriage-canopy) to a husband?"

On hearing this familiar voice the rabbi stood speechless. He gazed at the young woman. Now, indeed, he must regard her as one bereft of reason, rather than as a specter.

"Well, if you are she," he stammered out, after a pause, for it was with difficulty that he found words to answer, "why are you here and not in the place where you belong?"

"I know no other place to which I belong more than here where I now am!" she answered, severely.

These words puzzled the rabbi still more. Is it really an insane woman before him? He must have thought so, for he now addressed her in a gentle tone of voice, as we do those suffering from this kind of sickness, in order not to excite her, and said:

"The place where you belong, my daughter, is in the house of your parents, and, since you have today been made a wife, your place is in your husband's house."

The young woman muttered something which failed to reach the rabbi's ear. Yet he only continued to think that he saw before him some poor unfortunate whose mind was deranged. After a pause, he added, in a still gentler tone: "What is your name, then, my child?"

"God, god," she moaned, in the greatest anguish, "he does not even yet know my name!"

"How should I know you," he continued, apologetically, "for I am a stranger in this place?"

This tender remark seemed to have produced the desired effect upon her excited mind.

"My name is Veile," she said, quietly, after a pause.

The rabbi quickly perceived that he had adopted the right tone towards his mysterious guest.

"Veile," he said, approaching nearer her, "what do you wish of me?"

"Rabbi, I have a great sin resting heavily upon my heart," she replied despondently. "I do not know what to do."

"What can you have done," inquired the rabbi, with a tender look, "that cannot be discussed at any other time than just now? Will you let me advise you, Veile?"

"No, no," she cried again, violently, "I will not be advised. I see, I know what oppresses me. Yes, I can grasp it by the hand, it lies so near before me. Is that what you call to be advised?"

"Very well," returned the rabbi, seeing that this was the very way to get the young woman to talk—"very well, I say, you are not imagining anything. I believe that you have greatly sinned. Have you come here then to confess this sin? Do your parents or your husband know anything about it?"

"Who is my husband?" she interrupted him, impetuously.

Thoughts welled up in the rabbi's heart like a tumultuous sea in which opposing conjectures cross and recross each other's course. Should he speak with her as with an ordinary sinner?

"Were you, perhaps, forced to be married?" he inquired, as quietly as possible, after a pause.

A suppressed sob, a strong inward struggle, manifesting itself in the whole trembling body, was the only answer to this question.

"Tell me, my child," said the rabbi, encouragingly.

In such tones as the rabbi had never before heard, so strange, so surpassing any human sounds, the young woman began:

"Yes, rabbi, I will speak, even though I know that I shall never go from this place alive, which would be the very best thing for me! No, rabbi, I was not forced to be married. My parents have never once said to me 'you must,' but my own will, my own desire, rather, has always been supreme. My husband is the son of a rich man in the community. To enter his family was to be made the first lady in the *gasse*, to sit buried in gold and silver. And that very thing, nothing else, was what infatuated me with him. It was for that that I forced myself, my heart and will, to be married to him, hard as it was for me. But in my innermost heart I detested him. The more he loved me, the more I hated him. But the gold and silver had an influence over me. More and more they cried to me, 'You will be the first lady in the *gasse!*'"

"Continue," said the rabbi, when she ceased, almost exhausted by these words.

"What more shall I tell you, rabbi?" she began again. "I was never a liar, when a child, or older, and yet during my whole engagement it has seemed to me as if a big, gigantic he had followed me step by step. I have seen it on every side of me. But today, when I stood under the *chuppe*, rabbi, and he took the ring from his finger and put it on mine, and when I had to dance at my own wedding with him, whom I now recognized, now for the first time, as the lie, and—when they led me away—"

This sincere confession escaping from the lips of the young woman, she sobbed aloud and bowed her head still deeper over her breast. The rabbi gazed upon her in silence. No insane woman ever spoke like that! Only a soul conscious of its own sin, but captivated by a mysterious power, could suffer like this!

It was not sympathy which he felt with her; it was much more a living over the sufferings of the woman. In spite of the confused story, it was all clear to the rabbi. The cause of the flight from the father's house at this hour also required no explanation. "I know what you mean," he longed to say, but he could only find words to say: "Speak further, Veile!"

The young woman turned towards him. He had not yet seen her face. The golden hood with the shading lace hung deeply over it.

"Have I not told you everything?" she said, with a flush of scorn.

"Everything?" repeated the rabbi, inquiringly. He only said this, moreover, through embarrassment.

"Do you tell me now," she cried, at once passionately and mildly, "what am I to do?"

"Veile!" exclaimed the rabbi, entertaining now, for the first time, a feeling of repugnance for this confidential interview.

"Tell me now!" she pleaded; and before the rabbi could prevent it the young woman threw herself down at his feet and clasped his knees in her arms. This hasty act had loosened the golden wedding-hood from her head, and thus exposed her face to view, a face of remarkable beauty.

So overcome was the young rabbi by the sight of it that he had to shade his eyes with his hands, as if before a sudden flash of lightning.

"Tell me now, what shall I do?" she cried again. "Do you think that I have come from my parents' home merely to return again without help? You alone in the world must tell me. Look at me! I have kept all my hair just as God gave it me. It has never been touched by the shears. Should I, then, do anything to please my husband? I am no wife. I will not be a wife! Tell me, tell me, what am I to do?"

"Arise, arise," bade the rabbi; but his voice quivered, sounded almost painful.

"Tell me first," she gasped; "I will not rise till then!"

"How can I tell you?" he moaned, almost inaudibly.

"Naphtali!" shrieked the kneeling woman.

But the rabbi staggered backward. The room seemed ablaze before him, like a bright fire. A sharp cry rang from his breast, as if one suffering from some painful wound had been seized by a rough hand. In his hurried attempt to free himself from the embrace of the young woman, who still clung to his knees, it chanced that her head struck heavily against the floor.

"Naphtali!" she cried once again.

"Silence, silence," groaned the rabbi, pressing both hands against his head.

And still again she called out this name, but not with that agonizing cry. It sounded rather like a commingling of exultation and lamentation.

And again he demanded, "Silence! silence!" but this time so imperiously, so forcibly, that the young woman lay on the floor as if conjured, not daring to utter a single word.

The rabbi paced almost wildly up and down the room. There must have been a hard, terrible struggle in his breast. It seemed to the one lying on the floor that she heard him sigh from the depths of his soul. Then his pacing became calmer; but it did not last long. The fierce conflict again assailed him. His step grew hurried; it echoed loudly through the awful stillness of the room. Suddenly he neared the young woman, who seemed to lie there scarcely breathing. He stopped in front of her. Had any one seen the face of the rabbi at this moment the expression on it would have filled him with terror. There was a marvelous tranquility overlying it, the tranquility of a struggle for life or death.

"Listen to me now, Veile," he began, slowly. "I will talk with you."

"I listen, rabbi," she whispered.

"But do you hear me well?"

"Only speak," she returned.

"But will you do what I advise you? Will you not oppose it? For I am going to say something that will terrify you."

"I will do anything that you say. Only tell me," she moaned.

"Will you swear?"

"I will," she groaned.

"No, do not swear yet, until you have heard me," he cried. "I will not force you."

This time came no answer.

"Hear me, then, daughter of Ruben Klattaner," he began, after a pause. "You have a twofold sin upon your soul, and each is so great, so criminal, that it can only be forgiven by severe punishment. First you permitted yourself to be infatuated by the gold and silver, and then you forced your heart to lie. With the lie you sought to deceive the man, even though he had intrusted you with his all when he made you his wife. A lie is truly a great sin! Streams of water cannot drown them. They make men false and hateful to themselves. The worst that has been committed in the world was led in by a lie. That is the one sin."

"I know, I know," sobbed the young woman.

"Now hear me further," began the rabbi again, with a wavering voice, after a short pause. "You have committed a still greater sin than the first. You have not only deceived your husband, but you have also destroyed the happiness of another person. You could have spoken, and you did not. For life you have robbed him of his happiness, his light, his joy, but you did not speak. What can he now do, when he knows what has been lost to him?"

"Naphtali!" cried the young woman.

"Silence! silence! do not let that name pass your lips again," he demanded, violently. "The more you repeat it the greater becomes your sin. Why did you not speak when you could have spoken? God can never easily forgive you that. To be silent, to keep secret in one's breast what would have made another man happier than the mightiest monarch! Thereby you have made him more than unhappy. He will nevermore have the desire to be happy. Veile, God in heaven cannot forgive you for that."

"Silence! silence!" groaned the wretched woman.

"No, Veile," he continued, with a stronger voice, "let me talk now. You are certainly willing to hear me speak? Listen to me. You must do severe penance for this sin, the twofold sin which rests upon your head. God is long-suffering and merciful. He will perhaps look down upon your misery, and will blot out your guilt from the great book of transgressions. But you must become penitent. Hear, now, what it shall be."

The rabbi paused. He was on the point of saying the severest thing that had ever passed his lips.

"You were silent, Veile," then he cried, "when you should have spoken. Be silent now forever to all men and to yourself. From the moment you leave this house, until I grant it, you must be dumb; you dare not let a loud word pass from your mouth. Will you undergo this penance?"

"I will do all you say," moaned the young woman.

"Will you have strength to do it?" he asked, gently.

"I shall be as silent as death," she replied.

"And one thing more I have to say to you," he continued. "You are the wife of your husband. Return home and be a Jewish wife."

"I understand you," she sobbed in reply.

"Go to your home now, and bring peace to your parents and husband. The time will come when you may speak, when your sin will be forgiven you. Till then bear what has been laid upon you."

"May I say one thing more?" she cried, lifting up her head.

"Speak," he said.

"Naphtali!"

The rabbi covered his eyes with one hand, with the other motioned her to be silent. But she grasped his hand, drew it to her lips. Hot tears fell upon it.

"Go now," he sobbed, completely broken down.

She let go the hand. The rabbi had seized the candle, but she had already passed him, and glided through the dark hall. The door was left open. The rabbi locked it again.

* * * *

Veile returned to her home, as she had escaped, unnoticed. The narrow street was deserted, as desolate as death. The searchers were to be found everywhere

75

except there where they ought first to have sought for the missing one. Her mother, Selde, still sat on the same chair on which she had sunk down an hour ago. The fright had left her like one paralyzed, and she was unable to rise. What a wonderful contrast this wedding-room, with the mother sitting alone in it, presented to the hilarity reigning here shortly before! On Veile's entrance her mother did not cry out. She had no strength to do so. She merely said: "So you have come at last, my daughter?" as if Veile had only returned from a walk somewhat too long. But the young woman did not answer to this and similar questions. Finally she signified by gesticulations that she could not speak. Fright seized the wretched mother a second time, and the entire house was filled with her lamentations.

Ruben Klattaner and Veile's husband having now returned from their fruitless search, were horrified on perceiving the change which Veile had undergone. Being men, they did not weep. With staring eyes they gazed upon the silent young woman, and beheld in her an apparition which had been dealt with by God's visitation in a mysterious manner.

From this hour began the terrible penance of the young woman.

The impression which Veile's woeful condition made upon the people of the *gasse* was wonderful. Those who had danced with her that evening on the wedding now first recalled her excited state. Her wild actions were now first remembered by many. It must have been an "evil eye," they concluded—a jealous, evil eye, to which her beauty was hateful. This alone could have possessed her with a demon of unrest. She was driven by this evil power into the dark night, a sport of these malicious potencies which pursue men step by step, especially on such occasions. The living God alone knows what she must have seen that night. Nothing good, else one would not become dumb. Old legends and tales were revived, each more horrible than the other. Hundreds of instances were given to prove that this was nothing new in the *gasse*. Despite this explanation, it is remarkable that the people did not believe that the young woman was dumb. The most thought that her power of speech had been paralyzed by some awful fright, but that with time it would be restored. Under this supposition they called her "Veile the Silent."

There is a kind of human eloquence more telling, more forcible than the loudest words, than the choicest diction—the silence of woman! Ofttimes they cannot endure the slightest vexation, but some great, heart-breaking sorrow, some pain from constant renunciation, self-sacrifice, they suffer with sealed lips—as if, in very truth, they were bound with bars of iron.

It would be difficult to fully describe that long "silent" life of the young woman. It is almost impossible to cite more than one incident. Veile accompanied her husband to his home, that house resplendent with that gold and silver which had infatuated her. She was, to be sure, the "first" woman in the *gasse*; she had everything in abundance. Indeed, the world supposed that she had but little cause for complaint. "Must one have everything?" was sometimes queried in the *gasse*. "One has one thing; another, another." And, according to all appearances, the people were right. Veile continued to be the beautiful, blooming woman. Her penance of silence did not deprive her of a single charm. She was so very happy, indeed, that she did not seem to feel even the pain of her punishment. Veile could laugh and rejoice, but never did she forget to be silent. The seemingly happy days, however, were only qualified to bring about the proper time of trials and temptations. The beginning was easy enough for her, the middle and end were times of real pain. The first years of their wedded life were childless. "It is well," the people in the *gasse* said, "that she has no children, and God has rightly ordained it to be so. A mother who cannot talk to her child, that would be something awful!" Unexpectedly to all, she rejoiced one day in the birth of a daughter. And when that affectionate young creature, her own offspring, was laid upon her breast, and the first sounds were uttered by its lips—that nameless, eloquent utterance of an infant—she forgot herself not; she was silent!

She was silent also when from day to day that child blossomed before her eyes into fuller beauty. Nor had she any words for it when, in effusions of tenderness, it stretched forth its tiny arms, when in burning fever it sought for the mother's hand. For days—yes, weeks—together she watched at its bedside. Sleep never visited her eyes. But she ever remembered her penance.

Years fled by. In her arms she carried another child. It was a boy. The father's joy was great. The child inherited its mother's beauty. Like its sister, it grew in health and strength. The noblest, richest mother, they said, might be proud of such children! And Veile was proud, no doubt, but this never passed her lips. She remained silent about things which mothers in their joy often cannot find words enough to express. And although her face many times lighted up with beaming smiles, yet she never renounced the habitual silence imposed upon her.

The idea that the slightest dereliction of her penance would be accompanied with a curse upon her children may have impressed itself upon her mind. Mothers will understand better than other persons what this mother suffered from her penalty of silence.

Thus a part of those years sped away which we are wont to call the best. She still flourished in her wonderful beauty. Her maiden daughter was beside her, like the bud beside the full-blown rose. Suitors were already present from far and near, who passed in review before the beautiful girl. The most of them were excellent young men, and any mother might have been proud in having her own daughter sought by such. Even then Veile did not undo her penance. Those busy times of intercourse which keep mothers engaged in presenting the superiorities of their daughters in the best light were not allowed her. The choice of one of the most favored suitors was made. Never before did any couple in the *gasse* equal this in beauty and grace. A few weeks before the appointed time for the wedding a malignant disease stole on, spreading sorrow and anxiety over the greater part of the land. Young girls were principally its victims. It seemed to pass scornfully over the aged and infirm. Veile's daughter was also laid hold upon by it. Before three days had passed there was a corpse in the house—the bride!

Even then Veile did not forget her penance. When they bore away the corpse to the "good place," she did utter a cry of anguish which long after echoed in the ears of the people; she did wring her hands in despair, but no one heard a word of complaint. Her lips seemed dumb forever. It was then, when she was seated on the low stool in the seven days of mourning, that the rabbi came to her, to bring to her the usual consolation for the dead. But he did not speak with her. He addressed words only to her husband. She herself dared not look up. Only when he turned to go did she lift her eyes. They, in turn, met the eyes of the rabbi, but he departed without a farewell.

After her daughter's death Veile was completely broken down. Even that which at her time of life is still called beauty had faded away within a few days.

Her cheeks had become hollow, her hair gray. Visitors wondered how she could endure such a shock, how body and spirit could hold together. They did not know that that silence was an iron fetter firmly imprisoning the slumbering spirits. She had a son, moreover, to whom, as to something last and dearest, her whole being still clung.

The boy was thirteen years old. His learning in the Holy Scriptures was already celebrated for miles around. He was the pupil of the rabbi, who had treated him with a love and tenderness becoming his own father. He said that he was a remarkable child, endowed with rare talents. The boy was to be sent to Hungary, to one of the most celebrated teachers of the times, in order to lay the foundation for his sacred studies under this instructor's guidance and wisdom. Years might perhaps pass before she would see him again. But Veile let her boy go from her embrace. She did not say a blessing over him when he went; only her lips twitched with the pain of silence.

Long years expired before the boy returned from the strange land, a full-grown, noble youth. When Veile had her son with her again a smile played about her mouth, and for a moment it seemed as if her former beauty had enjoyed a second spring. The extraordinary ability of her son already made him famous. Wheresoever he went people were delighted with his beauty, and admired the modesty of his manner, despite such great scholarship.

The next Sabbath the young disciple of the Talmud, scarcely twenty years of age, was to demonstrate the first marks of this great learning.

The people crowded shoulder to shoulder in this great synagogue. Curious glances were cast through the lattice-work of the women's gallery above upon the dense throng. Veile occupied one of the foremost seats. She could see everything that took place below. Her face was extremely pale. All eyes were turned towards her—the mother, who was permitted to see such a day for her son! But Veile did not appear to notice what was happening before her. A weariness, such as she had never felt before, even in her greatest suffering, crept over her limbs. It was as if she must sleep during her son's address. He had hardly mounted the stairs before the ark of the laws—hardly uttered his first words—when a remarkable change crossed her face. Her cheeks burned. She arose. All her vital energy seemed aroused. Her son meanwhile was speaking down below. She could not have told what he was saying. She did not hear him—she only heard the murmur of approbation, sometimes low, sometimes loud, which came to her ears from the quarters of the men. The people were astonished at the noble bearing of the speaker, his melodious speech, and his powerful energy. When he stopped at certain times to rest it seemed as if one were in a wood swept by a storm. She could now and then hear a few voices declaring that such a one had never before been listened to. The women at her side wept; she alone could not. A choking pain pressed from her breast to her lips. Forces were astir in her heart which struggled for expression. The whole synagogue echoed with buzzing voices, but to her it seemed as if she must speak louder than these. At the very moment her son had ended she cried out unconsciously, violently throwing herself against the lattice-work:

"God! living God! shall I not now speak?" A dead silence followed this outcry. Nearly all had recognized this voice as that of the "silent woman." A miracle had taken place!

"Speak! speak!" resounded the answer of the rabbi from the men's seats below. "You may now speak!"

But no reply came. Veile had fallen back into her seat, pressing both hands
against her breast. When the women sitting beside her looked at her they were
terrified to find that the "silent woman" had fainted. She was dead! The unseal-
ing of her lips was her last moment.

Long years afterwards the rabbi died. On his death-bed he told those standing
about him this wonderful penance of Veile.

Every girl in the *gasse* knew the story of the "silent woman."

THE MIDDLE TOE OF THE RIGHT FOOT,
by Ambrose Bierce

I

It is well known that the old Manton house is haunted. In all the rural district near about, and even in the town of Marshall, a mile away, not one person of un-biased mind entertains a doubt of it; incredulity is confined to those opinionated persons who will be called "cranks" as soon as the useful word shall have pene-trated the intellectual demesne of the Marshall *Advance*. The evidence that the house is haunted is of two kinds; the testimony of disinterested witnesses who have had ocular proof, and that of the house itself. The former may be disre-garded and ruled out on any of the various grounds of objection which may be urged against it by the ingenious; but facts within the observation of all are mate-rial and controlling.

In the first place the Manton house has been unoccupied by mortals for more than ten years, and with its outbuildings is slowly falling into decay—a circum-stance which in itself the judicious will hardly venture to ignore. It stands a little way off the loneliest reach of the Marshall and Harriston road, in an opening which was once a farm and is still disfigured with strips of rotting fence and half covered with brambles overrunning a stony and sterile soil long unacquainted with the plow. The house itself is in tolerably good condition, though badly weather-stained and in dire need of attention from the glazier, the smaller male population of the region having attested in the manner of its kind its disapproval of dwelling without dwellers. It is two stories in height, nearly square, its front pierced by a single doorway flanked on each side by a window boarded up to the very top. Corresponding windows above, not protected, serve to admit light and rain to the rooms of the upper floor. Grass and weeds grow pretty rankly all about, and a few shade trees, somewhat the worse for wind, and leaning all in one direction, seem to be making a concerted effort to run away. In short, as the Marshall town humorist explained in the columns of the *Advance*, "the proposi-tion that the Manton house is badly haunted is the only logical conclusion from the premises." The fact that in this dwelling Mr. Manton thought it expedient one night some ten years ago to rise and cut the throats of his wife and two small children, removing at once to another part of the country, has no doubt done its share in directing public attention to the fitness of the place for supernatural phe-nomena.

To this house, one summer evening, came four men in a wagon. Three of them promptly alighted, and the one who had been driving hitched the team to the only remaining post of what had been a fence. The fourth remained seated in the wagon. "Come," said one of his companions, approaching him, while the others moved away in the direction of the dwelling—"this is the place."

The man addressed did not move. "By God!" he said harshly, "this is a trick, and it looks to me as if you were in it."

"Perhaps I am," the other said, looking him straight in the face and speaking in a tone which had something of contempt in it. "You will remember, however, that the choice of place was with your own assent left to the other side. Of course if you are afraid of spooks—"

"I am afraid of nothing," the man interrupted with another oath, and sprang to the ground. The two then joined the others at the door, which one of them had already opened with some difficulty, caused by rust of lock and hinge. All entered. Inside it was dark, but the man who had unlocked the door produced a candle and matches and made a light. He then unlocked a door on their right as they stood in the passage. This gave them entrance to a large, square room that the candle but dimly lighted. The floor had a thick carpeting of dust, which partly muffled their footfalls. Cobwebs were in the angles of the walls and depended from the ceiling like strips of rotting lace making undulatory movements in the disturbed air. The room had two windows in adjoining sides, but from neither could anything be seen except the rough inner surfaces of boards a few inches from the glass. There was no fireplace, no furniture; there was nothing: besides the cobwebs and the dust, the four men were the only objects there which were not a part of the structure.

Strange enough they looked in the yellow light of the candle. The one who had so reluctantly alighted was especially spectacular—he might have been called sensational. He was of middle age, heavily built, deep chested, and broad shouldered. Looking at his figure, one would have said that he had a giant's strength; at his features, that he would use it like a giant. He was clean shaven, his hair rather closely cropped and gray. His low forehead was seamed with wrinkles above the eyes, and over the nose these became vertical. The heavy black brows followed the same law, saved from meeting only by an upward turn at what would otherwise have been the point of contact. Deeply sunken beneath these, glowed in the obscure light a pair of eyes of uncertain color, but obviously enough too small. There was something forbidding in their expression, which was not bettered by the cruel mouth and wide jaw. The nose was well enough, as noses go; one does not expect much of noses. All that was sinister in the man's face seemed accentuated by an unnatural pallor—he appeared altogether blood-less.

The appearance of the other men was sufficiently commonplace; they were such persons as one meets and forgets that he met. All were younger than the man described, between whom and the eldest of the others, who stood apart, there was apparently no kindly feeling. They avoided looking at each other.

"Gentlemen," said the man holding the candle and keys, "I believe everything is right. Are you ready, Mr. Rosser?"

The man standing apart from the group bowed and smiled.

"And you, Mr. Grossmith?"

The heavy man bowed and scowled.

"You will be pleased to remove your outer clothing."

Their hats, coats, waistcoats, and neckwear were soon removed and thrown outside the door, in the passage. The man with the candle now nodded, and the fourth man—he who had urged Grossmith to leave the wagon—produced from the pocket of his overcoat two long, murderous-looking bowie-knives, which he drew now from their leather scabbards.

"They are exactly alike," he said, presenting one to each of the two principals —for by this time the dullest observer would have understood the nature of this meeting. It was to be a duel to the death.

Each combatant took a knife, examined it critically near the candle and tested the strength of the blade and handle across his lifted knee. Their persons were then searched in turn, each by the second of the other.

"If it is agreeable to you, Mr. Grossmith," said the man holding the light, "you will place yourself in that corner."

He indicated the angle of the room farthest from the door, whither Grossmith retired, his second parting from him with a grasp of the hand which had nothing of cordiality in it. In the angle nearest the door Mr. Rosser stationed himself, and after a whispered consultation his second left him, joining the other near the door. At that moment the candle was suddenly extinguished, leaving all in profound darkness. This may have been done by a draught from the opened door; whatever the cause, the effect was startling.

"Gentlemen," said a voice which sounded strangely unfamiliar in the altered condition affecting the relations of the senses—"gentlemen, you will not move until you hear the closing of the outer door."

A sound of trampling ensued, then the closing of the inner door; and finally the outer one closed with a concussion which shook the entire building.

A few minutes afterward a belated farmer's boy met a light wagon which was being driven furiously toward the town of Marshall. He declared that behind the two figures on the front seat stood a third, with its hands upon the bowed shoulders of the others, who appeared to struggle vainly to free themselves from its grasp. This figure, unlike the others, was clad in white, and had undoubtedly boarded the wagon as it passed the haunted house. As the lad could boast a considerable former experience with the supernatural thereabouts his word had the weight justly due to the testimony of an expert. The story (in connection with the next day's events) eventually appeared in the *Advance*, with some slight literary embellishments and a concluding intimation that the gentlemen referred to would be allowed the use of the paper's columns for their version of the night's adventure. But the privilege remained without a claimant.

II

The events that led up to this "duel in the dark" were simple enough. One evening three young men of the town of Marshall were sitting in a quiet corner of the porch of the village hotel, smoking and discussing such matters as three educated young men of a Southern village would naturally find interesting. Their names were King, Sancher, and Rosser. At a little distance, within easy hearing, but taking no part in the conversation, sat a fourth. He was a stranger to the others. They merely knew that on his arrival by the stage-coach that afternoon he had written in the hotel register the name of Robert Grossmith. He had not been observed to speak to anyone except the hotel clerk. He seemed, indeed, singularly fond of his own company—or, as the *personnel* of the *Advance* expressed it, "grossly addicted to evil associations." But then it should be said in justice to the stranger that the *personnel* was himself of a too convivial disposition fairly to judge one differently gifted, and had, moreover, experienced a slight rebuff in an effort at an "interview."

"I hate any kind of deformity in a woman," said King, "whether natural or— acquired. I have a theory that any physical defect has its correlative mental and moral defect."

"I infer, then," said Rosser, gravely, "that a lady lacking the moral advantage of a nose would find the struggle to become Mrs. King an arduous enterprise."

"Of course you may put it that way," was the reply; "but, seriously, I once threw over a most charming girl on learning quite accidentally that she had suffered amputation of a toe. My conduct was brutal if you like, but if I had married that girl I should have been miserable for life and should have made her so."

"Whereas," said Sancher, with a light laugh, "by marrying a gentleman of more liberal view she escaped with a parted throat."

"Ah, you know to whom I refer. Yes, she married Manton, but I don't know about his liberality; I'm not sure but he cut her throat because he discovered that she lacked that excellent thing in woman, the middle toe of the right foot."

"Look at that chap!" said Rosser in a low voice, his eyes fixed upon the stranger.

That chap was obviously listening intently to the conversation.

"Damn his impudence!" muttered King—"what ought we to do?"

"That's an easy one," Rosser replied, rising. "Sir," he continued, addressing the stranger, "I think it would be better if you would remove your chair to the other end of the veranda. The presence of gentlemen is evidently an unfamiliar situation to you."

The man sprang to his feet and strode forward with clenched hands, his face white with rage. All were now standing. Sancher stepped between the belligerents.

"You are hasty and unjust," he said to Rosser; "this gentleman has done nothing to deserve such language."

But Rosser would not withdraw a word. By the custom of the country and the time there could be but one outcome to the quarrel.

"I demand the satisfaction due to a gentleman," said the stranger, who had become more calm. "I have not an acquaintance in this region. Perhaps you, sir," bowing to Sancher, "will be kind enough to represent me in this matter."

Sancher accepted the trust—somewhat reluctantly it must be confessed, for the man's appearance and manner were not at all to his liking. King, who during the colloquy had hardly removed his eyes from the stranger's face and had not spoken a word, consented with a nod to act for Rosser, and the upshot of it was that, the principals having retired, a meeting was arranged for the next evening. The nature of the arrangements has been already disclosed. The duel with knives in a dark room was once a commoner feature of Southwestern life than it is likely to be again. How thin a veneering of "chivalry" covered the essential brutality of the code under which such encounters were possible we shall see.

III

In the blaze of a midsummer noonday the old Manton house was hardly true to its traditions. It was of the earth, earthy. The sunshine caressed it warmly and affectionately, with evident disregard of its bad reputation. The grass greening all the expanse in its front seemed to grow, not rankly, but with a natural and joyous exuberance, and the weeds blossomed quite like plants. Full of charming lights and shadows and populous with pleasant-voiced birds, the neglected shade trees no longer struggled to run away, but bent reverently beneath their burdens of sun and song. Even in the glassless upper windows was an expression of peace and contentment, due to the light within. Over the stony fields the visible heat danced with a lively tremor incompatible with the gravity which is an attribute of the supernatural.

Such was the aspect under which the place presented itself to Sheriff Adams and two other men who had come out from Marshall to look at it. One of these men was Mr. King, the sheriff's deputy; the other, whose name was Brewer, was a brother of the late Mrs. Manton. Under a beneficent law of the State relating to property which has been for a certain period abandoned by an owner whose residence cannot be ascertained, the sheriff was legal custodian of the Manton farm and appurtenances thereunto belonging. His present visit was in mere perfunctory compliance with some order of a court in which Mr. Brewer had an action to get possession of the property as heir to his deceased sister. By a mere coincidence, the visit was made on the day after the night that Deputy King had unlocked the house for another and very different purpose. His presence now was not of his own choosing: he had been ordered to accompany his superior, and at the moment could think of nothing more prudent than simulated alacrity in obedience to the command.

Carelessly opening the front door, which to his surprise was not locked, the sheriff was amazed to see, lying on the floor of the passage into which it opened, a confused heap of men's apparel. Examination showed it to consist of two hats, and the same number of coats, waistcoats, and scarves all in a remarkably good state of preservation, albeit somewhat defiled by the dust in which they lay. Mr. Brewer was equally astonished, but Mr. King's emotion is not of record. With a new and lively interest in his own actions the sheriff now unlatched and pushed open a door on the right, and the three entered. The room was apparently vacant —no; as their eyes became accustomed to the dimmer light something was visible in the farthest angle of the wall. It was a human figure—that of a man crouching close in the corner. Something in the attitude made the intruders halt when they had barely passed the threshold. The figure more and more clearly defined itself. The man was upon one knee, his back in the angle of the wall, his shoulders elevated to the level of his ears, his hands before his face, palms outward, the fingers spread and crooked like claws; the white face turned upward on the retracted neck had an expression of unutterable fright, the mouth half open, the eyes incredibly expanded. He was stone dead. Yet with the exception of a bowie-knife, which had evidently fallen from his own hand, not another object was in the room.

In thick dust that covered the floor were some confused footprints near the door and along the wall through which it opened. Along one of the adjoining walls, too, past the boarded-up windows was the trail made by the man himself in reaching his corner. Instinctively in approaching the body the three men followed that trail. The sheriff grasped one of the outthrown arms; it was as rigid as iron, and the application of a gentle force rocked the entire body without altering the relation of its parts. Brewer, pale with excitement, gazed intently into the distorted face. "God of mercy!" he suddenly cried, "it is Manton!"

"You are right," said King, with an evident attempt at calmness: "I knew Manton. He then wore a full beard and his hair long, but this is he."

He might have added: "I recognized him when he challenged Rosser. I told Rosser and Sancher who he was before we played him this horrible trick. When Rosser left this dark room at our heels, forgetting his outer clothing in the excitement, and driving away with us in his shirt sleeves—all through the discreditable proceedings we knew with whom we were dealing, murderer and coward that he was!"

But nothing of this did Mr. King say. With his better light he was trying to penetrate the mystery of the man's death. That he had not once moved from the corner where he had been stationed; that his posture was that of neither attack nor defense; that he had dropped his weapon; that he had obviously perished of sheer horror of something that he *saw*—these were circumstances which Mr. King's disturbed intelligence could not rightly comprehend.

Groping in intellectual darkness for a clew to his maze of doubt, his gaze, directed mechanically downward in the way of one who ponders momentous matters, fell upon something which, there, in the light of day and in the presence of living companions, affected him with terror. In the dust of years that lay thick upon the floor—leading from the door by which they had entered, straight across the room to within a yard of Manton's crouching corpse—were three parallel lines of footprints—light but definite impressions of bare feet, the outer ones those of small children, the inner a woman's. From the point at which they ended they did not return; they pointed all one way. Brewer, who had observed them at the same moment, was leaning forward in an attitude of rapt attention, horribly pale.

"Look at that!" he cried, pointing with both hands at the nearest print of the woman's right foot, where she had apparently stopped and stood. "The middle toe is missing—it was Gertrude!"

Gertrude was the late Mrs. Manton, sister to Mr. Brewer.

THE TOLL-HOUSE,
by W.W. Jacobs

"It's all nonsense," said Jack Barnes. "Of course people have died in the house; people die in every house. As for the noises—wind in the chimney and rats in the wainscot are very convincing to a nervous man. Give me another cup of tea, Meagle."

"Lester and White are first," said Meagle, who was presiding at the tea-table of the Three Feathers Inn. "You've had two."

Lester and White finished their cups with irritating slowness, pausing between sips to sniff the aroma, and to discover the sex and dates of arrival of the "strangers" which floated in some numbers in the beverage. Mr. Meagle served them to the brim, and then, turning to the grimly expectant Mr. Barnes, blandly requested him to ring for hot water.

"We'll try and keep your nerves in their present healthy condition," he remarked. "For my part I have a sort of half-and-half belief in the super-natural."

"All sensible people have," said Lester. "An aunt of mine saw a ghost once."

White nodded.

"I had an uncle that saw one," he said.

"It always is somebody else that sees them," said Barnes.

"Well, there is a house," said Meagle, "a large house at an absurdly low rent, and nobody will take it. It has taken toll of at least one life of every family that has lived there—however short the time—and since it has stood empty caretaker after care-taker has died there. The last caretaker died fifteen years ago."

"Exactly," said Barnes. "Long enough ago for legends to accumulate."

"I'll bet you a sovereign you won't spend the night there alone, for all your talk," said White, suddenly.

"And I," said Lester.

"No," said Barnes slowly. "I don't believe in ghosts nor in any supernatural things whatever; all the same I admit that I should not care to pass a night there alone."

"But why not?" inquired White.

"Wind in the chimney," said Meagle with a grin.

"Rats in the wainscot," chimed in Lester. "As you like," said Barnes coloring.

"Suppose we all go," said Meagle. "Start after supper, and get there about eleven. We have been walking for ten days now without an adventure—except Barnes's discovery that ditchwater smells longest. It will be a novelty, at any rate, and, if we break the spell by all surviving, the grateful owner ought to come down handsome."

"Let's see what the landlord has to say about it first," said Lester. "There is no fun in passing a night in an ordinary empty house. Let us make sure that it is haunted."

He rang the bell, and, sending for the landlord, appealed to him in the name of our common humanity not to let them waste a night watching in a house in which spectres and hobgoblins had no part. The reply was more than reassuring, and the landlord, after describing with considerable art the exact appearance of a head which had been seen hanging out of a window in the moonlight, wound up with a polite but urgent request that they would settle his bill before they went.

"It's all very well for you young gentlemen to have your fun," he said indulgently; "but supposing as how you are all found dead in the morning, what about me? It ain't called the Toll-House for nothing, you know."

"Who died there last?" inquired Barnes, with an air of polite derision.

"A tramp," was the reply. "He went there for the sake of half a crown, and they found him next morning hanging from the balusters, dead."

"Suicide," said Barnes. "Unsound mind."

The landlord nodded. "That's what the jury brought it in," he said slowly; "but his mind was sound enough when he went in there. I'd known him, off and on, for years. I'm a poor man, but I wouldn't spend the night in that house for a hundred pounds."

He repeated this remark as they started on their expedition a few hours later. They left as the inn was closing for the night; bolts shot noisily behind them, and, as the regular customers trudged slowly homewards, they set off at a brisk pace in the direction of the house. Most of the cottages were already in darkness, and lights in others went out as they passed.

"It seems rather hard that we have got to lose a night's rest in order to convince Barnes of the existence of ghosts," said White.

"It's in a good cause," said Meagle. "A most worthy object; and something seems to tell me that we shall succeed. You didn't forget the candles, Lester?"

"I have brought two," was the reply; "all the old man could spare."

There was but little moon, and the night was cloudy. The road between high hedges was dark, and in one place, where it ran through a wood, so black that they twice stumbled in the uneven ground at the side of it.

"Fancy leaving our comfortable beds for this!" said White again. "Let me see; this desirable residential sepulchre lies to the right, doesn't it?"

"Farther on," said Meagle.

They walked on for some time in silence, broken only by White's tribute to the softness, the cleanliness, and the comfort of the bed which was receding farther and farther into the distance. Under Meagle's guidance they turned oft at last to the right, and, after a walk of a quarter of a mile, saw the gates of the house before them.

The lodge was almost hidden by overgrown shrubs and the drive was choked with rank growths. Meagle leading, they pushed through it until the dark pile of the house loomed above them.

"There is a window at the back where we can get in, so the landlord says," said Lester, as they stood before the hall door.

"Window?" said Meagle. "Nonsense. Let's do the thing properly. Where's the knocker?"

He felt for it in the darkness and gave a thundering rat-tat-tat at the door.

"Don't play the fool," said Barnes crossly.

"Ghostly servants are all asleep," said Meagle gravely, "but I'll wake them up before I've done with them. It's scandalous keeping us out here in the dark."

He plied the knocker again, and the noise volleyed in the emptiness beyond. Then with a sudden exclamation he put out his hands and stumbled forward.

"Why, it was open all the time," he said, with an odd catch in his voice. "Come on."

"I don't believe it was open," said Lester, hanging back. "Somebody is playing us a trick."

"Nonsense," said Meagle sharply. "Give me a candle. Thanks. Who's got a match?"

Barnes produced a box and struck one, and Meagle, shielding the candle with his hand, led the way forward to the foot of the stairs. "Shut the door, somebody," he said, "there's too much draught."

"It is shut," said White, glancing behind him.

Meagle fingered his chin. "Who shut it?" he inquired, looking from one to the other. "Who came in last?"

"I did," said Lester, "but I don't remember shutting it—perhaps I did, though."

Meagle, about to speak, thought better of it, and, still carefully guarding the flame, began to explore the house, with the others close behind. Shadows danced on the walls and lurked in the corners as they proceeded. At the end of the passage they found a second staircase, and ascending it slowly gained the first floor.

"Careful!" said Meagle, as they gained the landing.

He held the candle forward and showed where the balusters had broken away. Then he peered curiously into the void beneath.

"This is where the tramp hanged himself, I suppose," he said thoughtfully.

"You've got an unwholesome mind," said White, as they walked on. "This place is qutie creepy enough without your remembering that. Now let's find a comfortable room and have a little nip of whiskey apiece and a pipe. How will this do?"

He opened a door at the end of the passage and revealed a small square room. Meagle led the way with the candle, and, first melting a drop or two of tallow, stuck it on the mantelpiece. The others seated themselves on the floor and watched pleasantly as White drew from his pocket a small bottle of whiskey and a tin cup.

"H'm! I've forgotten the water," he exclaimed. "I'll soon get some," said Meagle.

He tugged violently at the bell-handle, and the rusty jangling of a bell sounded from a distant kitchen. He rang again.

"Don't play the fool," said Barnes roughly.

Meagle laughed. "I only wanted to convince you," he said kindly. "There ought to be, at any rate, one ghost in the servants' hall."

Barnes held up his hand for silence.

"Yes?" said Meagle with a grin at the other two. "Is anybody coming?"

"Suppose we drop this game and go back," said Barnes suddenly. "I don't believe in spirits, but nerves are outside anybody's command. You may laugh as you like, but it really seemed to me that I heard a door open below and steps on the stairs."

His voice was drowned in a roar of laughter.

"He is coming round," said Meagle with a smirk. "By the time I have done with him he will be a confirmed believer. Well, who will go and get some water?

Will you, Barnes?"

"No," was the reply.

"If there is any it might not be safe to drink after all these years," said Lester. "We must do without it."

Meagle nodded, and taking a seat on the floor held out his hand for the cup. Pipes were lit and the clean, wholesome smell of tobacco filled the room. White produced a pack of cards; talk and laughter rang through the room and died away reluctantly in distant corridors.

"Empty rooms always delude me into the belief that I possess a deep voice," said Meagle. "Tomorrow—"

He started up with a smothered exclamation as the light went out suddenly and something struck him on the head. The others sprang to their feet. Then Meagle laughed.

"It's the candle," he exclaimed. "I didn't stick it enough."

Barnes struck a match and relighting the candle stuck it on the mantelpiece, and sitting down took up his cards again.

"What was I going to say?" said Meagle. "Oh, I know; tomorrow I—"

"Listen!" said White, laying his hand on the other's sleeve. "Upon my word I really thought I heard a laugh."

"Look here!" said Barnes. "What do you say to going back? I've had enough of this. I keep fancying that I hear things too; sounds of something moving about in the passage outside. I know it's only fancy, but it's uncomfortable."

"You go if you want to," said Meagle, "and we will play dummy. Or you might ask the tramp to take your hand for you, as you go downstairs."

Barnes shivered and exclaimed angrily. He got up and, walking to the half-closed door, listened.

"Go outside," said Meagle, winking at the other two. "I'll dare you to go down to the hall door and back by yourself."

Barnes came back and, bending forward, lit his pipe at the candle.

"I am nervous but rational," he said, blowing out a thin cloud of smoke. "My nerves tell me that there is something prowling up and down the long passage outside; my reason tells me that it is all nonsense. Where are my cards?"

He sat down again, and taking up his hand, looked through it carefully and led.

"Your play, White," he said after a pause. White made no sign.

"Why, he is asleep," said Meagle. "Wake up, old man. Wake up and play."

Lester, who was sitting next to him, took the sleeping man by the arm and shook him, gently at first and then with some roughness; but White, with his back against the wall and his head bowed, made no sign. Meagle bawled in his ear and then turned a puzzled face to the others.

"He sleeps like the dead," he said, grimacing. "Well, there are still three of us to keep each other company."

"Yes," said Lester, nodding. "Unless—Good Lord! suppose—"

He broke off and eyed them trembling.

"Suppose what?" inquired Meagle.

"Nothing," stammered Lester. "Let's wake him. Try him again. *White! White!*"

"It's no good," said Meagle seriously; "there's something wrong about that sleep."

"That's what I meant," said Lester; "and if he goes to sleep like that, why shouldn't—"

Meagle sprang to his feet. "Nonsense," he said roughly. "He's tired out; that's all. Still, let's take him up and clear out. You take his legs and Barnes will lead the way with the candle. Yes? Who's that?"

He looked up quickly towards the door. "Thought I heard somebody tap," he said with a shamefaced laugh. "Now, Lester, up with him. One, two—Lester! Lester!"

He sprang forward too late; Lester, with his face buried in his arms, had rolled over on the floor fast asleep, and his utmost efforts failed to awaken him.

"He—is—asleep," he stammered. "Asleep!"

Barnes, who had taken the candle from the mantel-piece, stood peering at the sleepers in silence and dropping tallow over the floor.

"We must get out of this," said Meagle. "Quick!" Barnes hesitated. "We can't leave them here—" he began.

"We must," said Meagle in strident tones. "If you go to sleep I shall go—Quick! Come."

He seized the other by the arm and strove to drag him to the door. Barnes shook him off, and putting the candle back on the mantelpiece, tried again to arouse the sleepers.

"It's no good," he said at last, and, turning from them, watched Meagle. "Don't you go to sleep," he said anxiously.

Meagle shook his head, and they stood for some time in uneasy silence. "May as well shut the door," said Barnes at last.

He crossed over and closed it gently. Then at a scuffling noise behind him he turned and saw Meagle in a heap on the hearthstone.

With a sharp catch in his breath he stood motionless. Inside the room the candle, fluttering in the draught, showed dimly the grotesque attitudes of the sleepers. Beyond the door there seemed to his over-wrought imagination a strange and stealthy unrest. He tried to whistle, but his lips were parched, and in a mechanical fashion he stooped, and began to pick up the cards which littered the floor.

He stopped once or twice and stood with bent head listening. The unrest outside seemed to increase; a loud creaking sounded from the stairs.

"Who is there?" he cried loudly.

The creaking ceased. He crossed to the door and flinging it open, strode out into the corridor. As he walked his fears left him suddenly.

"Come on!" he cried with a low laugh. "All of you! All of you! Show your faces—your infernal ugly faces! Don't skulk!"

He laughed again and walked on; and the heap in the fireplace put out his head tortoise fashion and listened in horror to the retreating footsteps. Not until they had become inaudible in the distance did the listeners' features relax.

"Good Lord, Lester, we've driven him mad," he said in a frightened whisper. "We must go after him."

There was no reply. Meagle sprang to his feet. "Do you hear?" he cried. "Stop your fooling now; this is serious. White! Lester! Do you hear?"

He bent and surveyed them in angry bewilderment. "All right," he said in a trembling voice. "You won't frighten me, you know."

He turned away and walked with exaggerated carelessness in the direction of the door. He even went outside and peeped through the crack, but the sleepers did not stir. He glanced into the blackness behind, and then came hastily into the room again.

He stood for a few seconds regarding them. The stillness in the house was horrible; he could not even hear them breathe. With a sudden resolution he snatched the candle from the mantelpiece and held the flame to White's finger. Then as he reeled back stupefied the footsteps again became audible.

He stood with the candle in his shaking hand listening. He heard them ascending the farther staircase, but they stopped suddenly as he went to the door. He walked a little way along the passage, and they went scurrying down the stairs and then at a jog-trot along the corridor below. He went back to the main staircase, and they ceased again.

For a time he hung over the balusters, listening and trying to pierce the blackness below; then slowly, step by step, he made his way downstairs, and, holding the candle above his head, peered about him.

"Barnes!" he called. "Where are you?" Shaking with fright, he made his way along the passage, and summoning up all his courage pushed open doors and gazed fearfully into empty rooms. Then, quite suddenly, he heard the footsteps in front of him.

He followed slowly for fear of extinguishing the candle, until they led him at last into a vast bare kitchen with damp walls and a broken floor. In front of him a door leading into an inside room had just closed. He ran towards it and flung it open, and a cold air blew out the candle. He stood aghast.

"Barnes!" he cried again. "Don't be afraid! It is I—Meagle!"

There was no answer. He stood gazing into the darkness, and all the time the idea of something close at hand watching was upon him. Then suddenly the steps broke out overhead again.

He drew back hastily, and passing through the kitchen groped his way along the narrow passages. He could now see better in the darkness, and finding himself at last at the foot of the staircase began to ascend it noiselessly. He reached the landing just in time to see a figure disappear round the angle of a wall. Still careful to make no noise, he followed the sound of the steps until they led him to the top floor, and he cornered the chase at the end of a short passage.

"Barnes!" he whispered. "Barnes!"

Something stirred in the darkness. A small circular window at the end of the passage just softened the blackness and revealed the dim outlines of a motionless figure. Meagle, in place of advancing, stood almost as still as a sudden horrible doubt took possession of him. With his eyes fixed on the shape in front he fell back slowly and, as it advanced upon him, burst into a terrible cry.

"Barnes! For God's sake! Is it you?"

The echoes of his voice left the air quivering, but the figure before him paid no heed. For a moment he tried to brace his courage up to endure its approach, then with a smothered cry he turned and fled.

The passages wound like a maze, and he threaded them blindly in a vain search for the stairs. If he could get down and open the hall door—

He caught his breath in a sob; the steps had begun again. At a lumbering trot they clattered up and down the bare passages, in and out, up and down, as though in search of him. He stood appalled, and then as they drew near entered a small room and stood behind the door as they rushed by. He came out and ran swiftly and noiselessly in the other direction, and in a moment the steps were after him.

He found the long corridor and raced along it at top speed. The stairs he knew were at the end, and with the steps close behind he descended them in blind haste. The steps gained on him, and he shrank to the side to let them pass, still continuing his headlong flight. Then suddenly he seemed to slip off the earth into space.

Lester awoke in the morning to find the sunshine streaming into the room, and White sitting up and regarding with some perplexity a badly blistered finger.

"Where are the others?" inquired Lester.

"Gone, I suppose," said White. "We must have been asleep."

Lester arose, and stretching his stiffened limbs, dusted his clothes with his hands, and went out into the corridor. White followed. At the noise of their approach a figure which had been lying asleep at the other end sat up and revealed the face of Barnes. "Why, I've been asleep," he said in surprise. "I don't remember coming here. How did I get here?"

"Nice place to come for a nap," said Lester, severely, as he pointed to the gap in the balusters. "Look there! Another yard and where would you have been?"

He walked carelessly to the edge and looked over. In response to his startled cry the others drew near, and all three stood gazing at the dead man below.

THE HAUNTED COVE,
by Sir George Douglas

Commonplace in itself and showing positive vulgarity in the style in which its pleasure-grounds are laid out, Clyffe, near Berwick-on-Tweed, has yet one delightful feature of its own—to wit, a private bay to which access is obtained by a tunnel seventy or eighty yards long, cut through the soft formation of the cliff from the sloping gardens above. The result is that, if you are a visitor at Clyffe, you have your own private bathing ground, your own private beach where the children may play, without fear of being encroached upon, unless, indeed, a boat should be run in among the rocks from seaward. In the early nineties of the last century, the only daughter of the house of Clyffe was engaged to be married to a young officer quartered at the military depot at Berwick. They were a blameless but not particularly interesting couple, and one of their hobbies was to meet and promenade on the smooth sands of Clyffe bay in the brilliant autumn moonlight. In order to prevent possible intrusion from the sea, the seaward end of the tunnel was closed by a heavy iron gate, and upon the inner side of this gate the Lieutenant was to wait until his fiancee should steal forth bringing with her the key which should give access to the beach. It was all very foolish and romantic, no doubt, for they might have met just as conveniently in the conservatory of Clyffe House, where their privacy would have been equally respected, and where Miss Alix's satin shoes and diaphanous draperies would have exposed her to no risk of a chill. Lovers are like that, however, and had they not been so on this occasion, I should have had no story to tell.

Like the exemplary swain he was, Dick arrived early at the rendezvous—that is to say, early in respect to the time agreed upon, though, as a matter of fact, it was nearly eleven o'clock. There he lit a cigarette, and approaching the heavy iron bars of the locked gate, looked forth upon the peaceful scene beyond. It was a perfect night, the harvest moon riding through fleecy cloud aloft, whilst the breaking of the sea between the rocky points to right and left was soothing in its gentle iteration. Dick had been on parade extremely early that morning, and, tell it not in Gath! his eyes involuntarily closed. Starting awake again, he saw with surprise that, though Alix had not yet come forward, he was no longer alone. No! the sacred beach had been invaded, and a female figure clad in light draperies was pacing slowly in the moonlight betwixt himself and the distant rocks. Who on earth could she be, and how had she got there? were the questions he asked himself, his first sensation being one of annoyance at so unexpected and so ill-timed an intrusion. But as the moments passed and the figure came more clearly into view, impatience gave way to curiosity, and curiosity to something like awe.

What he saw was the tall and slender form of a young girl whose hands were clasped in front of her, and whose eyes were fixed on the ground in a pensive, not to say sorrowful, attitude. Clear as was the moonlight, at least in the intervals of the moon's passage through the broken clouds, her features were not plainly visible; but her every movement was instinct with grace. What could she be doing there? Under other circumstances, possibly Dick might have felt inclined to pass the gate and himself step forth on to the sands. But, besides that the gate was locked, he gradually became conscious of a singular delicacy or unwillingness to intrude upon the privacy of this solitary, inexplicable, and impressive figure. He was content, therefore, to watch her noiseless progress, and, as he did so, even his untrained masculine eye seemed to note something unusual—out of date, it might be—in the fashion of her garments. So perhaps might some old-world portrait have appeared, had it stept down from its frame against the wall. This, however, stirred him little. What he was not prepared for was the gesture of anguish, nay, of positive despair, with which, when about opposite him, the figure threw her head back and her arms aloft, as if in mute and agonised appeal to Heaven. The action was heartrending even to look on; nor, to a male eye, did it lose aught from the fact that, as the moonlight now fell for the first time on her upturned face, it showed it to be deathly pale indeed, but also exquisitely lovely. Another moment or two, and the graceful and appealing form had passed beyond his field of vision, for, as the locked gate stood some little way back from the mouth of the tunnel, his view was restricted.

A short time only, though he knew not exactly how long, had passed when Alix stood beside him.

"I had some difficulty," she archly explained, "in eluding prying eyes."

For an ardent lover, Dick's greetings were perfunctory; after which, being still powerfully under the impression of what he had just seen, he told Alix all about it.

"We shall soon see who she is," replied that practical young lady, as she placed the heavy key in the cumbrous lock, "and I shall also take leave to inform her that this bit of coast is strictly private."

And strictly private it appeared to be when they emerged from the tunnel. For though their eyes swept the beach to right and left, and though the moon just then was unobscured, they saw no trace of any living form.

"She must have landed from a boat," said Alix; but as little trace of a boat could they discover.

Still it was quite possible that she might pass unobserved against the dark rocks, so they turned first to the right, then to the left, keeping a keen look-out for any sign of motion.

They detected nothing.

And by this time I am bound to confess that a slightly uncomplimentary suspicion had more than once crossed the brain of Alix. She knew that, as a rule, her Dick was a pattern of moderation. But even the most prudent may be liable to be occasionally overtaken. And she recalled his having mentioned that this was to be a guest-night at the mess. Indeed, it was chiefly upon that account that the assignation had been fixed so late. This present portentous solemnity was certainly most unlike him. Was it possible that the poor fellow had taken just one more whisky-and-soda than he could conveniently carry? Outspoken by nature, she blurted out her suspicion, which was strengthened rather than the reverse by the great earnestness with which he repelled it.

Less convinced than before, Alix then exclaimed: "Look here, Dick! If, as you say, the young woman passed this way, she must have left tracks on the smooth sand. Where do you say the place was?"

With some uncertainty, Dick then led her to what he took to be the place. No tracks were there. He then tried further back from the mouth of the tunnel, and with as little success. It was true the tide was coming up, but it could scarcely yet have reached footmarks which had been imprinted so far inshore as he supposed these to have been.

In a spirit of levity which jarred on him, Alix now recommended her lover to go back to his quarters and have a good sleep; and then, having again passed through the gate and pushed their way up the tunnel, the two young people parted in something very like a tiff.

Dick did not call at Clyffe House the next day, and when he called on the day following, Alix met him in a complaisant mood. After all, she had no wish to quarrel with him. And very soon she said, "Going back to what you told me you had seen the other night, Dick, it occurred to me, after you were gone, that it fits in rather curiously with an old story connected with this place." And then, at his request, she proceeded to tell him how, some thirty years ago, her grandmother had had a favourite maid, a friendless orphan girl named Barbara, to whom attached a mystery. Barbara was a very lovely creature of refinement and education above her station, and she had of course numerous admirers. Young as she was, her discretion was faultless, with the sole exception that her native amiability and desire to please sometimes betrayed her into conduct which meant less than her admirers wished to think it did. Well, at last Barbara became plighted to a respectable young fisherman, part-owner of a boat sailing from The Greenses, and, though details were vague, it was generally understood that, as a consequence, several hearts were severely damaged. As Barbara had no relatives, it was arranged by her employer that she should remain in her situation until the wedding-day and should be married from Clyffe House. Considerable preparations had also been made to do honour to the occasion, when—judge of the consternation of the inmates of the house!—upon the morning of the wedding-day Barbara was not to be found. She was believed to have retired to rest on the previous night as usual, yet her bed had not been slept in. Nor, although most of her clothes were packed in anticipation of her change of domicile, had she apparently taken anything with her. Nothing in the least unusual had been observed in her demeanour; nor could the unhappy bridegroom suggest any possible motive for her conduct. Exhaustive inquiries and exhaustive search were made; but, to cut the story short, nothing had ever again been seen or heard of the fair Barbara to that day. Her mistress, who had been sincerely attached to her, had long mourned for her, and in after times would often sing her praises. But, in order to be quite candid, it must be acknowledged that there were others, not a few, who declined to believe that the girl had come to an untimely end; and, who, knowing that she had several suitors, and had sometimes appeared uncertain which to favour, preferred to think that she had changed her mind at the last moment, and, deciding to throw over her fisherman, had made her escape from Clyffe House during the night to join some more eligible swain. This would have been a desperate step indeed; nor could her conduct in withholding subsequent explanations be absolved of heartlessness. But, after all, she was the sort of girl who, where no actual misconduct was involved, might easily allow herself to be over-persuaded. And certainly the tangled skein of love does sometimes present a knot which must be cut rather than untied.

The Lieutenant professed himself profoundly interested in this narrative, which he and Alix then proceeded to discuss in all its bearings, and more particularly, of course, in its relation to the figure seen by him in the cove. It is true that Alix never quite believed in the genuineness of the apparition; but, seeing that Dick really wished to have it taken seriously, she decided tactfully to humour him, and made quite a nine days' wonder of the mysterious occurrence. Their own wedding-day was, however, fast drawing on, so they soon found other things to talk and think of. To be brief, they were in due course married, and, amid the cares and pleasures of wedded life, the story, though not forgotten, came to be very seldom referred to. So twenty years passed; at the end of which time the Colonel (as he now was), accompanied by his wife and several youngsters, paid one of his not very frequent visits to his wife's parents at Clyffe House.

On the first night of the visit, after dinner, Alix's father had significantly recalled the story of the maid Barbara's disappearance, and, after stating that the mystery had now been finally cleared up, had gone on to relate the following particulars:—A few days previously there had lain at the point of death in the infirmary at Berwick an aged fisherman, who had long been known in the seaport town for his solitary habits and morose and violent ways. As death drew near, it became evident that his mind was sorely troubled, and to one of the nurses or doctors who had sought to comfort him he had been led to make the acknowledgment that a guilty secret weighed upon his soul, making him fearful to confront his Maker. He then told how, as a young man, he had passionately loved a pretty servant-girl employed at Clyffe House. Misled by those smiles and that graciousness of manner which in the guileless amiability of her nature the girl lavished upon all alike, he had for a moment imagined himself her favoured suitor. How bitter, then, was the blow, and how rude the awakening when he learned that a younger brother of his own, a mere boy, was preferred before himself! Nor was it only unrequited love that grieved him. No, he believed, or managed to persuade himself, that an unfair advantage had been taken of him, by which he had been made the lovers' dupe. A silent man, he took no one into his confidence, but abode his time until the eve of the wedding-day. On that day he had accidentally intercepted a note from the girl Barbara, addressed to his brother, in which she had agreed to meet her bridegroom of the morrow in the cove below Clyffe House one hour before midnight, to spend a final hour together before the momentous crisis in their lives. Instantly it had occurred to the elder brother to use the knowledge gained from the note in order to make one last desperate appeal on his own account to the sweet girl he loved so madly. Accordingly he kept back the missive, and, to make assurance doubly sure, mixed a soporific drug with his brother's drink when the latter came in from fishing. Then, whilst the youngster slumbered heavily, he himself embarked in a cockle-boat and, unobserved, rowed quietly round the headland, into Clyffe cove, where he ran his boat into a safe creek he knew of, and jumped ashore. Poor Barbara had come down to the water's edge to meet the boat, and great was her consternation on finding herself confronted by the wrong brother.

Then an impassioned scene was enacted, in which the seaman used every means of persuasion known to him to get the girl to give up his brother and plight herself to him. But though alternately distressed and terrified, Barbara had stood her ground, and, gentle and yielding though she appeared to be, neither threats nor vows had had the slightest effect upon her constancy. And then, of a sudden, the reckless brother had "seen red." If he could not have this girl to wife, then neither should another, and a moment later her white form lay stretched upon the dark rocks at his feet.

The sight brought him to himself. There was no room for doubt that life was extinct; and if he was to escape suspicion, he must act at once, for the summer night was short and the dread interview had lasted long. He accordingly placed the body in the boat, and, having collected several heavy stones, proceeded to make use of his seacraft by binding them closely and firmly about the poor girl's body by means of her clothing. Then he rowed out to sea, some mile or more, and there quietly dropped the body overboard. Such, in essentials, was the story told by the dying fisherman, and so it had come about that the bride of that fatal morning was never seen or heard of more. Though possibly intended to be regarded as confidential, certain it is that the confession had leaked out, and very soon became public property. For a few days it attracted great attention; and then, like other more important things which had preceded it, it ceased, save very occasionally, to be alluded to at all. But the Colonel never forgot it, any more than he ever forgot the lovely and inexplicable vision which had appeared to him for so brief an interval, in the moonlight, on the shore below Clyffe House. It is true that he seldom referred to it. Nor did that stately dame, who had once been Miss Alix and who was now believed to command the regiment, encourage him to do so. For she had observed that he was always most ready to tell the story after an exceptionally good dinner. And, with her high sense of what was due to his rank, she fancied that it made him mildly ridiculous. Neither, it might be, had her earliest doubts been ever wholly laid to rest. But members of the fair sex, when they are practical, are apt to be very practical indeed.

THE GHOST OF LORD CLARENCEUX,
by Arnold Bennett

In the chair which stood before the writing-table in the middle of the room sat the figure of Lord Clarenceux. The figure did not move as I went in; its back was towards me. At the other end of the room was the doorway, which led to the small bedroom, little more than an alcove, and the gaze of the apparition was fixed on this doorway. I closed the door behind me and locked it, and then stood still. In the looking-glass over the mantelpiece I saw a drawn, pale, agitated face, in which all the trouble in the world seemed to reside; it was my own face. I was alone in the room with the ghost—the ghost which, jealous of my love for the woman it had loved, meant to revenge itself by my death. The ghost, did I say? I looked at it; no one would have taken it for an apparition. Small wonder that till the previous evening I had never suspected it to be other than a man. It was dressed in black; it had the very aspect of life. I could follow the creases in the black coat, the direction of the nap of the silk hat. How well by this I knew the faultless black coat and that impeccable hat! Yet it seemed that I could not examine them too closely. I pierced them with the intensity of my fascinated glance. Yes, I pierced them, for, showing faintly through the coat, I could discern the outline of the table which should have been hidden by the man's figure, and through the hat I could see the handle of the French window.

As I stood motionless there, solitary in the glow of the electric light with this fearful visitor, I began to wish that it would move. I wanted to face it—to meet its gaze with my gaze, eye to eye, and will against will. The battle between us must start at once, I thought, if I was to have any chance of victory, for, moment by moment, I felt my resolution, my manliness, my mere physical courage slipping away.

But the apparition did not stir. Impassive, remorseless, sinister, it was content to wait, well aware that all suspense was in its favour. Then I said to myself that I would cross the room and so attain my object. I made a step and drew back, frightened by the quite sound of a creaking board. Absurd! but it was quite a minute before I dared to move another step. I had meant to walk straight across to the other door, passing in my course close by the occupied chair. I did do not so; I kept round by the wall, creeping on tiptoe, and my eye never leaving the figure in the chair. I did this in spite of myself, and the manner of my action was the first hint of my ultimate defeat.

At length I stood in the doorway leading to the bedroom. I could feel the perspiration on my forehead and at the back of my neck. I fronted the inscrutable white face of Lord Clarenceux, the lover of Rosetta Rosa; I met its awful eyes: dark, invidious, fateful. Ah, those eyes! Even in my terror I could read in them all the history and the characteristics of Lord Clarenceux. They were the eyes of one who could be of the highest and the lowest. Mingled in their hardness was a melting softness, with their cruelty a large benevolence, with their hate a pitying tenderness, with their spirituality a hellish turpitude. They were the eyes of two opposite men, and as I gazed into them they reconciled for me the conflicting accounts of Lord Clarenceux which I had heard from different people.

But, as far as I was concerned, that night the eyes held nothing but cruelty and disaster; though I could detect in them the other qualities, these qualities were not for me. We faced each other, the apparition and I, and the struggle, silent and bitter as the grave, began. Neither of us moved. My arms were folded easily, but my nails pressed into the palms of my clenched hands. My teeth were set, my lips tight together, my glance unswerving. By sheer strength of endeavour I cast aside my fear of defeat, and in my heart I said with the profoundest conviction that I would love Rosa though the seven seas and all the continents give up their dead to frighten me.

So we remained, for how long I do not know. It may have been only minutes —I cannot tell. Then gradually there came over me a feeling that the ghost in the chair was growing larger. The ghastly inhuman sneer on his thin widening lips assaulted me like a giant's malediction, and the light in the room seemed to become more brilliant till it was almost blinding. This went on for a time, and once more I pulled myself together, collected my scattering senses, and seized again the courage of determination which had nearly slipped from me; but I knew that I must get away, out of sight of this moveless and diabolic figure, which did not speak, but which made known its commands by means of its eyes. "Resign her," the eyes said. "Tear your love for her out of your heart! Swear that you will never see her again—or I will ruin you utterly, not now only but for evermore."

I think I trembled; my eyes answered "No." For some reason which I cannot at all explain, I suddenly took off my overcoat, and, drawing aside the screen which ran across the corner of the room at my right hand, forming a primitive sort of wardrobe, I hung it on one of the hooks. I had to feel with my fingers for the hook, because I kept my gaze on the figure. "I will go into the bedroom," I said; and I turned to pass through the doorway. Then I stopped. If I did so, the eyes of the ghost would be upon my back, and I felt that I could only withstand that glance by meeting it. To have it on my back.... Doubtless I was going mad. However, I went backwards to the doorway, and then rapidly stepped out of sight of the apparition and sat down upon the bed. Useless! I must return. The mere idea of the empty sitting-room—empty with the ghost in it—filled me with a new and considerable fear. Horrible happenings might occur in that room, and I must be there to see them! Moreover, the ghost's gaze must now fall on nothing; that would be too appalling (without doubt I was mad). Its gaze must meet something, otherwise it would travel out into space further and further till it had left all the stars and waggled aimless in the ether. The notion of such a calamity was unbearable. Besides, I was hungry for that gaze. My eyes desired those eyes: if that glance did not press against them, they would burst from my head and roll on the floor, and I should be compelled to go down on my hands and knees and grope in search for them. No, no. I must return to the sitting-room. And I returned. The gaze met mine in the doorway, and now there was something novel in it—an added terror, a more intolerable menace, the silent imprecation so frightful that no human being could suffer it. I sank to the ground, and as I did so I shrieked; but it was a weird shriek, sounding only within the brain, and in reply to that unheard shriek I heard an unheard voice of the ghost crying, "Yield!"

I would not yield. Crushed, maddened, tortured, I would not yield. I wanted to die. I felt that death would be sweet and truly desirable. And, so thinking, I faded into a kind of coma, or rather a state which was just short of coma. I had not lost consciousness, but I was conscious of nothing but the gaze. "Good-bye, Rosa," I whispered; "I am beaten, but my love has not been conquered." The next thing I remember was the paleness of the dawn at the window. The apparition had vanished for the night, and I was alive. But I knew that I had touched the skirts of death. I knew that after such another night I should die.

THE HAUNTED AUTOMATON,
by W. C. Morrow

Old man Erkins had three principal faults: he was rich, stingy, and a hard drinker. For the first of these he was to blame; for the second, pitied; for the third —but wait and read further before you express an opinion. At all events, by reason of these things and of others that I shall now write concerning him, I say and you will say that he should have been killed; which I am restrained from doing in this very line by the necessities of this story and not at all by fear either of the law or of punishment in the world to come.

Upon recovering from a hard spree, toward the end of which he would begin to see strange things, Erkins would not touch a drop for several days; then, recovering his nerve, he would laugh at his past timidity and—take a drink; the next day one, the next three, the next four, and so on, until snakes and other queer things would creep out of dark places.

There was an old servant, named Sarah, that kept his large prison (for such was his house) in order; and the one green spot in her shaky old life was a pretty girl, old Erkins' niece, ward and prisoner combined—Alice by name, and the prettiest girl in all the country thereabout, though a very unhappy one, to be sure. Alice had inherited Sarah, who was Alice's mother's trusted servant, and who vowed that she never, never would leave the poor young orphan, though the old house should swarm with snakes and things.

Now, the old miser loved his niece in a certain way. There are persons who love others so deeply that they murder them. There are various ways of committing murder, and one of the cruelest is to shut up a pretty girl in a big house and never let a young fellow even look at her.

Merely because she accidentally—entirely accidentally—fell in love with a poor but good-looking young machinist whom she met at church, her old guardian, in a spirit of mean tyranny, forbade her ever going out again, and in a most insulting and over-bearing manner told this young man, Howard Rankin, that the girl should never see him again, and that any mendicant fortune-hunter who should ever present himself at the house or seek to capture her for her quarter of a million would be riddled with buckshot.

Old Erkins had a mania for curious mechanisms. He had clocks that did all manner of wonderful things, and hundreds of other ingenious contrivances of various kinds. Whenever he read of some curious invention he would have it. He never tired of amusing himself with these things. There was one thing that Erkins needed to complete his happiness as well as his collection, and that was an automaton—a working counterfeit man. He had read everything that had ever been written on the subject of such automata. He had visited museums and wax-works shows, and had seen gladiators and Zouaves dying their several deaths again and again; but they were all too suggestive, for there were times when old Erkins' nerves were weak. Once he did buy a dying gladiator at enormous expense, but on the occasion of his next bad spell that gladiator's departing life seemed to take the form of numberless snakes and monkeys; and, frantic with fright, its owner chopped it to pieces with a hatchet.

Howard Rankin had a certain inventive genius. Knowing the old mans weakness, he conceived the idea of constructing an automaton, with which he hoped, he told a friend, to reinstate himself in the old man's good graces. However, this was a secret. All that he gave out was that he was going to construct an automaton—he knew what would result. He really did think that he loved Alice very, very deeply. Why shouldn't he? He promptly began to put his idea into execution, and selected the back room of his work-shop.

Very soon the project caused such talk that old Erkins heard of it. As the work progressed and favored bends were permitted to see the wonderful automaton as it grew under its author's hands, old Erkins, hearing the stories, became more and more interested. When a few months had passed he heard that the automaton was nearly finished.

Erkins could restrain himself no longer—he must see that automaton and must secure it. But how should he proceed? He had grossly insulted the inventor. This was a serious difficulty. He pondered over it a few days, and then boldly sent a polite note, asking permission to see the automaton. A formal note, granting the request, came in reply. The old man went at once.

The young man received him with polite condescension. Erkins' keen old eyes glittered eagerly; and Howard, noticing it, was secretly elated accordingly. Outwardly he was stiff and cold.

"And so you are at work on an automaton?" Erkins asked, as he was ushered into the back room.

"Yes," deliberately responded the young mechanic, as he quietly proceeded with his work.

"Cheerful one?"

"What?"

"Cheerful?"

"What do you mean?"

"It doesn't die, or anything of that sort, does it?"

"Oh, no!"

"'Cause I had a dying gladiator once, and it died so hard that sna—that—that it was unpleasant."

He stepped closer to the half finished automaton. It sat in an easy-chair. "So I killed it," he said.

"Killed what?"

"Gladiator."

He was devoured with curiosity concerning Howard's automaton, and yet felt such timidity that he hesitated about asking questions. Howard, volunteering no information, continued his work. Presently Erkins mustered up courage.

"I see you haven't put on its head yet," he essayed.

"No."

"Haven't got it ready?"

"No."

There was a pause.

"What will it do?"

"A good many things."

The old man went round it and examined it narrowly. It was the figure of a fop, dressed in the extreme of fashion, sitting in an indolent posture.

"Everything finished except the head, eh?"

"Yes," answered Howard; who seeing that he had carried his indifference far enough, left off his work, and said: "The head is to be the main part, because the more important work is to be done by it, and great care is required in making its wax face, its eyes, and so forth. Here is the block of it, with the machinery inside. That blonde wig will be its hair. As the automaton now is, however, it can give all the limb motions, though they are comparatively insignificant." Howard inserted a key in a hole in the back of the chair and wound up the automaton. The slight clicking of machinery was audible. Old Erkins trembled with excitement as he saw the automaton begin to move. It brought its right hand to the place where its mouth would be, then lowered it; brought up its left hand, and then crossed its legs.

"The right hand," explained Howard, "will carry a cigar, for the automaton will smoke. See—it will take a few puffs and then withdraw the cigar. The other hand is now taking up an eye-glass. I must now stop the machinery, as other attachments, not yet supplied, will have to be added, and still other machinery, the most intricate of all, is contained within the head."

"What will you do with the automaton?" asked Erkins, feeling his way.

"Don't know—probably keep it for my own amusement."

"Wouldn't you sell it?"

"Sell it! why, who is rich enough to buy it!"

Erkins' heart sank.

"What shall you ask for it?" he inquired in sheer desperation.

"A thousand dollars."

Erkins' heart leaped with joy.

"I'll take it," he eagerly said. He had expected to hear five-thousand. "It's a go," quietly responded Howard.

Then Erkins began to reflect that possibly he had been too hasty.

"I may be giving you too much," he said.

"Don't take it if you don't want it," coolly answered the young man.

"Will you give me a written guaranty of what it will do?" he asked.

Howard pondered a moment. "I will do not only that," he said, "but more; for I have great confidence in the automaton. Let me see. This is the 12th of November. I will be married on Wednesday, the 24th of next month, the day before Christmas. I shall want eight hundred dollars for my wedding and to start in life. I—"

"Married!" exclaimed old Erkins in astonishment.

"Yes. I will take eight hundred dollars down. If the automaton please you, you are to pay the balance; if in any particular it fall below your expectations, you may keep the two hundred. I will give you a written guaranty that the automaton shall cross and uncross its legs, smoke cigars, adjust its eye-glass, incline its head, open and close its eyes, wink and talk—speak two or three words."

"Good!" cried the old man. "It's a bargain." Erkins was very happy when he left. He had had two triumphs—secured the automaton and learned that Alice and her fortune were no longer in danger.

According to agreement the automaton was delivered on Saturday, December 20th, by a friend of Howard's, the inventor sending word that under the circumstances he had no desire to enter Mr. Erkins' house. The automaton was encased in a large box provided with handles, and four men were brought to carry it into the house. Old Erkins danced about in great excitement and high glee. It was a time of such rejoicing with him that he called Alice and Old Sarah to share his happiness and see the wonderful automaton. Much of his exhilaration was due to drink, for the old man was rapidly reaching the limit, and in two or three days his old wriggling friends would surely be upon him.

"How's Rankin getting along with his wedding?" asked Erkins of the friend.

The latter gave some offhand reply, and as he did so he saw Alice stagger backward to the wall and her face blanch. "By the way, Alice," said wicked old Erkins, delighting in the cruel stab he was giving, "Howard Rankin is to be married next Wednesday."

The poor girl could say nothing, for her heart was broken; but old Erkins did not notice her strange conduct nor see the agony of shame, humiliation and despair she suffered. Sarah saw it all, and it wrung her faithful old heart. She slipped her arm around the young girl's waist and would have led her away; but Erkins commanded them to remain, and Erkins' word was law.

The men set down the big box in the hall.

"Mr. Erkins," said the friend, "here are certain instructions that Howard sent for the management of the automaton. He insists that they be carried out to the letter, or he will not be responsible for failure."

The old man hastily read the instructions. Among them there was this one: "The automaton must be kept in a room with a temperature not below 65 degrees Fahrenheit nor above 75 degrees, otherwise the springs, catgut strings, the wax of the face and of the head, and the glue of the various parts will be ruined." Here was another: "There must be little light in the room, or the delicate colors in the face and hands will fade; and the automaton must not be placed with its face to the light." Another instruction made careful provision for ventilation, thus: "Exterior air, which at this time of year is either damp or frosty, must be excluded, and hence the window should never be opened; but as fresh air is necessary, the door must always be left slightly ajar—say six inches—and it must not open into any other room, but into a hall." Winding at night or more than once a day was forbidden. There were also minute instructions for preparing and lighting the cigars that the automaton should smoke.

Erkins reflected. There was only one room in the house which permitted of compliance with these instructions, and that was up-stairs. He slept down-stairs, and he had intended to place it in a room adjoining his bedroom; but as he used that one for an office and kept a hot fire in it, the automaton would be ruined there. The only objection he had to its going up-stairs was upon account of his fear that Sarah or Alice, who occupied rooms near the one that must receive the automaton, would surreptitiously wind up the treasure at unseasonable times and thus ruin it. But had he been shrewd enough to guess at the loathing they had for a thing that came from Howard's hands, he would have felt no uneasiness.

"Sarah," he sternly said, "I must put the automaton in the southwest room up-stairs; but if either you or Alice dare to touch it or enter the room where it is, I'll murder you. Do you understand that? I'll murder you both."

The four men carried the big box to the southwest room up-stairs and set it just where it should be, according to the instructions. Old Erkins, gleeful and brutal, forced Sarah and Alice to accompany it, and compelled them to stand and see it uncovered. This was done by removing the top, ends, and sides of the box and lifting a cloth that covered the figure. The wonderful automaton sat revealed.

Alice had secretly hoped that Howard had made the automaton to resemble himself, though ever so slightly; but when she saw the figure, with flaxen hair and mustache, so different from his, which were black; and the broad black eyebrows; and the painted cheeks, so different from his own pale face; and the foppish costume; and the effeminately curled hair; and the general air of impudence that pervaded the whole figure, her last hope departed. There was not a shadow of Howard's quiet manliness in anything about this mimic man.

Old Erkins regarded it otherwise. He saw only a wonderful mechanism, finished and decked out with fine art; and that was all he cared for. The artificial fop reclined indolently in an easy-chair. Its head hung upon its breast and its eyes were closed, its appearance being that of a slumbering man.

The four carriers were dismissed, and the friend produced a key, inserted it in a hole in the back of the chair, and wound up the automaton. It raised its head, opened its eyes sleepily, and with the greatest dignity it slowly turned its head as though regarding each member of the company, and then it smiled and very graciously bowed. Howard's friend produced a cigar and carefully prepared it, as a lesson to Erkins, the automaton meanwhile continuing to bow and smile. Following the instructions, the friend laid the cigar on a little stand convenient to the automaton's right hand, and the automaton with absolutely accurate movement brought the cigar to its mouth and with great deliberation took several puffs. Then it removed the cigar, and with its left hand adjusted an eyeglass, with which it gravely regarded the company; then puffed at the cigar again, and then crossed its legs.

"I must go now," said the friend. "The automaton will keep this up thirty minutes longer, and then it will have run down; but it must not be wound again till tomorrow. Remember the imtructions"; and he left.

Alice then begged to be allowed to go, as she was dying with a headache, she said, and had seen enough of the automaton; and so old Erkins, deeply disgusted, dismissed them.

He remained alone with the automaton, sitting directly in front of it and eagerly drinking with his eyes every one of the slow, dignified, accurate motions that it made. The only sound audible was a faint ticking, a very soft creaking, of the intricate machinery. This comparative silence, and the subtle wisdom that the automaton seemed to have and its deliberate manner, and its impudence, began to work upon Erkins' diseased imagination. As the thing continued to smoke, and adjust its eyeglass, and cross its legs, and open and close its eyes and bow so gravely, it took on, in Erkins' opinion, a kind of uncanny, supernatural air that disturbed its owner. Erkins' mind was not exactly right, and he knew it; but even making due allowance for it he was positive the thing was acting strangely. It seemed to be trying to exasperate him. This feeling was steadily growing upon Erkins; so that when there came a sharp little click in the machinery and the automaton dropped the cigar to the floor and boldly winked at Erkins, the old man began to experience downright fright. Yet he reflected that the guaranty called for winks. Still, this wink was too knowing. It was an insidious, wise, searching wink, that seemed to show cognizance of every sin that Erkins had ever committed. It was a leering, impudent wink; such a wink as innocence would be incapable of; a dangerous, mocking wink. It winked not only once, but twice, thrice, four times; taking a long time between winks, and accompanying each with a sinister leer. It did nothing but wink. Everything about it was perfectly still with the exception of that one eye-lid, and the stare that it kept fastened upon Erkins was a cold and deadly stare; a stare that saw through and through him, he thought, and that acted upon him with such strange effect that it held him bound, cold with terror, to his seat.

It was also in the guaranty that the automaton should speak. As yet it had not spoken. When it had winked several times there came another sharp little click, which startled Erkins. The old man had forgotten all about the speaking, but that little click warned him that something else was coming. What would it be? Something awful, he instinctively felt.

The automaton sat still for five long seconds, and then very slowly, very cautiously, very mysteriously, it leaned forward and said in a hollow, ghostly voice, that seemed to come up from the bowels of the earth:

"I'm haunted!" Erkins shivered, and he thought his heart had ceased beating. The automaton slowly resumed its former posture and fixed its dead stare upon its owner. It sat thus for what seemed to Erkins an age, and then again as before it leaned forward and in sepulchral tones it said:

"I'm haunted!"

Erkins could hear it no longer. White and trembling with fright, he backed out of the room, carefully left the door as the specifications required, and went out into the garden and shook himself like a dog.

"That thing," he muttered, "is worse than a sna—than the dying gladiator. But it's a beautiful piece of work," he presently added, when he had somewhat recovered his nerve; "and of course I shall get used to it. Of course."

Nevertheless, he needed something to help him in this and he sought it in his liquor. He drank frightfully all that day, and toward evening his old unwelcome visitors began to show themselves. And they were unusually bold. He went early to bed, and actually one hideous old monkey had the effrontery to pretend he was a dying gladiator. A young monkey assumed all the airs of a fop, and smoked a cigar, adjusted an eye-glass, crossed its legs, smiled and bowed, and then winked at the miserable old man in the most impudent and insulting manner; and, not satisfied with that, it leaned forward mysteriously from its perch on the foot-board of the bed, and in a rasping, sepulchral whisper, said:

"I'm haunted!"

Thus passed this hideous night—one of snakes, monkeys, dying gladiators, fops who declared they were haunted, and horrible nightmares.

But Sunday morning came at last, and old Erkins ushered in the new day with deep draughts of brandy. He was trying to steady himself for a second interview with the automaton.

At last he entered the automaton's room. There sat the ingeniously constructed thing, sound asleep in its chair. Erkins approached it gingerly, but it sat so quiet and harmless, and looked so weak and effeminate, and so unlike the ghostly thing that leered and winked at him the day before, declaring it was haunted, that his courage revived and he laughed at his fright. The old fellow was badly shattered from drinking, and his old knees tottered and his bony hands trembled as he went to the mantel and returned with the key to wind the automaton. He was very nervous and jerky about the winding; but he managed to get through with it in a fashion, and then he sat down in front of the automaton and awaited developments. The same old motions were exactly repeated, although the automaton had to puff an imaginary cigar, as Erkins was too badly shaken up to remember it. But the oversight soon began to trouble him. In his befogged condition of mind he imagined that the automaton laid it up against him. He was positive that under the smile lurked a wicked look, and he was thoroughly convinced of this when the first click came and the winking and leering commenced. There was then exhibited by that soft-appearing automaton a diabolical deviltry and a deeply mysterious cunning that no mechanical thing—so Erkins thought—could show; and when it came to the second click, and began slowly to lean forward, the horrible thought stole into the old man's mind that the devil himself sat before him.

"I'm haunted!"

Erkins' blood ran cold. He suffered an agony of fright. Every nerve quivered, and he gasped for breath. A deathly perspiration exuded from his face and trickled down his cheeks. With hands upraised and fingers outspread, with gaping mouth and wide-staring eyes, he gazed with a terrible, tragic fascination at the awful thing before him.

"I'm haunted!" The blind yet ever-watchful instinct of self-preservation dragged the old man tottering from his seat and thrust him out. Stumbling, staggering, mumbling, he found his way to his own room, and fell headlong upon the floor, and passed into grateful unconsciousness.

He lay thus an hour or more, and recovering, crawled to his bed. There he remained all day, discussing in his mind the ways and means for executing a design that he had conceived.

"He didn't exactly say it would be a cheerful one," he mused. "He said merely that it wouldn't die. But it does worse than that. The gladiator wasn't haunted. It was simply dying—dying all the time. Well, I put it out of its misery. I'll have to do another thing like that. I'm going to kill that haunted automaton if I die in the attempt."

Such was his design. But he was not yet able to put it into execution. He tried his strength; he could hardly stand. The day wore away, and still he was too weak. He drank more brandy. Night finally came, and then he dreaded the undertaking in the dark.

Finally twelve o'clock struck; then one o'clock. The frightful visitors had quit creeping about the halls, and all had congregated in his room. He drank more. He became stronger, and there came to him a boldness born of desperation. Not another minute would he delay the annihilation of the haunted automaton. He got out of bed and lighted a candle. He knew where to find the hatchet with which he had put a stop to the sufferings of the dying gladiator, and he desired to use that particular hatchet in the deadly work that lay before him. It was in the rear part of the house. He found it. He went cautiously upstairs and approached the room of the haunted automaton. As he drew near to it he became more and more violently agitated—so much so, in fact, that when he pushed the door to enter the room the candle fell from his trembling hand and was instantly extinguished. He nerved himself with all his might, for he was determined to accomplish the work.

As he approached stealthily, step by step, he imagined he felt that maddening wink, and momentarily he expected to hear that unearthly voice declare, "I'm haunted." So, he decided to strike from the rear. He crept around and got behind the chair. He took one step forward, and that brought him just close enough. He raised the heavy hatchet in both hands, and with all the strength of a madman brought down its keen edge upon the head of his unconscious victim.

The automaton must have turned to air, for the blow fell upon empty space; and the strength that he had thrown into it precipitated him headlong into the automatons chair. But the haunted automaton was gone!

The old man, mad with terror and raving in delirium tremens, ran from the room, shrieking for help. He burst into Sarah's room. She was gone. He tore into Alice's room. She too was gone.

Yelling, screaming, raving, pursued by a thousand demons, desperately mad, he flew out of the house and down the street, shrieking, "I'm haunted! I'm haunted! Help! Help!"

A policeman caught him and took him to prison. On Wednesday he was calm and rational, though somewhat ill and weak. A lawyer visited him at the hospital, whither he had been taken from jail, and handed him the following note, which the old man read several times before he could fully grasp its meaning:

My Dear Sir: I told you a few weeks ago that I should be married today, Wednesday, the 24th December. I have kept my word, as I was married an hour ago. If you want an automaton you may have that dummy that you saw in the back room of my workshop; for in reality that was the one you bought, and it has never left my shop. The money you paid me on account was just what I wanted to marry on. It is a little singular that when I told you I should marry today I had not even asked the girl! She never dreamed that such was my intention until last Saturday night, when I presented myself to her old servant, whose scream when she discovered me I greatly feared would betray my presence to a certain person who did not want me there. But the girl I wanted was sensible, and we made all necessary preparations and left the house Sunday. I feared that a certain person would hear our foot-falls, though we went on tiptoes and as softly as possible.

That certain person was the girl's uncle. He had done me a bad turn, and I am now even with him; for not only did I frighten him out of his wits but I stole his niece from under his very nose and made him pay all the expenses of the wedding.

She is an excellent girl and is rich besides. By the way, her name is Alice and she is your niece; and as I am now her legal guardian, I desire that you should make to Mr"—, the bearer of this, my attorney, a full accounting of all her property.

And by the way, further, we are to have a little dinner at our hotel this evening, at which our friends are expected. Can't you come? Do so, and let's be friends; for Christmas is a time when we should all make up. Hope you are better.

Howard Rankin, alias The Haunted Automaton.

The old man thought it all over—and went; and I am happy to add that he never drank another drop.

THE GHOSTS AT GRANTLEY,
by Leonard Kip

CHAPTER I

The London stagecoach dropped me at the gatelodge of Grantley Grange, and according to my usual custom I started up to the Hall on foot. It was such a pleasant Christmas morning as perhaps is not often seen, and might well have tempted to a longer walk than that short mile up the carefully trimmed avenue. There had been a slight fall of snow, a mere sprinkle indeed; but it was sufficient to clothe the brown turf with a dainty tint of pearl, and to make the dry leaves rattle crisp beneath the feet, and to project the great oaks in seemingly more ancient grandeur against the brightened background and generally to give an unusually cheery and exhilerating aspect to the whole scenery of the park.

When I had nearly reached the Hall, the church clock struck noon, and immediately all the bells began to ring out a merry Christmas peal. Up and down, hither and thither, now a snatch of tune and again a meaningless clashing of all the bells at once—single notes and double and triple concords, and, in fact, everything that well-disposed bells ever can or will do—so it ran on right cheerily. Now it was that I anticipated my Uncle Ruthven would hasten out to meet and welcome me. For I knew that he was fond of listening to the chimes; and when the changes were being sounded upon them he would not unfrequently sit at the open window, the better to enjoy them.

And of course, as I could now plainly see the Hall through the leafless trees, he from his open window could as readily watch my approach. Somewhat to my momentary chagrin, however, he did not come forth or even meet me at the door, and I was suffered to enter unannounced. And passing through the main hall, I wandered into the library.

There I found my Uncle Ruthven standing in the middle of the floor, his head thrown back, his eyes fixed intently upon the opposite wall, one arm raised in front to the level of his face, the other hand thrown behind him, an expression of resolute determination impressed upon every feature, his whole appearance and position resembling that of the antique Quolt Thrower.

Evidently he had been engaged in similar action; for, in a moment, he stepped to the other side of the room, picked up a short, fat book which had been thrown thither, and replaced it upon the table.

"Anatomy of Melancholy," he remarked, turning to me with a little chuckling laugh. "The first person who for a long while has got the book all through him—eh, Geoffrey? Though, of course, we all relish a little of it, now and then. Hit him directly upon the breast, and it went through him as through a summer mist, dropping out behind between his shoulder blades. Of course he has vanished, taking the hint of not being longer wanted here."

"Who, Uncle Ruthven?" I asked.

"Why, the ghost, of course," was the answer.

I was a little startled at this. It is true that I had sometimes thought that the library at Grantley Grange might be just the place for ghosts. It was wainscoted heavily with carved oak darkened in tint with the seasoning of four centuries. Above, the walls were covered with hangings of Spanish leather, stamped in quaint pattern. The fireplace was deep set and broad—so deep and broad, indeed, that the great logs smoldering within appeared no larger than ordinary sticks. The windows were projected into oriels with heavy mullions and let in the light, encumbered with a thousand stray shadows. The tables and chairs and high bookcases seemed almost immovable with their sculptured massiveness, and as though designed for a race of giants. Queer lamps hung from the ceiling and grotesque candlesconces projected themselves from the walls, each with heavy metal shades that would shut in more light than they sent forth. Over the mantel and beside the doors were paintings blackened with age; a Salvator Rosa, turned by the grime of time into a mere confusion of different shadows, with only here and there a touch of faded light for contrast, and, on either hand, eight or ten old portraits in ruffs and crimson coats and armor, cracked and worm-eaten and sometimes almost undistinguishable in face, but serving in costume to show the different careers into which, in times past, the fates or inclinations of the originals had carried them. A gloomy old library, indeed, full of crevices that would not stay closed, and cobwebs that could not be got at, and drafts that came from no one knew where, and flickering shades that seemed to obey no philosophic law, but stole here and there across wall and ceiling as their fancy led them. So that not unnaturally it appeared at times as though the place could never have been made for man's enjoyment, but rather as a hall for witches' Sabbath or ghostly revels; and as I watched the subdued and hesitating flickering of an errant sunbeam across the tarnished gilt pattern of the Spanish leather, it was not difficult for queer fancies and imaginings to take hold of me. But, after all, they were mere idle conceits, and at the most I had not for an instant anticipated the actual presentment of unearthly visitants.

"The ghost, did you say?" I therefore repeated, in some amazement.

"Yes, the ghost. Has been here every Christmas for many a year. Always comes just as the chimes strike up at noon, as regularly as though they had waked him. If you had ever before this happened to spend a Christmas with us, you might have met him yourself. Assumes that he belongs to the house, and that therefore he has his vested rights in it. Frightened me a little at the first, but have become used to him now and do not care. Am rather disposed, indeed, to lord it over him with high hand; and he is such a patient ghost that it hardly seems to make much difference with him. Am sorry always, in fact, if I speak crossly to him. But, then, you know my temper, Geoffrey, and how little I can brook presumption. How, then, would you feel if a ghost were to come, implying that he was the master of the house and that you were merely a visitor? Getsjust so far, indeed, and then vanishes without telling anything important."

I looked wonderingly at Uncle Ruthven thus calmly discoursing about the supernatural.

"But do you ever let him get further than that?" I suggested, my eyes wandering to the book upon the table.

"Perhaps not, Geoffrey—perhaps not. I suppose that if I were more patient he would talk a little better to the purpose. But then I am very quick tempered, and it is so exasperating, every Christmas to go through the very same thing. I always throw a book at him and am sorry for it afterward. It is certainly not the hospitable thing upon my part. But then to be so constantly beset, year after year, and not to know how many more there may be of them. For there is at least one other ghost somewhere about the house, Geoffrey. I have never seen him, but Bidgers the butler has, and he says it is as like this fellow as two peas. And if I am too polite to them, who knows but that they may be encouraged to come in swarms and make the house very uncomfortable? But let us leave all that for the present. You will be wanting to see your room, I suppose. The South Oriel, just past the second landing. Bidgers will carry up your portmanteau. Am sorry, by the way, that Lilian has not yet returned from the continent. She could, of course, make your stay much more pleasant for you than I can. But will do my best, Geoffrey. Luncheon at one, as usual."

Escorted by Bidgers, I proceeded upstairs to the South Oriel. It was a large apartment upon the south side of the house, with a broad octagonal window projection. If possible, the furniture was heavier and more antiquated than that of the library. There were quaint old tapestry hangings to the bedstead, so queer and faded that it seemed almost as though they might have been embroidered during the Crusades. The wardrobe was a marvel of size and solidity, and gave the impression that in troublous times, obnoxious owners of the estate might have safely been concealed in a false recess. Other articles of furniture were in similar style, and all together gave quite a gloomy aspect to an apartment that naturally, if left to itself, might have been well disposed to be cheerful. The effect was not diminished by a dingy picture over the mantelshelf, representing a funeral urn and drooping willow worked in hair, with an exceedingly numerous and mournfully dressed family coming two by two down a winding path to weep in concert around the tomb.

While I gazed solemnly at this work of art, a ragged yew tree kept striving at every breath of wind to thrust one of its gnarled old branches in at the window; and putting all things together, the cheerfulness went out of me entirely, and the idea of ghosts came in quite as naturally as in the library. I tried to shake it off, remembering my late experience and not wishing to have my mind burdened with any further queer fancies of the kind; and after a moment or two, indeed, seemed to be succeeding very tolerably and became able to hum an operatic drinking song with comparative ease and correctness. Just then, however, happening to turn my head, I saw a strange figure standing near the foot of the bed and gazing at me with fixed but not unpleasing or unfriendly expression.

The figure of a pleasant young fellow; hot, to all appearance, over twenty-two years of age, and exhibiting a lifelike rotundity and opacity that would have prevented any suspicion in my mind of the supernatural, if I had not had my uncle's word for it, or if I had discovered any way in which the stranger could have entered the room without my seeing him. A handsome young fellow, courtly in manner and dress, with coat of purple velvet, slashed and embroidered the whole length of the sleeves, a dainty little rapier swinging at his side and a plumed cap held in his hand. Hair falling in long curls over his broad lace collar, and the beard twisted into a point, while the small mustachios also twined into points turned up against the cheeks. A mild, responsive kind of face, with courteous smiles and replete with indications of gentle disposition.

"I am exceedingly happy to meet you," he remarked, playing with the gold-lace upon his sword hilt. "The more so that since I have been ill, so few persons come to visit me at all. I do not know that I have seen anybody of late, excepting the butler; and even he appears to be a new butler, most unaccountably put into possession by some other and pretended authority. I must in-quire into it when I am completely restored."

"You say that you have been ill?"

"Yes; a faintness and much uneasy want of rest at night, principally arising from this lump in my chest; and that, in turn, coming from the attack upon me by my brother Harold. Would be glad to introduce him to you if it were not for that. But I put it to you now: after what has happened, could I show him any such attention, or, indeed, associate with him at all? If cousin Beatrice were here, now —"

At this moment there came a rap at the door; and the ghost, shrinking a little toward one side, began to pale before me, and I saw that he was slowly fading away, beginning at the legs, and so the line of invisibility extending upward until gradually the whole figure had entirely vanished. Again I saw in its entirety the carved footboard which he had hitherto partially obscured; there was nothing left, indeed, to remind me of the strange visitant.

And opening the door I saw only Bidgers, the butler.

"Luncheon is ready, Master Geoffrey," he said. "No fish today, for the West stage is not in, but the mushrooms is particularly fine. Heard you talking to the ghost as I came along—the upstairs ghost, not Sir Ruthven's downstairs ghost. Sir Ruthven has only seen the downstairs one, but I've seen both. Saw this one last Christmas, about this time. He would not speak to me, however, it being that I am only the butler. They're very much alike, Master Geoffrey. There's a very nice haunch of venison for dinner today, let me recommend; and the kidneys is not to be despised, either."

CHAPTER II

After that, and during the remainder of my visit, nothing else happened especially worthy of mention. The Christmas festivities passed off as they generally do; and the next morning I returned to London, where my recollection of the ghosts soon began to die away. At first, indeed, as is natural, I could think of nothing else. But inasmuch as my Uncle Ruthven had taken the matter so coolly, I began to be impressed by a careful and more deliberate consideration of his manner, and to wonder whether I might not have imagined many of the most singular circumstances attending the incident; until, at last, I concluded that there could have been no ghost at all, but that I must have dreamed the whole story.

In addition, my time became so fully occupied that I had few occasions in which I might engage in desultory wandering of idle curiosity or speculation; for during the first eight months I was diligently employed reading for my admission to the Bar. After that, I was actively forgetting most of what I had learned, giving myself up as escort to my cousin Lilian. She had returned from her travels upon the continent, and with her father was stopping awhile in London before continuing on to the Grange. It was my pleasing duty to remain at Lilian's side most of the time, Sir Ruthven being glad to avoid the toil of active companionship. I was very much in love with Lilian, but would not for the world have prematurely told her of it—it would have made her so tyrannical. At last, of course, we quarreled. It was the day before Sir Ruthven and Lilian returned home; and she informed me that she was going on the 10.45 stagecoach, and that she would be seriously displeased if I attempted to see her off. This looked well for me upon the whole, I thought, and I started for the coach at once. As ill luck would have it, I missed it, a circumstance which really helped my cause; since Lilian, being thereby persuaded that I understood it to be a lasting quarrel, felt suitably piqued into anxiety and regret.

A little before Christmas, Sir Ruthven wrote me to run down to the Grange as usual. With his letter came a perfumed note from Lilian, stating that if she could, she would gladly be away at Christmas with her Aunt Eleanor; but since she could not, but was obliged to remain home, she would consider it a great insult if I presumed to visit the Grange before she could get away in some other direction. I was wonderfully encouraged at this, feeling that all was going on well; and packing my trunk at once, I went down by the earliest stage on Christmas morning.

Again the chimes happened to be ringing just as I alighted; and, as before, no one coming forth to meet me, I pressed on to the library, there to make my respects to Uncle Ruthven, feeling well assured that I should find him in his accustomed seat beside the fireplace. He was in the room, indeed, but not sitting down. He was standing beside the chair and bowing with great affection of cordiality to some one in the further corner of the room. Looking in that direction, I beheld a young fellow in court suit of two centuries ago, with hand upon his heart, bowing back to my uncle with still greater excess of old-fashioned courtesy and cordiality; and I did not for an instant doubt that I was looking upon the downstairs ghost. Almost the duplicate of the other one, indeed. Evidently about the same age, with equally agreeable, sunny, ingratiating expression.

Like the other, he had thick curls falling over the collar, beard cultivated to a point, slashed velvet coat, laces, gold tassels, and a slim, daintily decorated rapier. The most notable differences consisted in his complexion and hair being a shade darker, and his coat being of a lively crimson. It was a pleasant thing to see these two persons salaaming cordially and ceremoniously to each other; my uncle bowing until he struck the table behind him, and the ghost bending over in responsive courtesy until the point of the scabbard of his sword tipping up, made a new scratch upon the worm-eaten picture of Salvator Rosa.

"You see, Geoffrey," my uncle whispered between his repeated genuflexions, "he has come again to the very minute. The very same time as last year, just as though the chimes waked him up. I remember that you then thought that perhaps I was accustomed to cut him short rather too suddenly. We will be more cautious now, and will not end until we get his whole story out of him." Then to the ghost "I am rejoiced to see you once more, kind sir."

"It gives me equal and exceeding pleasure," responded the ghost. "And I know that my brother Arthur would be similarly gratified could he only know about your arrival. But, then, how is he to know? After his conduct toward me— the obloquy he has thrown around me, in fact—it certainly would be beneath my dignity to approach him, even for the sake of imparting information. I can, therefore, merely myself welcome you."

"Now, just listen to that!" muttered Uncle Ruthven, beginning to flush up angrily. "I have done my best; but is it possible to continue politeness with a person who insists upon treating me as his guest? I treat him with all the cordiality I can muster, and the only result of it is that he turns around and seems to patronize me."

It chanced that, moved by the first warmth of my uncle's courtesy, the ghost had advanced a little, as though to meet us, and thereby he now stood between us and the window. This change of position seemed to produce a marvelous alteration in his appearance. The face so fair and genial and prepossessing became at once a queer confusion of lines, every feature being obscured by what looked like converging cuts and wrinkles, making the whole expression of the countenance unintelligible. It was only for an instant, however. The next moment, the ghost moving away from the window, his face became as before—clear, distinct, filled with amiable and courteous refinement and intelligence. It was not until afterward that the mystery explained itself. Now, indeed, the singular appearance had lasted for such a brief moment that it seemed scarcely worth while to seek an explanation. The only thing, in fact, that particularly struck me was a red line extending around the throat, as though the result of a forced compression. This was observable even after the ghost had passed from directly before the window, and until he had moved completely out of reach of the entire spread of sunlight.

"If Cousin Beatrice were here," remarked the ghost in continuation, "she would undoubtedly be very happy to take part in entertaining you. But where is she now? It is some days since I have seen her. Do you think it possible that Brother Arthur, in addition to the ignominy to which he has subjected me by his unjust suspicions, can have influenced her mind against me? If so, as long as I live, I will never—"

"Listen again to that! As long as he lives! How can anybody stand such drivel?" cried Uncle Ruthven. "I suppose, Geoffrey, you will now see that it is as well to put an end to this first as last?"

With that, as upon the previous Christmas, my uncle seized a large book and vindictively let fly at the stranger. If until that time I had had any doubts as to his unsubstantial nature, they were now relieved. Corporeal and opaque as he had seemed, it was none the less true that the volume, striking him in the stomach, passed completely through him as through a stratum of air, falling upon the floor behind, while the figure remained unblemished and uninjured; with this exception, however, that naturally he seemed scarcely pleased with the roughness of the reception, and a shadow of discontent flickered across his face. Then appearing to comprehend that possibly he might be unwelcome, he slowly faded away.

"Middleton's Cicero, this time," remarked my uncle, wiping his face and gazing toward the weapon he had just so successfully used. "And the fellow has digested that as well as the volume last year. At this rate he will get my whole library into him before long. I cannot help it, Geoffrey. You saw that I tried my best to be polite. But when a ghost acts as though he owned the house, and moreover talks as though he were alive, mortal man could not withstand the temptation to cut him down. Well, well, get ready for lunch, Geoffrey. The South Oriel, as last year."

Of course, being sent up to the same room and the old program seeming to begin being played, I expected once again to meet the purple-coated ghost. And as is natural, I went up with some little trepidation. For it is one thing to have a ghost appear to you; good natured and smiling from the first; and another thing deliberately to throw one's self in the way of a ghost who might not happen at the moment to be in a very pleasant humor, and might exert some supernatural power to make himself extremely disagreeable. All the time I was dressing, I looked uneasily over my shoulder, in search of apparitions. But inasmuch as we seldom find what we most surely expect to see, I was left entirely undisturbed, and finally began my descent to the dining room with feelings greatly relieved and composed.

Passing the drawing-room, I heard the subdued rustle of silk, and entering, found Cousin Lilian all arrayed for luncheon and smoothing herself out before the fire. Of course after what had passed in London, she swept me a stately courtesy, addressing me by my surname as though I were a stranger whom she had casually met the previous day; and of course I bowed in her presence with ceremonious reverence befitting the first presentation of Raleigh to Queen Elizabeth. Then Lilian, slightly lifting her eyebrows in spirit of wonderment at my intrusion, remarked that she believed Sir Ruthven was in the library. I replied that I had already seen Sir Ruthven and had found him busily engaged with a ghost; and that as this seemed to be their reception day and others might be expected by him, I would not intrude upon him for a while, but with her permission would prefer to remain where I was.

These preambles having been thus satisfactorily entered into, of course we began making up by throwing at each other little spiteful remarks of an epigrammatic nature; now and then spontaneous, but for the most part carefully manufactured weeks before and treasured up for the occasion. Snapping these off from side to side like torpedoes, and mutually rebounding them harmlessly from our casemated natures, we gradually composed our feelings and began getting along very well on the path to reconciliation. How long it might have taken under ordinary circumstances I cannot tell; but it happened all at once that Lilian was startled into an unexpectedly rapid advance. For of a sudden I felt her hand grasping my arm, and she called me by my first name in the old familiar manner; and turning, I saw her gaze fixed with a wondering but not altogether alarmed expression upon the opposite corner of the room.

"See, Geoffrey!" she whispered. "The upstairs ghost! How comes he in here?"

CHAPTER III

Turning, I saw the purple velvet ghost at last, bowing low to the floor, with a humble courtesy that disarmed wrath, though nonetheless did an explanation seem necessary.

"Really, my good sir," I therefore said, "this intrusion—"

"I must apologize for it, certainly," he remarked, again bowing low. "I was a little behindhand this morning in reaching the South Oriel. And passing through the hall, I saw a female figure inside this room. I entered, expecting to meet my Cousin Beatrice. I see that I am mistaken. Last night I slumbered more uneasily than usual—the lump in my chest causing me very great disturbance, and doubtless it has excited my nerves and made me easily deceived. It has all come from Brother Harold's outrage upon me, I suppose. Which being so, it only remains for me to take my leave, with apology for the intrusion."

"Stay yet a moment," I said. "This is my cousin Miss Lilian, who certainly will not! fear you and will forgive your slight mistake. And—and I have so much to say to you."

In fact, I felt that this might be the last time I should see him; and that it would be no more than a charity to enlighten him as to his true condition. It was a very sad thing to see a bright, amiable young ghost going around century after century as though he were still alive, and I decided that it would be a kind action to correct his error. Moreover, it happened that just at this moment, chance threw a convincing explanation within my reach. For as the ghost stepped a little to one side preparatory to taking his departure, it came about that he stood between me and the window, just as the other ghost had done; and in like manner, every feature seemed obscured with a network of contrary lines and wrinkles. But as he chanced to remain there a little longer than the other one had done, the mystery became almost at once revealed. I saw that the singular appearance was caused by the strong sunlight showing through him, whereby his whole head appeared as a transparent object. It was exhibited as a mass of dim, lurid light, not entirely endowed with all the bright translucent qualities of glass, but rather as when a sheet of thin porcelain is held up to the light, so that its semicloudy transparency is revealed, and with it, any dark spots or imperfections in the surface are brought to notice. In like manner, our visitor's head now seemed transformed with the brightness of the sunlight behind it, so that its former opacity was gone and there was a light, cloudy appearance as of a dissolving mist, marked in every direction with straight and curved lines of greater or less intensity. At first, the features, excepting as they appeared in profile, seemed entirely to have vanished beneath a confusion of other lines; but a moment's observation assured me of the contrary. They were all still there—the sparkling eye, the delicate mouth, the well-shapen ear. With a little attention, I could still trace the sweep of their several outlines. It was merely that those outlines were now somewhat confused by the addition of other lines appearing from within the skull. These also, I found that with a little study, I could still make out. There was a broad, irregularly-curved mark showing the outline of the lobes of the brain. I could follow the whole ball of the eye beneath its socket and the fainter lines which connect the eye with the brain behind. The drum and the small bones of the ear, and the twisted passages from the nose to the ear were all now clearly defined. The palate, too, and the sides of the throat, until hidden at last beneath the laced collar of that courtly coat. In fine, under the influence of that bright sunlight behind it, the young fellow's head became something like one of the modern medical wax preparations, exhibiting every portion of its frame in exact position; except that, far superior to any work of art, it did not require to be taken apart for study, but could be examined in detail, just as it stood.

"How long," I said, myself moving a little one side so that he might not appear between me and the window; by which judicious movement he became at once like any other person, his features returning to their usual distinctness of outline, unclouded by any rival lines and curves from behind; "how long have you been thus ill and disturbed at night by pain within your chest?"

"A week, or even more, I think," he said.

"Pardon me," I responded; "here is where you have made a trifling mistake in your chronology—you, and the other, as well. This little episode which you believe has occupied a few days or so, has lasted, in reality, upward of two centuries. You have been thrown into a certain condition of mind in which you are unable to take due note of time. Why this is so, I cannot attempt to explain. The melancholy fact remains that you have already been wandering some two hundred years, and for all we know, may be destined to wander to all eternity. In proof of this, I might refer you to your costume, which is of the fashion of Charles the Second; while, in fact, we are living in the thirty-eighth of Victoria."

I paused for a moment here, thinking that he might wish to ask some question. But as he maintained a perplexed silence, I continued:

"You are in further error in believing that the only consequence of some injury you have received has been mere restlessness at night. Instead of which, you died and of course were suitably buried. And consequently, you are not now a man, but merely a ghost. It may be unpleasant to be told this, but it is as well that you should know it first as last. And, after all, there can be no harm in being a well-conducted, creditable ghost. As such, you are allowed to appear each Christmas day for a few minutes, at the expiration of which, doubtless, you return to your grave. There, I presume, you slumber until the next Christmas day, for you seem to have no definite knowledge of your whereabouts. At the least you must be comfortable, which perhaps is more than can be said of many ghosts. Even Hamlet's father seems to have suffered torments; though there is presumptive evidence that he was a very good man, and totally unlike his brother.

"You are incredulous about what I am now telling you? In proof of it, let me stand you directly in front of the window, so that the sunlight will strike full upon your person. Then let me hold this looking-glass before you. Now studying your reflection carefully, you will see that you are transparent; which, I take it, is the surest proof any man can enjoy of his being a ghost. You can trace out the passages of your ears, the convolutions of your brain, the course of your jugular vein. This line, which you might easily mistake for a nerve or cord, is merely a crack in the looking-glass. Should you feel disposed, hereafter, for your amusement, to study your internal anatomy more thoroughly, I would advise a new and more perfect mirror. But can you any longer doubt your condition?"

"I can no longer doubt, indeed," groaned the ghost. "But what, alas, can I now do?"

"A thousand things," I responded. "I take it that, inasmuch as men must not live idle lives, in like manner ghosts, also, may have their duties to perform. Surely, it can scarcely be intended, in the economy of the unseen world, that they should pass lives—or, rather, existences—of careless idleness. I know that, were I a ghost, I would do my best to find some useful employment. I think that I would endeavor to obtain some occupation that might be of benefit to the world I had left behind. Suppose, for instance, that you endeavored to retain some, even trifling, recollection of the nature of your abode in the unseen world, how you are associated, whither you are sent, and other facts of a kindred character, and were to impart them to the human race from time to time through myself. Do you not think that you would be doing great good, as well as entitling yourself to the gratitude of all living men?"

The ghost mutely shook his head. Evidently he did not care particularly about the gratitude of living men.

"Or suppose," I continued, struck with a new, and, in my estimation, better idea—for it happened that I had lately been interesting myself deeply in medical jurisprudence—"suppose that you were to apply yourself to the benefit of the human race in an anatomical or pathological capacity. There is on record the case of a man who had a hole in the side of his stomach through which processes of digestion could be watched, to the great service of medical science. Need I say that, for every purpose of interest or utility, you surpass him infinitely? I must assume, with tolerable certainty, that if your head is transparent, so, also, is your whole body; and that the workings of your inner system are simply hidden from sight by your clothing. Divested of that, you could easily unfold, in the strong light of the sun, the entire operations of your heart, your lungs and your stomach. Daily could you have your seances, and new discoveries could be noted down. There must be some thin, ghostly, almost impalpable fluid in your system answering the purpose of blood in the human frame, and of this physicians might succeed in watching the circulation and flow. There are vexed questions in medical science as to the real use of certain vessels and attachments—whether they are actually necessary in the human constitution, or whether they are mere rudimentary relics of a lower organization. These questions you might succeed in determining. In fact—"

I had reached thus far, becoming so transported with the increasing magnitude of my speculations that I no longer looked at the ghost, but with half-closed eyes gazed upward at the ceiling; when suddenly Lilian plucked me gently by the sleeve, and, with quiet movement of the eyes, called my attention more directly to our visitor. He was standing motionless beside the window; but I observed that the pleasant expression had faded from his face, an angry flush was mounting into every feature, grim, transporting rage was clouding every line. And, as I paused in natural hesitation, he turned roughly toward me.

"Have you done?" he cried, bursting out with an old-fashioned oath of the days of the royal Stuarts. "Have you come to the end of your base proposals? Have you reflected sufficiently what it is to dare to suggest to Sir Arthur Grantley, of the Court of Charles, that he should pass his time illustrating the labors and theories of leeches, quacks, and charlatans?"

Another old-fashioned oath, a half withdrawal of the slender rapier from its sheath, a driving it down again with impetuous, angry energy, and the ghost strode wildly out of the drawing room, and was no more seen. But for two or three moments we could hear him growling forth his queer old court oaths as he rattled away along the outside passage.

CHAPTER IV

Lilian and I gazed at each other in speechless wonderment. The bell rung for luncheon, and we passed toward the dining room; still with thoughts too deep for words.

"Can it be," I said at length, as we entered the other room, "that this person, whom we had supposed to be merely some retainer of the family, was in reality its head? That he could have been an ancestor of yours, Lilian?"

"Papa will know," she answered. "We will ask him at luncheon." Then, when the old gentleman sat eating his nuts and raisins and sipping his wine—before which time he disliked to be disturbed about anything excepting the occupation immediately in view—she began:

"Was there ever a Sir Arthur Grantley, papa?"

"Let me think," mumbled Uncle Ruthven. "Yes, there was a Sir Arthur about two centuries ago. And now the story begins to come to me. There were two brothers—twins; the oldest having the estate and title, and the youngest being a captain in the Royal Guard. One would have supposed that, being so nearly of an age and closely related, they would have kept the peace; but the contrary was the fact. They quarreled so that one of them murdered the other, and was suitably hanged for it."

"Is there record of the fact, Uncle Ruthven?"

"Nowhere, unless it may be in the State Trials. I have never looked there. You will find no allusion to it in Burke or Debrett. Those useful and accommodating compilers, out of regard for the family honor, I suppose, merely state that Harold Grantley died, aged twenty-two: a piece of reticence which, after all, was scarcely worthwhile, considering that it happened so long ago. Time is a great cleanser of family escutcheons. It would be unpleasant to have a murder attached to the reputation of one's father or grandfather; but carry it two centuries backs and no one seems to care. If it were not so, there is scarcely a royal family on earth which would not be hanging its head. I do not read that Her Most Gracious Majesty Victoria ever makes herself miserable about any suspicions attaching to the memory of Queen Mary of Scotland. In fact, rather a disreputable ancestry, if distinguished, is better than none at all. It is scarcely to be supposed, for instance, that any of us would take it much to heart at finding Guy Fawkes seated upon one of the limbs of the family tree. At any rate, we have no reason to complain of this little murder in the Grantley line, seeing that it finished up the direct descent in that quarter and sent down the entail to us through a collateral branch."

With that, having exhausted his knowledge upon the subject, Uncle Ruthven went on sipping his wine and turned the subject upon the culture of turnips. But after luncheon Lilian and myself, feeling by no means contented, slipped up to the library again and took down one of the time-worn dusty volumes of the State Trials. The books had evidently not been moved out of place for years; but it was easy, having the reign, to find all that we wanted, and in a few minutes we opened at the case of Rex Grantley. The book was very heavy, and at the first we spread upon the table. This proving inconveniently high we took to the sofa, where we let the volume rest on both our laps and read together. It was very pleasant, altogether. It was necessary for Lilian to lean over so that her curls brushed across my shoulder, and at times I could feel her breath warm upon my cheek. That she might have greater strength to hold her share of the book, I passed my arm sustainingly about her waist; a fact which she did not seem to realize, so intent was she upon the story of the murder. We have often read about young men and maidens looking upon the same book and in just such positions. In those narrations it is generally a book of poetry, or at least a novel that interests them. I question if very often a young lady sits with her lover absorbed in the story of a murder committed by one of her own family and reads it without any feeling except of curiosity about its mere incidents, and as coolly as though it were Jack Shepperd or Oliver Twist.

But then, as Uncle Ruthven justly observed, it was so long ago.

It appeared, then, from the account in the State Trials, that Arthur and Harold Grantley were twin brothers of the age of twenty-two. As Uncle Ruthven had stated, Arthur was the oldest and in possession of the title and estate, while Harold held commission in the Palace Guard.

Naturally the two brothers were thrown much together, and were supposed to be greatly attached to each other. Of course, they sometimes had their little disagreements; but, until the period of the murder, it was never supposed that there was any especial ill feelings between them. The trouble ensued about noon one Christmas day. Harold had obtained leave to visit his brother at the Grange; and after an early dinner—for they were alone and much form and ceremony was dispensed with—they sat at the table, conversing, eating filberts and drinking their wine.

Possibly they had been drinking too much; but not so much, in fact, as to exhibit its effects upon them to any great extent. The most that could be said was, that it might have tended to make them quarrelsome; but as it turned out, this after all was the whole mischief in the case, and much worse in its results than downright and less harmful intoxication. It chanced that Sir Arthur had taken the opportunity of exhibiting to his brother a certain valuable heirloom, known in the family as the great Lancaster diamond, having come into the line from a collateral Lancaster branch. It had lain concealed in a secret closet during the Cromwellian troubles, and had just been brought to light again. It is supposed that Sir Arthur, being attached to their cousin Beatrice and wishing marriage with her, had designed presenting her with the diamond; and that Harold, being equally in love with her and perhaps with no less prospect of success, had made objection; and that from this fact the quarrel had arisen. Be that as it may, their voices were heard in loud dispute; and suddenly Harold calling out for help, his brother was found lying upon his back lifeless and with every appearance about the throat of having been foully dealt with. Harold's account of the circumstance was to the effect that Sir Arthur all at once had thrown himself back in his chair and gasped and seemed to have been seized with a fit. On the other hand, it was argued that young men of his vigorous constitution did not readily die in fits—that the appear-ances of foul play by strangulation were too evident—that there had certainly been high words between them, a fact, indeed, which Harold was obliged to admit—that the known passion of both the young men for the same lady would have been sufficient of itself to produce fraternal hatred and strife—and furthermore, that Harold would have a supreme interest in his brother's death, by reason of the succession to the estate. And then again, the diamond had disappeared. If the death had been a natural one, the diamond would not have been disturbed; but inasmuch as it was the leading cause of the dissension, nothing was more natural than that the murderer should have made away with it, by throwing it out of the window, into the lake, most likely, so as to remove one great evidence of the crime. Altogether the feeling ran very high against the surviving brother, political prejudices that could scarcely now be explained intervened to increase the excitement, while certain favorites of the king, desiring promotion in the Guard by removal of one person of higher rank, prejudiced the royal mind against pity or pardon. In fine, after much agitation and a protracted trial, young Harold was found guilty and executed.

"And this explains," I said to Lilian, "many circumstances that hitherto have not been clear to me. The red line around the throat of the downstairs ghost; the pain in the chest of the upstairs ghost—a difficulty most naturally resulting from outside pressure—all these things now tell the story very clearly, and agree most wonderfully with the State trials account. Only—which at first seems strange—the murdered now does not seem to remember that he was put to death, nor the murderer that he was executed for it."

"That is, indeed, singular," said Lilian. "But, then, ghosts are so silly!"

"At first sight, it may seem strange," I answered; "but not after a moment's reflection. Violence endured by us in life is very often with difficulty afterward brought to our memory. One has a fall or is stricken down by a club and made senseless; he recovers after awhile, and knows that in some way he has been injured, but does not remember the actual fall or blow. And why should it be different if the injury leads to death? Looking upon it in this light, and with this philosophy, we see the young baronet awakening in the grave with no conception of ever having been killed, but merely with some indistinct idea of previous attack or vituperation. And, in the same manner, we find the younger brother awakening in the belief that he is still alive, and remembering not his execution at the hands of the law, but only the fact of having been charged with some outrage against the other, the nature of which he cannot comprehend, while the circumstance of any charge being made at all grievously offends and distresses him."

"All very plausible, indeed," responded Lilian. "But suppose that, after all, he was innocent?"

"A thing very hard to believe, with so much contrary evidence," I said. "All that is a mere woman's unreasoning supposition, with endeavor to wipe off a blemish from the family escutcheon."

"*Pho!* for the family escutcheon," responded Lilian, putting up her lips in pholike form. And as she spoke she looked so pretty that, having my arm still about her waist, I began seriously to consider whether I had not better improve the opportunity and now make my offer. So much was already understood between us, indeed; and everyone, even Lilian herself, knew very well that it was destined some day to come about, as a suitable family arrangement long foreseen and often talked about; and, therefore, what better moment than the present to unburden my heart?

"I think, Lilian," I said, "that it is about time I spoke a word or two to you about our future."

"Well, Geoffrey," she replied.

I saw the flush gather in her face, that she knew what must be coming, that she anticipated tender avowal with loving expression. In this last respect, at least, mindful of recent aggravations on her part, I determined that I would disappoint her.

"No," I said, "it is not probable that Harold was innocent. And therefore you must see for yourself, Lilian, that your family have been a most disreputable lot. But for all that, having unfortunately a strong personal prejudice in your favor, I am inclined to believe that I shall not be doing myself too great injustice in offering you my alliance."

"You are very kind, certainly, Geoffrey," she responded. "I cannot but feel intensely gratified at the preference. I suppose that every family must at some time or other meet its misfortune of a public execution or some similar disgrace. I consider it particularly fortunate that with us it has already happened. In your line of the family it is yet to come; and if I may judge by circumstances, it will probably take place during the present generation. And merely that I may legally enjoy the privilege of standing at your side and comforting you during that closing ordeal, I take pleasure in accepting your offer."

And this is how Lilian and I became engaged.

CHAPTER V

It was understood that the wedding would not take place immediately. Uncle Ruthven had some old-fashioned notions about matrimony, prominent among which was the idea that no young man should marry without having the means of support from his profession, so as to be independent of the fluctuations and liabilities to loss of private fortune. Upon this basis, it was determined that we should not wed until I had made a public and credible appearance at the Bar.

This came about in the following October. I had been engaged as third counsel in the great case of Charity-boy v. Church-warden, for assault. Churchwarden had boxed the ears of Charity-boy for playing marbles on a tombstone; but unfortunately had not succeeded in catching him to do so until they were over the boundary-line of the graveyard. Upon this defect, want of jurisdiction as to place was alleged, and action brought. The suit had been running nearly five years, and therefore could now reasonably be moved for trial. The rector, curate, half the vestry and three of the bell-ringers had been subpoenaed to give evidence and stood ready. It was necessary to have, in addition, the testimony of the toy-maker who had sold the marbles; and he, it happened, was on his deathbed at the north of Scotland. A commission had been issued to take his testimony.

The toy-maker lay delirious for the most part, having a lucid interval of about half an hour each day, during which he desired to make his will. He was constantly prevented from doing so, however, by the entrance of the commissioners demanding to take his testimony, which so confused him that he always went off wandering again. Pending the execution of the commission, of course an adjournment was desired.

Now it happened that, both the senior counsel being away, it devolved upon me to make the application for the adjournment, and with a little difficulty about the pitch of my voice, I succeeded in doing so. The judge said that if the other side were agreed, there could be no objection; and the other side having duly consented, the adjournment was ordered. Whereupon I wrote down to Sir Ruthven that I had made my first appearance. Sir Ruthven immediately wrote back, asking whether my speech would be reported in the Times. I replied that I did not suppose it would, as the papers were unusually interested in the Montenegro difficulty, to the exclusion of much other valuable news. Uncle Ruthven thereupon responded that he was satisfied, upon the whole, even if the Times was silent about me; and that now that I had resources for support independent of inherited estate, the wedding might come off immediately after Christmas. And he told me to run down the day before Christmas, so that we could have a pleasant little Christmas dinner by ourselves, before the invited visitors began to arrive.

Accordingly, I arrived at Grantley Grange upon the after-noon of the twenty-fourth, and was at once shown to my room by Bidgers, who not only lighted me up, but followed me in to assist in unpacking my wardrobe. And while doing so, naturally with the self-allowance of an old family servant he let his tongue run loose with the gossip and events of the day.

"A hamper just come in, Master Geoffrey, with a fine large salmon; but that is for tomorrow. You must praise it when you see it, for Sir Ruthven sets great store in having got it. There has been no ghosts seen since you was here last—perhaps they have all gone away for good. There is talk that the Earl of Kildare will be at the wedding next week; but any which way, he has sent a silver pitcher. Maybe, after all, the ghosts have all been locked lip where they are. Miss Lilian's Aunt Eleanor has done better than the Earl of Kildare though. She cannot come, they say; but such diamond earrings as she has sent—almost as large as filberts, Mr. Geoffrey! As to the grapes today, I am fearful there's a little mold on some of them; but the oysters—"

"That will do—thank you, Bidgers," I said, tired of the running stream; and Bidgers, taking the hint, affected to blow a speck of dirt off the sleeve of my wedding coat, and gently glided out of the room. I was not so much tired, indeed, as that I felt I would like to be alone for thought.

Something in Bidgers last remark had awakened an association of ideas in my mind; but of such intangible, confused character that I could not follow it up to any definite purpose. Diamonds as large as filberts—filberts and diamonds, so ran the words, through and through my mind like the strain of a tune; but out of it all I could not, with the utmost concentration of thought, gain any clue that I might—follow up to a satisfactory certainty. At night the same—I fell asleep with the old sequence of words running in my head, still like the strain of a tune, as sometimes we will set to meter the thumping of a railroad car. In the middle of the night I awoke; and then there flashed upon mx' mind a solution of the puzzle, but so wild and improbable, so idiotic and fantastic did it seem, that at once I discouraged it. Even then, when scarcely half aroused, and at an hour when the waking fancies run riot in premonition and alliance with hardly more fanciful dreams, did I laugh at the crude conception and try to beat it down, falling asleep again at last with mind apparently entirely relieved of the foolish notion. But when in the morning I awoke with the sun broadly shining in upon me, there again was the queer idea; and now, wonderful to relate, though I lay with the collectedness of thought appertaining to the open day, and with little chance of crude fancies any longer overwhelming me, the idea, though still as strange and ghostlike as before, no longer bore that first impress of the ridiculous, but was as something real and to be soberly and carefully considered. At least the experiment suggested by it might be tried, though secretly and cautiously, so as not to provoke ridicule in case it came to nothing.

Dressing myself, I stole softly downstairs. It was still very early, and there was no one stirring below, excepting a housemaid dusting the furniture. She merely looked up and then continued her task, my habit of morning walks being too well known to excite observation. I passed through the long window and came upon the bare winter-stained lawn. There was the gardener, muffling anew some plants in straw; but he too, merely touching his hat, said nothing. Then I followed a gravel path around the terrace to the rear of the house, and thence struck off to a little grove of pines a hundred yards or so away.

In the midst of these was the burial vault of the Grantley family. It was by no means a repulsive object, being merely a brick erection a few feet above the surface of the ground, and originally constructed with some pretense of architectural symmetry. Neither was it an object of superstitious or sentimental reverence. In fact, at the present time there were not more than twelve or fifteen of the family laid away in it. It had been built four centuries ago, and with accommodation for a hundred or so; but at the time of the rebellion a party of Cromwell's troops came sweeping down upon the house, and, being in want of material for bullets, turned all the dead Grantleys out of doors and took their leaden coffins to cast into ammunition. After that time the burials continued for only a few generations; since which, the yard around the village church had received the family dead. About ten years ago it had been found necessary to open the vault in order to get the date of some particular death for legal evidence. The long-closed door had stoutly resisted, and at length the lock was obliged to be broken. It was intended, of course, to restore the fastenings; but equally of course, and as happens so often with matters that can be done any day, the duty was postponed from time to time, and gradually came to be no longer remembered. The closed door then warped open a little of itself, and the gardeners leaned their tools against it, and after awhile pushed the door further back, and slipped their tools just inside out of the rain; and so, step by step, the almost empty vault became only used as a toolhouse.

Vines were trained to grow over it, ferns gathered around its base, and a stranger would have taken it for a somewhat dilapidated icehouse.

I pushed the door open yet a little further and peeped within. The sunbeams, still low and shut out by the screen of trees, could not now enter; but enough light stole in to show a pile of rakes and hoes just inside, and a little further along, a row of empty recesses, built for coffins, but long since made vacant. Entering, I could see that the recesses ran in double rows for some distance in front of me, being at the further end shrouded in darkness. I drew out my cigar lighter and by the aid of repeated tapers proceeded to explore. Then I could see that at the further end, a few of the recesses were filled with coffins. These were in various stages of decay. In all cases, the dark coverings of cloth had moldered away and lay in fragments at the side or on the stone floor below. In some, the outer wooden shells were nearly whole; but in others, they had crumbled into dust and splinters. With a few of the recesses, the names and dates of the remains within were fastened at the lower edge upon brass plates; with others, the plates had entirely disappeared. There was one recess which contained a worm-eaten coffin of somewhat plain construction, but no name or date or even evidence that any such had ever been affixed. I could not resist the impression that here lay the unfortunate Harold Grantley; given, as matter of right, a place in this ancestral vault, but, through some charitable idea of letting his unhappy fate become forgotten, denied all record that could lead to future identification. Passing onward, with gathering assurance that my search would not prove unavailing, at each minute renewing my quickly expiring tapers, I carefully read every name, now and then rubbing the brass plates with my handkerchief before I could decipher the blurred old-fashioned letterings. Then, for a while, as the number of remaining niches one by one was lessened without rewarding my search, hope began to give way to disappointment. Only for a moment, however; for soon, to my abundant gratification, I read upon one of the plates, the words and characters, "Arthur Grantley, Obt. Dec. 25, 1663, Aet 22."

Here then, lay he whom I sought, and I scrutinized attentively all that remained. A moth-eaten, rat-torn pall, a nest of coffins, and that was all. Uneasily for the instant I turned my head, dreading lest the blithe young apparition with its purple and laced coat and dangling sword should arise and demand wherefore I was about to disturb him; hut all remained quiet about me. I was alone with my own thoughts and purposes, and could prosecute my designs unquestioned and unimpeded.

I had feared lest I might be obliged to seek for assistance, but it was not so. Every thing, in fact, seemed made ready and convenient for me. The outer box was worm-eaten, warped and decayed, so that it could be broken and brushed away in places with a mere stroke of the hand; the leaden coffin inside had corroded, and the solder of the seams parted, so that the joints had spread apart, and, with no great effort, I was able to bend open the end; the mahogany coffin inside of all had suffered similar decay with the outer box, and readily parted. In a moment the outer end of all three coffins lay open, and I could easily insert my hand.

For a moment I hesitated. What if, as sometimes happens, the remains had not suffered corruption, and my touch were to encounter a solid form! Repressing this fear, I passed my hand stealthily within, finding no obstruction. Only a little dust at the bottom, hardly deep enough for a finger to write a name upon. This was all that was left of the gay young courtier, twelfth baronet of Grantley. Slowly I let my hand wander up along the bottom of the coffin, groping among the dust, until two-thirds up to the top; then I struck against a small, hard lump. My heart gave a loud thump of excitement. What could it be? Was it the prize that I had hoped for, or was it merely some fragment of unpulverized bone? Half wild with tremulous expectation, I grasped the little lump of substance firmly between thumb and forefinger, and hurried with it to the door of the vault. Even as I approached the dim, lurid light just within the half-opened entrance, I began to feel my assurances grow more sure; and when I emerged into the bright glow of day beyond, and held my prize up against the golden rays of the risen sun, I could no longer doubt that I had gained possession of the long lost Lancaster diamond.

CHAPTER VI

When I returned to the house, I said nothing about what I had been doing. It seemed as though the time for explanation would not come until toward evening. How, in that broad garish light of morning, could I venture to reveal that secret of dreams and darkness and rifled tombs? How, indeed, would my story be believed, unless with the glow of nightfall thrown around it to attune the listeners to credence?

Moreover, what if, during the day, the ghost were to appear, condemn my invasion of his sepulcher, demand his diamond, and possibly, by threats of supernatural force and terrors, obtain it? Certainly the accustomed hour for the ghosts was close at hand, and at any moment they might visit us. Already Sir Ruthven sat in the library awaiting his especial apparition. My uncle was, for the time, in no particularly friendly mood toward ghosts; and he now loudly declared that, whatever might before have been his courtesy, his forbearance had at last ceased, and he would not tolerate their coming. Certainly not now, he said, seeing that the house was preparing for a season of festivity, and had other things than the next world to think about. Accordingly he sat, watching, in his great elbow chair, with the heaviest volume of the Encyclopaedia Brittanica at his side, in readiness to crush out the first sign of ghost before even a word of salutation could be uttered.

But to the wonder of all and greatly to Sir Ruthven's disgust as well—seeing that, having made up his mind for action, he did not like to feel that his time had been thrown away—no ghost appeared, upstairs or down. Punctually at twelve, indeed, the chimes rang out the merriest peal we had enjoyed for years—the changes were sounded by the hundred with unusual exactness and celerity; yet all the time my uncle sat unmolested, with his Encyclopaedia lying idle beside him.

At length the day wore itself out, the bell sounded for dinner, and we repaired to the dining room.

It was to be our last little dinner by ourselves; a very small Christmas party, indeed, but on the morrow the guests would begin to arrive and to break up our privacy, and then there could be no complaint about lack of excitement in the household. This last day Sir Ruthven had desired we should have for ourselves. But few as we were, no one had forgotten that it was the Christmas season and should be honored accordingly. Holly and mistletoe decked the room in every direction. A great yule log lay cosily esconced in the chimney-back and good humoredly tried to blaze up as merrily as the smaller branches that crackled around it; though being so unwieldy, it was not very successful in the attempt. But those smaller branches, invading the yule log's smoldering dignity with their blithe sport of gaiety, snapped and sputtered around it with uproarious mirthfulness; sending none but the prettiest colored smoke wreaths up the chimney, and casting out bright tongues of flames that lighted up every corner of the room and gave a ruddy glow to the time-faded portraits, and even brought out patches of cheerful sunlight upon an old cracked Rembrandt that no one had ever been able to decipher.

The table was set for us three only; but, in honor of the day, with as much ceremony as though there were to be twenty present. A tall branch wax-light, used only on occasions of great festivity, was brought out from its green baize covering and planted in the center. Treasures of antique silver, the very existence of which Sir Ruthven had nearly forgotten, were exhumed from their places of long concealment, and now once more, as in past centuries, pleasantly glimmered in the gentle gleam of wax-light. Flowers here and there unobtrusively exhaled sweet odors from tiny vases. There was to be a boar's head brought out and placed on the table at the proper time for each of us to look at and taste and pretend to enjoy. The plum-pudding was turning out a great success—the greatest for many years, as Bidgers whispered to me. All the circumstances of the scene around us were soft, harmonious and cheerful; certainly now was the time for me to tell my story.

With some little affectation of ceremony, perhaps, I drew forth the Lancaster diamond and placed it in Lilian's hand. I told her that I could make her no more valuable Christmas gift than to restore this rich family relic of the past. Lightly I touched upon the process whereby I had found it; rather elaborating, instead, the train of thought that had led me to suspect where it had lain hidden. I explained how the finding of the diamond gave new illustration to the record in the State Trials, proving that the younger brother had not been guilty of any murder at all —that during the agitation of a quarrel the older brother must have accidentally swallowed the diamond, mistaking it for one of the filberts that lay beside it near his plate, and which were of similar size—how that this unfortunate error had been sufficient of itself to cause his death by suffocation—how that thereby the discoloration around the neck of the deceased, as Well as the disappearance of the diamond were properly accounted for—how that, most probably, it also gave an explanation of the unpleasant lump in the chest of the crimson-coated ghost.

"It is doubtless so," a soft voice thereat interrupted. We all looked up; and, at the further side of the table, we beheld both the ghosts. More alike now than ever before, it seemed to me; only with that single difference of color of the coats. The same bright engaging faces, the same gentle manner; as now, all heart burnings seemingly healed, they stood with their arms bound lovingly about each other in fraternal embrace.

126

"We have heard it all," continued the crimson ghost, "and thereby we find an explanation of some things that we never thought of before. Both Brother Arthur and myself now know that we are dead; and that it is fitting, therefore, that we should no longer haunt these scenes, to which indeed, we have no claim. I know that I have been hanged; a matter, however, which occasions me no concern, seeing that I deserved it not. I should at any rate have been dead long before this; and since my family can be satisfied of my innocence and I know that my Brother Arthur, in spite of a few harsh words, loves me still the same, I care not for others' opinions."

"And I," said the purple ghost, "cannot sufficiently thank you for the relief you have given me. Nightly have I lain in what I now perceive was my grave, unable to sleep by reason of the strange lump in my chest. This morning about eight, there came sudden relief; such sweet relief, indeed, that I overslept myself, and for the first time in many years have missed the chimes, and neglected at the appointed hour to make my usual Christmas visit. Even this bodily relief, perhaps, is not equal to what I feel at knowing that in reality I have suffered no wrong at the hands of Brother Harold. I think that if now we could only agree about the only subject which has ever estranged us—by which I refer to our mutual attachment to Cousin Beatrice we might—"

"I think I can easily make your mind easy about that matter," remarked Uncle Ruthven, coming forward. "If you will bear with me a minute, I will show you the lifelike picture of your Cousin Beatrice in after days."

He lifted one of the branch candlesticks from the table, and directed its light upon a painting on the wall. The portrait of Cousin Beatrice in more advanced life. A cracked, blackened and moth-eaten picture; but in which, by singular chance, the face had remained intact. The face of a woman who had long survived the natural freshness and graces of youth, and had gained in place of them none of those more matured and ennobling qualities that dignify age. The patched and painted and powdered face of a woman given up to all lightness and frivolity; a face in which there was nothing sweet or pleasant or kindly; in which all the art of Sir Godfrey Kneller had not succeeded in mingling with accurate likeness one spark of generous nature or blotting out the appearance of sordid vanity that pervaded it throughout all.

"The portrait of your Cousin Beatrice in her fiftieth year," remarked my Uncle Ruthven. "She never married, and was noted at Court for her skill in cheating at cards."

The two young ghosts gazed for a moment intently at the picture. As they did so, it seemed as though their embrace grew more intimate and fraternal. At last they turned again, as satisfied.

"I do not think that we shall ever quarrel again about Cousin Beatrice, even if at times we forget that we are all dead," the older ghost then said, with a sweet smile. "And now that all differences are so pleasantly made up, it remains for us only to bid you farewell. And since Brother Harold can now rest in his grave untroubled by any idea of wrong from me, and I can sleep, no longer annoyed by the lump that pained my chest, it is probable that we shall never be aroused to visits you again."

"But stay a moment," cried Uncle Ruthven, fairly touched at heart, and no longer remembering the Encyclopaedia. "You will not go so soon? At least you will take dinner with us?" As he spoke the ghosts had already begun to vanish, the line of invisibility starting at the feet, as before, and working upward until they were half gone. Then, for a moment, the line trembled irresolutely, and so began to descend until again they stood entirely revealed. It was as though a person going out at a door had indeterminately held the handle for an instant and then returned.

"Moreover," continued my uncle, "I have apologies to make for many a past act of rudeness toward one of you."

"It is forgotten already," said the crimson ghost, bowing.

"What do you say Brother Arthur, can we wait a little longer?"

"A very few minutes, Brother Harold, if only to give myself time to make amends for an act of impoliteness on my part toward this other gentleman only last year."

So they seated themselves at the table and the dinner began. It was pleasant to watch the old-fashioned politeness with which they conducted themselves—the courtesy with which they bowed to Lilian at each word they addressed to her—the grace with which, wishing to cause no remark, they affected to eat and drink. Not able to do so, indeed, by reason of their incorporeal nature, but all the time lifting the full glasses and laden forks to their mouths and dropping them again untouched. It was delightful to listen to their conversation, marked here and there indeed, after the fashion of their time, with a light oath, but bright and sparkling throughout all, with vivacity and wit. At first, indeed; the time was somewhat occupied by Uncle Ruthven giving sketches of the late history of the family; but after that the ghosts were encouraged to talk, and pleasantly beguiled half an hour with hitherto unknown anecdotes of the Court of the Merry Monarch. As I listened my thoughts naturally strayed from the present back to the romantic past, and my imagination carried me, unresisting, into the olden days of the Stuarts. I was no longer in the prosaic nineteenth century, I was in the midst of a laughing, careless throng of king and courtiers, all busily making up for their enforced deprivations during the somber period of the Commonwealth. Hamilton and Nelly Gwynn, De Grammont and Villiers and Frances Stewart, these and others of those long dead disreputables, whose actions may not have been comely but whose names live vividly in story, and to whose memories some glamor of romance still kindly attaches us, now crowded around and made the past a reality and the present a mere unstable myth. In the hallucination of the moment even the portrait of the poor old card-cheating Beatrice Grantley seemed to invest itself with something of her long-departed youthfulness; and as the mingled gleam of wax-lights and yule log flickered upon it, it was as though some hitherto unnoted beauties of expression came to the surface, and the whole countenance became once more aglow with that youthful loveliness which, doubtless, in the time of it, and during her occasional visits to the Court, must have enticed Charles himself awhile from his more stable attachments in order to enjoy passing flirtation with her.

"A joyous Court, indeed; and sadly now coming to my memory as I feel that I can never mingle with it more," said the purple ghost. "A Court to which I know that my fair young kinswoman would have done ample honor, could she have been there," he added, bowing to Lilian; "even more abundantly, indeed, than Cousin Beatrice. Growing old with more grace and dignity than did Beatrice, I am very sure. And that she may live to grow old in such gentle manner, let her take heed and not make my sad mistake."

128

As he spoke, he pointed significantly to the Lancaster diamond which chanced at that moment to be beside her plate, and, by a singular coincidence, among a little pile of filberts.

"Yet I am sure," he added, still with the courtly manner of his period, "that such sweet lips could never make mistake about anything. Rather should the diamond, with its appropriate mate, be reserved to grace those beauteous ears."

"Its mate, do you say?" I remarked; not sure, for the moment, but that the young ghost had swallowed two diamonds, and that I had not carried my researches far enough.

"Yes, its mate," he said. "Surely you must know? Not so, indeed? Well, there were two of these great diamonds, the Lancaster and the York. They had come into possession of one family through union of adherents of those two rival parties, and thence into our own line, through subsequent alliance of that family with the Grantleys. In Cromwell's time, the diamonds were hidden in separate places to preserve them from confiscation, the knowledge of those places being handed down only by word of mouth, for greater security. At the Restoration, I alone knew the secret. At the time of my death I had already brought the Lancaster diamond to light, as you are well aware. The York still remains hidden. Permit us now, my brother and myself, to offer it to you as our joint Christmas present. You will find it in a little metal box close beside—"

At that very moment it chanced that a small bantam rooster outside the window set up a crow.

It was a miserable little banty, scarcely half fledged. It had a drooping wing, and a twisted toe; and for these defects and others, perhaps, which we had not noticed, was constantly driven away from the general society of the poultry-yard. Even the hens were accustomed to pick at it. Its crow was weak, and piping, like a school-boy's first attempt at whistling. Nor was this the hour of midnight or early dawn, but merely seven in the evening. There seemed no reason why any ghost with self-respect should be moved by such a feeble crow from such a despicable source, and at such an early hour. And yet there may be a certain, inflexible rule for well-constituted ghosts; and perhaps, in cock-crowing, the line cannot easily be drawn between different styles.

Be that as it may, at the very first pretense of sound from the little banty, the ghost stopped speaking, gazed inquiringly at his brother and received an answering nod; and then without another word they slowly faded away.

"Ghosts are so ridiculous!" said Lilian. But I thought that as she gazed at the Lancaster diamond and reflected how well the two Christmas gifts would have looked if worn together, she seemed sadly disappointed that the little banty had not put off his crowing for a minute longer.

THE SPECTRE COOK OF BANGLETOP,
by John Kendrick Bangs

For the purposes of this bit of history, Bangletop Hall stands upon a grassy knoll on the left bank of the River Dee, about eighteen miles from the quaint old city of Chester. It does not in reality stand there, nor has it ever done so, but consideration for the interests of the living compels me to conceal its exact location, and so to befog the public as to its whereabouts that its identity may never be revealed to its disadvantage. It is a rentable property, and were it known that it has had a mystery connected with it of so deep, dark, and eerie a nature as that about to be related, I fear that its usefulness, save as an accessory to romance, would be seriously impaired, and that as an investment it would become practically worthless.

The hall is a fair specimen of the architecture which prevailed at the time of Edward the Confessor; that is to say, the main portion of the structure, erected in Edward's time by the first Baron Bangletop, has that square, substantial, stony aspect which to the eye versed in architecture identifies it at once as a product of that enlightened era. Later owners, the successive Barons Bangletop, have added to its original dimensions, putting Queen Anne wings here, Elizabethan ells there, and an Italian-Renaissance façade on the river front. A Wisconsin water tower, connected with the main building by a low Gothic alleyway, stands to the south; while toward the east is a Greek chapel, used by the present occupant as a store-room for his wife's trunks, she having lately returned from Paris with a wardrobe calculated to last through the first half of the coming London season. Altogether Bangletop Hall is an impressive structure, and at first sight gives rise to various emotions in the aesthetic breast; some cavil, others admire. One leading architect of Berlin travelled all the way from his German home to Bangletop Hall to show that famous structure to his son, a student in the profession which his father adorned; to whom he is said to have observed that, architecturally, Bangletop Hall was "cosmopolitan and omniperiodic, and therefore a liberal education to all who should come to study and master its details." In short, Bangletop Hall was an object-lesson to young architects, and showed them at a glance that which they should ever strive to avoid.

Strange to say, for quite two centuries had Bangletop Hall remained without a tenant, and for nearly seventy-five years it had been in the market for rent, the barons, father and son, for many generations having found it impossible to dwell within its walls, and for a very good reason: no cook could ever be induced to live at Bangletop for a longer period than two weeks. Why the queens of the kitchen invariably took what is commonly known as French leave no occupant could ever learn, because, male or female, the departed domestics never returned to tell, and even had they done so, the pride of the Bangletops would not have permitted them to listen to the explanation. The Bangletop escutcheon was clear of blots, no suspicion even of a conversational blemish appearing thereon, and it was always a matter of extreme satisfaction to the family that no one of its scions since the title was created had ever been known to speak directly to any one of lesser rank than himself, communication with inferiors being always had through the medium of a private secretary, himself a baron, or better, in reduced circumstances.

The first cook to leave Bangletop under circumstances of a Gallic nature—that is, without known cause, wages, or luggage—had been employed by Fitzherbert Alexander, seventeenth Baron of Bangletop, through Charles Mortimor de Herbert, Baron Peddlington, formerly of Peddlington Manor at Dunwoodie-on-the-Hike, his private secretary, a handsome old gentleman of sixty-five, who had been deprived of his estates by the crown in 1629 because he was suspected of having inspired a comic broadside published in those troublous days, and directed against Charles the First, which had set all London in a roar.

This broadside, one of very few which are not preserved in the British Museum—and a greater tribute to its rarity could not be devised—was called, "A Good Suggestion as to ye Proper Use of ye Chinne Whisker," and consisted of a few lines of doggerel printed beneath a caricature of the king, with the crown hanging from his goatee, reading as follows:

> "Ye King doth sporte a gallous grey goatee
> Uponne ye chinne, where evey one may see.
> And since ye Monarch's head's too small to holde
> With comfort to himselfe ye crowne of gold,
> Why not enwax and hooke ye goatee rare,
> And lette ye British crown hang down from there?"

Whether or no the Baron of Peddlington was guilty of this traitorous effusion no one, not even the king, could ever really make up his mind. The charge was never fully proven, nor was De Herbert ever able to refute it successfully, although he made frantic efforts to do so. The king, eminently just in such matters, gave the baron the benefit of the doubt, and inflicted only half the penalty prescribed, confiscating his estates, and letting him keep his head and liberty. De Herbert's family begged the crown to reverse the sentence, permitting them to keep the estates, the king taking their uncle's head in lieu thereof, he being unmarried and having no children who would mourn his loss. But Charles was poor rather than vindictive at this period, and preferring to adopt the other course, turned a deaf ear to the petitioners. This was probably one of the earliest factors in the decadence of literature as a pastime for men of high station.

De Herbert would have starved had it not been for his old friend Baron Bangletop, who offered him the post of private secretary, lately made vacant by the death of the Duke of Algeria, who had been the incumbent of that office for ten years, and in a short time the Baron of Peddlington was in full charge of the domestic arrangements of his friend. It was far from easy, the work that devolved upon him. He was a proud, haughty man, used to luxury of every sort, to whom contact with those who serve was truly distasteful; to whom the necessity of himself serving was most galling; but he had the manliness to face the hardships Fate had put upon him, particularly when he realized that Baron Bangle-top's attitude towards servants was such that he could with impunity impose on the latter seven indignities for every one that was imposed on him. Misery loves company, particularly when she is herself the hostess, and can give generously of her stores to others.

Desiring to retrieve his fallen fortunes, the Baron of Peddlington offered large salaries to all those whom he employed to serve in the Bangletop menage, and on payday, through an ingenious system of fines, managed to retain almost seventy-five per cent of the funds for his own use. Of this Baron Bangletop, of course, could know nothing. He was aware that under De Herbert the running expenses of his house-hold were nearly twice what they had been under the dusky Duke of Algeria; but he also observed that repairs to the property, for which the late duke had annually paid out several thousands of pounds sterling, with very little to show for it, now cost him as many hundreds with no fewer tangible results. So he winked his eye—the only unaristocratic habit he had, by-the-way—and said nothing. The revenue was large enough, he had been known to say, to support himself and all his relatives in state, with enough left over to satisfy even Ali Baba and the forty thieves.

Had he foreseen the results of his complacency in financial matters, I doubt if he would have persisted therein.

For some ten years under De Herbert's management everything went smoothly and expensively for the Bangletop Hall people, and then there came a change. The Baron Bangletop rang for his breakfast one morning, and his breakfast was not. The cook had disappeared.

Whither or why she had gone, the private secretary professed to be unable to say. That she could easily be replaced, he was certain. Equally certain was it that Baron Bangletop stormed and raved for two hours, ate a cold breakfast—a thing he never had been known to do before—and then departed for London to dine at the club until Peddlington had secured a successor to the departed cook, which the private secretary succeeded in doing within three days. The baron was informed of his manager's success, and at the end of a week returned to Bangletop Hall, arriving there late on a Saturday night, hungry as a bear, and not too amiable, the king having negotiated a forcible loan with him during his sojourn in the metropolis.

"Welcome to Bangletop, Baron," said De Herbert, uneasily, as his employer alighted from his coach.

"Blast your welcome, and serve the dinner," returned the baron, with a somewhat ill grace.

At this the private secretary seemed much embarrassed. "Ahem!" he said. "I'll be very glad to have the dinner served, my dear Baron; but the fact is I—er—I have been unable to provide anything but canned lobster and apples."

"What, in the name of Chaucer, does this mean?" roared Bangletop, who was a great admirer of the father of English poetry; chiefly because, as he was wont to say, Chaucer showed that a bad speller could be a great man, which was a condition of affairs exactly suited to his mind, since in the science of orthography he was weak, like most of the aristocrats of his day. "I thought you sent me word you had a cook?"

"Yes, Baron, I did; but the fact of the matter is, sir, she left us last night, or, rather, early this morning."

"Another one of your beautiful Parisian exits, I presume?" sneered the baron, tapping the floor angrily with his toe.

"Well, yes, somewhat so; only she got her money first."

"Money!" shrieked the baron. "Money! Why in Liverpool did she get her money? What did we owe her money for? Rent?"

"No, Baron; for services. She cooked three dinners."

"Well, you'll pay the bill out of your perquisites, that's all. She's done no cooking for me, and she gets no pay from me. Why do you think she left?"

"She said—"

"Never mind what she said, sir," cried Bangletop cutting De Herbert short. "When I am interested in the table-talk of cooks, I'll let you know. What I wish to hear is what do you think was the cause of her leaving?"

"I have no opinion on the subject," replied the private secretary, with becoming dignity. "I only know that at four o'clock this morning she knocked at my door, and demanded her wages for four days, and vowed she'd stay no longer in the house."

"And why, pray, did you not inform me of the fact, instead of having me travel away down here from London?" queried Bangletop.

"You forget, Baron," replied De Herbert, with a deprecatory gesture—"you forget that there is no system of telegraphy by which you could be reached. I may be poor, sir, but I'm just as much of a baron as you are, and I will take the liberty of saying right here, in what would be the shadow of your beard, if you had one, sir, that a man who insists on receiving cable messages when no such things exist is rather rushing business."

"Pardon my haste, Peddlington, old chap," returned the baron, softening. "You are quite right. My desire was unreasonable; but I swear to you, by all my ancestral Bangletops, that I am hungry as a pit full of bears, and if there's one thing I can't eat, it is lobster and apples. Can't you scare up a snack of bread and cheese and a little cold larded fillet? If you'll supply the fillet, I'll provide the cold."

At this sally the Baron of Peddlington laughed and the quarrel was over. But none the less the master of Bangletop went to bed hungry; nor could he do any better in the morning at breakfast-time.

The butler had not been trained to cook, and the coachman's art had once been tried on a boiled egg, which no one had been able to open, much less eat, and as it was the parlor-maid's Sunday off, there was absolutely no one in the house who could prepare a meal. The Baron of Bangletop had a sort of sneaking notion that if there were nobody around he could have managed the spit or grid-iron himself; but, of course, in view of his position, he could not make the attempt.

And so he once more returned to London, and vowed never to set his foot within the walls of Bangletop hall again until his ancestral home was provided with a cook "copper-fastened and riveted to her position."

And Bangletop Hall from that time was as a place deserted. The baron never returned, because he could not return without violating his oath; for De Herbert was not able to obtain a cook for the Bangletop cuisine who would stay, nor was any one able to discover why. Cook after cook came, stayed a day, a week, and one or two held on for two weeks, but never longer. Their course was invariably the same—they would leave without notice; nor could any inducement be offered which would persuade them to remain. The Baron of Peddlington became, first round-shouldered, then deaf, an then insane in his search for a permanent cook, landing finally in an asylum, where he died, four years after the demise of his employer in London, of softening of the brain. His last words were, "Why did you leave your last place?"

And so time went on. Barons of Bangle-top were born, educated, and died. Dynasties rose and fell, but Bangletop Hall remained uninhabited, although it was not until 1799 that the family gave up all hopes of being able to use their ancestral home. Tremendous alterations, as I have already hinted, were made. The drainage was carefully inspected, and a special apartment connected with the kitchen, finished in hardwood, handsomely decorated, and hung with rich tapestries, was provided for the cook, in the vain hope that she might be induced permanently to occupy her position. The Queen Anne wing and Elizabethan ell were constructed, the latter to provide bowling-alleys and smoking-rooms for the probable cousins of possible culinary queens, and many there were who accepted the office with alacrity, throwing it up with still greater alacrity before the usual fortnight passed. Then the Bangletops saw clearly that it was impossible for them to live there, and moving away, the house was announced to be "for rent, with all modern improvements, conveniently located, spacious grounds, especially adapted to the use of those who do their own cooking." The last clause of the announcement puzzled a great many people, who went to see the mansion for no other reason than to ascertain just what the an-nouncement meant, and the line, which was inserted in a pure spirit of facetious bravado, was probably the cause of the mansion's quickly renting, as hardly a month had passed before it was leased for one year by a retired London brewer, whose wife's curiosity had been so excited by the strange wording of the advertisement that she travelled out to Bangletop to gratify it, fell in love with the place, and insisted upon her husband's taking it for a season. The luck of the brewer and his wife was no better than that of the Bangletops. Their cooks—and they had fourteen during their stay there—fled after an average service of four days apiece, and later the tenants themselves were forced to give up and return to London, where they told their friends that the "'all was 'aunted," which might have filled the Bangletops with concern had they heard of it. They did not hear of it, however, for they and their friends did not know the brewer and the brewers friends, and as for complaining to the Bangletop agent in the matter, the worthy beer-maker thought he would better not do that, because he had hopes of being knighted some day, and he did not wish to antagonize so illustrious a family as the Bangletops by running down their famous hall—an antagonism which might materially affect the chances of himself and his good wife when they came to knock at the doors of London society. The lease was allowed to run its course, the rent was paid when due, and at the end of the stipulated term Bangletop Hall was once more on the lists as for rent.

II

For fourscore years and ten did the same hard fortune pursue the owners of Bangletop. Additions to the property were made immediately upon request of possible lessees. The Greek chapel was constructed in 1868 at the mere suggestion of a Hellenic prince, who came to England to write a history of the American rebellion, finding the information in back files of British newspapers exactly suited to the purposes of picturesque narrative, and no more misleading than most home-made history. Bangletop was retired, "far from the gadding crowd," as the prince put it, and therefore just the place in which a historian of the romantic school might produce his magnum opus without disturbance; the only objection being that there was no place whither the eminently Christian sojourner could go to worship according to his faith, he being a communicant in the Greek Church. This defect Baron Bangletop immediately remedied by erecting and endowing the chapel; and his youngest son, having been found too delicate morally for the army, was appointed to the living and placed in charge of the chapel, having first embraced with considerable ardor the faith upon which the soul of the princely tenant was wont to feed. All of these improvements—chapel, priest, the latter's change of faith, and all—the Bangletop agent put at the exceedingly low sum of forty-two guineas per annum and board for the priest; an offer which the prince at once accepted, stipulating, however, that the lease should be terminable at any time he or his landlord should see fit. Against this the agent fought nobly, but without avail. The prince had heard rumors about the cooks of Bangletop, and he was wary. Finally the stipulation was accepted by the baron, with what result the reader need hardly be told. The prince stayed two weeks, listened to one sermon in classic university Greek by the youthful Bangletop, was deserted by his cook, and moved away.

After the departure of the prince the estate was neglected for nearly twenty-two years, the owner having made up his mind that the case was hopeless. At the end of that period there came from the United States a wealthy shoemaker, Hankinson J. Terwilliger by name, chief owner of the Terwilliger Three-dollar Shoe Company (Limited), of Soleton, Massachusetts, and to him was leased Bangletop Hall, with all its rights and appurtenances, for a term of five years. Mr.

Terwilliger was the first applicant for the hall as a dwelling to whom the agent, at the instance of the baron, spoke in a spirit of absolute candor. The baron was well on in years, and he did not feel like getting into trouble with a Yankee, so he said, at his time of life. The hall had been a thorn in his flesh all his days, and he didn't care if it was never occupied, and therefore he wished nothing concealed from a prospective tenant. It was the agent's candor more than anything else that induced Mr. Terwilliger to close with him for the term of five years. He suspected that the Bangletops did not want him for a tenant, and from the moment that notion entered his head, he was resolved that he would be a tenant.

"I'm as good a man as any baron that ever lived," he said; "and if it pleases Hankinson J. Terwilliger to live in a baronial hail, a baronial hall is where Hankinson J. Terwilliger puts up."

"We certainly have none of the feeling which your words seem to attribute to us, my dear sir," the agent had answered. "Baron Bangletop would feel highly honored to have so distinguished a sojourner in England as yourself occupy his estate, but he does not wish you to take it without fully understanding the circumstances. Desirable as Bangletop Hall is, it seems fated to be unoccupied because it is thought to he haunted, or something of that sort, the effect of which is to drive away cooks, and without cooks life is hardly an ideal."

Mr. Terwilliger laughed. "Ghosts and me are not afraid of each other," he said. "'Let 'em haunt,' I say; and as for cooks, Mrs. H. J. T. hasn't had a liberal education for nothing. We could live if all the cooks in creation were to go off in a whiff. We have daughters too, we have. Good smart American girls, who can adorn a palace or grace a hut on demand, not afraid of poverty, and able to take care of good round dollars. They can play the piano all the morning and cook dinner all the afternoon if they're called on to do it; so your difficulties ain't my difficulties. I'll take the hall at your figures; term, five years; and if the baron'll come down and spend a month with us at any time, I don't care when, we'll show him what a big lap Luxury can get up when she tries."

And so it happened. The New York papers announced that Hankinson J. Terwilliger, Mrs.

Terwilliger, the Misses Terwilliger, and Master Hankinson J. Terwilliger, Jun., of Soleton, Massachusetts, had plunged into the dizzy whirl of English society, and that the sole of the three-dollar shoe now trod the baronial halls of the Bangletops. Later it was announced that the Misses Terwilliger, of Bangletop Hall, had been presented to the queen; that the Terwilligers had entertained the Prince of Wales at Bangletop; in fact, the Terwilligers became an important factor in the letters of all foreign correspondents of American papers, for the president of the Terwilliger Three-dollar Shoe Company, of Soleton, Massachusetts (Limited), was now in full possession of the historic mansion, and was living up to his surroundings.

For a time everything was plain sailing for the Americans at Bangle top. The dire forebodings of the agent did not seem to be fulfilled, and Mr. Terwilliger was beginning to feel aggrieved. He had hired a house with a ghost, and he wanted the use of it; but when he reflected upon the consequences below stairs, he held his peace. He was not so sure, after he had stayed at Bangletop awhile, and had had his daughters presented to the queen, that he could be so independent of cooks as he had at first supposed. Several times he had hinted rather broadly that some of the old New England homemade flap-jacks would be most pleasing to his palate; but since the prince had spent an afternoon on the lawn of Bangletop, the young ladies seemed deeply pained at the mere mention of their accomplishments in the line of griddles and batter; nor could Mrs. Terwilliger, after having tasted the joys of aristocratic life, bring herself to don the apron which so became her portly person in the early American days, and prepare for her lord and master one of those delicious platters of poached eggs and breakfast bacon, the mere memory of which made his mouth water. In short, palatial surroundings had too obviously destroyed in his wife and daughters all that capacity for happiness in a hovel of which Mr.

Terwilliger had been so proud, and concerning which he had so eloquently spoken to Baron Bangletop's agent, and he now found himself in the position of Damocles. The hall was leased for a term, entertainment had been provided for the county with lavish hand; but success was dependent entirely upon his ability to keep a cook, his family having departed from their republican principles, and the history of the house was dead against a successful issue. So he decided that, after all, it was better that the ghost should he allowed to remain quiescent, and he uttered no word of complaint.

It was just as well, too, that Mr. Terwilliger held his peace, and refrained from addressing a complaining missive to the agent of Bangletop Hall; for before a message of that nature could have reached the person addressed, its contents would have been misleading, for at a quarter after midnight on the morning of the date set for the first of a series of grand banquets to the county folk, there came from the kitchen of Bangletop Hall a quick succession of shrieks that sent the three Misses Terwilliger into hysterics, and caused Hankinson J. Terwilliger's sole remaining lock to stand erect. Mrs. Terwilliger did not hear the shrieks, owing to a lately acquired habit of hearing nothing that proceeded from below stairs.

The first impulse of Terwilliger père was to dive down under the bedclothes, and endeavor to drown the fearful sound by his own labored breathing, but he never yielded to first impulses. So he awaited the second, which came simultaneously with a second series of shrieks and a cry for help in the unmistakable voice of the cook; a lady, by-the-way, who had followed the Terwilliger fortunes ever since the Terwilligers began to have fortunes, and whose first capacity in the family had been the dual one of mistress of the kitchen and confidante of madame. The second impulse was to arise in his might, put on a stout pair of the Terwilliger three-dollar brogans—the strongest shoe made, having been especially devised for the British Infantry in the Soudan—and garments suitable to the occasion, namely, a mackintosh and pair of broadcloth trousers, and go to the rescue of the distressed domestic. This Hankinson J. Terwilliger at once proceeded to do, arming himself with a pair of horse-pistols, murmuring on the way below a soft prayer, the only one he knew, and which, with singular inappropriateness on this occasion, began with the words, "Now I lay me down to sleep."

"What's the matter, Judson?" queried Mrs. Terwilliger, drowsily, as she opened her eyes and saw her husband preparing for the fray.

She no longer called him Hankinson, not because she did not think it a good name, nor was it less euphonious to her ear than Judson, but Judson was Mr. Terwilliger's middle name, and middle names were quite the thing, she had observed, in the best circles. It was doubtless due to this discovery that her visiting cards had been engraved to read "Mrs. H. Judson-Terwilliger."

the hyphen presumably being a typographical error, for which the engraver was responsible.

"Matter enough," growled Hankinson. "I have reason to believe that that jackass of a ghost is on duty tonight."

At the word ghost a pseudo-aristocratic shriek pervaded the atmosphere, and Mrs. Terwilliger, forgetting her social position for a moment, groaned "Oh, Hank!" and swooned away. And then the president of the Terwilliger Three-dollar Shoe Company of Soleton, Massachusetts (Limited), descended to the kitchen.

Across the sill of the kitchen door lay the culinary treasure whose lobster croquettes the Prince of Wales had likened unto a dream of Lucullus. Within the kitchen were signs of disorder. Chairs were upset the table was lying flat on its back, with its four legs held rigidly up in the air; the kitchen library, consisting of a copy of Marie Antoinette's Dream-Book; a yellow-covered novel bearing the title Little Lucy: or, The Kitchen-maid who Became a Marchioness; and Sixty Soups, by One who Knows, lay strewn about the room, the Dream-Book sadly torn, and Little Lucy disfigured forever with batter. Even to the unpractised eye it was evident that something had happened, and Mr. Terwilliger felt a cold chill mounting his spine three sections at a time.

Whether it was the chill or his concern for the prostrate cook that was responsible or not I cannot say, but for some cause or other Mr. Terwilliger immediately got down on his knees, in which position he gazed fearfully about him for a few minutes, and then timidly remarked, "Cook!"

There was no answer.

"Mary, I say. Cook," he whispered, "what the deuce is the meaning of all this?"

A low moan was all that came from the cook, nor would Hankinson have listened to more had there been more to hear, for simultaneously with the moan he became uncomfortably conscious of a presence. In trying to describe it afterwards, Hankinson said that at first he thought a cold draught from a dank cavern filled with a million eels, and a rattlesnake or two thrown in for luck, was blowing over him, and he avowed that it was anything but pleasant; and then it seemed to change into a mist drawn largely from a stagnant pool in a malarial country, floating through which were great quantities of finely chopped seaweed, wet hair, and an indescribable atmosphere of something the chief quality of which was a sort of stale clamminess that was awful in its intensity.

"I'm glad," Mr. Terwilliger murmured to himself, "that I ain't one of those delicately reared nobles. If I had anything less than a right-down regular republican constitution I'd die of fright."

And then his natural grit came to his rescue, and it was well it did, for the presence had assumed shape, and now sat on the window-ledge in the form of a hag, glaring at him from out of the depths of her unfathomable eyes, in which, despite their deadly greenness, there lurked a tinge of red caused by small specks of that hue semi-occasionally seen floating across her dilated pupils.

"You are the Bangletop ghost, I presume?" said Terwilliger, rising and standing near the fire to thaw out his system.

The spectre made no reply, but pointed to the door.

"Yes," Terwilliger said, as if answering a question. That's the way out, madame. It's a beautiful exit, too. Just try it."

"H'I knows the wi out," returned the spectre, rising and approaching the tenant of Bangletop, whose solitary lock also rose, being too polite to remain seated while the ghost walked. "H'I also knows the wi in, 'Ankinson Judson Terwilliger."

"That's very evident, madame, and between you and me I wish you didn't," returned Hankinson, somewhat relieved to hear the ghost talk, even if her voice did sound like the roar of a conch-shell with a bad case of grip. "I may say to von that, aside from a certain uncanny satisfaction which I feel at being permitted for the first time in my life to gaze upon the linaments of a real live misty musty spook, I regard your coming here as an invasion of the sacred rights of privacy which is, as you might say, 'hinexcusable.'"

"Hinvaision?" retorted the ghost, snapping her fingers in his face with such effect that his chin dropped until Terwilliger began to fear it might never resume its normal position. "Hinvaision? H'I'd like to know 'oo's the hinvaider. H'I've occupied hese 'ere 'alls for hover two 'undred years."

"Then its time you moved, unless per chance you are the ghost of a medieval porker," Hankinson said, his calmness returning now that he had succeeded in plastering his iron-gray lock across the top of his otherwise bald head. "Of course, if you are a spook of that kind you want the earth, and maybe you'll get it."

"H'I'm no porker," returned the spectre. "H'I'm simply the shide of a poor abused cook which is hafter revenge."

"Ah!" ejaculated Terwilliger, raising his eyebrows, "this is getting interesting. You're a spook with a grievance, eh? Against me? I've never wronged a ghost that I know of."

"No, h'I've no 'ard feelinks against you, sir," answered the ghost. "Hin fact h'I don't know nothink about you. My trouble's with them Baingletops, and h'I'm a-pursuin' of 'em. H'I've cut 'em out of two 'undred years of rent 'ere. They might better 'ave pide me me waiges hin full."

"Oho!" cried Terwilliger; "it's a question of wages, is it? The Bangletops were hard up?"

"'Ard up? The Baingletops?" laughed the ghost. "When they gets 'ard up the Baink o' Hengland will be in all the sixty soups mentioned in that there book."

"You seem to be up in the vernacular," returned Terwilliger, with a smile. "I'll bet you are an old fraud of a modern ghost."

Here he discharged all six chambers of his pistol into the body of the spectre.

"No taikers," retorted the ghost, as the bullets whistled through her chest, and struck deep into the wall on the other side of the kitchen. "That's a noisy gun you've got, but you carn't ly a ghost with cold lead hany more than you can ly a corner-stone with a chicken. H'I'm 'ere to sty until I gets me waiges."

"What was the amount of your wages due at the time of your discharge?" asked Hankinson.

"Hi was gettin' ten pounds a month," returned the spectre.

"Geewhittaker!" cried Terwilliger, "you must have been an all-fired fine cook."

"H'I was," assented the ghost, with a proud smile. "H'I cooked a boar's 'ead for 'is Royal 'Ighness King Charles when 'e visited Baingletop 'All as which was the finest 'e hever taisted, so 'e said, hand 'e'd 'ave knighted me hon the spot honly me sex wasn't suited to the title. 'You carn't make a knight out of a woman,' says the king, 'but give 'er my compliments, and tell 'er 'er monarch says as 'ow she's a cook as is too good for 'er staition.'"

"That was very nice," said Terwilliger. "No one could have desired a higher recommendation than that."

"My words hexackly when the baron's privit secretary told me two dys laiter as 'ow the baron's heggs wasn't done proper," said the ghost. "H'I says to 'im, says I: 'The baron's heggs be blowed. My monarch's hopinion is worth two of any ten barons's livin', and Mister Baingletop,' (h'I allus called 'im mister when 'e was ugly,) 'can get 'is heggs cooked helsewhere if 'e don't like the wy h'I boils 'em.' Hand what do you suppose the secretary said then?"

"I give it up," replied Terwilliger. "What?"

"'E said as 'ow h'I 'ad the big 'eadl."

"How disgusting of him!" murmured Terwilliger. "That was simply low."

"Hand then 'e accuged me of bein' himpudent."

"No!"

"'E did, hindeed; hand then 'e discharged me without me waiges. Hof course h'I wouldn't sty after that; but h'I says to 'im, 'Hif I don't get me py, h'I'll 'aunt this place from the dy of me death;' hand 'e says, ''Aunt awy.'"

"And you have kept your word."

"H'I 'ave that! H'I've made it 'ot for 'em, too."

"Well, now, look here," said Terwilliger, "I'll tell you what I'll do. I'll pay you your wages if you'll go back to Spookland and mind your own business. Ten pounds isn't much when three-dollar shoes cost fifteen cents a pair and sell like hot waffles. Is it a bargain?"

"H'I was sent off with three months' money owin' me," said the ghost.

"Well, call it thirty pounds, then," replied Terwilliger.

"With hinterest—compound hinterest at six per cent—for two 'undred and thirty years," said the ghost.

"Phew!" whistled Terwilliger. "Have you any idea how much money that is?"

"Certingly," replied the ghost. "Hit's just 63,609,609 pounds 6 shillings 4 ½ pence. When h'I gets that, h'I flies; huntil I gets it h'I stys 'ere an' I 'aunts."

"Say," said Terwilliger, "haven't you been chumming with an Italian ghost named Shylock over on the other shore?"

"Shylock!" said the ghost. "No, h'I've never 'eard the naime. Perhaps 'e's stoppin' at the hother place."

"Very likely," said Terwilliger. "He is an eminent saint alongside of you. But I say now, Mrs. Spook, or whatever your name is, this is rubbing it in, to try to collect as much money as that, particularly from me, who wasn't to blame in any way, and on whom you haven't the spook of a claim."

"H'I'm very sorry for you, Mr. Terwilliger," said the ghost. "But my vow must be kept sacrid."

"But why don't you come down on the Bangletops up in London, and squeeze it out of them?"

"H'I carn't. H'I'm bound to 'aunt this 'all, an' that's hall there is about it. H'I carn't find a better wy to ly them Baingletops low than by attachin' of their hin-come, hand the rent of this 'all is the honly bit of hincome within my reach."

"But I've leased the place for five years," said Terwilliger, in despair; "and I've paid the rent in advance."

"Carn't 'elp it," returned the ghost. "Hif you did that, hit's your own fault."

"I wouldn't have done it, except to advertise my shoe business," said Terwilliger, ruefully. "The items in the papers at home that arise from my occupancy of this house, together with the social cinch it gives me, are worth the money; but I'm hanged if it's worth my while to pay back salaries to every grasping apparition that chooses to rise up out of the moat and dip his or her clammy hand into my surplus. The shoe trade is a blooming big thing, but the profits aren't big enough to divide with tramp ghosts."

"Your tone is very 'aughty, 'Ankinson J. Terwilliger, but it don't haffeck me. H'I don't care 'oo pys the money, an' h'I 'aven't got you into this scripe. You've done that yourself. Hon the other 'and, sir, h'I've showed you 'ow to get out of it."

"Well, perhaps you're right," returned Hankinson. "I can't say I blame you for not perjuring yourself, particularly since you've been dead long enough to have discovered what the probable consequences would be. But I do wish there was some other way out of it. I couldn't pay you all that money without losing a controlling interest in the shoe company, and that's hardly worth my while, now is it?"

"No, Mr. Terwilliger; hit is not."

"I have a scheme," said Hankinson, after a moment or two of deep thought. "Why don't you go back to the spirit world and expose the Bangletops there? They have spooks, havent they?"

"Yes," replied the ghost, sadly. "But the spirit world his as bad as this 'ere. The spook of a cook carn't reach the spook of a baron there hany more than a scullery-maid can reach a markis 'ere. H'I tried that when the baron died and came over to the hother world, but 'e 'ad 'is spook flunkies on 'and to tell me 'e was hout drivin' with the ghost of William the Conqueror and the shide of Solomon. H'I knew 'e wasn't, but what could h'I do?"

"It was a mean game of bluff," said Terwilliger. "I suppose, though, if you were the shade of a duchess, you could simply knock Bangletop silly?"

"Yes, and the Baron of Peddlington too. 'E was the private secretary as said h'I 'ad the big 'ead."

"H'm!" said Terwilliger, meditatively. "Would you—er—would you consent to retire from this haunting business of yours, and give me a receipt for that bill for wages, interest and all, if I had you made over into the spook of a duchess? Revenge is sweet, you know, and there are some revenges that are simply a thousand times more balmy than riches."

"Would h'I?" ejaculated the ghost, rising and looking at the clock. "Would h'I?" she repeated.

"Well, rather. If h'I could enter spook society as a duchess, you can wager a year's hincome them Bangletops wouldn't be hin it."

"Good I am glad to see that you are a spook of spirit. If you had veins, I believe there'd be sporting blood in them."

"Thainks," said the ghost, dryly. "But 'ow can it hever be did?"

"Leave that to me," Terwilliger answered. "We'll call a truce for two weeks, at the end of which time you must come back here, and we'll settle on the final arrangements. Keep your own counsel in the matter, and don't breathe a word about your intentions to anybody. Above all, keep sober."

"H'I'm no cannibal," retorted the ghost.

"Who said you were?" asked Terwilliger.

"You intimated as much," said the ghost, with a smile. "You said as 'ow I must keep sober, and 'ow could I do hotherwise hunless I swallered some spirits?"

Terwilliger laughed. He thought it was a pretty good joke For a ghost—especially a cook's ghost—and then, having agreed on the hour of midnight one fortnight thence for the next meeting, they shook hands and parted.

"What was it, Hankinson?" asked Mrs. Terwilliger, as her husband crawled back into bed.

"Burglars?"

"Not a burglar," returned Hankinson. "Nothing but a ghost—a poor, old, female ghost."

"Ghost!" cried Mrs. Terwilliger, trembling with fright. "In this house?"

"Yes, my dear. Haunted us by mistake, that's all. Belongs to another place entirely; got a little befogged, and came here without intending to, that's all. When she found out her mistake, she apologized, and left."

"What did she have on?" asked Mrs. Terwilliger, with a sigh of relief.

But the president of the Three-dollar Shoe Company, of Soleton, Massachusetts (Limited), said nothing. He had dropped off into a profound slumber.

III

For the next two weeks Terwilliger lived in a state of preoccupation that worried his wife and daughters to a very considerable extent. They were afraid that something had happened, or was about to happen, in connection with the shoe corporation; and this deprived them of sleep, particularly the elder Miss Terwilliger, who had danced four times at a recent ball with an impecunious young earl, whom she suspected of having intentions. Ariadne was in a state of grave apprehension, because she knew that much as the earl might love her, it would be difficult for them to marry on his income, which was literally too small to keep the roof over his head in decent repair.

But it was not business troubles that occupied every sleeping and waking thought of Hankinson Judson Terwilliger. His mind was now set upon the hardest problem it had ever had to cope with, that problem being how to so ennoble the spectre cook of Bangletop that she might outrank the ancestors of his landlord in the other world—the shady world, he called it. The living cook had been induced to remain partly by threats and partly by promises of increased pay; the threats consisting largely of expressions of determination to leave her in England, thousands of miles from her home in Massachusetts, deserted and forlorn, the poor woman being insufficiently provided with funds to get back to America, and holding in her veins a strain of Celtic blood quite large enough to make the idea of remaining an outcast in England absolutely intolerable to her. At the end of seven days Terwilliger was seemingly as far from the solution of his problem as ever, and at the grand fête given by himself and wife on the afternoon of the seventh day of his trial, to the Earl of Mugley, the one in whom Ariadne was interested, he seemed almost rude to his guests, which the latter overlooked, taking it for the American way of entertaining. It is very hard for a shoemaker to entertain earls, dukes, and the plainest kind of every-day lords under ordinary circumstances; but when, in addition to the duties of host, the maker of soles has to think out a recipe for the making of an aristocrat out of a deceased plebe, a polite drawing-room manner is hardly to be expected. Mr. Terwilliger's manner remained of the kind to be expected under the circumstances, neither better nor worse, until the flunky at the door announced, in stentorian tones, "The Hearl of Mugley."

The "Hearl" of Mugley seemed to be the open sesame to the door betwixt Terwilliger and success. Simultaneously with the entrance of the earl the solution of his problem flashed across the mind of the master of Bangletop, and his affronting demeanor, his preoccupation and all disappeared in an instant. Indeed, so elegantly enthusiastic was his reception of the earl that Lady Maud Sniffles, on the other side of the room, whispered in the ear of the Hon. Miss Pottleton that Mugley's creditors were in luck; to which the Hon. Miss Pottleton, whose smiles upon the nobleman had been returned unopened, curved her upper lip spitefully, and replied that they were indeed, but she didn't envy Ariadne that pompous little error of nature's, the earl.

"Howdy do, Earl?" said Terwilliger. "Glad to see you looking so well. How's your mamma?"

"The countess is in her usual state of health, Mr. Terwilliger," returned the earl.

"Ain't she coming this afternoon?"

"I really can't say," answered Mugley. "I asked her if she was coming, and all she did was to call for her salts. She's a little given to fainting-spells, and the slightest shock rather upsets her."

And then the earl turned on his heel and sought out the fair Ariadne, while Terwilliger, excusing himself, left the assemblage, and went directly to his private office in the crypt of the Greek chapel. Arrived there, he seated himself at his desk and wrote the following formal card, which he put in an envelope and addressed to the Earl of Mugley "If the Earl of Mugley will call at the private office of Mr. H. Judson Terwilliger at once, he will not only greatly oblige Mr. H. Judson Terwilliger, but may also hear of something to his advantage."

The card written, Terwilliger summoned an attendant, ordered a quantity of liqueurs, whiskey, sherry, port, and lemon squash for two to be brought to the office, and then sent his communication to the earl.

Now the earl was a great stickler for etiquette, and he did not at all like the idea of one in his position waiting upon one of Mr. Terwilliger's rank or lack of rank, and, at first thought, he was inclined to ignore the request of his host, but a combination of circumstances served to change his resolution. He so seldom heard anything to his advantage that, for mere novelty's sake, he thought he would do as he was asked; but the question of his dignity rose up again, and shoving the note into his pocket he tried to forget it. After five minutes he found he could not forget it, and putting his hand into the pocket for the missive, meaning to give it a second reading, he drew out another paper by mistake, which was, in brief, a reminder from a firm of London lawyers that he owed certain clients of theirs a few thousands of pounds for the clothing that had adorned his back for the last two years, and stating that proceedings would be begun if at the expiration of three months the account was not paid in full. The reminder settled it. The Earl of Mugley graciously concluded to grant Mr. H. Judson Terwilliger an audience in the private office under the Greek chapel.

"Sit down, Earl, and have a cream de mint with me," said Terwilliger, as the earl, four minutes later, entered the apartment.

"Thanks," returned the earl. "Beautiful color that," he added, pleasantly, smacking his lips with satisfaction as the soft green fluid disappeared from the glass into his inner earl.

"Fine," said Terwilliger. "Little unripe, perhaps, but pleasant to the eye. I prefer the hue of the Maraschino, myself. Just taste that Maraschino, Earl. It's A1; thirty-six dollars a case."

"You wanted to see me about some matter of interest to both of us, I believe, Mr. Terwilliger," said the earl, declining the proffered Maraschino.

"Well, yes," returned Terwilliger. "More of interest to you, perhaps, than to me. The fact is, Earl, I've taken quite a shine to you, so much of a one in fact, that I've looked you up at a commercial agency, and H. J. Terwilliger never does that unless he's mightily interested in a man."

"I—er—I hope you are not to be prejudiced against me," the earl said, uneasily, "by—er—by what those cads of tradesmen say about me."

"Not a bit," returned Terwilliger—"not a bit. In fact, what I've discovered has prejudiced me in your favor. You are just the man I've been looking for for some days. I've wanted a man with three A blood and three Z finances for 'most a week now, and from what I gather from Burke and Bradstreet, you fill the bill. You owe pretty much everybody from your tailor to the collector of pew rents at your church, eh?"

"I've been unfortunate in financial matters," returned the earl; "but I have left the family name untarnished."

"So I believe, Earl. That's what I admire about you. Some men with your debts would be driven to drink or other pastimes of a more or less tarnishing nature, and I admire you for the admirable restraint you have put upon yourself. You owe, I am told, about twenty-seven thousand pounds."

"My secretary has the figures I believe," said the earl, slightly bored.

"Well, we'll say thirty thousand in round figures. Now what hope have you of ever paying that sum off?"

"None—unless I—er—well, unless I should be fortunate enough to secure a rich wife."

"Precisely; that is exactly what I thought," rejoined Terwilliger. "Marriage is your only asset, and as yet that is hardly negotiable. Now I have called you here this afternoon to make a proposition to you. If you will marry according to my wishes I will give you an income of five thousand pounds a year for the next five years."

"I don't quite understand you," the earl replied, in a disappointed tone. It was evident that five thousand pounds per annum was too small a figure for his tastes.

"I think I was quite plain," said Terwilliger, and he repeated his offer.

"I certainly admire the lady very much," said the earl; "but the settlement of income seems very small." Terwilliger opened his eyes wide with astonishment. "Oh, you admire the lady, eh?" he said.

"Well, there is no accounting for tastes."

"You surprise me slightly," said the earl, in response to this remark. "The lady is certainly worthy of any man's admiration. She is refined, cultivated, beautiful, and—"

"Ahem!" said Terwilliger. "May I ask, my dear Earl, to whom you refer?"

"To Ariadne, of course. I thought your course somewhat unusual, but we do not pretend to comprehend you Americans over here. Your proposition is that I shall marry Ariadne?"

I hesitate to place on record what Terwilliger said in answer to this statement. It was forcible rather than polite, and the earl from that moment adopted a new simile for degrees of profanity, substituting "to swear like an American" for the old forms having to do with pirates and troopers.

The string of expletives was about five minutes in length, at the end of which time Terwilliger managed to say:

"No such damn proposition ever entered my mind. I want you to marry a cold, misty, musty spectre, nothing more or less, and I'll tell you why."

And then he proceeded to tell the Earl of Mugley all that he knew of the history of Bangletop Hall, concluding with a narration of his experiences with the ghost cook.

"My rent here," he said, in conclusion, "is five thousand pounds per annum. The advertising I get out of the fact of my being here and swelling it with you nabobs is worth twenty-five thousand pounds a year, and I'm willing to pay, in good hard cash, twenty *per cent*. of that amount rather than he forced to give up. Now here's your chance to get an income without an encumbrance and stave off your creditors. Marry the spook, so that she can go back to the spirit land a countess and make it hot for the Bangletops, and don't be so allfired proud. She'll be disappointed enough I can tell you, when I inform her that an earl was the best I could do, the promised duke not being within reach. If she says earls are drugs in the market, I won't be able to deny it; and, after all, my lad, a good cook is a greater blessing in this world than any earl that ever lived, and a blamed sight rarer."

"Your proposition is absolutely ridiculous, Mr. Terwilliger," replied the earl.

"I'd look well marrying a draught from a dark cavern, as you call it, now wouldn't I? To say nothing of the impossibility of a Mugley marrying a cook. I cannot entertain the proposition."

"You'll find you can't entertain anything if you don't watch out," fumed Terwilliger, in return.

"I'm not so sure about that," replied the earl, haughtily, sipping his lemon squash. "I fancy Miss Ariadne is not entirely indifferent to me."

"Well, you might just as well understand on this 18 th day of July, 18—, as any other time, that my daughter Ariadne never becomes the Earless of Mugley," said Terwilliger, in a tone of exasperation.

"Not even when her father considers the commercial value of such an alliance for his daughter?" retorted the earl, shaking his tinger in Terwilliger's face. "Not even when the President of the Three-dollar Shoe Company, of Soleton, Massachusetts (Limited), considers the advertising sure to result from a marriage between his house and that of Mugley, with presents from her majesty the queen, the Duke of York acting as best man, and telegrams of congratulation from the crowned heads of Europe pouring in at the rate of two an hour for half as many hours as there are thrones?"

Terwilliger turned pale.

The picture painted by the earl was terribly alluring.

He hesitated.

He was lost.

"Mugley," he whispered, hoarsely—"Mugley, I have wronged you. I thought you were a fortune-hunter. I see you love her. Take her, my boy, and pass me the brandy."

"Certainly, Mr. Terwilliger," replied the earl, affably. "And then, if you've no objection, you may pass it back, and I'll join you in a thimbleful myself."

And then the two men drank each other's health in silence, which was prolonged for at least five minutes, during which time the earl and his host both appeared to be immersed in deep thought.

"Come," said Terwilliger at last. "Let us go back to the drawing-room, or they'll miss us, and, by the way, you might speak of that little matter to Ariadlne tonight. It'll help the fall trade to have the engagement announced."

"I will, Mr. Terwilliger," returned the earl, as they started to leave the room; "but I say, father-in-law elect," he whispered, catching Terwilliger's coat sleeve and drawing him back into the office for an instant, "you couldn't let me have five pounds on account this evening, could you?"

Two minutes later Terwilliger and the earl appeared in the drawing-room, the former looking haggard and worn, his eyes feverishly bright, and his manner betraying the presence of disturbing elements in his nerve centres; the latter smiling more affably than was consistent with his title, and jingling a number of gold coins in his pocket, which his intimate friend and old college chum, Lord Dufferton, on the other side of the room, marvelled at greatly, for he knew well that upon the earl's arrival at Bangle-top Hall an hour before his pockets were as empty as a flunky's head.

IV

Terwilliger's time was almost up. The hour for his interview with the spectre cook of Bangletop was hardly forty-eight hours distant, and he was wellnigh distracted. No solution of the problem seemed possible since the earl had so peremptorily declined to fall in with his plan. He was glad the earl had done so, for otherwise he would have been denied the tremendous satisfaction which the consummation of an alliance between his own and one of the oldest and noblest houses of England was about to give him, not to mention the commercial phase of the situation, which had been so potent a factor in bringing the engagement about; for Ariadne had said yes to the earl that same nights and the betrothal was shortly to be announced. It would have been announced at once, only the earl felt that he should break the news himself first to his mother, the countess—an operation which he dreaded, and for which he believed some eight or ten weeks of time were necessary.

"What is the matter, Judson?" Mrs. Terwilliger asked finally, her husband was growing so careworn of aspect.

"Nothing, my dear, nothing."

"But there is something, Judson, and as your wife I demand to know what it is. Perhaps I can help you."

And then Mr. Terwilliger broke down, and told the whole story to Mrs. Terwilliger, omitting no detail, stopping only to bring that worthy lady to on the half-dozen or more occasions when her emotions were too strong for her nerves, causing her to swoon. When he had quite done, she looked him reproachfully in the eye, and said that if he had told her the truth instead of deceiving her on the night of the spectral visitation, he might have been spared all his trouble.

"For you know, Judson," she said, "I have made a study of the art of acquiring titles. Since I read the story of the girl who started in life as an innkeeper's daughter and died a duchess, by Elizabeth Harley Hicks, of Salem, and realized how one might be lowly born and yet rise to lofty heights, it has been my dearest wish that my girls might become noblewomen, and at times, Judson, I have even hoped that you might yet become a duke."

"Great Scott!" ejaculated Terwilliger. "That would be awful. Hankinson, Duke of Terwilliger! Why, Molly, I'd never be able to hold up my head in shoe circles with a name on me like that."

"Is there nothing in the world but shoes, Judson?" asked his wife, seriously.

"You'll find shoes are the foundation upon which society stands," chuckled Terwilliger in return.

"You are never serious," returned Mrs. Terwilliger; "but now you must be. You are coping with the supernatural. Now I have discovered," continued the lady, "that there are three methods by which titles are acquired—birth, marriage, and purchase."

"You forget the fourth—achievement," suggested Terwilliger.

"Not these days, Judson. It used to be so, but it is not so now. Now the spectre hasn't birth, we can't get any living duke to marry her, dead dukes are hard to find, so there's nothing to do but to buy her a title."

"But where?"

"In Italy. You can get 'em by the dozen. Every hand-organ grinder in America grinds away in the hope of going back to Italy and purchasing a title. Why can't you do the same?"

"Me? Me grind a hand-organ in America?" cried Jlankinson.

"No, no; purchase a dukedom."

"I don't want a dukedom; I want a duchessdom."

"That's all right. Buy the title, give it to the cook, and let her marry some spectre of her own rank; she can give him the title; and there you are!"

"Good scheme!" cried Terwilliger. "But I say, Molly, don't you think it would be better to get her to bring the spectre over here, and have me give him the title, and then let him marry her here?"

"No, I don't. If you give it to him first, the chances are he would go back on his bargain. He'd say that, being a duke, he couldn't marry a cook."

"You have a large mind, Molly," said Terwilliger.

"I know men!" snapped Mrs. Terwilliger.

And so it happened. Hankinson Judson Terwilliger applied by wire to the authorities in Rome for all right, title, and interest in one dukedom, free from encumbrances irrevocable, and duly witnessed by the proper dignitaries of the Italian government, and at the second interview with the spectre cook of Bangletop, he was able to show her a cablegram received from the Eternal City stating that the papers would be sent upon receipt of the applicant's check for one hundred lire.

"'Ow much his that?" asked the ghost.

"One hundred lire?" returned Terwilliger, repeating the sum to gain time to think. He was himself surprised at the cheapness of the duchy, and he was afraid that if the ghost knew its real value she would decline to take it. "One hundred lire? Why, that's about 750,000 dollars—150,000 pounds. They charge high for their titles," he added, blushing slightly.

"Pretty 'igh," returned the ghost. "But h'I carn't be a duke, ye know. 'Ow'll I manidge that?"

Hankinson explained his wife's scheme to the spectre.

"That's helegant," said she. "H'I've loved a butler o' the Bangletops for nigh hon to two 'undred years, but, some 'ow or hother, he's kep' shy o' me. This'll fix 'im. But h'I say, Mr. Terwilliger, his one o' them Heyetalian dukes as good as a Henglish one?"

"Every bit," said Terwilliger. "A duke's a duke the world over. Don't you know the lines of Burns, 'A duke's a duke for a' that'?"

"Never 'eard of 'im," replied the ghost.

"Well, you look him up when you get settled down at home. He was a smart man here, and, if his ghost does him justice, you'll be mighty glad to know him," Terwilliger answered.

And thus was Bangletop Hall delivered of its uncanny visitor. The ducal appointment, entitling its owner to call himself "Duke of Cavalcadi," was received in due time, and handed over to the curse of the kitchen, who immediately disappeared, and permanently, from the haunts that had known her for so long and so disadvantageously. Bangletop Hall is now the home of a happy family, to whom all are devoted, and from whose ménage no cook has ever been known to depart, save for natural causes, despite all that has gone before.

Ariadne has become Countess of Mugley, and Mrs. Terwilliger is content with her Judson, whom, however, she occasionally calls Duke of Cavalcadi, claiming that he is the representative of that ancient and noble family on earth. As for Judson, he always smiles when his wife calls him Duke, but denies the titular impeachment, for he is on good terms with his landlord, whose admiration for his tenant's wholly unexpected ability to retain his cook causes him to regard him as a supernatural being, and therefore worthy of a Bangletop's regard.

"All of which," Terwilliger says to Mrs. Terwilliger, "might not be so, my dear, were I really the duke, for I honestly believe that if there is a feud of long standing anywhere in the universe, it is between the noble families of Bangletop and Cavalcadi over on the other shore."

THE SUPERSTITIOUS MAN'S STORY,
by Thomas Hardy

"There was something very strange about William's death—very strange indeed!" sighed a melancholy man in the back of the van. It was the seedman's father, who had hitherto kept silence.

"And what might that have been?" asked Mr Lackland.

"William, as you may know, was a curious, silent man; you could feel when he came near 'ee; and if he was in the house or anywhere behind you without your seeing him, there seemed to be something clammy in the air, as if a cellar door opened close by your elbow. Well, one Sunday, at a time that William was in very good health to all appearance, the bell that was ringing for church went very heavy all of a sudden; the sexton, who told me o't, said he had not known the bell go so heavy in his hand for years—it was just as if the gudgeons wanted oiling. That was on the Sunday, as I say.

"During the week after, it chanced that William's wife was staying up late one night to finish her ironing, she doing the washing for Mr and Mrs Hardcome. Her husband had finished his supper, and gone to bed as usual some hour or two before. While she ironed she heard him coming downstairs; he stopped to put on his boots at the stair-foot, where he always left them, and then came on into the living-room where she was ironing, passing through it towards the door, this being the only way from the staircase to the outside of the house. No word was said on either side, William not being a man given to much speaking, and his wife being occupied with her work. He went out and closed the door behind him. As her husband had now and then gone out in this way at night before when unwell, or unable to sleep for want of a pipe, she took no particular notice, and continued at her ironing. This she finished shortly after, and, as he had not come in, she waited awhile for him, putting away the irons and things, and preparing the table for his breakfast in the morning. Still he did not return, but supposing him not far off, and wanting to go to bed herself, tired as she was, she left the door unbarred and went to the stairs, after writing on the back of the door with chalk: *Mind and do the door* (because he was a forgetful man).

"To her great surprise, and I might say alarm, on reaching the foot of the stairs his boots were standing there as they always stood when he had gone to rest. Going up to their chamber, she found him in bed sleeping as sound as a rock. How he could have got back again without her seeing or hearing him was beyond her comprehension. It could only have been by passing behind her very quietly while she was bumping with the iron. But this notion did not satisfy her: it was surely impossible that she should not have seen him come in through a room so small. She could not unravel the mystery, and felt very queer and uncomfortable about it. However, she would not disturb him to question him then, and went to bed herself.

"He rose and left for his work very early the next morning, before she was awake, and she waited his return to breakfast with much anxiety for an explanation, for thinking over the matter by daylight made it seem only the more startling. When he came in to the meal he said, before she could put her question, 'What's the meaning of them words chalked on the door?'

"She told him, and asked him about his going out the night before. William declared that he had never left the bedroom after entering it, having in fact undressed, lain down, and fallen asleep directly, never once waking till the clock struck five, and he rose up to go to his labour.

"Betty Privett was as certain in her own mind that he did go out as she was of her own existence, and was little less certain that he did not return. She felt too disturbed to argue with him, and let the subject drop as though she must have been mistaken. When she was walking down Longpuddle Street later in the day she met Jim Weedle's daughter Nancy, and said: 'Well Nancy, you do look sleepy today!'

"'Yes, Mrs Privett,' said Nancy. 'Now, don't tell anybody, but I don't mind letting you know what the reason o't is. Last night, being Old Midsummer Eve, some of us church porch, and didn't get home till near one.'

"'Did ye?' says Mrs Privett. 'Old Midsummer yesterday was it? Faith, I didn't think whe'r 'twas Midsummer or Michaelmas; I'd too much work to do.'

"'Yes. And we were frightened enough, I can tell 'ee by what we saw.'

"'What did ye see?'

"(You may not remember, sir, having gone off to foreign parts so young, that on Midsummer Night it is believed hereabout that the faint shapes of all the folk in the parish who are going to be at death's door within the year can be seen entering the church. Those who get over their illness come out again after awhile; those that are doomed to die do not return.)

"'What did you see?' asked William's wife.

"'Well,' says Nancy, backwardly—'we needn't tell what we saw or who we saw.'

"'You saw my husband,' said Betty Privett in a quiet way.

"'Well, since you put it so,' says Nancy, hanging fire, 'we—thought we did see him; but it was darkish and we was frightened, and of course it might not have been he.'

"'Nancy, you needn't mind letting it out, though 'tis kept back in kindness. And he didn't come out of the church again: I know it as well as you.'

"Nancy did not answer yes or no to that, and no more was said. But three days after, William Privett was mowing with John Chiles in Mr Hardcome's meadow, and in the heat of the day they sat down to their bit o' nunch under a tree, and empty their flagon. Afterwards both of 'em fell asleep as they sat. John Chiles was the first to wake, and, as he looked towards his fellow-mower, he saw one of those great white miller's-souls as we call 'em—that is to say, a miller moth—come from William's open mouth while he slept and fly straight away. John thought it odd enough, as William had worked in a mill for several years when he was a boy. He then looked at the sun, and found by the place o't that they had slept a long while, and, as William did not wake, John called to him and said it was high time to begin work again. He took no notice, and then John went up and shook him and found he was dead.

150

"Now on that very day old Philip Hookhorn was down at Longpuddle Spring, dipping up a pitcher of water; and, as he turned away, who should he see coming down to the spring on the other side but William, looking very pale and old? This surprised Philip Hookhorn very much, for years before that time William's little son—his only child—had been drowned in that spring while at play there, and this had so preyed upon William's mind that he'd never been seen near the spring afterwards, and had been known to go half a mile out of his way to avoid the place. On enquiry, it was found that William in body could not have stood by the spring, being in the mead two miles off; and it also came out that at the time at which he was seen at the spring was the very time when he died."

"A rather melancholy story," observed the emigrant, after a minute's silence.

"Yes, yes. Well, we must take ups and downs together," said the seedman's father.

THE SPECTRE BRIDEGROOM,
by William Hunt

Long, long ago a farmer named Lenine lived in Boscean. He had but one son, Frank Lenine, who was indulged into waywardness by both his parents. In addition to the farm servants, there was one, a young girl, Nancy Trenoweth, who especially assisted Mrs Lenine in all the various duties of a small farmhouse.

Nancy Trenoweth was very pretty, and although perfectly uneducated, in the sense in which we now employ the term education, she possessed many native graces, and she had acquired much knowledge, really useful to one whose aspirations would probably never rise higher than to be mistress of a farm of a few acres. Educated by parents who had certainly never seen the world beyond Penzance, her ideas of the world were limited to a few miles around the Land's-End. But although her book of nature was a small one, it had deeply impressed her mind with its influences. The wild waste, the small but fertile valley, the rugged hills, with their crowns of cairns, the moors rich in the golden furze and the purple heath, the sea-beaten cliffs and the silver sands, were the pages she had studied, under the guidance of a mother who conceived, in the sublimity of her ignorance, that everything in nature was the home of some spirit form. The soul of the girl was imbued with the deeply religious dye of her mother's mind, whose religion was only a sense of an unknown world immediately beyond our own. The elder Nancy Trenowethexerted over the villagers around her considerable power. They did not exactly fear her. She was too free from evil for that; but they were conscious of a mental superiority, and yielded without complaining to her sway.

The result of this was, that the younger Nancy, although compelled to service, always exhibited some pride, from a feeling that her mother was a superior woman to any around her.

She never felt herself inferior to her master and mistress, yet she complained not of being in subjection to them. There were so many interesting features in the character of this young servant girl that she became in many respects like a daughter to her mistress. There was no broad line of division in those days, in even the manorial hall, between the lord and his domestics, and still less defined was the position of the employer and the employed in a small farmhouse. Consequent on this condition of things, Frank Lenine and Nancy were thrown as much together as if they had been brother and sister. Frank was rarely checked in anything by his over-fond parents, who were especially proud of their son, since he was regarded as the handsomest young man in the parish. Frank conceived a very warm attachment for Nancy, and she was not a little proud of her lover. Although it was evident to all the parish that Frank and Nancy were seriously devoted to each other, the young man's parents were blind to it, and were taken by surprise when one day Frank asked his father and mother to consent to his marrying Nancy.

The Lenines had allowed their son to have his own way from his youth up; and now, in a matter which brought into play the strongest of human feelings, they were angry because he refused to bend to their wills.

The old man felt it would be a degradation for a Lenine to marry a Trenoweth, and, in the most unreasoning manner, he resolved it should never be.

The first act was to send Nancy home to Alsia Mill, where her parents resided; the next was an imperious command to his son never again to see the girl.

The commands of the old are generally powerless upon the young where the affairs of the heart are concerned. So were they upon Frank. He who was rarely seen of an evening beyond the garden of his father's cottage, was now as constantly absent from his home. The house, which was wont to be a pleasant one, was strangely altered. A gloom had fallen over all things; the father and son rarely met as friends—the mother and her boy had now a feeling of reserve. Often there were angry altercations between the father and son, and the mother felt she could not become the defender of her boy, in his open acts of disobedience, his bold defiance of his parents' commands.

Rarely an evening passed that did not find Nancy and Frank together in some retired nook. The Holy Well was a favourite meeting-place, and here the most solemn vows were made. Locks of hair were exchanged; a wedding-ring, taken from the finger of a corpse, was broken, when they vowed that they would be united either dead or alive; and they even climbed at night the granite-pile at Treryn, and swore by the Logan Rock the same strong vow.

Time passed onward unhappily, and as the result of the endeavours to quench out the passion by force, it grew stronger under the repressing power, and, like imprisoned steam, eventually burst through all restraint.

Nancy's parents discovered at length that moonlight meetings between two untrained, impulsive youths, had a natural result, and they were now doubly earnest in their endeavours to compel Frank to marry their daughter.

The elder Lenine could not be brought to consent to this, and he firmly resolved to remove his son entirely from what he considered the hateful influences of the Trenoweths. He resolved to go to Plymouth, to take his son with him, and, if possible, to send him away to sea, hoping thus to wean him from his folly, as he considered this love-madness. Frank, poor fellow, with the best intentions, was not capable of any sustained effort, and consequently he at length succumbed to his father; and, to escape his persecution, he entered a ship bound for India, and bade adieu to his native land.

Frank could not write, and this happened in days when letters could be forwarded only with extreme difficulty, consequently Nancy never heard from her lover.

A babe had been born into a troublesome world, and the infant became a real solace to the young mother. As the child grew, it became an especial favourite with its grandmother; the elder Nancy rejoiced over the little prattler, and forgot her cause of sorrow. Young Nancy lived for her child, and on the memory of its father. Subdued in spirit she was, but her affliction had given force to her character, and she had been heard to declare that wherever Frank might be, she was ever present with him, whatever might be the temptations of the hour, that her influence was all powerful over him for good. She felt that no distance could separate their souls, that no time could be long enough to destroy the bond between them.

A period of distress fell upon the Trenoweths, and it was necessary that Nancy should leave her home once more, and go again into service. Her mother took charge of the babe, and she found a situation in the village of Kimyall, in the parish of Paul. Nancy, like her mother, contrived by force of character to maintain an ascendancy amongst her companions. She had formed an acquaintance, which certainly never grew into friendship, with some of the daughters of the small farmers around. These girls were all full of the superstitions of the time and place.

The winter was coming on, and nearly three years had passed away since Frank Lenine left his country. As yet there was no sign. Nor father, nor mother, nor maiden had heard of him, and they all sorrowed over his absence. The Lenines desired to have Nancy's child, but the Trenoweths would not part with it. They went so far even as to endeavour to persuade Nancy to live again with them, but Nancy was not at all disposed to submit to their wishes.

It was All-Hallows' eve, and two of Nancy's companions persuaded her—no very difficult task—to go with them and sow hemp-seed.

At midnight the three maidens stole out unperceived into Kimyall town-place to perform their incantation. Nancy was the first to sow, the others being less bold than she.

Boldly she advanced, saying, as she scattered the seed—

> *"Hemp-seed I sow thee,*
> *Hemp-seed grow thee;*
> *And he who will my true love be,*
> *Come after me*
> *And shaw thee."*

This was repeated three times, when, looking back over her left shoulder, she saw Lenine; but he looked so angry that she shrieked with fear, and broke the spell. One of the other girls, however, resolved now to make trial of the spell, and the result of her labours was the vision of a white coffin. Fear now fell on all, and they went home sorrowful, to spend, each one, a sleepless night.

November came with its storms, and during one terrific night a large vessel was thrown upon the rocks in Bernowhall Cliff, and, beaten by the impetuous waves, she was soon in pieces. Amongst the bodies of the crew washed ashore, nearly all of whom had perished, was Frank Lenine. He was not dead when found, but the only words he lived to speak were begging the people to send for Nancy Trenoweth, that he might make her his wife before he died.

Rapidly sinking, Frank was borne by his friends on a litter to Boscean, but he died as he reached the town-place. His parents, overwhelmed in their own sorrows, thought nothing of Nancy, and without her knowing that Lenine had returned, the poor fellow was laid in his last bed, in Burian Churchyard.

On the night of the funeral, Nancy went, as was her custom, to lock the door of the house, and as was her custom too, she looked out into the night. At this instant a horseman rode up in hot haste, called her by name, and hailed her in a voice that chilled her blood.

The voice was the voice of Lenine. She could never forget that; and the horse she now saw was her sweetheart's favourite colt, on which he had often ridden at night to Alsia.

The rider was imperfectly seen; but he looked very sorrowful, and deathly pale, still Nancy knew him to be Frank Lenine.

He told her that he had just arrived home, and that the first moment he was at liberty he had taken horse to fetch his loved one, and to make her his bride.

Nancy's excitement was so great, that she was easily persuaded to spring on the horse behind him, that they might reach his home before the morning.

When she took Lenine's hand a cold shiver passed through her, and as she grasped his waist to secure herself in her seat, her arm became as stiff as ice. She lost all power of speech, and suffered deep fear, yet she knew not why. The moon had arisen, and now burst out in a full flood of light, through the heavy clouds which had obscured it. The horse pursued its journey with great rapidity, and whenever in weariness it slackened its speed, the peculiar voice of the rider aroused its drooping energies. Beyond this no word was spoken since Nancy had mounted behind her lover. They now came to Trove Bottom, where there was no bridge at that time; they dashed into the river. The moon shone full in theirfaces. Nancy looked into the stream, and saw that the rider was in a shroud and other grave-clothes. She now knew that she was being carried away by a spirit, yet she had no power to save herself; indeed, the inclination to do so did not exist.

On went the horse at a furious pace, until they came to the blacksmith's shop, near Burian Church-town, when she knew by the light from the forge fire thrown across the road that the smith was still at his labours. She now recovered speech. "Save me! save me! save me!" she cried with all her might. The smith sprang from the door of the smithy, with a red-hot iron in his hand, and as the horse rushed by, caught the woman's dress, and pulled her to the ground. The spirit, however, also seized Nancy's dress in one hand, and his grasp was like that of a vice. The horse passed like the wind, and Nancy and the smith were pulled down as far as the old Alms-houses, near the churchyard. Here the horse for a moment stopped. The smith seized that moment, and with his hot iron burned off the dress from the rider's hand, thus saving Nancy, more dead than alive; while the rider passed over the wall of the churchyard, and vanished on the grave in which Lenine had been laid but a few hours before.

The smith took Nancy into his shop, and he soon aroused some of his neighbours, who took the poor girl back to Alsia. Her parents laid her on her bed. She spoke no word, but to ask for her child, to request her mother to give up her child to Lenine's parents, and her desire to be buried in his grave. Before the morning light fell on the world Nancy had breathed her last breath.

A horse was seen that night to pass through the Church-town like a ball from a musket, and in the morning Lenine's colt was found dead in Bernowhall Cliff, covered with foam, its eyes forced from its head, and its swollen tongue hanging out of its mouth. On Lenine's grave was found the piece of Nancy's dress which was left in the spirit's hand when the smith burnt her from his grasp.

It is said that one or two of the sailors who survived the wreck related after the funeral, how, on the 30th of October, at night, Lenine was like one mad; they could scarcely keep him in the ship. He seemed more asleep than awake, and, after great excitement, he fell as if dead upon the deck, and lay so for hours. When he came to himself, he told them that he had been taken to the village of Kimyall, and that if he ever married the woman who had cast the spell, he would make her suffer the longest day she had to live for drawing his soul out of his body.

Poor Nancy was buried in Lenine's grave, and her companion in sowing hemp-seed, who saw the white coffin, slept beside her within the year.

THE SPECTRE IN THE CART,
by Thomas Nelson Page

I had not seen my friend Stokeman since we were at college together, and now naturally we fell to talking of old times. I remembered him as a hard-headed man without a particle of superstition, if such a thing be possible in a land where we are brought up on superstition, from the bottle. He was at that time full of life and of enjoyment of whatever it brought. I found now that his wild and almost reckless spirits had been tempered by the years which had passed as I should not have believed possible, and that gravity had taken place of the gaiety for which he was then noted.

He used to maintain, I remember, that there was no apparition or supernatural manifestation, or series of circumstances pointing to such a manifestation, however strongly substantiated they appeared to be, that could not be explained on purely natural grounds.

During our stay at college a somewhat notable instance of what was by many supposed to be a supernatural manifestation occurred in a deserted house on a remote plantation in an adjoining county.

It baffled all investigation, and got into the newspapers, recalling the Cock Lane ghost, and many more less celebrated apparitions. Parties were organized to investigate it, but were baffled. Stokeman, on a bet of a box of cigars, volunteered to go out alone and explode the fraud; and did so, not only putting the restless spirit to flight, but capturing it and dragging it into town as the physical and indisputable witness both of the truth of his theory and of his personal courage. The exploit gave him immense notoriety in our little world.

I was, therefore, no little surprised to hear him say seriously now that he had come to understand how people saw apparitions.

"I have seen them myself," he added, gravely.

"You do not mean it!" I sat bolt upright in my chair in my astonishment. I had myself, largely through his influence, become a sceptic in matters relating to the supernatural.

"Yes, I have seen ghosts. They not only have appeared to me, but were as real to my ocular vision as any other external physical object which I saw with my eyes."

"Of course, it was an hallucination. Tell me; I can explain it."

"I explained it myself," he said, dryly. "But it left me with a little less conceit and a little more sympathy with the hallucinations of others not so gifted."

It was a fair hit.

"In the year—," he went on, after a brief period of reflection, "I was the State's Attorney for my native county, to which office I had been elected a few years after I left college, and the year we emancipated ourselves from carpet-bag rule, and I so remained until I was appointed to the bench. I had a personal acquaintance, pleasant or otherwise, with every man in the county. The district was a close one, and I could almost have given the census of the population. I knew every man who was for me and almost every one who was against me. There were few neutrals. In those times much hung on the elections. There was no borderland. Men were either warmly for you or hotly against you.

"We thought we were getting into smooth water, where the sailing was clear, when the storm suddenly appeared about to rise again. In the canvass of that year the election was closer than ever and the contest hotter.

"Among those who went over when the lines were thus sharply drawn was an old darky named Joel Turnell, who had been a slave of one of my nearest neighbors, Mr. Eaton, and whom I had known all my life as an easygoing, palavering old fellow with not much principle, but with kindly manners and a likable way. He had always claimed to be a supporter of mine, being one of the two or three negroes in the county who professed to vote with the whites.

"He had a besetting vice of pilfering, and I had once or twice defended him for stealing and gotten him off, and he appeared to be grateful to me. I always doubted him a little; for I believed he did not have force of character enough to stand up against his people, and he was a chronic liar. Still, he was always friendly with me, and used to claim the emoluments and privileges of such a relation. Now, however, on a sudden, in this campaign he became one of my bitterest opponents. I attributed it to the influence of a son of his, named Absalom, who had gone off from the county during the war when he was only a youth, and had stayed away for many years without anything being known of him, and had now returned unexpectedly. He threw himself into the fight. He claimed to have been in the army, and he appeared to have a deep-seated animosity against the whites, particularly against all those whom he had known in boyhood. He was a vicious-looking fellow, broad-shouldered and bow-legged, with a swagger in his gait. He had an ugly scar on the side of his throat, evidently made by a knife, though he told the negroes, I understood, that he had got it in the war, and was ready to fight again if he but got the chance. He had not been back long before he was in several rows, and as he was of brutal strength, he began to be much feared by the negroes. Whenever I heard of him it was in connection with some fight among his own people, or some effort to excite race animosity. When the canvass began he flung himself into it with fury, and I must say with marked effect.

"His hostility appeared to be particularly directed against myself, and I heard of him in all parts of the district declaiming against me. The negroes who, for one or two elections, had appeared to have quieted down and become indifferent as to politics were suddenly revivified. It looked as if the old scenes of the Reconstruction period, when the two sides were like hostile armies, might be witnessed again. Night meetings, or 'camp-fires,' were held all through the district, and from many of them came the report of Absalom Turnell's violent speeches stirring up the blacks and arraying them against the whites. Our side was equally aroused and the whole section was in a ferment. Our effort was to prevent any outbreak and tide over the crisis.

"Among my friends was a farmer named John Halloway, one of the best men in my county, and a neighbor and friend of mine from my boyhood. His farm, a snug little homestead of fifty or sixty acres, adjoined our plantation on one side; and on the other, that of the Eatons, to whom Joel Turnell and his son Absalom had belonged, and I remember that as a boy it was my greatest privilege and reward to go over on a Saturday and be allowed by John Halloway to help him plough, or cut his hay. He was a big, ruddy-faced, jolly boy, and even then used to tell me about being in love with Fanny Peel, who was the daughter of another farmer in the neighborhood, and a Sunday-school scholar of my mother's. I thought him the greatest man in the world. He had a fight once with Absalom Turnell when they were both youngsters, and, though Turnell was rather older and much the heavier, whipped him completely. Halloway was a good soldier and a good son, and when he came back from the war and won his wife, who was a belle among the young farmers, and settled down with her on his little place, which he proceeded to make a bower of roses and fruit-trees, there was not a man in the neighborhood who did not rejoice in his prosperity and wish him well. The Halloways had no children and, as is often the case in such instances, they appeared to be more to each other than are most husbands and wives. He always spoke of his wife as if the sun rose and set in her. No matter where he might be in the county, when night came he always rode home, saying that his wife would be expecting him. 'Don't keer whether she's asleep or not,' he used to say to those who bantered him, 'she knows I'm a-comin', and she always hears my click on the gate-latch, and is waitin' for me.'

"It came to be well understood throughout the county.

"'I believe you are hen-pecked,' said a man to him one night.

"'I believe I am, George,' laughed Hallo-way, 'and by Jings! I like it, too.'

"It was impossible to take offence at him, he was so good-natured. He would get out of his bed in the middle of the night, hitch up his horse and pull his bitterest enemy out of the mud. He had on an occasion ridden all night through a blizzard to get a doctor for the wife of a negro neighbor in a cabin near by who was suddenly taken ill. When someone expressed admiration for it, especially as it was known that the man had not long before been abusing Halloway to the provost-marshal, who at that time was in supreme command, he said:

"'Well, what's that got to do with it? Wa'n't the man's wife sick? I don't deserve no credit, though; if I hadn't gone, my wife wouldn' 'a' let me come in her house.'

"He was an outspoken man, too, not afraid of the devil, and when he believed a thing he spoke it, no matter whom it hit. In this way John had been in trouble several times while we were under 'gun-rule'; and this, together with his personal character, had given him great influence in the county, and made him a power. He was one of my most ardent friends and supporters, and to him, perhaps, more than to any other two men in the county, I owed my position.

"Absalom Turnell's rancorous speeches had stirred all the county, and the apprehension of the outbreak his violence was in danger of bringing might have caused trouble but for John Halloway's coolness and level-headedness. John offered to go around and follow Absalom up at his meetings. He could 'spike his guns,' he said.

"Some of his friends wanted to go with him. 'You'd better not try that,' they argued. That fellow, Ab. Turnell's got it in for you.' But he said no. The only condition on which he would go was that he should go alone.

"'They ain't any of 'em going to trouble me. I know 'em all and I git along with 'em first rate. I don't know as I know this fellow Ab.; he's sort o' grown out o' my recollection; but I want to see. He knows me, I know. I got my hand on him once when he was a boy—about my age, and he ain't forgot that, I know. He was a blusterer; but he didn't have real grit. He won't say nothin' to my face. But I must go alone. You all are too flighty.'

"So Halloway went alone and followed Ab. up at his 'camp-fires,' and if report was true his mere presence served to curb Ab.'s fury, and take the fire out of his harangues. Even the negroes got to laughing and talking about it 'Ab. was jest like a dog when a man faced him,' they said; 'he couldn' look him in the eye.'

"The night before the election there was a meeting at one of the worst places in the county, a country store at a point known as Burley's Fork, and Halloway went there, alone—and for the first time in the canvass thought it necessary to interfere. Absalom, stung by the taunts of some of his friends, and having stimulated himself with mean whiskey, launched out in a furious tirade against the whites generally, and me in particular; and called on the negroes to go to the polls next day prepared to 'wade in blood to their lips.' For himself, he said, he had 'drunk blood' before, both of white men and women, and he meant to drink it again. He whipped out and flourished a pistol in one hand and a knife in the other.

"His language exceeded belief, and the negroes, excited by his violence, were showing the effect on their emotions of his wild declamation, and were beginning to respond with shouts and cries when Halloway rose and walked forward. Absalom turned and started to meet him, yelling his fury and threats, and the audience were rising to their feet when they were stopped. It was described to me afterward.

"Halloway was in the midst of a powder magazine, absolutely alone, a single spark would have blown him to atoms and might have caused a catastrophe which would have brought untold evil. But he was as calm as a May morning. He walked through them, the man who told me said, as if he did not know there was a soul in a hundred miles of him, and as if Absalom were only something to be swept aside.

"'He wa'n't exac'ly laughin', or even smilin', said my informant, 'but he jest looked easy in his mine.'

"They were all waiting, he said, expecting Absalom to tear him to pieces on the spot; but as Halloway advanced, Absalom faltered and stopped. He could not stand his calm eye.

"'It was jest like a dog givin' way before a man who ain't afraid of him,' my man said. 'He breshed Absalom aside as if he had been a fly, and began to talk to us, and I never heard such a speech.'

"I got there just after it happened; for some report of what Absalom intended to do had reached me that night and I rode over hastily, fearing that I might arrive too late. When, however, I arrived at the place everything was quiet, Absalom had disappeared. Unable to face his downfall, he had gone off, taking old Joel with him. The tide of excitement had changed and the negroes, relieved at the relaxing of the tension, were laughing among themselves at their champion's defeat and disavowing any sympathy with his violence. They were all friendly with Halloway.

"'Dat man wa'n' nothin' but a' outside nigger, nohow,' they said. 'And he always was more mouth then anything else,' etc.

"'Good Lord! He say he want to drink blood!' declared one man to another, evidently for us to hear, as we mounted our horses.

"'Drink *whiskey*!' replied the other, dryly, and there was a laugh of derision.

"I rode home with Halloway.

"I shall never forget his serenity. As we passed along, the negroes were lining the roads on their way homeward, and were shouting and laughing among themselves; and the greetings they gave us as we passed were as civil and good-humored as if no unpleasantness had ever existed. A little after we set out, one man, who had been walking very fast just ahead of us, and had been keeping in advance all the time, came close to Halloway's stirrup and said something to him in an undertone. All I caught was, layin' up something against him.'

"'That's all right, Dick; let him lay it up, and keep it laid up,' Halloway laughed.

"'Dat's a bad feller!' the negro insisted, uneasily, his voice kept in an undertone. 'You got to watch him. I'se knowed him from a boy.'

"He added something else in a whisper which I did not catch.

"'All right; certainly not! Much obliged to you, Dick. I'll keep my eyes open. Goodnight.'

"'Good-night, gent'men'; and the negro fell back and began to talk with the nearest of his companions effusively.

"'Who is that?' I asked, for the man had kept his hat over his eyes.

"'That's Dick Winchester. You remember that old fellow 't used to belong to old Mr. Eaton—lived down in the pines back o' me, on the creek 't runs near my place. His wife died the year of the big snow.'

"It was not necessary for him to explain further. I remembered the negro for whom Hal-loway had ridden through the storm that night.

"I asked Halloway somewhat irrelevantly, if he carried a pistol. He said no, he had never done so.

"'Fact is, I'm afraid of killin' somebody. And I don't want to do that, I know. Never could bear to shoot my gun even durin' o' the war, though I shot her 'bout as often as any of 'em, I reckon—always used to shut my eyes right tight whenever I pulled the trigger. I reckon I was a mighty pore soldier,' he laughed. I had heard that he was one of the best in the army.

"'Besides, I always feel sort o' cowardly if I've got a pistol on. Looks like I was afraid of somebody—an' I ain't. I've noticed if two fellows have pistols on and git to fightin', mighty apt to one git hurt, maybe both. Sort o' like two dogs growling—long as don't but one of 'em growl it's all right. If don't but one have a pistol, t' other feller always has the advantage and sort o' comes out top, while the man with the pistol looks mean.'

"I remember how he looked in the dim moonlight as he drawled his quaint philosophy.

"'I'm a man o' peace, Mr. Johnny, and I learnt that from your mother—I learnt a heap o' things from her,' he added, presently, after a little period of reflection. 'She was the lady as used always to have a kind word for me when I was a boy. That's a heap to a boy. I used to think she was an angel. You think it's *you* I'm a fightin' for in this canvass? 'Tain't. I like you well enough, but I ain't never forgot your mother, and her kindness to my old people durin' the war when I was away. She give me this handkerchief for a weddin' present when I was married after the war—said 'twas all she had to give, and my wife thinks the world and all of it; won't let me have it 'cept as a favor; but this mornin' she told me to take it—said 'twould bring me luck.' He took a big bandana out of his pocket and held it up in the moonlight. I remembered it as one of my father's.

"'She'll make me give it up tomorrow night when I git home,' he chuckled.

"We had turned into a road through the plantations, and had just come to the fork where Halloway's road turned off toward his place.

"'I lays a heap to your mother's door—purty much all this, I reckon.' His eye swept the moon-bathed scene before him. 'But for her I mightn't 'a got *her*. And ain't a' man in the world got a happier home, or as good a wife.' He waved his hand toward the little homestead that was sleeping in the moonlight on the slope the other side of the stream, a picture of peace.

"His path went down a little slope, and mine kept along the side of the hill until it entered the woods. A great sycamore tree grew right in the fork, with its long, hoary arms extending over both roads, making a broad mass of shadow in the white moonlight.

"The next day was the day of election. Hal-loway was at one poll and I was at another; so I did not see him that day. But he sent me word that evening that he had carried his poll, and I rode home knowing that we should have peace.

"I was awakened next morning by the news that both Halloway and his wife had been murdered the night before. I at once galloped over to his place, and was one of the first to get there. It was a horrible sight. Halloway had evidently been waylaid and killed by a blow of an axe just as he was entering his yard gate, and then the door of the house had been broken open and his wife had been killed, after which Halloway's body had been dragged into the house, and the house had been fired with the intention of making it appear that the house had burned by accident. But by one of those inscrutable fatalities, the fire, after burning half of two walls, had gone out.

"It was a terrible sight, and the room looked like a shambles. Halloway had plainly been caught unawares while leaning over his gate. The back of his head had been crushed in with the eye of an axe, and he had died instantly. The pleasant thought which was in his mind at the instant—perhaps, of the greeting that always awaited him on the click of his latch; perhaps, of his success that day; perhaps, of my mother's kindness to him when he was a boy—was yet on his face, stamped there indelibly by the blow that killed him. There he lay, face upward, as the murderer had thrown him after bringing him in, stretched out his full length on the floor, with his quiet face upturned! looking in that throng of excited, awe-stricken men, just what he had said he was: a man of peace. His wife, on the other hand, wore a terrified look on her face. There had been a terrible struggle. She had lived to taste the bitterness of death, before it took her."

Stokeman, with a little shiver, put his hand over his eyes as though to shut out the vision that recurred to him. After a long breath he began again.

"In a short time there was a great crowd there, white and black. The general mind flew at once to Absalom Turnell. The negroes present were as earnest in their denunciation as the whites; perhaps, more so, for the whites were past threatening. I knew from the grim-ness that trouble was brewing, and I felt that if Absalom were caught and any evidence were found on him, no power on earth could save him. A party rode off in search of him, and went to old Joel's house. Neither Absalom nor Joel were there; they had not been home since the election, one of the women said.

"As a law officer of the county I was to a certain extent in charge at Halloway's and in looking around for all the clews to be found, I came on a splinter of 'light-wood' not as large or as long as one's little finger, stuck in a crack in the floor near the bed: a piece of a stick of 'fat-pine,' such as negroes often carry about, and use as tapers. One end had been burned; but the other end was clean and was jagged just as it had been broken off. There was a small scorched place on the planks on either side, and it was evident that this was one of the splinters that had been used in firing the house. I called a couple of the coolest, most level-headed men present and quietly showed them the spot, and they took the splinter out and I put it in my pocket.

"By one of those fortuitous chances which so often happen in every lawyer's experience, and appear inexplicable, Old Joel Turnell walked up to the house just as we came out. He was as sympathetic as possible, appeared outraged at the crime, professed the highest regard for Halloway, and the deepest sorrow at his death. The sentiment of the crowd was rather one of sympathy with him, that he should have such a son as Absalom.

"I took the old man aside to have a talk with him, to find out where his son was and where he had been the night before. He was equally vehement in his declarations of his son's innocence, and of professions of regard for Halloway. And suddenly to my astonishment he declared that his son had spent the night with him and had gone away after sunrise.

"Then happened one of those fatuous things that have led to the detection of so many negroes and can almost be counted on in their prosecution. Joel took a handkerchief out of his pocket and wiped his face, and as he did so I recognized the very handkerchief Halloway had shown me the night before. With the handkerchief, Joel drew out several splinters of light-wood, one of which had been broken off from a longer piece. I picked it up and it fitted exactly into the piece that had been stuck in the crack in the floor. At first, I could scarcely believe my own senses. Of course, it became my duty to have Joel arrested immediately. But I was afraid to have it done there, the crowd was so deeply incensed. So I called the two men to whom I had shown the light-wood splinter, told them the story, and they promised to get him away and arrest him quietly and take him safely to jail, which they did.

"Even then we did not exactly believe that the old man had any active complicity in the crime, and I was blamed for arresting the innocent old father and letting the guilty son escape. The son, however, was arrested shortly afterward.

"The circumstances from which the crime arose gave the case something of a political aspect, and the prisoners had the best counsel to be procured, both at our local bar and in the capital. The evidence was almost entirely circumstantial, and when I came to work it up I found, as often occurs, that although the case was plain enough on the outside, there were many difficulties in the way of fitting all the circumstances to prove the guilt of the accused and to make out every link in the chain. Particularly was this so in the prosecution of the young man, who was supposed to be the chief criminal, and in whose case there was a strong effort to prove an alibi.

"As I worked, I found to my surprise that the guilt of the old man, though based wholly on circumstantial evidence, was established more clearly than that of his son—not indeed, as to the murders, but as to the arson, which served just as well to convict on. The handkerchief, which Joel had not been able to resist the temptation to steal, and the splinter of light-wood in his pocket, which fitted exactly into that found in the house, together with other circumstances, proved his guilt conclusively. But although there was an equal moral certainty of the guilt of the young man, it was not so easy to establish it by law.

"Old Dick Winchester was found dead one morning and the alibi was almost completely proved, and only failed by the incredibility of the witnesses for the defence. Old Joel persistently declared that Absalom was innocent, and but for a confession by Absalom of certain facts intended to shift the suspicion from himself to his father, I do not know how his case might have turned out.

"I believed him to be the instigator as well as the perpetrator of the crime.

"I threw myself into the contest, and prosecuted with all the vigor I was capable of. And I finally secured the conviction of both men. But it was after a hard fight. They were the only instances in which, representing the Commonwealth, I was ever conscious of strong personal feeling, and of a sense of personal triumph. The memory of my last ride with Hal-loway, and of the things he had said to me; the circumstances under which he and his wife were killed; the knowledge that in some sort it was on my account; and the bitter attacks made on me personally;(for in some quarters I was depicted as a bloodthirsty ruffian, and it was charged that I was for political reasons prosecuting men whom I personally knew to be innocent), all combined to spur me to my utmost effort. And when the verdicts were rendered, I was conscious of a sense of personal triumph so fierce as to shock me.

"Not that I did not absolutely believe in the guilt of both prisoners; for I considered that I had demonstrated it, and so did the jurors who tried them.

"The day of execution was set. An appeal was at once taken in both cases and a stay was granted, and I had to sustain the verdicts in the upper court. The fact that the evidence was entirely circumstantial had aroused great interest, and every lawyer in the State had his theory. The upper court affirmed in both cases and appeals were taken to the highest court, and again stay of execution was granted.

"The prisoners' counsel had moved to have the prisoners transferred to another county, which I opposed. I was sure that the people of my county would observe the law. They had resisted the first fierce impulse, and were now waiting patiently for justice to take its course. Months passed, and the stay of execution had to be renewed. The road to Halloway's grew up and I understood that the house had fallen in, though I never went that way again. Still the court hung fire as to its conclusion.

"The day set for the execution approached for the third time without the court having rendered its decision.

"On the day before that set for the execution, the court gave its decision. It refused to interfere in the case of old Joel, but reversed and set aside the verdict in that of the younger man. Of a series of over one hundred bills of exception taken by his counsel as a 'drag-net,' one held; and owing to the admission of a single question by a juror, the judgment was set aside in Absalom's case and a new trial was ordered.

"Being anxious lest the excitement might increase, I felt it my duty to stay at the county-seat that night, and as I could not sleep I spent the time going over the records of the two cases; which, like most causes, developed new points every time they were read.

"Everything was perfectly quiet all night, though the village was filling up with people from the country to see the execution, which at that time was still public. I determined next morning to go to my home in the country and get a good rest, of which I began to feel the need. I was detained, however, and it was well along in the forenoon before I mounted my horse and rode slowly out of town through a back street. The lane kept away from the main road except at one point just outside of town, where it crossed it at right angles.

"It was a beautiful spring day—a day in which it is a pleasure merely to live, and as I rode along through the quiet lane under the leafy trees I could not help my mind wandering and dwelling on the things that were happening. I am not sure, indeed, that I was not dozing; for I reached the highway without knowing just where I was.

"I was recalled to myself by a rush of boys up the street before me, with a crowd streaming along behind them. It was the head of the procession. The sheriff and his men were riding, with set faces, in front and on both sides of a slowly moving vehicle; a common horse-cart in which in the midst of his guards, and dressed in his Sunday clothes, with a clean white shirt on, seated on his pine coffin, was old Joel. I unconsciously gazed at him, and at the instant he looked up and saw me. Our eyes met as naturally as if he had expected to find me there, and he gave me as natural and as friendly a bow—not a particle reproachful; but a little timid, as though he did not quite know whether I would speak to him.

"It gave me a tremendous shock. I had a sudden sinking of the heart, and nearly fell from my horse.

"I turned and rode away; but I could not shake off the feeling. I tried to reassure myself with the reflection that he had committed a terrible crime. It did not compose me. What insisted on coming to my mind was the eagerness with which I had prosecuted him and the joy I had felt at my success.

"Of course, I know now it was simply that I was overworked and needed rest; but at that time the trouble was serious.

"It haunted me all day, and that night I could not sleep. For many days afterwards, it clung to me, and I found myself unable to forget it, or to sleep as I had been used to do.

"The new trial of Absalom came on in time, and the fight was had all over again. It was longer than before, as every man in our county had an opinion, and a jury had to be brought from another county. But again the verdict was the same. And again an appeal was taken; was refused by the next higher court; and allowed by the highest; this time because a talesman had said he had expressed an opinion, but had not formed one. In time the appeal was heard once more, and after much delay, due to the number of cases on the docket and the immense labor of studying carefully so huge a record, it was decided. It was again reversed, on the technicality mentioned, and a new trial was ordered.

"That same day the court adjourned for the term.

"Having a bed-room adjoining my office, I spent that night in town. I did not go to sleep until late, and had not been asleep long when I was awakened by the continual repetition of a monotonous sound. At first I thought I was dreaming, but as I aroused it came to me distinctly: the sound of blows in the distance struck regularly. I awoke fully. The noise was in the direction of the jail. I dressed hastily and went down on the street. I stepped into the arms of a half-dozen masked men who quietly laid me on my back, blindfolded me and bound me so that I could not move. I threatened and struggled; but to no purpose, and finally gave it up and tried expostulation. They told me that they intended no harm to me; but that I was their prisoner and they meant to keep me. They had come for their man, they said, and they meant to have him. They were perfectly quiet and acted with the precision of old soldiers.

"All the time I could hear the blows at the jail as the mob pounded the iron door with sledges, and now and then a shout or cry from within.

"The blows were on the inner door, for the mob had quickly gained access to the outer corridor. They had come prepared and, stout as the door was, it could not resist long. Then one great roar went up and the blows ceased suddenly, and then one cry.

"In a little while I heard the regular tramp of men, and in a few minutes the column came up the street, marching like soldiers. There must have been five hundred of them. The prisoner was in the midst, bare-headed and walking between two mounted men, and was moaning and pleading and cursing by turns.

"I asked my captors if I might speak, and they gave me ten minutes. I stood up on the top step of the house, and for a few minutes I made what I consider to have been the best speech I ever made or shall make. I told them in closing that I should use all my powers to find out who they were, and if I could do so I should prosecute them, everyone, and try and have them hanged for murder.

"They heard me patiently, but without a word, and when I was through, one of the leaders made a short reply. They agreed with me about the law; but they felt that the way it was being used was such as to cause a failure of justice. They had waited patiently, and were apparently no nearer seeing justice executed than in the beginning. So they proposed to take the law into their own hands. The remedy was, to do away with all but proper defences and execute the law without unreasonable delay.

"It was the first mob I had ever seen, and I experienced a sensation of utter powerlessness and insignificance; just as in a storm at sea, a hurricane, or a conflagration. The individual disappeared before the irresistible force.

"An order was given and the column moved on silently.

"A question arose among my guards as to what should be done with me.

"They wished to pledge me to return to my rooms and take no steps until morning, but I would give no pledges. So they took me along with them.

"From the time they started there was not a word except the orders of the leader and his lieutenants and the occasional outcry of the prisoner, who prayed and cursed by turns.

"They passed out of the village and turned in at Halloway's place.

"Here the prisoner made his last struggle. The idea of being taken to Halloway's place appeared to terrify him to desperation. He might as well have struggled against the powers of the Infinite. He said he would confess everything if they would not take him there. They said they did not want his confession. He gave up, and from this time was quiet; and he soon began to croon a sort of hymn.

"The procession stopped at the big sycamore under which I had last parted from Halloway.

"I asked leave to speak again; but they said no. They asked the prisoner if he wanted to say anything. He said he wanted something to eat. The leader said he should have it; that it should never be said that any man—even he—had asked in vain for food in that county.

"Out of a haversack food was produced in plenty, and while the crowd waited, amidst profound silence the prisoner squatted down and ate up the entire plateful.

"Then the leader said he had just five minutes more to live and he had better pray.

"He began a sort of wild incoherent ramble; confessed that he had murdered Halloway and his wife, but laid the chief blame on his father, and begged them to tell his friends to meet him in heaven.

"I asked leave to go, and it was given me on condition that I would not return for twenty minutes. This I agreed to.

"I went to my home and aroused someone, and we returned. It was not much more than a half-hour since I had left, but the place was deserted. It was all as silent as the grave. There was no living creature there. Only under the great sycamore, from one of its long, pale branches that stretched across the road, hung that dead thing with the toes turned a little in, just out of our reach, turning and swaying a little in the night wind.

"We had to climb to the limb to cut the body down.

"The outside newspapers made a good deal of the affair. I was charged with indifference, with cowardice, with venality. Some journals even declared that I had instigated the lynching and participated in it, and said that I ought to be hanged.

"I did not mind this much. It buoyed me up, and I went on with my work without stopping for a rest, as I had intended to do.

"I kept my word and ransacked the county for evidence against the lynchers. Many knew nothing about the matter; others pleaded their privilege and refused to testify on the ground of self-crimination.

"The election came on again, and almost before I knew it I was in the midst of the canvass.

"I held that election would be an indorsement of me, and defeat would be a censure. After all, it is the indorsement of those about our own home that we desire.

"The night before the election I spoke to a crowd at Burley's Fork. The place had changed since Halloway checked Absalom Turnell there. A large crowd was in attendance. I paid Halloway my personal tribute that night, and it met with a deep response. I denounced the lynching. There was a dead silence. I was sure that in my audience were many of the men who had been in the mob that night.

"When I rode home quite a company started with me.

"The moon, which was on the wane, was, I remember, just rising as we set ont It was a soft night, rather cloudy, but not dark, for the sad moon shone a little now and then, looking wasted and red. The other men dropped off from time to time as we came to the several roads that led to their homes and at last I was riding alone. I was dead tired and after I was left by my companions sat loungingly on my horse. My mind ran on the last canvass and the strange tragedy that had ended it, with its train of consequences. I was not aware when my horse turned off from the main road into the by-lane that led through the Halloway place to my own home. My horse was the same I had ridden that night. I awaked suddenly to a realization of where I was, and regretted for a second that I had come by that road. The next moment I put the thought away as a piece of cowardice and rode on, my mind perfectly easy. My horse presently broke into a canter and I took a train of thought distinctly pleasant. I mention this to account for my inability to explain what followed. I was thinking of old times and of a holiday I had once spent at Halloway's when old Joel came through on his way to his wife's house. It was the first time I remembered ever seeing Joel. I was suddenly conscious of something white moving on the road before me. At the same second my horse suddenly wheeled with such violence as to break my stirrup-leather and almost throw me over his neck. I pulled him up and turned him back, and there before me, coming along the unused road up the hill from Hallo way's, was old Joel, sitting in a cart, looking at me, and bowing to me politely just as he had done that morning on his way to the gallows; while dangling from the white limb of the sycamore, swaying softly in the wind, hung the corpse of Absalom. At first I thought it was an illusion and I rubbed my eyes. But there they were. Then I thought it was a delusion; and I reined in my horse and reasoned about it. But it was not; for I saw both men as plainly as I saw my stirrup-leather lying there in the middle of the road, and in the same way. My horse saw them too, and was so terrified that I could not keep him headed to them. Again and again I pulled him around and looked at the men and tried to reason about them; but every time I looked there they were, and my horse snorted and wheeled in terror. I could see the clothes they wore: the clean, white shirt and neat Sunday suit old Joel had on, and the striped, hickory shirt, torn on the shoulders, and the gray trousers that the lynched man wore—I could see the white rope wrapped around the limb and hanging down, and the knot at his throat; I remembered them perfectly. I could not get near the cart, for the road down to Halloway's, on which it moved steadily without ever approaching, was stopped up. But I rode right under the limb on which the other man hung, and there he was just above my head. I reasoned with myself, but in vain. There he still hung silent and limp, swinging gently in the night wind and turning a little back and forth at the end of the white rope.

"In sheer determination to fight it through I got off my horse and picked up my stirrup. He was trembling like a leaf. I remounted and rode back to the spot and looked again, confident that the spectres would now have disappeared. But there they were, old Joel, sitting in his cart, bowing to me civilly with timid, sad, friendly eyes, as much alive as I was, and the dead man, with his limp head and arms and his toes turned in, hanging in mid-air.

"I rode up under the dangling body and cut at it with my switch. At the motion my horse bolted. He ran fully a mile before I could pursue him in.

"The next morning I went to my stable to get my horse to ride to the polls. The man a the stable said:

"'He ain't fit to take out, sir. You must 'a gi'n him a mighty hard ride last night—he won't tetch a moufful; he's been in a cold sweats all night.'

"Sure enough, he looked it.

"I took another horse and rode out by Halloway's to see the place by daylight.

"It was quiet enough now. The sycamore shaded the grass-grown track, and a branch, twisted and broken by some storm, hung by a strip of bark from the big bough that stretched across the road above my head, swaying, with limp leaves, a little in the wind; a dense dogwood bush in full bloom among the young pines, filled a fence-corner down the disused road where old Joel had bowed to me from his phantom cart the night before. But it was hard to believe that these were the things which had created such impressions on my mind—as hard to believe as that the quiet cottage peering out from amid the mass of peach-bloom on the other slope was one hour the home of such happiness, and the next the scene of such a tragedy." Once more he put his hand suddenly before his face as though to shut out something from his vision. "Yes, I have seen apparitions," he said, thoughtfully, "but I have seen what was worse."

THE TALE OF THE PORCELAIN-GOD,
by Lafcadio Hearn

It is written in the Fong-ho-chin-tch'ouen, *that whenever the artist Thsang-Kong was in doubt, he would look into the fire of the great oven in which his vases were baking, and question the Guardian-Spirit dwelling in the flame. And the Spirit of the Oven-fires so aided him with his counsels, that the porcelains made by Thsang-Kong were indeed finer and lovelier to look upon than all other porcelains. And they were baked in the years of Khang-hi—sacredly called Jin Houang-ti.*

THE TALE OF THE PORCELAIN-GOD

Who first of men discovered the secret of the *Kao-ling*, of the *Pe-tun-tse*—the bones and the flesh, the skeleton and the skin, of the beauteous Vase? Who first discovered the virtue of the curd-white clay? Who first prepared the ice-pure bricks of *tun*: the gathered-hoariness of mountains that have died for age; blanched dust of the rocky bones and the stony flesh of sun-seeking Giants that have ceased to be? Unto whom was it first given to discover the divine art of porcelain?

Unto Pu, once a man, now a god, before whose snowy statues bow the myriad populations enrolled in the guilds of the potteries. But the place of his birth we know not; perhaps the tradition of it may have been effaced from remembrance by that awful war which in our own day consumed the lives of twenty millions of the Black-haired Race, and obliterated from the face of the world even the wonderful City of Porcelain itself—the City of King-te-chin, that of old shone like a jewel of fire in the blue mountain-girdle of Feou-liang.

Before his time indeed the Spirit of the Furnace had being; had issued from the Infinite Vitality; had become manifest as an emanation of the Supreme Tao. For Hoang-ti, nearly five thousand years ago, taught men to make good vessels of baked clay; and in his time all potters had learnedto know the God of Oven-fires, and turned their wheels to the murmuring of prayer. But Hoang-ti had been gathered unto his fathers for thrice ten hundred years before that man was born destined by the Master of Heaven to become the Porcelain-God.

And his divine ghost, ever hovering above the smoking and the toiling of the potteries, still gives power to the thought of the shaper, grace to the genius of the designer, luminosity to the touch of the enamellist. For by his heaven-taught wisdom was the art of porcelain created; by his inspiration were accomplished all the miracles of Thao-yu, maker of the *Kia-yu-ki*, and all the marvels made by those who followed after him;—

All the azure porcelains called *You-kouo-thien-tsing*; brilliant as a mirror, thin as paper of rice, sonorous as the melodious stone *Khing*, and colored, in obedience to the mandate of the Emperor Chi-tsong, "blue as the sky is after rain, when viewed through the rifts of the clouds." These were, indeed, the first of all porcelains, likewise called *Tchai-yao*, which no man, howsoever wicked, could find courage to break, for they charmed the eye like jewels of price;—

And the *Jou-yao*, second in rank among all porcelains, sometimes mocking the aspect and the sonority of bronze, sometimes blue as summer waters, and deluding the sight with mucid appearance of thickly floating spawn of fish;—

And the *Kouan-yao*, which are the Porcelains of Magistrates, and third in rank of merit among all wondrous porcelains, colored with colors of the morning—skyey blueness, with the rose of a great dawn blushing and bursting through it, and long-limbed marsh-birds flying against the glow;

Also the *Ko-yao*—fourth in rank among perfect porcelains—of fair, faint, changing colors, like the body of a living fish, or made in the likeness of opal substance, milk mixed with fire; the work of Sing-I, elder of the immortal brothers Tchang;

Also the *Ting-yao*—fifth in rank among all perfect porcelains—white as the mourning garments of a spouse bereaved, and beautiful with a trickling as of tears—the porcelains sung of by the poet Son-tong-po;

Also the porcelains called *Pi-se-yao*, whose colors are called "hidden," being alternately invisible and visible, like the tints of ice beneath the sun—the porcelains celebrated by the far-famed singer Sin-in;

Also the wondrous *Chu-yao*—the pallid porcelains that utter a mournful cry when smitten—the porcelains chanted of by the mighty chanter, Thou-chao-ling;

Also the porcelains called *Thsin-yao*, white or blue, surface-wrinkled as the face of water by the fluttering of many fins.... And ye can see the fish!

Also the vases called *Tsi-hong-khi*, red as sunset after a rain; and the *T'o-t'ai-khi*, fragile as the wings of the silkworm-moth, lighter than the shell of an egg;

Also the *Kia-tsing*—fair cups pearl-white when empty, yet, by some incomprehensible witchcraft of construction, seeming to swarm with purple fish the moment they are filled with water;

Also the porcelains called *Yao-pien*, whose tints are transmuted by the alchemy of fire; for they enter blood-crimson into the heat, and change there to lizard-green, and at last come forth azure as the cheek of the sky;

Also the *Ki-tcheou-yao*, which are all violet as a summer's night; and the *Hing-yao* that sparkle with the sparklings of mingled silver and snow;

Also the *Sieouen-yao*—some ruddy as iron in the furnace, some diaphanous and ruby-red, some granulated and yellow as the rind of an orange, some softly flushed as the skin of a peach;

Also the *Tsoui-khi-yao*, crackled and green as ancient ice is; and the *Tchou-fou-yao*, which are the Porcelains of Emperors, with dragons wriggling and snarling in gold; and those *yao* that are pink-ribbed and have their angles serrated as the claws of crabs are;

Also the *Ou-ni-yao*, black as the pupil of the eye, and as lustrous; and the *Hou-tien-yao*, darkly yellow as the faces of men of India; and the *Ou-kong-yao*, whose color is the dead-gold of autumn-leaves;

Also the *Long-kang-yao*, green as the seedling of a pea, but bearing also paintings of sun-silvered cloud, and of the Dragons of Heaven;

Also the *Tching-hoa-yao*—pictured with the amber bloom of grapes and the verdure of vine-leaves and the blossoming of poppies, or decorated in relief with figures of fighting crickets;

Also the *Khang-hi-nien-ts'ang-yao*, celestial azure sown with star-dust of gold; and the *Khien-long-nien-thang-yao*, splendid in sable and silver as a fervid night that is flashed with lightnings.

Not indeed the *Long-Ouang-yao*—painted with the lascivious *Pi-hi*, with the obscene *Nan-niu-ssé-sie*, with the shameful *Tchun-hoa*, or "Pictures of Spring"; abominations created by command of the wicked Emperor Moutsong, though the Spirit of the Furnace hid his face and fled away;

But all other vases of startling form and substance, magically articulated, and ornamented with figures in relief, in cameo, in transparency—the vases with orifices belled like the cups of flowers, or cleft like the bills of birds, or fanged like the jaws of serpents, or pink-lipped as the mouth of a girl; the vases flesh-colored and purple-veined and dimpled, with ears and with earrings; the vases in likeness of mushrooms, of lotos-flowers, of lizards, of horse-footed dragons woman-faced; the vases strangely translucid, that simulate the white glimmering of grains of prepared rice, that counterfeit the vapory lace-work of frost, that imitate the efflorescences of coral;—

Also the statues in porcelain of divinities: the Genius of the Hearth; the Long-pinn who are the Twelve Deities of Ink; the blessed Lao-tseu, born with silver hair; Kong-fu-tse, grasping the scroll of written wisdom; Kouan-in, sweetest Goddess of Mercy, standing snowy-footed upon the heart of her golden lily; Chi-nong, the god who taught men how to cook; Fo, with long eyes closed in meditation, and lips smiling the mysterious smile of Supreme Beatitude; Cheou-lao, god of Longevity, bestriding his aërial steed, the white-winged stork; Pou-t'ai, Lord of Contentment and of Wealth, obese and dreamy; and that fairest Goddess of Talent, from whose beneficent hands eternally streams the iridescent rain of pearls.

* * * *

And though many a secret of that matchless art that Pu bequeathed unto men may indeed have been forgotten and lost forever, the story of the Porcelain-God is remembered; and I doubt not that any of the aged *Jeou-yen-liao-kong*, any one of the old blind men of the great potteries, who sit all day grinding colors in the sun, could tell you Pu was once a humble Chinese workman, who grew to be a great artist by dint of tireless study and patience and by the inspiration of Heaven. So famed he became that some deemed him an alchemist, who possessed the secret called *White-and-Yellow*, by which stones might be turned into gold; and others thought him a magician, having the ghastly power of murdering men with horror of nightmare, by hiding charmed effigies of them under the tiles of their own roofs; and others, again, averred that he was an astrologer who had discovered the mystery of those Five Hing which influence all things—those Powers that move even in the currents of the star-drift, in the milky *Tien-ho*, or River of the Sky. Thus, at least, the ignorant spoke of him; but even those who stood about the Son of Heaven, those whose hearts had been strengthened by the acquisition of wisdom, wildly praised the marvels of his handicraft, and asked each other if there might be any imaginable form of beauty which Pu could not evoke from that beauteous substance so docile to the touch of his cunning hand.

And one day it came to pass that Pu sent a priceless gift to the Celestial and August: a vase imitating the substance of ore-rock, all aflame with pyritic scintillation—a shape of glittering splendor with chameleons sprawling over it;

chameleons of porcelain that shifted color as often as the beholder changed his position. And the Emperor, wondering exceedingly at the splendor of the work, questioned the princes and the mandarins concerning him that made it. And the princes and the mandarins answered that he was a workman named Pu, and that he was without equal among potters, knowing secrets that seemed to have been inspired either by gods or by demons. Whereupon the Son of Heaven sent his officers to Pu with a noble gift, and summoned him unto his presence.

So the humble artisan entered before the Emperor, and having performed the supreme prostration—thrice kneeling, and thrice nine times touching the ground with his forehead—awaited the command of the August.

And the Emperor spake to him, saying: "Son, thy gracious gift hath found high favor in our sight; and for the charm of that offering we have bestowed upon thee a reward of five thousand silver *liang*. But thrice that sum shall be awarded thee so soon as thou shalt have fulfilled our behest. Hearken, therefore, O matchless artificer! it is now our will that thou make for us a vase having the tint and the aspect of living flesh, but—mark well our desire!—*of flesh made to creep by the utterance of such words as poets utter—flesh moved by an Idea, flesh horripilated by a Thought!* Obey, and answer not! We have spoken."

* * * *

Now Pu was the most cunning of all the *P'ei-se-kong*—the men who marry colors together; of all the *Hoa-yang-kong*, who draw the shapes of vase-decoration; of all the *Hoei-sse-kong,* who paint in enamel; of all the *T'ien-thsai-kong*, who brighten color; of all the *Chao-lou-kong*, who watch the furnace-fires and the porcelain-ovens. But he went away sorrowing from the Palace of the Son of Heaven, notwithstanding the gift of five thousand silver *liang* which had been given to him. For he thought to himself: "Surely the mystery of the comeliness of flesh, and the mystery of that by which it is moved, are the secrets of the Supreme Tao. How shall man lend the aspect of sentient life to dead clay? Who save the Infinite can give soul?"

Now Pu had discovered those witchcrafts of color, those surprises of grace, that make the art of the ceramist. He had found the secret of the *feng-hong*, the wizard flush of the Rose; of the *hoa-hong*, the delicious incarnadine; of the mountain-green called *chan-lou*; of the pale soft yellow termed *hiao-hoang-yeou*; and of the *hoang-kin*, which is the blazing beauty of gold. He had found those eel-tints, those serpent-greens, those pansy-violets, those furnace-crimsons, those carminates and lilacs, subtle as spirit-flame, which our enamellists of the Occident long sought without success to reproduce. But he trembled at the task assigned him, as he returned to the toil of his studio, saying: "How shall any miserable man render in clay the quivering of flesh to an Idea—the inexplicable horripilation of a Thought? Shall a man venture to mock the magic of that Eternal Moulder by whose infinite power a million suns are shapen more readily than one small jar might be rounded upon my wheel?"

* * * *

Yet the command of the Celestial and August might never be disobeyed; and the patient workman strove with all his power to fulfil the Son of Heaven's desire. But vainly for days, for weeks, for months, for season after season, did he strive; vainly also he prayed unto the gods to aid him; vainly he besought the

Spirit of the Furnace, crying: "O thou Spirit of Fire, hear me, heed me, help me! how shall I—a miserable man, unable to breathe into clay a living soul—how shall I render in this inanimate substance the aspect of flesh made to creep by the utterance of a Word, sentient to the horripilation of a Thought?"

For the Spirit of the Furnace made strange answer to him with whisperingof fire: "*Vast thy faith, weird thy prayer! Has Thought feet, that man may perceive the trace of its passing? Canst thou measure me the blast of the Wind?*"

* * * *

Nevertheless, with purpose unmoved, nine-and-forty times did Pu seek to fulfil the Emperor's command; nine-and-forty times he strove to obey the behest of the Son of Heaven. Vainly, alas! did he consume his substance; vainly did he expend his strength; vainly did he exhaust his knowledge: success smiled not upon him; and Evil visited his home, and Poverty sat in his dwelling, and Misery shivered at his hearth.

Sometimes, when the hour of trial came, it was found that the colors had become strangely transmuted in the firing, or had faded into ashen pallor, or had darkened into the fuliginous hue of forest-mould. And Pu, beholding these misfortunes, made wail to the Spirit of the Furnace, praying: "O thou Spirit of Fire, how shall I render the likeness of lustrous flesh, the warm glow of living color, unless thou aid me?"

And the Spirit of the Furnace mysteriously answered him with murmuring of fire: "*Canst thou learn the art of that Infinite Enameller who hath made beautiful the Arch of Heaven—whose brush is Light; whose paints are the Colors of the Evening?*"

Sometimes, again, even when the tints had not changed, after the pricked and labored surface had seemed about to quicken in the heat, to assume the vibratility of living skin—even at the last hour all the labor of the workers proved to have been wasted; for the fickle substance rebelled against their efforts, producing only crinklings grotesque as those upon the rind of a withered fruit, or granulations like those upon the skin of a dead bird from which the feathers have been rudely plucked. And Pu wept, and cried out unto the Spirit of the Furnace: "O thou Spirit of Flame, how shall I be able to imitate the thrill of flesh touched by a Thought, unless thou wilt vouchsafe to lend me thine aid?"

And the Spirit of the Furnace mysteriously answered him with muttering of fire: "*Canst thou give ghost unto a stone? Canst thou thrill with a Thought the entrails of the granite hills?*"

Sometimes it was found that all the work indeed had not failed; for the color seemed good, and all faultless the matter of the vase appeared to be, having neither crack nor wrinkling nor crinkling; but the pliant softness of warm skin did not meet the eye; the flesh-tinted surface offered only the harsh aspect and hard glimmer of metal. All their exquisite toil to mock the pulpiness of sentient substance had left no trace; had been brought to nought by the breath of the furnace. And Pu, in his despair, shrieked to the Spirit of the Furnace: "O thou merciless divinity! O thou most pitiless god!—thou whom I have worshipped with ten thousand sacrifices!—for what fault hast thou abandoned me? for what error hast thou forsaken me? How may I, most wretched of men! ever render the aspect of flesh made to creep with the utterance of a Word, sentient to the titillation of a Thought, if thou wilt not aid me?"

And the Spirit of the Furnace made answer unto him with roaring of fire: "*Canst thou divide a Soul? Nay!... Thy life for the life of thy work!—thy soul for the soul of thy Vase!*"

And hearing these words Pu arose with a terrible resolve swelling at his heart, and made ready for the last and fiftieth time to fashion his work for the oven.

One hundred times did he sift the clay and the quartz, the *kao-ling* and the *tun*; one hundred times did he purify them in clearest water; one hundred times with tireless hands did he knead the creamy paste, mingling it at last with colors known only to himself. Then was the vase shapen and reshapen, and touched and retouched by the hands of Pu, until its blandness seemed to live, until it appeared to quiver and to palpitate, as with vitality from within, as with the quiver of rounded muscle undulating beneath the integument. For the hues of life were upon it and infiltrated throughout its innermost substance, imitating the carnation of blood-bright tissue, and the reticulated purple of the veins; and over all was laid the envelope of sun-colored *Pe-kia-ho*, the lucid and glossy enamel, half diaphanous, even like the substance that it counterfeited—the polished skin of a woman. Never since the making of the world had any work comparable to this been wrought by the skill of man.

Then Pu bade those who aided him that they should feed the furnace well with wood of *tcha*; but he told his resolve unto none. Yet after the oven began to glow, and he saw the work of his hands blossoming and blushing in the heat, he bowed himself before the Spirit of Flame, and murmured: "O thou Spirit and Master of Fire, I know the truth of thy words! I know that a Soul may never be divided! Therefore my life for the life of my work!—my soul for the soul of my Vase!"

And for nine days and for eight nights the furnaces were fed unceasingly with wood of *tcha*; for nine days and for eight nights men watched the wondrous vase crystallizing into being, rose-lighted by the breath of the flame. Now upon the coming of the ninth night, Pu bade all his weary comrades retire to, rest, for that the work was well-nigh done, and the success assured. "If you find me not here at sunrise," he said, "fear not to take forth the vase; for I know that the task will have been accomplished according to the command of the August." So they departed.

But in that same ninth night Pu entered the flame, and yielded up his ghost in the embrace of the Spirit of the Furnace, giving his life for the life of his work—his soul for the soul of his Vase.

And when the workmen came upon the tenth morning to take forth the porcelain marvel, even the bones of Pu had ceased to be; but lo! the Vase lived as they looked upon it: seeming to be flesh moved by the utterance of a Word, creeping to the titillation of a Thought. And whenever tapped by the finger it uttered a voice and a name—the voice of its maker, the name of its creator: PU.

* * * *

And the son of Heaven, hearing of these things, and viewing the miracle of the vase, said unto those about him: "Verily, the Impossible hath been wrought by the strength of faith, by the force of obedience! Yet never was it our desire that so cruel a sacrifice should have been; we sought only to know whether the skill of the matchless artificer came from the Divinities or from the Demons—from heaven or from hell. Now, indeed, we discern that Pu hath taken his place

175

among the gods." And the Emperor mourned exceedingly for his faithful servant. But he ordained that godlike honors should be paid unto the spirit of the marvellous artist, and that his memory should be revered forevermore, and that fair statues of him should be set up in all the cities of the Celestial Empire, and above all the toiling of the potteries, that the multitude of workers might unceasingly call upon his name and invoke his benediction upon their labors.

THE BELL IN THE FOG,
by Gertrude Atherton

I

The great author had realized one of the dreams of his ambitious youth, the possession of an ancestral hall in England. It was not so much the good American's reverence for ancestors that inspired the longing to consort with the ghosts of an ancient line, as artistic appreciation of the mellowness, the dignity, the aristocratic aloofness of walls that have sheltered, and furniture that has embraced, generations and generations of the dead. To mere wealth, only his astute and incomparably modern brain yielded respect; his ego raised its goose-flesh at the sight of rooms furnished with a single check, conciliatory as the taste might be. The dumping of the old interiors of Europe into the glistening shells of the United States not only roused him almost to passionate protest, but offended his patriotism—which he classified among his unworked ideals. The average American was not an artist, therefore he had no excuse for even the affectation of cosmopolitanism. Heaven knew he was national enough in everything else, from his accent to his lack of repose; let his surroundings be in keeping.

Orth had left the United States soon after his first successes, and, his art being too great to be confounded with locality, he had long since ceased to be spoken of as an American author. All civilized Europe furnished stages for his puppets, and, if never picturesque nor impassioned, his originality was as overwhelming as his style. His subtleties might not always be understood—indeed, as a rule, they were not—but the musical mystery of his language and the penetrating charm of his lofty and cultivated mind induced raptures in the initiated, forever denied to those who failed to appreciate him.

His following was not a large one, but it was very distinguished. The aristocracies of the earth gave to it; and not to understand and admire Ralph Orth was deliberately to relegate one's self to the ranks. But the elect are few, and they frequently subscribe to the circulating libraries; on the Continent, they buy the Tauchnitz edition; and had not Mr. Orth inherited a sufficiency of ancestral dollars to enable him to keep rooms in Jermyn Street, and the wardrobe of an Englishman of leisure, he might have been forced to consider the tastes of the middle-class at a desk in Hampstead. But, as it mercifully was, the fashionable and exclusive sets of London knew and sought him. He was too wary to become a fad, and too sophisticated to grate or bore; consequently, his popularity continued evenly from year to year, and long since he had come to be regarded as one of them. He was not keenly addicted to sport, but he could handle a gun, and all men respected his dignity and breeding. They cared less for his books than women did, perhaps because patience is not a characteristic of their sex. I am alluding, however, in this instance, to men-of-the-world. A group of young literary men—and one or two women—put him on a pedestal and kissed the earth before it. Naturally, they imitated him, and as this flattered him, and he had a kindly heart deep among the cere-cloths of his formalities, he sooner or later wrote "appreciations" of them all, which nobody living could understand, but which owing to the sub-title and signature answered every purpose.

With all this, however, he was not utterly content. From the 12th of August until late in the winter—when he did not go to Homburg and the Riviera—he visited the best houses in England, slept in state chambers, and meditated in historic parks; but the country was his one passion, and he longed for his own acres.

He was turning fifty when his great-aunt died and made him her heir: "as a poor reward for his immortal services to literature," read the will of this phenomenally appreciative relative. The estate was a large one. There was a rush for his books; new editions were announced. He smiled with cynicism, not unmixed with sadness; but he was very grateful for the money, and as soon as his fastidious taste would permit he bought him a country-seat.

The place gratified all his ideals and dreams—for he had romanced about his sometime English possession as he had never dreamed of woman. It had once been the property of the Church, and the ruin of cloister and chapel above the ancient wood was sharp against the low pale sky. Even the house itself was Tudor, but wealth from generation to generation had kept it in repair; and the lawns were as velvety, the hedges as rigid, the trees as aged as any in his own works. It was not a castle nor a great property, but it was quite perfect; and for a long while he felt like a bridegroom on a succession of honeymoons. He often laid his hand against the rough ivied walls in a lingering caress.

After a time, he returned the hospitalities of his friends, and his invitations, given with the exclusiveness of his great distinction, were never refused. Americans visiting England eagerly sought for letters to him; and if they were sometimes benumbed by that cold and formal presence, and awed by the silences of Chillingsworth—the few who entered there—they thrilled in anticipation of verbal triumphs, and forthwith bought an entire set of his books. It was characteristic that they dared not ask him for his autograph.

Although women invariably described him as "brilliant," a few men affirmed that he was gentle and lovable, and any one of them was well content to spend weeks at Chillingsworth with no other companion. But, on the whole, he was rather a lonely man.

It occurred to him how lonely he was one gay June morning when the sunlight was streaming through his narrow windows, illuminating tapestries and armor, the family portraits of the young profligate from whom he had made this splendid purchase, dusting its gold on the black wood of wainscot and floor. He was in the gallery at the moment, studying one of his two favorite portraits, a gallant little lad in the green costume of Robin Hood. The boy's expression was imperious and radiant, and he had that perfect beauty which in any disposition appealed so powerfully to the author. But as Orth stared today at the brilliant youth, of whose life he knew nothing, he suddenly became aware of a human stirring at the foundations of his aesthetic pleasure.

"I wish he were alive and here," he thought, with a sigh. "What a jolly little companion he would be! And this fine old mansion would make a far more complementary setting for him than for me."

He turned away abruptly, only to find himself face to face with the portrait of a little girl who was quite unlike the boy, yet so perfect in her own way, and so unmistakably painted by the same hand, that he had long since concluded they had been brother and sister. She was angelically fair, and, young as she was—she could not have been more than six years old—her dark-blue eyes had a beauty of mind which must have been remarkable twenty years later. Her pouting mouth was like a little scarlet serpent, her skin almost transparent, her pale hair fell waving—not curled with the orthodoxy of childhood—about her tender bare shoulders. She wore a long white frock, and clasped tightly against her breast a doll far more gorgeously arrayed than herself. Behind her were the ruins and the woods of Chillingsworth.

Orth had studied this portrait many times, for the sake of an art which he understood almost as well as his own; but today he saw only the lovely child. He forgot even the boy in the intensity of this new and personal absorption.

"Did she live to grow up, I wonder?" he thought. "She should have made a remarkable, even a famous woman, with those eyes and that brow, but—could the spirit within that ethereal frame stand the enlightenments of maturity? Would not that mind—purged, perhaps, in a long probation from the dross of other existences—flee in disgust from the commonplace problems of a woman's life? Such perfect beings should die while they are still perfect. Still, it is possible that this little girl, whoever she was, was idealized by the artist, who painted into her his own dream of exquisite childhood."

Again he turned away impatiently. "I believe I am rather fond of children," he admitted. "I catch myself watching them on the street when they are pretty enough. Well, who does not like them?" he added, with some defiance.

He went back to his work; he was chiselling a story which was to be the foremost excuse of a magazine as yet unborn. At the end of half an hour he threw down his wondrous instrument—which looked not unlike an ordinary pen—and making no attempt to disobey the desire that possessed him, went back to the gallery. The dark splendid boy, the angelic little girl were all he saw—even of the several children in that roll-call of the past—and they seemed to look straight down his eyes into depths where the fragmentary ghosts of unrecorded ancestors gave faint musical response.

"The dead's kindly recognition of the dead," he thought. "But I wish these children were alive."

For a week he haunted the gallery, and the children haunted him. Then he became impatient and angry. "I am mooning like a barren woman," he exclaimed. "I must take the briefest way of getting those youngsters off my mind."

With the help of his secretary, he ransacked the library, and finally brought to light the gallery catalogue which had been named in the inventory. He discovered that his children were the Viscount Tancred and the Lady Blanche Mortlake, son and daughter of the second Earl of Teignmouth. Little wiser than before, he sat down at once and wrote to the present earl, asking for some account of the lives of the children. He awaited the answer with more restlessness than he usually permitted himself, and took long walks, ostentatiously avoiding the gallery.

"I believe those youngsters have obsessed me," he thought, more than once. "They certainly are beautiful enough, and the last time I looked at them in that waning light they were fairly alive. Would that they were, and scampering about this park."

Lord Teignmouth, who was intensely grateful to him, answered promptly.

"I am afraid," he wrote, "that I don't know much about my ancestors—those who didn't do something or other; but I have a vague remembrance of having been told by an aunt of mine, who lives on the family traditions—she isn't mar-ried—that the little chap was drowned in the river, and that the little girl died too —I mean when she was a little girl—wasted away, or something—I'm such a beastly idiot about expressing myself, that I wouldn't dare to write to you at all if you weren't really great. That is actually all I can tell you, and I am afraid the painter was their only biographer."

The author was gratified that the girl had died young, but grieved for the boy. Although he had avoided the gallery of late, his practised imagination had evoked from the throngs of history the high-handed and brilliant, surely adven-turous career of the third Earl of Teignmouth. He had pondered upon the deep delights of directing such a mind and character, and had caught himself envying the dust that was older still. When he read of the lad's early death, in spite of his regret that such promise should have come to naught, he admitted to a secret thrill of satisfaction that the boy had so soon ceased to belong to any one. Then he smiled with both sadness and humor.

"What an old fool I am!" he admitted. "I believe I not only wish those chil-dren were alive, but that they were my own."

The frank admission proved fatal. He made straight for the gallery. The boy, after the interval of separation, seemed more spiritedly alive than ever, the little girl to suggest, with her faint appealing smile, that she would like to be taken up and cuddled.

"I must try another way," he thought, desperately, after that long communion. "I must write them out of me."

He went back to the library and locked up the *tour de force* which had ceased to command his classic faculty. At once, he began to write the story of the brief lives of the children, much to the amazement of that faculty, which was little ac-customed to the simplicities. Nevertheless, before he had written three chapters, he knew that he was at work upon a masterpiece—and more: he was experienc-ing a pleasure so keen that once and again his hand trembled, and he saw the page through a mist. Although his characters had always been objective to him-self and his more patient readers, none knew better than he—a man of no delu-sions—that they were so remote and exclusive as barely to escape being mere mentalities; they were never the pulsing living creations of the more full-blooded genius. But he had been content to have it so. His creations might find and leave him cold, but he had known his highest satisfaction in chiselling the statuettes, extracting subtle and elevating harmonies, while combining words as no man of his tongue had combined them before.

But the children were not statuettes. He had loved and brooded over them long ere he had thought to tuck them into his pen, and on its first stroke they danced out alive. The old mansion echoed with their laughter, with their delight-ful and original pranks. Mr. Orth knew nothing of children, therefore all the pranks he invented were as original as his faculty. The little girl clung to his hand or knee as they both followed the adventurous course of their common idol, the boy. When Orth realized how alive they were, he opened each room of his home to them in turn, that evermore he might have sacred and poignant memories with all parts of the stately mansion where he must dwell alone to the end. He selected their bedrooms, and hovered over them—not through infantile disorders, which were beyond even his imagination—but through those painful intervals incident upon the enterprising spirit of the boy and the devoted obedience of the girl to fraternal command. He ignored the second Lord Teignmouth; he was himself their father, and he admired himself extravagantly for the first time; art had chastened him long since. Oddly enough, the children had no mother, not even the memory of one.

He wrote the book more slowly than was his wont, and spent delightful hours pondering upon the chapter of the morrow. He looked forward to the conclusion with a sort of terror, and made up his mind that when the inevitable last word was written he should start at once for Homburg. Incalculable times a day he went to the gallery, for he no longer had any desire to write the children out of his mind, and his eyes hungered for them. They were his now. It was with an effort that he sometimes humorously reminded himself that another man had fathered them, and that their little skeletons were under the choir of the chapel. Not even for peace of mind would he have descended into the vaults of the lords of Chillingsworth and looked upon the marble effigies of his children. Nevertheless, when in a superhumorous mood, he dwelt upon his high satisfaction in having been enabled by his great-aunt to purchase all that was left of them.

For two months he lived in his fool's paradise, and then he knew that the book must end. He nerved himself to nurse the little girl through her wasting illness, and when he clasped her hands, his own shook, his knees trembled. Desolation settled upon the house, and he wished he had left one corner of it to which he could retreat unhaunted by the child's presence. He took long tramps, avoiding the river with a sensation next to panic. It was two days before he got back to his table, and then he had made up his mind to let the boy live. To kill him off, too, was more than his augmented stock of human nature could endure. After all, the lad's death had been purely accidental, wanton. It was just that he should live—with one of the author's inimitable suggestions of future greatness; but, at the end, the parting was almost as bitter as the other. Orth knew then how men feel when their sons go forth to encounter the world and ask no more of the old companionship.

The author's boxes were packed. He sent the manuscript to his publisher an hour after it was finished—he could not have given it a final reading to have saved it from failure—directed his secretary to examine the proof under a microscope, and left the next morning for Homburg. There, in inmost circles, he forgot his children. He visited in several of the great houses of the Continent until November; then returned to London to find his book the literary topic of the day. His secretary handed him the reviews; and for once in a way he read the finalities of the nameless. He found himself hailed as a genius, and compared in astonished phrases to the prodigiously clever talent which the world for twenty years had isolated under the name of Ralph Orth. This pleased him, for every writer is human enough to wish to be hailed as a genius, and immediately. Many are, and many wait; it depends upon the fashion of the moment, and the needs and bias of those who write of writers. Orth had waited twenty years; but his past was bedecked with the headstones of geniuses long since forgotten. He was gratified to come thus publicly into his estate, but soon reminded himself that all the adulation of which a belated world was capable could not give him one thrill of the pleasure which the companionship of that book had given him, while creating. It was the keenest pleasure in his memory, and when a man is fifty and has written many books, that is saying a great deal.

He allowed what society was in town to lavish honors upon him for something over a month, then cancelled all his engagements and went down to Chillingsworth.

His estate was in Hertfordshire, that county of gentle hills and tangled lanes, of ancient oaks and wide wild heaths, of historic houses, and dark woods, and green fields innumerable—a Wordsworthian shire, steeped in the deepest peace of England. As Orth drove towards his own gates he had the typical English sunset to gaze upon, a red streak with a church spire against it. His woods were silent. In the fields, the cows stood as if conscious of their part. The ivy on his old gray towers had been young with his children.

He spent a haunted night, but the next day stranger happenings began.

II

He rose early, and went for one of his long walks. England seems to cry out to be walked upon, and Orth, like others of the transplanted, experienced to the full the country's gift of foot-restlessness and mental calm. Calm flees, however, when the ego is rampant, and today, as upon others too recent, Orth's soul was as restless as his feet. He had walked for two hours when he entered the wood of his neighbor's estate, a domain seldom honored by him, as it, too, had been bought by an American—a flighty hunting widow, who displeased the fastidious taste of the author. He heard children's voices, and turned with the quick prompting of retreat.

As he did so, he came face to face, on the narrow path, with a little girl. For the moment he was possessed by the most hideous sensation which can visit a man's being—abject terror. He believed that body and soul were disintegrating. The child before him was his child, the original of a portrait in which the artist, dead two centuries ago, had missed exact fidelity, after all. The difference, even his rolling vision took note, lay in the warm pure living whiteness and the deeper spiritual suggestion of the child in his path. Fortunately for his self-respect, the surrender lasted but a moment. The little girl spoke.

"You look real sick," she said. "Shall I lead you home?"

The voice was soft and sweet, but the intonation, the vernacular, were American, and not of the highest class. The shock was, if possible, more agonizing than the other, but this time Orth rose to the occasion.

"Who are you?" he demanded, with asperity. "What is your name? Where do you live?"

The child smiled, an angelic smile, although she was evidently amused. "I never had so many questions asked me all at once," she said. "But I don't mind, and I'm glad you're not sick. I'm Mrs. Jennie Root's little girl—my father's dead. My name is Blanche—you *are* sick! No?—and I live in Rome, New York State. We've come over here to visit pa's relations."

Orth took the child's hand in his. It was very warm and soft.

"Take me to your mother," he said, firmly; "now, at once. You can return and play afterwards. And as I wouldn't have you disappointed for the world, I'll send to town today for a beautiful doll."

The little girl, whose face had fallen, flashed her delight, but walked with great dignity beside him. He groaned in his depths as he saw they were pointing for the widow's house, but made up his mind that he would know the history of the child and of all her ancestors, if he had to sit down at table with his obnoxious neighbor. To his surprise, however, the child did not lead him into the park, but towards one of the old stone houses of the tenantry.

"Pa's great-great-great-grandfather lived there," she remarked, with all the American's pride of ancestry. Orth did not smile, however. Only the warm clasp of the hand in his, the soft thrilling voice of his still mysterious companion, prevented him from feeling as if moving through the mazes of one of his own famous ghost stories.

The child ushered him into the dining-room, where an old man was seated at the table reading his Bible. The room was at least eight hundred years old. The ceiling was supported by the trunk of a tree, black, and probably petrified. The windows had still their diamond panes, separated, no doubt, by the original lead. Beyond was a large kitchen in which were several women. The old man, who looked patriarchal enough to have laid the foundations of his dwelling, glanced up and regarded the visitor without hospitality. His expression softened as his eyes moved to the child.

"Who 'ave ye brought?" he asked. He removed his spectacles. "Ah!" He rose, and offered the author a chair. At the same moment, the women entered the room.

"Of course you've fallen in love with Blanche, sir," said one of them. "Everybody does."

"Yes, that is it. Quite so." Confusion still prevailing among his faculties, he clung to the naked truth. "This little girl has interested and startled me because she bears a precise resemblance to one of the portraits in Chillingsworth— painted about two hundred years ago. Such extraordinary likenesses do not occur without reason, as a rule, and, as I admired my portrait so deeply that I have written a story about it, you will not think it unnatural if I am more than curious to discover the reason for this resemblance. The little girl tells me that her ancestors lived in this very house, and as my little girl lived next door, so to speak, there undoubtedly is a natural reason for the resemblance."

His host closed the Bible, put his spectacles in his pocket, and hobbled out of the house.

"He'll never talk of family secrets," said an elderly woman, who introduced herself as the old man's daughter, and had placed bread and milk before the guest. "There are secrets in every family, and we have ours, but he'll never tell those old tales. All I can tell you is that an ancestor of little Blanche went to wreck and ruin because of some fine lady's doings, and killed himself. The story is that his boys turned out bad. One of them saw his crime, and never got over the shock; he was foolish like, after. The mother was a poor scared sort of creature, and hadn't much influence over the other boy. There seemed to be a blight on all the man's descendants, until one of them went to America. Since then, they haven't prospered, exactly, but they've done better, and they don't drink so heavy."

"They haven't done so well," remarked a worn patient-looking woman. Orth typed her as belonging to the small middle-class of an interior town of the eastern United States.

"You are not the child's mother?"

"Yes, sir. Everybody is surprised; you needn't apologize. She doesn't look like any of us, although her brothers and sisters are good enough for anybody to be proud of. But we all think she strayed in by mistake, for she looks like any lady's child, and, of course, we're only middle-class."

Orth gasped. It was the first time he had ever heard a native American use the term middle-class with a personal application. For the moment, he forgot the child. His analytical mind raked in the new specimen. He questioned, and learned that the woman's husband had kept a hat store in Rome, New York; that her boys were clerks, her girls in stores, or type-writing. They kept her and little Blanche—who had come after her other children were well grown—in comfort; and they were all very happy together. The boys broke out, occasionally; but, on the whole, were the best in the world, and her girls were worthy of far better than they had. All were robust, except Blanche. "She coming so late, when I was no longer young, makes her delicate," she remarked, with a slight blush, the signal of her chaste Americanism; "but I guess she'll get along all right. She couldn't have better care if she was a queen's child."

Orth, who had gratefully consumed the bread and milk, rose. "Is that really all you can tell me?" he asked.

"That's all," replied the daughter of the house. "And you couldn't pry open father's mouth."

Orth shook hands cordially with all of them, for he could be charming when he chose. He offered to escort the little girl back to her playmates in the wood, and she took prompt possession of his hand. As he was leaving, he turned suddenly to Mrs. Root. "Why did you call her Blanche?" he asked.

"She was so white and dainty, she just looked it."

Orth took the next train for London, and from Lord Teignmouth obtained the address of the aunt who lived on the family traditions, and a cordial note of introduction to her. He then spent an hour anticipating, in a toy shop, the whims and pleasures of a child—an incident of paternity which his book-children had not inspired. He bought the finest doll, piano, French dishes, cooking apparatus, and playhouse in the shop, and signed a check for thirty pounds with a sensation of positive rapture. Then he took the train for Lancashire, where the Lady Mildred Mortlake lived in another ancestral home.

Possibly there are few imaginative writers who have not a leaning, secret or avowed, to the occult. The creative gift is in very close relationship with the Great Force behind the universe; for aught we know, may be an atom thereof. It is not strange, therefore, that the lesser and closer of the unseen forces should send their vibrations to it occasionally; or, at all events, that the imagination should incline its ear to the most mysterious and picturesque of all beliefs. Orth frankly dallied with the old dogma. He formulated no personal faith of any sort, but his creative faculty, that ego within an ego, had made more than one excursion into the invisible and brought back literary treasure.

The Lady Mildred received with sweetness and warmth the generous contributor to the family sieve, and listened with fluttering interest to all he had not told the world—she had read the book—and to the strange, Americanized sequel.

"I am all at sea," concluded Orth. "What had my little girl to do with the tragedy? What relation was she to the lady who drove the young man to destruction—?"

"The closest," interrupted Lady Mildred. "She was herself!"

Orth stared at her. Again he had a confused sense of disintegration. Lady Mildred, gratified by the success of her bolt, proceeded less dramatically:

"Wally was up here just after I read your book, and I discovered he had given you the wrong history of the picture. Not that he knew it. It is a story we have left untold as often as possible, and I tell it to you only because you would probably become a monomaniac if I didn't. Blanche Mortlake—that Blanche—there had been several of her name, but there has not been one since—did not die in childhood, but lived to be twenty-four. She was an angelic child, but little angels sometimes grow up into very naughty girls. I believe she was delicate as a child, which probably gave her that spiritual look. Perhaps she was spoiled and flattered, until her poor little soul was stifled, which is likely. At all events, she was the coquette of her day—she seemed to care for nothing but breaking hearts; and she did not stop when she married, either. She hated her husband, and became reckless. She had no children. So far, the tale is not an uncommon one; but the worst, and what makes the ugliest stain in our annals, is to come.

"She was alone one summer at Chillingsworth—where she had taken temporary refuge from her husband—and she amused herself—some say, fell in love—with a young man of the yeomanry, a tenant of the next estate. His name was Root. He, so it comes down to us, was a magnificent specimen of his kind, and in those days the yeomanry gave us our great soldiers. His beauty of face was quite as remarkable as his physique; he led all the rural youth in sport, and was a bit above his class in every way. He had a wife in no way remarkable, and two little boys, but was always more with his friends than his family. Where he and Blanche Mortlake met I don't know—in the woods, probably, although it has been said that he had the run of the house. But, at all events, he was wild about her, and she pretended to be about him. Perhaps she was, for women have stooped before and since. Some women can be stormed by a fine man in any circumstances; but, although I am a woman of the world, and not easy to shock, there are some things I tolerate so hardly that it is all I can do to bring myself to believe in them; and stooping is one. Well, they were the scandal of the county for months, and then, either because she had tired of her new toy, or his grammar grated after the first glamour, or because she feared her husband, who was returning from the Continent, she broke off with him and returned to town. He followed her, and forced his way into her house. It is said she melted, but made him swear never to attempt to see her again. He returned to his home, and killed himself. A few months later she took her own life. That is all I know."

"It is quite enough for me," said Orth.

The next night, as his train travelled over the great wastes of Lancashire, a thousand chimneys were spouting forth columns of fire. Where the sky was not red it was black. The place looked like hell. Another time Orth's imagination would have gathered immediate inspiration from this wildest region of England. The fair and peaceful counties of the south had nothing to compare in infernal grandeur with these acres of flaming columns. The chimneys were invisible in the lower darkness of the night; the fires might have leaped straight from the angry caldron of the earth.

But Orth was in a subjective world, searching for all he had ever heard of occultism. He recalled that the sinful dead are doomed, according to this belief, to linger for vast reaches of time in that borderland which is close to earth, eventually sent back to work out their final salvation; that they work it out among the descendants of the people they have wronged; that suicide is held by the devotees of occultism to be a cardinal sin, abhorred and execrated.

Authors are far closer to the truths enfolded in mystery than ordinary people, because of that very audacity of imagination which irritates their plodding critics. As only those who dare to make mistakes succeed greatly, only those who shake free the wings of their imagination brush, once in a way, the secrets of the great pale world. If such writers go wrong, it is not for the mere brains to tell them so.

Upon Orth's return to Chillingsworth, he called at once upon the child, and found her happy among his gifts. She put her arms about his neck, and covered his serene unlined face with soft kisses. This completed the conquest. Orth from that moment adored her as a child, irrespective of the psychological problem.

Gradually he managed to monopolize her. From long walks it was but a step to take her home for luncheon. The hours of her visits lengthened. He had a room fitted up as a nursery and filled with the wonders of toyland. He took her to London to see the pantomimes; two days before Christmas, to buy presents for her relatives; and together they strung them upon the most wonderful Christmas-tree that the old hall of Chillingsworth had ever embraced. She had a donkey-cart, and a trained nurse, disguised as a maid, to wait upon her. Before a month had passed she was living in state at Chillingsworth and paying daily visits to her mother. Mrs. Root was deeply flattered, and apparently well content. Orth told her plainly that he should make the child independent, and educate her, meanwhile. Mrs. Root intended to spend six months in England, and Orth was in no hurry to alarm her by broaching his ultimate design.

He reformed Blanche's accent and vocabulary, and read to her out of books which would have addled the brains of most little maids of six; but she seemed to enjoy them, although she seldom made a comment. He was always ready to play games with her, but she was a gentle little thing, and, moreover, tired easily. She preferred to sit in the depths of a big chair, toasting her bare toes at the log-fire in the hall, while her friend read or talked to her. Although she was thoughtful, and, when left to herself, given to dreaming, his patient observation could detect nothing uncanny about her. Moreover, she had a quick sense of humor, she was easily amused, and could laugh as merrily as any child in the world. He was resigning all hope of further development on the shadowy side when one day he took her to the picture-gallery.

It was the first warm day of summer. The gallery was not heated, and he had not dared to take his frail visitor into its chilly spaces during the winter and spring. Although he had wished to see the effect of the picture on the child, he had shrunk from the bare possibility of the very developments the mental part of him craved; the other was warmed and satisfied for the first time, and held itself aloof from disturbance. But one day the sun streamed through the old windows, and, obeying a sudden impulse, he led Blanche to the gallery.

It was some time before he approached the child of his earlier love. Again he hesitated. He pointed out many other fine pictures, and Blanche smiled appreciatively at his remarks, that were wise in criticism and interesting in matter. He never knew just how much she understood, but the very fact that there were depths in the child beyond his probing riveted his chains.

Suddenly he wheeled about and waved his hand to her prototype. "What do you think of that?" he asked. "You remember, I told you of the likeness the day I met you."

She looked indifferently at the picture, but he noticed that her color changed oddly; its pure white tone gave place to an equally delicate gray.

"I have seen it before," she said. "I came in here one day to look at it. And I have been quite often since. You never forbade me," she added, looking at him appealingly, but dropping her eyes quickly. "And I like the little girl—and the boy—very much."

"Do you? Why?"

"I don't know"—a formula in which she had taken refuge before. Still her candid eyes were lowered; but she was quite calm. Orth, instead of questioning, merely fixed his eyes upon her, and waited. In a moment she stirred uneasily, but she did not laugh nervously, as another child would have done. He had never seen her self-possession ruffled, and he had begun to doubt he ever should. She was full of human warmth and affection. She seemed made for love, and every creature who came within her ken adored her, from the author himself down to the litter of puppies presented to her by the stable-boy a few weeks since; but her serenity would hardly be enhanced by death.

She raised her eyes finally, but not to his. She looked at the portrait.

"Did you know that there was another picture behind?" she asked.

"No," replied Orth, turning cold. "How did you know it?"

"One day I touched a spring in the frame, and this picture came forward. Shall I show you?"

"Yes!" And crossing curiosity and the involuntary shrinking from impending phenomena was a sensation of aesthetic disgust that *he* should be treated to a secret spring.

The little girl touched hers, and that other Blanche sprang aside so quickly that she might have been impelled by a sharp blow from behind. Orth narrowed his eyes and stared at what she revealed. He felt that his own Blanche was watching him, and set his features, although his breath was short.

There was the Lady Blanche Mortlake in the splendor of her young womanhood, beyond a doubt. Gone were all traces of her spiritual childhood, except, perhaps, in the shadows of the mouth; but more than fulfilled were the promises of her mind. Assuredly, the woman had been as brilliant and gifted as she had been restless and passionate. She wore her very pearls with arrogance, her very hands were tense with eager life, her whole being breathed mutiny.

Orth turned abruptly to Blanche, who had transferred her attention to the picture.

"What a tragedy is there!" he exclaimed, with a fierce attempt at lightness. "Think of a woman having all that pent up within her two centuries ago! And at the mercy of a stupid family, no doubt, and a still stupider husband. No wonder —Today, a woman like that might not be a model for all the virtues, but she certainly would use her gifts and become famous, the while living her life too fully to have any place in it for yeomen and such, or even for the trivial business of breaking hearts." He put his finger under Blanche's chin, and raised her face, but he could not compel her gaze. "You are the exact image of that little girl," he said, "except that you are even purer and finer. She had no chance, none whatever. You live in the woman's age. Your opportunities will be infinite. I shall see to it that they are. What you wish to be you shall be. There will be no pent-up energies here to burst out into disaster for yourself and others. You shall be trained to self-control—that is, if you ever develop self-will, dear child—every faculty shall be educated, every school of life you desire knowledge through shall be opened to you. You shall become that finest flower of civilization, a woman who knows how to use her independence."

She raised her eyes slowly, and gave him a look which stirred the roots of sensation—a long look of unspeakable melancholy. Her chest rose once; then she set her lips tightly, and dropped her eyes.

"What do you mean?" he cried, roughly, for his soul was chattering. "Is—it—do you—?" He dared not go too far, and concluded lamely, "You mean you fear that your mother will not give you to me when she goes—you have divined that I wish to adopt you? Answer me, will you?"

But she only lowered her head and turned away, and he, fearing to frighten or repel her, apologized for his abruptness, restored the outer picture to its place, and led her from the gallery.

He sent her at once to the nursery, and when she came down to luncheon and took her place at his right hand, she was as natural and childlike as ever. For some days he restrained his curiosity, but one evening, as they were sitting before the fire in the hall listening to the storm, and just after he had told her the story of the erl-king, he took her on his knee and asked her gently if she would not tell him what had been in her thoughts when he had drawn her brilliant future. Again her face turned gray, and she dropped her eyes.

"I cannot," she said. "I—perhaps—I don't know."

"Was it what I suggested?"

She shook her head, then looked at him with a shrinking appeal which forced him to drop the subject.

He went the next day alone to the gallery, and looked long at the portrait of the woman. She stirred no response in him. Nor could he feel that the woman of Blanche's future would stir the man in him. The paternal was all he had to give, but that was hers forever.

He went out into the park and found Blanche digging in her garden, very dirty and absorbed. The next afternoon, however, entering the hall noiselessly, he saw her sitting in her big chair, gazing out into nothing visible, her whole face settled in melancholy. He asked her if she were ill, and she recalled herself at once, but confessed to feeling tired. Soon after this he noticed that she lingered longer in the comfortable depths of her chair, and seldom went out, except with himself. She insisted that she was quite well, but after he had surprised her again looking as sad as if she had renounced every joy of childhood, he summoned from London a doctor renowned for his success with children.

The scientist questioned and examined her. When she had left the room he shrugged his shoulders.

"She might have been born with ten years of life in her, or she might grow up into a buxom woman," he said. "I confess I cannot tell. She appears to be sound enough, but I have no X-rays in my eyes, and for all I know she may be on the verge of decay. She certainly has the look of those who die young. I have never seen so spiritual a child. But I can put my finger on nothing. Keep her out-of-doors, don't give her sweets, and don't let her catch anything if you can help it."

Orth and the child spent the long warm days of summer under the trees of the park, or driving in the quiet lanes. Guests were unbidden, and his pen was idle. All that was human in him had gone out to Blanche. He loved her, and she was a perpetual delight to him. The rest of the world received the large measure of his indifference. There was no further change in her, and apprehension slept and let him sleep. He had persuaded Mrs. Root to remain in England for a year. He sent her theatre tickets every week, and placed a horse and phaeton at her disposal. She was enjoying herself and seeing less and less of Blanche. He took the child to Bournemouth for a fortnight, and again to Scotland, both of which outings benefited as much as they pleased her. She had begun to tyrannize over him amiably, and she carried herself quite royally. But she was always sweet and truthful, and these qualities, combined with that something in the depths of her mind which defied his explorations, held him captive. She was devoted to him, and cared for no other companion, although she was demonstrative to her mother when they met.

It was in the tenth month of this idyl of the lonely man and the lonely child that Mrs. Root flurriedly entered the library of Chillingsworth, where Orth happened to be alone.

"Oh, sir," she exclaimed, "I must go home. My daughter Grace writes me—she should have done it before—that the boys are not behaving as well as they should—she didn't tell me, as I was having such a good time she just hated to worry me—Heaven knows I've had enough worry—but now I must go—I just couldn't stay—boys are an awful responsibility—girls ain't a circumstance to them, although mine are a handful sometimes."

Orth had written about too many women to interrupt the flow. He let her talk until she paused to recuperate her forces. Then he said quietly:

"I am sorry this has come so suddenly, for it forces me to broach a subject at once which I would rather have postponed until the idea had taken possession of you by degrees—"

"I know what it is you want to say, sir," she broke in, "and I've reproached myself that I haven't warned you before, but I didn't like to be the one to speak first. You want Blanche—of course, I couldn't help seeing that; but I can't let her go, sir, indeed, I can't."

"Yes," he said, firmly, "I want to adopt Blanche, and I hardly think you can refuse, for you must know how greatly it will be to her advantage. She is a wonderful child; you have never been blind to that; she should have every opportunity, not only of money, but of association. If I adopt her legally, I shall, of course, make her my heir, and—there is no reason why she should not grow up as great a lady as any in England."

The poor woman turned white, and burst into tears. "I've sat up nights and nights, struggling," she said, when she could speak. "That, and missing her. I couldn't stand in her light, and I let her stay. I know I oughtn't to, now—I mean, stand in her light—but, sir, she is dearer than all the others put together."

"Then live here in England—at least, for some years longer. I will gladly relieve your children of your support, and you can see Blanche as often as you choose."

"I can't do that, sir. After all, she is only one, and there are six others. I can't desert them. They all need me, if only to keep them together—three girls unmarried and out in the world, and three boys just a little inclined to be wild. There is another point, sir—I don't exactly know how to say it."

"Well?" asked Orth, kindly. This American woman thought him the ideal gentleman, although the mistress of the estate on which she visited called him a boor and a snob.

"It is—well—you must know—you can imagine—that her brothers and sisters just worship Blanche. They save their dimes to buy her everything she wants —or used to want. Heaven knows what will satisfy her now, although I can't see that she's one bit spoiled. But she's just like a religion to them; they're not much on church. I'll tell you, sir, what I couldn't say to any one else, not even to these relations who've been so kind to me—but there's wildness, just a streak, in all my children, and I believe, I know, it's Blanche that keeps them straight. My girls get bitter, sometimes; work all the week and little fun, not caring for common men and no chance to marry gentlemen; and sometimes they break out and talk dreadful; then, when they're over it, they say they'll live for Blanche— they've said it over and over, and they mean it. Every sacrifice they've made for her—and they've made many—has done them good. It isn't that Blanche ever says a word of the preachy sort, or has anything of the Sunday-school child about her, or even tries to smooth them down when they're excited. It's just herself. The only thing she ever does is sometimes to draw herself up and look scornful, and that nearly kills them. Little as she is, they're crazy about having her respect. I've grown superstitious about her. Until she came I used to get frightened, terribly, sometimes, and I believe she came for that. So—you see! I know Blanche is too fine for us and ought to have the best; but, then, they are to be considered, too. They have their rights, and they've got much more good than bad in them. I don't know! I don't know! It's kept me awake many nights."

Orth rose abruptly. "Perhaps you will take some further time to think it over," he said. "You can stay a few weeks longer—the matter cannot be so pressing as that."

The woman rose. "I've thought this," she said; "let Blanche decide. I believe she knows more than any of us. I believe that whichever way she decided would be right. I won't say anything to her, so you won't think I'm working on her feelings; and I can trust you. But she'll know."

"Why do you think that?" asked Orth, sharply. "There is nothing uncanny about the child. She is not yet seven years old. Why should you place such a responsibility upon her?"

"Do you think she's like other children?"

"I know nothing of other children."

"I do, sir. I've raised six. And I've seen hundreds of others. I never was one to be a fool about my own, but Blanche isn't like any other child living—I'm certain of it."

"What *do* you think?"

And the woman answered, according to her lights: "I think she's an angel, and came to us because we needed her."

"And I think she is Blanche Mortlake working out the last of her salvation," thought the author; but he made no reply, and was alone in a moment.

It was several days before he spoke to Blanche, and then, one morning, when she was sitting on her mat on the lawn with the light full upon her, he told her abruptly that her mother must return home.

To his surprise, but unutterable delight, she burst into tears and flung herself into his arms.

"You need not leave me," he said, when he could find his own voice. "You can stay here always and be my little girl. It all rests with you."

"I can't stay," she sobbed. "I can't!"

"And that is what made you so sad once or twice?" he asked, with a double eagerness.

She made no reply.

"Oh!" he said, passionately, "give me your confidence, Blanche. You are the only breathing thing that I love."

"If I could I would," she said. "But I don't know—not quite."

"How much do you know?"

But she sobbed again and would not answer. He dared not risk too much. After all, the physical barrier between the past and the present was very young.

"Well, well, then, we will talk about the other matter. I will not pretend to disguise the fact that your mother is distressed at the idea of parting from you, and thinks it would be as sad for your brothers and sisters, whom she says you influence for their good. Do you think that you do?"

"Yes."

"How do you know this?"

"Do you know why you know everything?"

"No, my dear, and I have great respect for your instincts. But your sisters and brothers are now old enough to take care of themselves. They must be of poor stuff if they cannot live properly without the aid of a child. Moreover, they will be marrying soon. That will also mean that your mother will have many little grandchildren to console her for your loss. I will be the one bereft, if you leave me. I am the only one who really needs you. I don't say I will go to the bad, as you may have very foolishly persuaded yourself your family will do without you, but I trust to your instincts to make you realize how unhappy, how inconsolable I shall be. I shall be the loneliest man on earth!"

She rubbed her face deeper into his flannels, and tightened her embrace. "Can't you come, too?" she asked.

"No; you must live with me wholly or not at all. Your people are not my people, their ways are not my ways. We should not get along. And if you lived with me over there you might as well stay here, for your influence over them would be quite as removed. Moreover, if they are of the right stuff, the memory of you will be quite as potent for good as your actual presence."

"Not unless I died."

Again something within him trembled. "Do you believe you are going to die young?" he blurted out.

But she would not answer.

He entered the nursery abruptly the next day and found her packing her dolls. When she saw him, she sat down and began to weep hopelessly. He knew then that his fate was sealed. And when, a year later, he received her last little scrawl, he was almost glad that she went when she did.

THE HAUNTING OF WHITE GATES,
by G. M. Robins

I

In a Vault not far from this Tablet
Repose the mortal Remains of
two Protestant Gentlewomen,
Mrs. **ANNA** and Mrs. **CLARA KENTON**,of White Gates, in this Parish.
For many Years they led a Life of
Virtuous Retirement, united in Sisterly Affection.

They lived to mourn the loss of amiable Parents,
of three Brothers, and two Sisters,
Whose names are duly recorded on a
Tablet in the Chancel,
and after presenting to the World
a shining Example of Christian Patience,
Fortitude, and Resignation, quitted this Life
for a better, in sure and certain
Expectation of future Glory.

Mrs. **ANNA** deceased Dec. 8, 18—,

Mrs. **CLARA** surviving her beloved Sisteronly one month and three days.

This Monument is erected by the Piety
of their Nephew and sole Descendant,

JOSHUA KENYON HACKETT,

In Commemoration of Qualities in this life, Alas! too rare!

* * * *

The soft, dark eyes of a young girl in a shady black hat and feathers perused with languid interest the information recorded on the square, ugly marble tablet, mounted upon slate, which adorned the wall just above the mouldering oak pew labelled "White Gates." The piety of the sole descendant of the Kenyon family had limited itself to a very plain, not to say bald memorial of his maiden aunts. Not a carving, not a flourish, no death's-head, nor dove, nor weeping willow, testified to the depth of his affection.

Muriel North, whose imagination was keen, found herself taking a definite dislike to the idea of Mr. Joshua Hackett's personality, while she speculated as to the grammatical accuracy of his description of himself as the *descendant* of these irreproachable ladies.

The date of the tablet was twenty years earlier than the dull November Sunday upon which Miss North formed, for the first time, a part of the scanty con-

192

gregation in the ramshackle village church.

"Why doesn't he live at White Gates himself, instead of letting it?" she idly mused, as the Litany came to an end, and the aged clerk, pulling himself to his feet with an effort, gave out a hymn.

Terrible groans in the west gallery announced the preliminary spasms of the harmonium; and then the shrill quavering voices of the schoolchildren broke out into song.

The place, the ritual, were survivals such as are yet to be found in the remoter agricultural districts of England. Muriel had never been in such a church, never assisted at such a function before; and it added to a curious sense of remoteness from the world she knew, which had assailed her as soon as she arrived at White Gates yesterday.

The chambers which, in London, she shared with two girl friends, and the city office in which her daily lot was cast, with a typewriter, were things alien, far removed from the moaning, desolate wolds, the silent, depopulated waste which surrounded the village of Longstreet Parva.

Coming at last out of church, from the oppression of mustiness and dry-rot, and the suggestion of wet vaults and gaping coffins under the uneven stone slabs of the floor, there encompassed her a heaving expanse of country sown with the graves of a race that had ceased to be, before the armed tread of Caesar's legions shook the land. Even in summer a wind always moaned about the hill where the church stood; now, in the dreary November, the gusts whistled and screamed, and sprinkled Muriel's dainty hat and feathers with the first drops of the water they had drawn as they scudded over the cold bosom of the Atlantic.

Below her a creeping mist hid the village—rent here and there by a desultory wind that had no heart to persevere. The contorted chimneys of White Gates showed against black fir-trees.

"No wonder they let it cheap," reflected Muriel, as she descended the hill. The few worshippers dispersed in silence.

Nobody spoke to the girl. The natives of the Wolds are not a friendly race. Perhaps in their blood still lurks the memory of a time when they dwelt in pile-raised villages in the marshes to escape their foes.

"It may have been bearable in summer," Miss North was thinking, as she pushed open one of the white gates and walked among the yellow leaves to the unpretentious house door, "but in winter—rather they than I!"

"They" were Muriel's father and his second wife. Being very poor and in weak health, it was but natural that Major North should marry again; and still more natural that he should become the property of the most impecunious of the ladies who showed him special attention at the boarding-houses frequented by him and his daughters. Two of these daughters, Evie and Constance, married; Muriel, the youngest, chose to be independent. But the chronic ill-health of the major had now developed into positive disease; and Mrs. North had implored Muriel to come and relieve her for a time of a portion of her heavy nursing duties.

The firm in whose employ the girl worked well knew her value, and readily agreed to keep her post for her during her father's illness; so she repaired, as in duty bound, to the remote village where the couple resided in a house of some pretensions, which they had procured ridiculously cheap.

"Oh, he's better today," said Mrs. North, as she and her step-daughter sat down to their Sunday roast beef and apple tart. "I think your coming cheered him up. The church is rather depressing, isn't it?"

"The whole place seems to me a little depressing," said Muriel with a shiver, thinking of her terribly cold drive from the station the previous day, eleven miles across the wold in a cart. "I dare say it's better in summer."

"It's very pretty," said Mrs. North eagerly, "and such a nice house! Stables, you know, and the rent so low, owing to the distance from the railway; your father is able to keep his horse, his great pleasure. He was so counting upon the hunting this winter." She sighed regretfully.

"He may get some yet," said Muriel hopefully. "He is not nearly so ill as I expected to find him."

"He's been so well all the autumn, and taking such an interest in the place," regretted his wife. "Really it is so far beyond anything we thought our means would allow, and yet not a big house, not expensive to keep up. And the garden so well stocked! Mr. Hackett had it all attended to in spite of the house being empty for so long."

"Was the house long empty?"

"Oh, dear yes. People don't care for remote places nowadays. Every one is for railways and telephones and automobiles. The house-agent told us he had only to say, 'In the Cotswolds,' and intending tenants fled!"

"I wonder Mr. Hackett should let it, if it is his family place," mused Muriel. "One's own place never seems remote—at least, so I should have fancied."

"He did live here for a time," was the reply, "but I don't think he was popular in the neighbourhood; anyhow, he left, and all kinds of people have had it since. But it suits us admirably. Not a large neighbourhood, but everyone has called; your father's position, you know." And the poor soul, whose life's ambition had been fulfilled when she married an "army man," smiled in satisfaction.

Muriel would not for worlds have damped Agnes's simple pride, so she said nothing; but she felt that, personally, she did not consider the house comfortable.

It was not old enough to be picturesque or quaint. The rooms were square, with early Victorian sash windows. A horrible green iron verandah made dark the interior of the dining-and drawing-rooms. It was hard to believe that, at any season of the year, the Cotswolds would feel themselves in harmony with that flimsy erection.

* * * *

This girl was quick to feel local influences. Her own mother had been a Celt, pure-blooded, the descendant of a race of Irish kings; and Muriel had inherited, with her clear skin and wonderful eyes, the sensitive temperament which is so curiously alive to the pressure of the unseen through nature's visible order.

More than one curious experience, of a nature almost too elusive to be chronicled, had fallen to her lot; and once, as quite a small child, she had declined to sleep in a certain house where lodgings had been taken by the family, and had sobbed without reason, refusing to be left alone, and next day it was discovered that a corpse lay that night in the room next that in which the child slept.

Her thoughts, as that afternoon she sat by her father's bed, were of the two old Protestant gentlewomen whose bones had lain somewhere not far from the soles of her boots as she sat in the melancholy church that morning.

What kind of lives had they really led, concealed in that Virtuous Retirement which figured so well upon their tombstone? Had they quarrelled? Or had they clung together the closer, as Fate tore from them, one by one, all those who had formerly played and romped with them through the gardens of White Gates? Had their hearts broken, under the stroke of some forsaking lover, keener even than the death of brother or sister? Or had they been content to vegetate and make up their lives out of servants' shortcomings, fruit preserving, and the gossip of a scanty neighbourhood? Food for much conjecture floated in the brain of Muriel, sitting where they might have sat, beside a sickbed—perhaps the very same bed which had held the pining, dying limbs of many Kenyons. It was a mahogany four-poster, upholstered in gay new chintz, according to the taste of Mrs. North. Muriel wished it still wore the green damask hangings and woollen fringe which formed, she was certain, its original garment.

This room looked to the front of the house, and had a communicating dress-ing-room. The two best bedrooms were at the back, over the dining-and drawing-rooms, and these also had a communicating door. Muriel felt certain that it was these two latter rooms which had watched over the virgin slumbers of the Protes-tant gentlewomen.

On the other side of the landing was a bachelor's room, now assigned to her own use, as it was possible, even in this weather, to warm it with a fire. Here she felt certain that Joshua had slept, when he came on a visit to his maiden aunts.

It was a bitterly cold night. Muriel passed it on a sofa at the foot of her fa-ther's bed, Mrs North occupying the bachelor's room, that she might get a sound night's rest for the first time in many weeks.

All through the dark hours the girl's dreams were confused. The thoughts she had cherished during the gloomy day, of death and dissolution, in that house, that bed, filled her brain with curious imaginings. The light tread of watchers, the slow shuffling step of undertaker's men, the murmur of voices round a bed, and of deep groaning breaths, woke her again and again, but always to find the room quiet and her father sleeping peacefully. Yet, as soon as her eyes, still weary with her long cold journey of yesterday, closed again, the weird procession passed be-fore her brain, the ceaseless out-going of the dead from White Gates! The tolling of the bell in the crazy church tower smote her ear, every room contained a corpse, watched with candles. People moved to and fro, doing the last sad of-fices. The very smell of death was in her nostrils as she struggled awake again. The night-light burned beside her watch; it was half-past five.

Rising noiselessly she put fresh billets on the dying fire, and kindled it afresh, listened with satisfaction to the major's even breathing, and was just about to lie down again when she heard a door softly close.

In the absolute stillness the sound seemed all the more audible because it was manifestly made with extreme caution, by one not desiring to be heard.

"How vexing of Agnes to be awake and on the fidget when she might be hav-ing a good night," she thought; and, hurrying swiftly to the door, she peeped across the passage with the design of assuring her step-mother that all was well. A lamp was burning upon a small table on the landing, as the two women thought it quite possible that communication between them during the night might be necessary.

Just outside the door of the room in which Mrs. North was sleeping, and im-mediately opposite Muriel, a young woman stood, her hand still on the latch of the door. She was tall, fair, pale, with a look of great determination, and a rigid line of jaw which was especially noticeable. Her eyes gave the impression of being artificially darkened beneath, and her fair hair was elaborately puffed and waved.

As Muriel peeped out, she was in the act of turning quickly away from the door which she bad just closed; her face was hut for a moment visible, then she turned round and walked swiftly along the passage leading to the other end of the house, where the servants' rooms were.

This passage was considerably to the right of where Muriel stood, beyond the stair-head; and the woman was thus completely lost to view the moment she reached it.

Two things in her appearance struck the gazing girl as odd. One was the expression—as of a mind tensely nerved to some special effort—which appeared on her strong face—the thin lips compressed, the eyes narrowed; the other was a small point, but curious. As she turned her back, it could be seen that her conspicuous-looking hair was arranged in a large ball behind, and that this ball was encircled by a string of beads, apparently tied beneath with ribbon streamers, which hung down her dress to the waist.

Her presence mildly surprised Muriel. She knew that there was only one indoor servant—a capable, elderly person, whom she had already seen; but she had heard her step-mother mention a young dressmaker from the village, who had come in to help her with the nursing, and she took it for granted that this was she. Still, it was both annoying and puzzling to find her prowling about the passage at such an hour; and her appearance conveyed anything but a favourable impression.

Leaving the door at which she stood slightly ajar, she slipped noiselessly across the landing, turned the handle of Mrs. North's door, and peeped in.

The night-light showed the occupant of the bed motionless in the heavy sleep of the thoroughly tired woman.

On reflection it was perhaps natural to suppose that the dressmaker had come to ascertain that the worn-out watcher was really getting the rest she needed; but Muriel had not liked her expression, and returned to bed somewhat displeased at the incident.

"What is the name of the young woman, the dressmaker you told me of, who is sleeping in the house?" she asked when she and Agnes met down-stairs at breakfast, having left the patient comfortable after his good night.

"What, Miss Abel? But she is not sleeping in the house now; she went home yesterday morning."

"She was sleeping, or, I should say, walking about the house at half-past five this morning," replied Muriel. "I was making up the fire, and heard your door shut. I thought you were on the fidget, and looked out to see; and she was standing just outside your door listening. I thought it rather queer, for she was fully dressed; but I supposed she thought she might be wanted."

Mrs. North, who had listened with open mouth, turned extremely red.

"Oh," she said nervously, "then—then, I suppose Miss Abel came back. I did not know; now I think of it, I believe I remember her saying something of the kind. She has been very attentive, and probably thought, as you say, that I might want her."

196

"Very attentive; but she doesn't look like a country dressmaker, her dress did fit and hang so remarkably well."

"I will ask Caroline," murmured Agnes, and, taking up her keys, she hurriedly went out of the room, leaving Muriel rather mystified. Miss Abel's appearance had impressed her most disagreeably, and she wondered at Mrs. North's liking to have such a person about; but then Agnes was always odd—apt to foregather with the most unlikely people.

II

At about eleven o'clock that morning the doctor arrived: a hale, elderly man, who seemed imbued with the strong, robust air of the Cotswolds, and whose general appearance captivated Muriel. She soon found that he knew all there was to know of every house, church, family, estate, barrow, or cromlech in the district; and with the keenest interest she began to ply him with questions about the Kenyons and White Gates.

"I remember them well, of course," he said. "I knew the whole family from a boy, but I had been already ten years in practice here when Miss Anna was found dead in her bed."

"Was she found dead in her bed?" asked the girl, with breathless interest.

He nodded. "Sudden failure of the heart's action," he said. "But what caused it, my dear—what caused it is another matter, and did not come within the scope of my certificate."

"Then you knew what caused it?"

"Certainly not; nobody knew. I do not suppose anybody ever will."

"What kind of old ladies were they, really?" asked Muriel.

"They were about the most detestable people I ever was personally acquainted with," responded the doctor simply. The girl's eager eyes drew him on, and after a bit he resumed. "The whole family of Kenyon was as odious as it is possible for people to be who live within the narrowest borders of respectability. The father of these two old women had made money in Bristol, and built this house upon the site of a farm which had belonged to his family for generations. He was a morose, evil-tempered man, repulsively ugly; and his wife was worse. The children were most of them sickly in constitution, and all hideous. One of the seven was an idiot—they used to say she was ill-treated, and had been heard to scream o' nights; she died in her early teens. The eldest son also died young. The eldest daughter ran away with a gamekeeper named Hackett. She was the least ill-favoured of the lot, but as ill-conditioned as any, I should say. The second son went to London, and formed a *liaison* with some woman, so was not received at home. The others all died unmarried, fortunately for society; it was a stock one could not wish to see preserved. The Hacketts had one son; shortly after his birth they quarrelled—going, as I understand, to the length of fire-irons and carving-knives—and separated. I imagine he had thought he should get money out of the old man, and ill-treated his wife when he found he could not. She came back home with the child, who was brought up in this house; he was about thirty years old when his aunts died, and for nearly twenty years they had been his only living relations."

"Were they rich?"

"They were commonly reported to be so. All the neighbourhood knew them as misers. They lived almost without servants, for their temper was so bad that

197

nobody would stay with them. One woman, who had been their nurse when they were children, remained faithful; she survived them a few years. Except for her there was no indoor servant, save such women as could be persuaded to come in by the day from the village; and they kept no horses. But the curious thing, the thing that has never been explained, was—what became of their money?.... They left Hackett, their nephew, heir of all they possessed, on the sole condition of his erecting a suitable monument to their memory in the church. But when he came to examine their affairs, there was found to be just enough invested stock to bring in about £300 a year—a sum which would have more than covered their annual expenses for years past. Their lawyer—a solicitor of very good standing in Bristol—told Hackett that, ever since they had been mistress of their fortune they had been realizing large sums of money, whenever the condition of the market was advantageous. They had sold land, they had sold shares, they were constantly having big consignments of bank-notes sent down to them at White Gates. He had an idea that they turned this money into gems, or gold plate, or something concrete, which they could look at and treasure. There was something like forty thousand pounds to be accounted for. You look interested, Miss North."

"I should think so! Do go on! Who would have thought that Virtuous Retirement could he so sensational? Please—what happened?"

"Why, nothing. The money was not forthcoming, that was all."

"Surely the heir searched—"

"Searched? I should think so! After due investigation of the safe—"

"The safe! What safe?"

"Oh, haven't you seen the safe? The one built into the wall of Miss Anna's room!"

"Do show me," urged Muriel.

They were talking in the dressing-room adjoining the patient's room, and the doctor, laughing to find so charming a listener to his gossip, led the girl across the landing, and opened the door into one of the two large communicating bedrooms at the back of the house.

In the wall between these rooms was fixed the iron door of a safe: and there were signs that the wall had been artificially thickened for its reception, for the doorway leading from one room to the next was furnished with two doors, and between these was comfortable space for a person to stand.

"The will," said the doctor, "Particularly included the contents of the safe, in the list of the possessions to which Hackett was to succeed. But, when opened, it contained only a few trinkets which had belonged to the sisters, and a fair quantity of silver plate, the total value of the whole collection being perhaps fifty pounds. Everything was neatly arranged, packed, and labelled. There was no appearance of anything having been disturbed.

"Hackett had the place pretty well pulled down, the safe taken from the wall, the space between the walls examined, inch by inch, the interior and exterior measurements of every inch of space ascertained mathematically. Then the floor, both of this and the adjoining room, was taken up, bit by bit, the beams and rafters overhauled, every scrap of furniture taken to pieces, the frames of the beds, the very rungs of the chairs subjected to the minutest scrutiny, since miserly old maiden ladies have strange ideas of securing the safety of their treasures. Every scrap of writing existing in the house was carefully gone through to see if any clue could be found. The old servant, of whom I spoke—her name was Deborah Blaize—declared most positively that her mistresses had frequent dealings with diamond merchants, that she had actually seen a sapphire which they told her was worth two thousand pounds; and that she knew for a fact that these treasures were packed in the safe, the gems being secured inside a dispatch-box with a triple lock, of which Miss Anna always wore the three keys on a slender gold chain round her neck, under her clothes."

"Surely the diamond merchants could have been found," broke in Muriel.

"Hackett could not discover them. Neither were there any keys found round Miss Anna's neck at her death. There was no document found bearing the slightest reference to any such transactions. You see," said the doctor, "the difficulty was this. Nothing of the terms of the will, nor of the existence of the secret hoard, came to light till the death of Miss Clara, who was the elder, but much the weaker-minded of the couple. In fact, I never used to think her quite 'all there,' as the saying is; but she was left by her father absolute mistress of the house and the money, because he had a spite against Anna, the only one of the family who used to dare to browbeat him. Anna ruled the roast, however, but it was thought extremely likely that her desire to realize the property was the result of a fear that she might die first, and Clara be induced to alter her will, or otherwise imposed upon. Clara survived her sister more than a month, so there was no question of opening the will until her death. It is perfectly possible, indeed most likely, that she, who was the one to find her sister dead, would instantly remove from her neck the chain and keys that guarded the treasure, and hide or dispose of them as best occurred to her. The two seem to have acted completely in concert about most things, though it was always Anna who led, and Clara who followed."

"What did the elder, Miss Clara, die of?"

"Primarily, of the family scourge—consumption; they all had either weak hearts or weak lungs. The shock of her sister's death, and exposure to the cold in her night-dress, brought on a paralytic stroke, and bronchitis supervened."

"Exposure?" queried Muriel.

The doctor nodded, pointing to the adjoining room.

"She slept in there. The door of communication was always open, and they burned a light all night—their solitary extravagance. One terribly cold night—a bitter black frost and an icy wind, such as we revel in here in Longstreet—old Deborah was aroused by being violently shaken in her bed, and sitting up in the pitch darkness, cried aloud to know who was there, getting in reply only curious, inarticulate sounds. Wild with terror she struck a light, expecting to find herself in the clutches of a lunatic; but it was Miss Clara who stood there, speechless, and with her mouth drawn horribly to one side. She wore only her nightdress, and was as cold as ice. Huddling on some clothes, Deborah ran with her along the passage to Miss Anna's room; and there, in that place"—the doctor pointed —"though not in that bed you see before you—the old one was simply cut to bits afterwards to find treasure—there sat Miss Anna, still grim, erect, facing them— glaring at them in her frilled nightcap, with eyes astare, stone dead!"

Muriel gave an involuntary gasp. The horror of that situation, and of the two lonely old women in the grip of it, made her shudder.

"Was the nephew in the house?" she asked. "No, oh no, he was in Bristol."

"Were there any signs of confusion in the room?"

"None whatever, nothing to make any one fancy that any special thing had oc-curred in the night. Miss Clara could not speak, and the idea of writing does not seem to have occurred to her feeble brain in the first moments of horror, so no suspicion was aroused. On ascertaining that Miss Anna was dead, old Deborah tried to force the body into a recumbent position. But it was frozen stiff; and, at that culminating horror, the old woman told me that her nerve deserted her, and she rushed screaming from the room. Her first care was to bestow the shivering, trembling old Miss Clara in her own bed, then she rushed from the house, roused the gardener, who then lived in the cottage across the road, and sent him for me.

"When I got here Miss Clara was delirious—quite wandering in the head. She had still the use of her hands at that time, and had her brain been clear, she could have written us some account of what had passed in the dead hours of that night. She was icy cold when she aroused Deborah, we felt sure she must have been long out of bed. But she was never sensible again till very near death, when she evidently wished to say something, but by that time all power of communicating anything had left her. On the day of Miss Anna's death there was a severe snow-fall, I never remember a worse in all my winters on these wolds. It was some days before we could send a telegram to Hackett, two or three more before he could reach White Gates. When he came, it was evident that his surviving aunt was dying, and he could do nothing but wait for the end. He knew of the treasure in the safe, though I fancy he had no idea of its comprising the bulk of their for-tune; but nobody said a word that could lead him to suppose it had been tam-pered with. The shock of finding her sister dead was more than enough to ac-count for Miss Clara's seizure. It was not until her death that old Deborah first awoke his suspicions by saying that she could not find the triple keys, and at there dawned upon us all the extreme probability that something might have hap-pened on that night to cause the failure of heart which had killed Miss Anna.

"It was then too late to search for traces—the snow out of doors and house-cleaning within had eliminated all such; the only thing that could be called a clue at all, was the testimony of a charwoman to the effect that, some weeks after Miss Anna's death, she had found the remains of burnt paper in the stove in the hall, which was never by any chance lighted."

"You suppose, then, that the valuables really were in the safe, but were carried off by a thief?"

"Against that theory is the fact that no such person was ever seen or heard of; and that the safe was apparently quite undisturbed, being securely locked when Hackett first examined it, the key in its usual position in the old ladies' key-box. On the other hand, the triple keys, of whose existence old Deborah was positive, were gone. There was no sort of reason, either then or afterwards, to doubt old Deborah's complete fidelity. Most people inclined strongly to the idea that the jewels were concealed somewhere in the house, and this opinion grew when months went by and no sales of important gems could be discovered to have taken place, though Hackett had people on the watch everywhere. He and his wife came and lived here for a bit, for it turned out that he was married, had been secretly married for more than a year. He did nothing all the time but ransack the place, quite fruitlessly. Soon his wife died, in her first confinement. He said then that the house was no better than a grave, and he went back to Bristol with his little boy. Then there was a rush of people anxious to rent White Gates; everybody thought that they were sure to discover the treasure. But it has never been found; perhaps you may hit upon it, Miss North."

"Perhaps; I shall dream of it, at least," she laughed. "Why, here comes Agnes, wondering what on earth we are plotting here in the cold!"

Mrs. North looked surprised, and anything but pleased, to find them in this room.

"I am showing Miss North the safe," said Dr. Forrest. "You ought to get her to find the treasure for you, ma'am; she looks a bit of a *clairvoyante.*"

"Oh, I don't believe that nonsense about the treasure," said Mrs. North frigidly. "Muriel dear, go to your father, I want to speak to the doctor;" and, as the girl left the room, she heard her begin, urgently, "I do hope you have not—" The rest was lost in the shutting of the door; but as she moved away, she caught the doctor's hearty response—

"No, no, my dear madam, certainly not!"

That night Muriel slept soundly and undisturbed in the small front room, never moving until awakened at eight o'clock. The major also slept well, so well that on the morrow his wife declared that she did not want her "night off" again; but Muriel insisted.

"While I am here, I may as well do my share," she urged. Accordingly she slept again on the sofa, and slept well until two o'clock, when her father woke, and grew restless. As it soon appeared that he was not likely to sleep again, Muriel suggested reading aloud; he seemed pleased with the idea. She had a volume of Kipling with her, which she had left in the drawing-room, so, lighting a candle, she softly stole from the room to get it. There was, perhaps, a half-thought in her mind that Miss Abel might be prowling on the landing; but she was not there, nor in the house at all, as far as Muriel knew. She went with noiseless feet to the stair-head, the thoughts that occupied her being, as nearly as she could afterwards remember, as to which of the stories in *Life's Handicap* she should select to soothe the major.

She was half-way down; her candle flung long, wavering shadows across the hall; something light, something that moved, caught her eye in the darkness near the floor. She turned her light fully upon the place, grasping the balustrade, and with an undefined feeling of expectation in her heart she stood still.

There was a woman, stooping, crawling on her hands and knees, upon the black and red diamond tiles that paved the hall. The curiously fair hair, with its conspicuous arrangement, could only belong to Miss Abel. What in the world was she about? The momentary terror became merged in curiosity; she was picking up something from the floor.

Muriel saw the quick movement of her hand as it pounced on an apparently very small object, took it up, glanced at it, bestowed it in some receptacle. Then, as though attracted by a sound, the searcher raised her head; the attitude was that of listening—keen, furtive. Her glance travelled up to the landing above her; she remained a moment motionless, then, like one reassured, she stooped and again felt carefully about her, to and fro, shifted her position slightly, repeated the movement of picking up something. After a little she sat upon her heels, took the box, or what it was that she held, from the ground, and seemed to examine the contents; then bowed herself afresh, and again searched the floor.

Muriel watched like one petrified, a consideration creeping into her consciousness that made her shiver. Until the coming of her light Miss Abel must have been searching for those minute objects she had dropped *in the pitch dark.* The coming of the candle and the spectator made no effect upon her movements; she neither started nor turned her head.

An urgent need to make sure was the first imperative impulse. Leaning over the rail, and subduing her voice that the invalid above might not hear it, she spoke—

"Miss Abel, what are you doing?"

The quavering accents fell dead upon the silence, the crouching figure took no heed. It was just possible that she might be deaf; and Muriel, taking her courage in both hands, cleared the remaining stairs at a run, and, gaining the hail, circled round so as to face the intruder.

The woman with the sinister jaw and heavily shaded eyes now stood up. Her movements all suggested a fierce necessity for noiseless haste. She made a dart at the house door, and with one last backward gaze of alarmed watchfulness seemed to let herself out instantly. The sound of the cautious click of the latch as it closed behind her, echoed through the still house to its remotest end, like the widening of ripples on a pool when a stone is gently dropped. The first momentary impression of the listening girl was the conviction that her step-mother must he aroused by a noise so solitary, so incisive.

Shaking all over she approached the door. The chain was up, the bolts drawn. The whole figure of this woman was delusion then—stark and sheer delusion. Her knees knocked together, she almost lost grip on her own consciousness; only the thought of her father's critical state kept her from abject panic. For his sake she mastered fear, compelled her limbs to obey her will—to enter the drawing-room, take thence the book she needed, and to walk, not to stampede, up the stairs again.

The bedroom, with its fire and lamp, seemed the essence of comfort and friendliness. She crouched by the generous blaze, warming her chilled fingers, steadying her convulsive shaking.

"This *is* a cold house," she said to her father, forcing her wan lips to a smile. "Is Agnes awake?" asked the major.

She looked up quickly. "No! What makes you ask?"

"I thought I heard you speak to her; and I thought I heard her door close."

III

"Ah, Dr. Forrest," said Muriel, archly, next day, "I have made a discovery! Not treasure—no! But I have found out what Agnes was so anxious you should not tell me yesterday White Gates is haunted!"

"Ah!" said the doctor, retaining her hand that he might feel her pulse, "so you have been dreaming of horrors, have you? I'm not surprised; I should not have told you all that yarn."

"You cannot be responsible for my dreaming; you left out the essential person in the story; who is she?"

He looked genuinely puzzled. "Tell me what you saw, Miss North."

"Tell me first—you knew the house is haunted?"

"I have heard people say so."

"And tenants left, and the rent went down, in consequence?"

"Folks are superstitious."

"Now, doctor, what did people see, or fancy they saw?"

202

"'Pon my life, I hardly know. Noises, rustlings, doors opened, some one about the house at night—the usual thing. The manner of the old ladies' death was more than enough to give the place a bad name."

"But the person—the individual that walks and rustles, that opens or closes doors—who is she? No Kenyon, I am quite sure, from your description of the family. Do tell me how she comes into the story."

"My dear young lady, I have no notion what you are talking about; please explain." She told him, then, of the two appearances of the fair-haired woman—told him so simply and directly, that he could not help but feel in some sort impressed.

"The first time I saw her," she said, "nothing could have been more totally unexpected. Now, do tell me who she is!"

"But I have no idea who she is." He looked thoroughly puzzled. "The idea of her being Miss Abel is absurd, of course. The little dressmaker is a dark-haired hunchback."

"Is she not one of the treasure-hunters who occupied the house in such numbers for the last twenty years?"

"No, certainly not. There have been five sets of tenants, and I have known them all. You see, folks here are at my mercy completely. If they fall ill, they must either die or call me in." He laughed. "Nobody at all like the person you describe has ever, to my knowledge, set foot in the house. And yet, oddly enough, I do know of a person to whom your description applies in some curious points: the hair especially—the unusual style of it. She is a Mrs. Gibson, the wife of a farmer who lives at Cloverhead, nearly twelve miles from here, on the wolds. She isn't young now by any means; and she is no ghost—as much alive as you or I—and I would take my oath she never was at White Gates in her life."

"Who is she? A native of these parts?"

"A native of God knows where. She was a barmaid in Bristol, and turned the heads of half the young men in the place, in my day. I don't know why she married Gibson of Cloverhead; he's rich, of course; but she might have done better, I should think."

"I should like to see her," said Muriel suddenly. "Was she married at the time of Miss Kenyon's death?"

He pondered. "Was she? No. That spring, I think it was. Yes, of course, that spring. I remember it now, because Hackett's wife and she were confined much the same time. Her child—Mrs. Gibson's—was born prematurely, about six months after her marriage, and did not live. She was left without a baby, and poor little Hackett without a mother."

"I *should* like to see her," said Muriel.

"If it was summer-time, I'd drive you over," said the doctor. "But this time of year it's out of the question."

The human brain weaves threads faster than any spider; and Muriel's was busy indeed after the doctor left her.

Mrs. Gibson—ex-barmaid in Bristol—very attractive. Young Hackett was in business in Bristol.... Her sudden marriage, immediately after the announcement of his—for Dr. Forrest had said that the fact of his being married came as a surprise to the neighbourhood.... The birth of her child.... Oh, surely, surely there was some thread of connection here! Was it not possible that after all Mrs. Gibson, and she alone, knew the secret of the disappearance of the bulk of Joshua's fortune? The motive?—Revenge.

It all seemed to unroll itself before her like a drama. Young Hackett, the doctor said, knew of the secret hoard; if Muriel's suspicions hit the mark, the one person to whom he would be likely to mention such a thing would be the barmaid. How easy to gain access to a house inhabited solely by three women, all advanced in years! In so many empty rooms, how easy concealment to one who had learned the ways of the house from the nephew and heir of its owners!

And no possible clue to connect the woman and her secret could, as far as one saw, have been forthcoming, short of her own haunting presence there! In the very place!

Muriel was divided between a great desire to pass a night in the room containing the safe, and a great fear of doing so. The thought of Agnes was the casting vote; her distress and disapproval would be so great, and Muriel could think of no device by which permission to change her room could be obtained, without speaking of the second apparition which was so far, a secret between herself and the doctor. Neither he nor she had the least reason to suppose that Mrs. North had ever been disturbed nocturnally, though she knew the house was reputed haunted, and was most anxious that her step-daughter should be kept in ignorance.

Major North's turn for the better became so marked, that very soon there was no more night-nursing required. The weather changed, and grew soft and genial, which was very favourable to him.

Dr. Forrest and Muriel more than once discussed the fanciful theories which she had based upon his casual mention of Mrs. Gibson: the doctor inclining to the belief that, had she really abstracted the jewels, she would have taken herself off and lived in wealth upon the proceeds; Muriel strongly urging that such a theory was opposed to the motive of the theft, as she conceived it, and that Mrs. Gibson's possession of the treasures accounted entirely for the undoubted fact that no sale of them had been attempted.

One evening, unusually late, the doctor dropped in, finding the girl, as he expected, alone in the library.

"Miss Muriel," he said, "I'm sent for, to Cloverhead. Mrs. Gibson is ill. I shall start early tomorrow morning, and as it's so fine, if you like. I'll take you; but you must wrap up."

Mrs. North eagerly accepted the chance for Muriel to get a good long drive; and the following morning, amid the chill, still smiles of a sunny, quiet December day, they set off in the clog-cart over the wolds, to the remote farm known as Cloverhead.

A more desolate drive than that which lies between the two places could hardly be imagined. The wold, in its most treeless, exposed form, heaved in sullen savagery all about it. The square, grey, hard-looking house, with its ricks and outbuildings, stood out as a landmark for miles and miles.

A pebble-capped walk, edged with pointed cypress bushes, led from the gate to the house door; and, as the doctor's cart stopped, a tall woman, wrapped in a shawl, came slowly down the dark entrance passage, and paused on the threshold, holding her shawl over her mouth as though she feared the keen air.

"Good-morning, Mrs. Gibson," called the doctor. "May I bring in this young lady out of the cold?"

The woman nodded silently; and, with some tumult of nerves, Muriel found herself approaching, facing, actually speaking to—the spectre that haunted White Gates.

There was no doubt it was she. The face was gaunt, aged, haggard, the hard line of jaw was even more pronounced; but the sunken eyes were still accented with artificial pencilling, the abundant hair was not grey, and was still elaborately dressed. As she preceded them into her parlour, the grandeur of her carriage, and the fine lines of her build, showed traces of a personality not usual in farmers' wives.

"Sit down," she said abruptly to Muriel, pulling forward a solid old Chippendale chair.

"You must have had a chilly drive. There s a good fire. I'll go and have a chat with the doctor, and tell the girl to bring you some cake." Muriel sat down, bewildered. The corporeal touch of the woman's fingers upon her own jarred with probabilities. Many people in these days have heard of Phantasms of the living. Muriel never had. It seemed uncanny, even to the point of horror, that she should have spoken face to face with a woman whom she had recently seen vanish through barred doors.

The room was hot and stuffy, the big clock ticked lazily, the wood fire crackled. An armchair, such as one sees in old pictures, with very high back, drawn near the fire and piled with tumbled pillows, showed that Mrs. Gibson had been sitting here until the doctor's arrival. There was an inkstand on the table near, and a litter of papers and pens. It was a relief to see signs of habitation among the wool mats, albums, and wax-flower groups.

Muriel's eye rested idly on a folded vellum document that looked legal, thence it wandered to a packet of letters, carefully tied up. There was sealing-wax upon the package—newly spilt, as one could see by the adjacent candle and smell by the unmistakable fragrance. There was in the girl's mind no smallest intent to spy, but her eye fell on the inscription, written in a large, flowing hand.

"To be given, with all the other contents of this box, to Maurice Kenyon Hackett, on the death of his father. The contents to justify my entire course of conduct."

A hot flush mounted slowly to Muriel's brow. Springing up, she turned her back upon the table, and walked to the window. Her heart beat uncomfortably. She was ashamed, yet triumphant. She felt like a spy, yet she longed—oh, how ardently—to break the seal, and possess herself of the secret those letters hid!

After a long hesitation she took a sudden resolution—with a swift movement back to the table she turned the package over so that the wax lay uppermost, and the inscription was hidden from view. Then she went back to the window. A minute later a servant-girl brought in a tray of cake and currant wine; and, to beguile the time of waiting, Muriel presently ate some, for her long drive had made her hungry. More than an hour was she alone with that packet of mystery, before the doctor and his patient rejoined her.

The woman's face was more drawn, her eyes more sunken than ever. "I'm sorry you've had to wait so long," she said.

Muriel murmured a word of deprecation, and thanked her for her hospitality. Mrs. Gibson approached the table, against which she leaned, like one who needs support; the girl saw a sudden swift start, as her eye fell on the package; she saw her note that it lay so that no writing could be seen, saw her glance from it to her visitor, and push it away as though inadvertently, under some loose sheets of blotting-paper.

"We must get off, Miss Muriel, or we shall be benighted," said Dr. Forrest.

"Are you staying with the doctor?" asked Mrs. Gibson.

"Oh no, I am staying at White Gates," replied Muriel, smiling full into her eyes. There was not a flicker, not a ray of recognition, nor of consciousness.

"White Gates? Where's that?" said the slow, hard voice. For a moment Muriel held her breath; then she replied simply—"I think you know the house; I have seen you there."

The woman looked at her in blank, broad surprise. "I don't know what you mean," she said.

The doctor drew back, watching Muriel, his hand hiding his amused lips.

"I have been staying a month at White Gates, in Longstreet," said Muriel, "and I have twice seen you there; the second time, you were picking up those things that you dropped in the hall, you remember."

Still the woman faced her with unmoved muscles; but a red spot crept into her cheeks. "You make a mistake," she said coldly, "I have not been beyond the garden since October."

"Nevertheless, I have seen you at White Gates," steadily repeated the girl. "Next time, do you think you will know me?"

"I don't understand your insinuation," replied her antagonist, after a pause. "I have hardly been in Longstreet village in my life, and I do not know the house you allude to."

"Nor the owner?" softly suggested Muriel.

Nothing could daunt this woman; her lips tightened themselves like cords. "Nor its owner," she replied unflinchingly. Then she turned to the doctor.

"This young lady has—a bee in her bonnet."

"She seems to be asking queer questions," said Dr. Forrest, twinkling. "I will ask no more," said Muriel, her face relaxing into a smile. "I have found out all I wished to know. Good-bye, Mrs. Gibson; do speak to me next time we meet. We have been introduced now, you know."

"I am sure she must be cracked," was the only answer vouchsafed by the hostess. The woman had strung herself to a point, but, as they shook hands, Muriel felt that she was quivering, and her breath came in quick, short pants. They drove away in silence from the desolate place, and, standing at the door, she watched them go, her shawl over her mouth.

"She sent for rue chiefly to tell me that she has made me sole executor of her will," said the doctor, speaking at last. "I don't fancy she and Gibson get on over well. Poor soul! Her days are numbered, I hardly think she will get through the winter."

Mrs. Gibson never moved until the dog-cart dipped down out of sight, over the brow of the moor. Then she turned back to the sitting-room, and, closing the door, stood motionless in the middle of the room. After a silence, she flung her arms upwards and outwards, with a gesture that sent her shawl to the ground, and showed the attenuation of her finely-proportioned figure.

"My God!" she said aloud, "after twenty years!... My God! How long it takes to die!"

IV

Of course Muriel told Dr. Forrest of the inscription on the packet of letters, and he gave her in return the information that Maurice was certainly the name of Joshua Hackett's son. It began to seem to him almost probable that the wronged woman had chosen so to avenge herself and that the box to be given to the young man might actually prove to contain the missing fortune. Meanwhile, no action was possible; all was surmise; and Mrs. Gibson so near death that the doctor could not find it in his heart to break confidence, and confide his suspicions to Joshua Hackett.

For several days the image of the miserable woman, her desolate house, and her haggard eyes, so dwelt in Muriel's mind that she went about the house expecting to meet her at every corner. But as days went by, and all things at White Gates pursued their normal course, the strength of the impression began to fade. Several external circumstances combined in this direction. The weather continued "saft," the major liked her to exercise his horse, she was introduced by the doctor to the young people at the Manor House, and with them she rode and also played hockey, and had something of a good time. But soon after Christmas the weather became severe. A heavy snowfall, accompanied by a driving gale, plunged the Cotswolds into a mass of drifts; and White Gates, when communication with the outer world was practically severed, was a weird and gruesome abode.

On the third night of the siege Muriel went to bed wearied out. The weather made the major worse, the doctor could not be sent for, and she had sat up with him the previous night, scarcely sleeping at all. Tonight, no sooner was her head on the pillow than she was wrapped in the healthy slumber of a thoroughly tired girl.

How long she had been asleep she did not know; but suddenly she found herself wide awake, with an impression that some one had called her. She sat up; the expanse of snow without cast a reflection of light into the room, and, truth to tell, she expected to see Mrs. Gibson; but there was no one.

Concluding that Mrs. North might have called her, and her father be worse, she slipped out of bed, wrapped her warm gown about her, and opened the door. All was still. She crossed the passage, and from the bedroom came the sound of the major's snores. Reassured she turned to go back, when her attention was caught by a curious phenomenon.

Between her and the open door of her own room there hovered a pale, nebulous light. It was of no particular shape, and perhaps two feet in height, seeming not to touch the floor. As the girl's eyes fell upon it, it began to move, crossed the stair-head, and passed slowly on until it was in front of the door leading to the bedroom which contained the safe. Muriel caught her breath. Oh, if it went in there, she dared not, could not follow!

But it did go in—or rather, it vanished, seeming to pass through the wooden panels; and suddenly fear fell away from her like an external thing, and she knew that she must follow. As she turned the key, she heard the hall clock strike three, and thought, "I am not asleep; I hear the clock."

The waning moon was on this side of the house, and objects in the room could be clearly distinguished; but quite distinct from its pallid radiance was the blue, quivering mass of light near the safe. It grew in size and height until it was the shape and size of a human figure—and slowly, as it seemed to her, it took on the likeness of Mrs. Gibson.

The details of her appearance were not like the former ones; she now wore the shawl in which Muriel had seen her in the flesh; her eyes were fixed upon the girl with eagerness and recognition; after a moment, words were clearly audible.

"It was the keys—can you hear me? Do you hear me? You say you have seen me—hear me now. The keys, I left that out, and the doctor ought to know. I buried them in my baby's coffin; I shut them in his little dead hand, for it should all have been his; he was the heir. Three keys on a little chain…"

Muriel had no recollection of the end of the episode, nor of how she got back to bed. When she next awoke, in the broad sunshine, she was strongly inclined to consider the whole thing as a dream, in spite of the clock. However, as soon as she was up, she wrote down the curious words of the message. It was not until after the episode was finished that she heard that her step-mother, coming out of her room early that morning, had been startled to see the door of the spare room standing wide open.

Two days after, Dr. Forrest succeeded in braving the drifts, and arrived shortly after breakfast. The first thing he said to Muriel was—"Mrs. Gibson died the night before last, between two and three in the morning."

The girl turned very white.

"She came to me with a message," said she. "A very curious message about a key. I wonder if there is any sense in it."

"About a key!" cried the doctor. "If it should be the missing one! I was there when she died, but she had been unconscious for hours when I arrived, and she never spoke or moved. After it was over, her husband showed me her will. She had no property of any kind to bequeath; all I have to do, is to take in charge the box mentioned in the inscription you saw, and to hand it and its contents intact to Maurice. Hackett immediately on his father's death. There was no stipulation that we should not see what was inside, so I unlocked the box. It contains the letters you told me of, a quantity of babies' clothes, a wedding-ring, one or two photographs, and a dispatch-box, of an expensive kind, with a lock which is evidently a complicated one, and no key that we can find. I really feel pretty sure that it is *the* dispatch-box, and I must take legal advice about withholding it from Hackett, I think."

Muriel handed him the message, as she had written it. He was profoundly struck. At last—"They will have to open the vault to bury the mother," he said. "If Gibson will consent, we might at least test the truth of this."

* * * *

Within a fortnight it was known that Joshua Hackett, of White Gates, had died on the same night as that in which Josephine Gibson passed away. He was found dead in bed—heart failure—the Kenyon scourge, they said. Whether the vision that visited Muriel that night passed on to his bedside, who can say?

The dispatch-box was handed over at once, by the much relieved doctor, to Maurice, and with it the keys, taken from the hand of a dead baby, in Mr. Gibson's family vault.

The jewels were all there; with them was a sheaf of Bank of England notes, the total value of which was £25,000.

The packet of letters from Joshua to the woman whom he had deceived by a mock marriage, were a full explanation of her wrongs. There was no doubt that her intention in making the theft was to secure a part of Joshua's fortune for her unborn child. A written statement which accompanied the letters showed that she had no idea of the amount of the hoard beforehand; but dare not afterwards send any of it back. This statement also related in full how she had opened the box, when she got safely out of the room, to remove any papers which might supply a clue to the owner of the property; how, not clearly understanding how the intricate lock worked, she had failed to re-fasten it securely, and how, just as she was in the act of flight, the box flew open, and the jewels rolled about the hall, on which she gave up all for lost, till emboldened by the fact that, although she knew Miss Anna had been awakened by her theft of the keys from her neck, still there was no sign or sound of any one moving in the house. She then ventured to light her lantern, to pick up every single gem, and to make good her escape; and it was not until weeks after that she heard the horrible news that she had been the unintentional murderer of the old lady.

The above curious facts remain the solitary psychic experience in the life of Muriel North. No doubt the girl arrived at the house just when the thoughts of the woman, by reason of approaching death, were constantly and strongly turned upon the events immediately preceding her marriage: the period into which had been crowded all the tragedy and bitterness of her afterwards monotonous existence. The influence was potent, the girl's temperament of a quality to respond. She has been inclined to avoid haunted houses since. White Gates no longer belongs to this interesting category.

THE SHADOW ON THE BLIND,
by Mrs. Alfred (Louisa) Baldwin

Harbledon Hall had stood empty for seven years. For seven years no smoke had issued from its chimneys telling of the cheerful hearth within, no voice or laughter had been heard under its roof, no footstep coming or going across its threshold. A straggling growth of ivy and Virginia creeper that covered the walls and veiled the windows made the front of the house look as forlorn and neglected as the face of a sick man who has grown a ragged beard during a long illness. The window-sills were green with the drip of rain from the spouts choked with decaying leaves, and the brickwork was stained with dark patches of damp. The birds had built their nests undisturbed in every gable and projection of the roof, and in the wide chimneys, secure from danger of being smoked out of their comfortable quarters.

And within the house, though man had withdrawn his presence from it, other tenants were in possession. Rats and mice held revels in the empty rooms and passages, that resounded with the patter of their feet, the squeak of their voices, and the nibbling of their teeth. In the dead of night, bold as they had grown, they scared themselves by catching in wires that set bells ringing and echoing through the house, and an army of rats would rush helter-skelter down the great staircase, bounding over one another's backs in their panic, as we see them depicted in illustrations of the famous history of Whittington and his cat.

If desolation reigned in Harbledon Hall, its gardens were returning to a state of savage nature, and the rank growth of weeds choked and overtopped the flowers and shrubs. No seeds had been sown, no lawns mown, no hedges clipped or tree or bush pruned in seven long years, and the once orderly gardens had become a tangled thicket where the fairy prince might seek the sleeping beauty. A bramble had sprung up by the sundial, and clasping it in its thorny arms, threw its branches about it, effectually hiding it from the light of day. The stone basin of the disused fountain had become a nursery of young frogs, that hopped, swam, and croaked undisturbed, and nature was endeavouring to re-establish her sway where man had withdrawn his cultivating and restraining hand.

It was a radiant day in June. The hot sun poured down on the tangled overgrowth in the gardens of Harbledon Hall, the birds were in a perfect riot of song, and a south-west wind rocked them on the bough. Even the old forsaken house on such a day wore its least sombre aspect. One could imagine there had been happy household life within its walls, and it was possible to conceive that they might again resound to the laughter and voices of children at play.

Some such thought as this must have entered the mind of an elderly gentleman driving by in an open carriage, with his wife, a pale grey-haired lady, seated beside him. Mr. Stackpoole was a cheerful, energetic man of sixty years of age, of strong likes and dislikes and sudden impulses. As he caught sight of the wide front of Harbledon Hall with its red gables glowing in the sun, its confused mass of creepers almost hiding the lower storeys from view, he told the coachman to draw up at the iron gates at the entrance.

"This is a very picturesque house, my dear; I should like to have a look at it," he said to his wife; "it may be the kind of place we are in search of," and he alighted from the carriage as nimbly as a young man to read the notice painted on the weather-stained board fastened to the gates.:

For admission to view these premises,apply to Mr. Judd, sexton, by the church.

Mr. Stackpoole returned to the carriage and bade the coachman drive to the church, the tower of which they could see embowered among trees, apparently not more than a quarter of a mile distant. As they drove, he continued, "I like the look of the place very much. I am sure I could do something with it. I should just enjoy setting to work upon it to call order out of chaos, and in six months I would undertake to effect an entire transformation in the house and grounds and make it one of the prettiest places in the neighbourhood. What do you think, my dear? Hey?"

The frail-looking elderly lady thus addressed made but a faint rejoinder, and her husband's sanguine enthusiasm by no means communicated itself to her. Harbledon Hall was the sixth old house to which Mr. Stackpoole had taken a fancy in the last ten years, and fallen out of love with as quickly, after exercising his ingenuity in putting it in perfect order and living in it for a short time. It was his diversion, now that he had retired from business and had nothing particular to do, to hunt up old country houses, put them in thorough modern repair and working order, live in them just long enough to induce his wife to hope that he had pitched his tent finally, when the demon of unrest would break out in him once more, and he was off again on the old quest.

This hunting of houses, catching them, and then letting them go that he might pursue game of the same kind elsewhere was naturally more entertaining to Mr. Stackpoole than it could be to his wife and daughter. But the elder lady was patient and philosophic, and when her daughter said petulantly, "Oh, Mamma, what a shame it is that we have to be dragged about the country like this! We have not been a year in this lovely house, and Papa is tired of it already, and looking out again for some tumble-down old place to put that in good order, and leave it too, I suppose!" Mrs. Stackpoole would say, "Never mind, Ella. Papa must do as he thinks best. The excitement and interest he finds in frequently changing house are necessary to him now that he has done with business; and remember, my dear, he has no home occupations to pass the time like you and I have." But Ella Stackpoole was now married and settled in a home of her own, and the only other child, a son, was stationed with his regiment in Malta.

Therefore it was that when Mr. Stackpoole became suddenly interested in the appearance of Harbledon Hall his wife was unable to feel any enthusiasm on the subject. Their last home had been in Cornwall, where, after six months spent in its most westerly corner, Mr. Stackpoole discovered what everyone else had always known, that he was in a decidedly rainy part of England. He could scarcely have been more astonished at the quantity of rain that fell if it had been in Egypt, and he fled to London to make that his headquarters while he looked about for an old house to suit his fancy in the drier county of Surrey.

And on this bright June day, he and his wife were driving through the fair country house-hunting, and the more dilapidated a house looked, provided that his experienced eye saw capacities of improvement about it, the more attractive it appeared to Mr. Stackpoole, as affording wider scope for his particular form of genius. His was a costly hobby, and strangers reaped the benefit of his lavish outlay on houses he perfected, tired of, and left so soon.

* * * *

Mr. Judd, the sexton, was found without difficulty; for, indeed, he was a conspicuous object, sitting in a large armchair by his cottage door reading the newspaper, and taking an occasional sip from a glass of cold brandy-and-water that stood beside him on the window-sill. He was a person of dignity in the village, accustomed to waste his own time and that of others; but Mr. Stackpoole hurried him off to the carriage as soon as he had found the keys and compelled him to unwonted activity. "The garden be a wilderness, sir," said the old man, opening one of the great iron gates, "and it's four years since e'er an inquiry was made about the place."

"It wouldn't be to everyone's taste, you see; it'll need a considerable outlay upon it before it is fit for habitation," said Mr. Stackpoole complacently as he stooped to disentangle a briar from his wife's skirt. "Who were the last tenants, and how long had they lived here?" he said, turning to the old man and asking two questions at once.

"Sir Eoland Shawe and his family had it last, sir. They took the place on a twenty-one years' lease, and they left uncommon sudden when it had five years and more to run. There was a deal o' talk about what made 'em leave it that way," and Judd opened wide the front door as he spoke, and they entered a large, lofty hall, smelling mouldy as though there were vaults below.

"Folks did say there was reasons more 'n what they'd own up to, for a large fam'ly to turn out all of a sudden, as if they was running away from the plague," and the old sexton looked mysterious and as though he longed to be questioned. Mr. Stackpoole, however, was too much interested in pacing the length of the dining room to notice any hints he might throw out.

"My dear," he said to his wife, who was resting on the low window seat, "we will have the whole of this oak floor polished, and Turkish rugs laid down at intervals."

"That is just what we did in our house in Cumberland," said Mrs. Stackpoole gently, "and if you remember you were not pleased with it when it was done;" then, turning to the old man: "You were going to tell us why Sir Koland Shawe left so suddenly."

"Forbid, ma'am, that I should say definite why he left, not knowing for certain," said Mr. Judd, swelling with importance as he spoke. "I never believe more 'n 'alf o' what I hear, and puts no faith in tales, whether master's or man's. But by what I can make out and old Jimmy Judd can see through a stone wall as fer as most folks I should say as ghosts was at the bottom of the whole kick-up."

Mrs. Stackpoole smiled at the old man's mode of expressing himself, and then looked anxiously towards her husband, who laughed heartily, and they left the dining room for the upstairs regions, which he was impatient to explore.

"They fled before ghosts, did they?" said Mr. Stackpoole, still laughing at the idea. "If the house is supposed to be haunted I should like it all the better for its reputation," and he swung open the door of a large, low room, with a deep projecting chimney-place and wide window letting in a flood of sunshine.

"This is certainly a very cheerful aspect," said his wife, stepping to the window and looking out upon the wild garden enclosed by ragged yew hedges; "there is nothing ghostly about this room, at all events!"

"Pooh! Ghosts indeed! those who believe in them deserve to see them," said Mr. Stackpoole contemptuously. "If we take the house this shall be your morning-room; you'll get plenty of sunshine, which is a great thing for you; and if I like the room under it I will have it done up for a business-room for myself." And they wandered from cellar to attic of the big house, Mr. St ackpoole delighted with the possibilities of the place, and noting in his pocket-book the dimensions of the chief rooms and of the entrance hall.

"At all events I shall inquire on what terms the house is to be let," he said, after spending two hours in energetically inspecting the premises, and as he slipped five shillings into Mr. Judd's expectant palm, "By the way, I have not asked who is the landlord?"

"The landlord, sir, be a many and not one," and the old man named a well-known city company to which the property belonged.

"I've rented from landlords, and landladies, and trustees, but never yet from a company. It's all one to me, and I shall see their agent in town tomorrow." Then Mr. Stackpoole took a farewell look at the room on the ground floor, immediately under the cheerful room at the head of the stairs that he had assigned to his wife's prospective use, and decided that it was exactly adapted to his requirements, after which they threaded their way back to the gates through the neglected maze of the garden.

"And how do you like the look of Harbledon Hall?" he asked his wife as they drove away; "what do you think of the old place?"

"I confess that I was not very favourably impressed with it, though it is a handsome, well-built house, and might be made very comfortable, no doubt. But it struck me with a kind of chill."

"So would any place, my dear, that had been shut up for seven years. I feel it in my back now; I wish it may not mean an attack of lumbago for me." Mrs. Stackpoole smiled at the literal interpretation of her words.

"I don't mean that kind of chill, but a sort of depressed, foreboding feeling that I have never had before in any of the houses you and I have been over together, and their name is legion."

"Why, Anna, you don't mean to say that the tedious old sexton has frightened you with his gossip! It was merely some nonsense or other he had made up to increase his importance. If I take the place I shall put an army of workmen in an army of workmen in a week from now, and when next you see it, with good fires drying the rooms, windows bright and clean, and paperers and painters busy upon it, it will look very different, I can assure you. Any house that has been uninhabited as long as Harbledon Hall wears a forlorn look, but for all that I see the possibilities of it, and I could make it the prettiest place we have lived in yet." And Mrs. Stackpoole felt certain that her husband would take the old house.

* * * *

The following day, when Mr. Stackpoole saw the company's agent, he was surprised at the very moderate rent asked for the house. Whether he wished to take it on lease or as a yearly tenant, the sum demanded was small enough to arouse suspicion in the most unwary.

"Why do you ask such a low rent for a fine old place likethat?" he asked.

"It is so much out of repair from standing empty so long, that I suppose the company is willing to submit to a certain loss, for the sake of having it inhabited again."

"But with such a temptingly low rent, how is it that it has not been taken long ago?"

"There have been any number of applications for it."

"Indeed! The old fellow in charge of the keys who showed me over the place yesterday said that no one had inquired about it for four years." A peculiar expression passed over the agent's face, but it was not one of surprise.

"He said so, did he? I've had plenty of inquiries."

"He certainly said so. He was a talkative old man, and anxious to impress us with the idea that Sir Eoland Shawe left Harbledon Hall suddenly, some considerable time before his lease was up, in consequence of an absurd notion that the house was haunted. Now, personally I care nothing about it, but my wife is sometimes nervous, and I thought I would ask you if you know anything of any unusual circumstances connected with his leaving so abruptly."

"Judd is a chattering old fool! Did he tell you anything definite about it himself?" asked the agent.

"Nothing whatever, but he said some nonsense about ghosts driving them away from the place."

"Of course there was an absurd story that got about at the time! It was some hocus-pocus with a magic-lantern, I believe, got up by the young fellows to frighten the servants, with pictures of a skeleton on a sheet hung up somewhere or other. The whole thing was a stupid practical joke, only too successful, for the scare spread to the ladies of the house, and of course Sir Eoland had to leave; they made the place too hot for him," and the agent laughed uproariously. "I remember all about it now you come to ask me. The young Shawes got up the panic for their own purposes. They found the country too slow for them, they wanted to live in London, so with the simple apparatus of a magic-lantern and a sheet or blind they frightened the family back into town and got what they wanted. Naturally Sir Eoland used not to speak of it when he found it out, for no one is proud of having been made a fool of. And now, my dear sir," he said, assuming an air of great candour, "you know as much about this childish folly as I do myself. It has been magnified into something wonderful till we've had that tempting property on our hands all these years in consequence."

Mr. Stackpoole was pleased and amused with the agent's frank explanation of the basis of Mr. Judd's mysterious allusions and he and his wife laughed at it together over their evening dinner. Mrs. Stackpoole was now willing that her husband should take Harbledon Hall, which he did as a yearly tenant, with the right of taking the property on a lease, if at the end of three years he felt inclined to prolong his stay.

Then began all the delightful bustle that Mr. Stackpoole's soul loved—the drying, warming, painting, lighting, decorating, and furnishing of the house; the taming and reclaiming of the garden; the stubbing up of old lawns and laying down of new turf; the cleaning and regravelling of weed-grown paths. Such an army of workmen was engaged that Mr. Stackpoole calculated that in less than five months the house would be ready to go into, and the gardens be all clean, smooth, and bare in their winter tidiness. "It must be finished by the middle of

December," he said, "that I may keep Christmas here with my family; and if every man has done his work well, and is out of the house by the twelfth of December, I will give each one a bonus on his wages, and a Christmas supper to you all."

No wonder that the workmen caught something of Mr. Stackpoole's enthusiasm, and that every time he brought his wife to see what was going on she was delighted with the progress made. All their friends were informed of the lucky find of the beautiful old house in Surrey, and invitations were issued long before for a series of entertainments, dances, and private theatricals that they intended to give at Harbledon Hall in the following January, when their daughter, Mrs. Beaumont, and her husband would be staying with them.

Shortly before Mr. and Mrs. Stackpoole removed to Harbledon Hall they were dining out one evening, and after the ladies had left the room and the gentlemen had rearranged their chairs comfortably and were seated at their wine, Mr. Stackpoole began on his favourite theme, the furnishing and repairing of the old house in Surrey. As most of those present had frequently heard him on the subject before, he was not much heeded, and prosed on without interruption till a tall, bald-headed gentleman opposite him caught the words Harbledon Hall and became an attentive listener.

"Harbledon Hall, did you say? Do you mean the old gabled, red-brick house three miles from Mendleton in Surrey? I hope no friend of yours is thinking of taking it."

Mr. Stackpoole smiled. "Not exactly a friend of mine, though probably I know him better than anyone else. I have taken Harbledon Hall myself and intend moving into it next December."

"The deuce you do!" said the bald-headed gentleman, setting down his glass.

"I don't know why it should surprise you," said Mr. Stackpoole.

"Surprise me? Certainly not. Only I thought that the house was empty and likely to remain so."

"Surely it has stood empty long enough for seven years. It requires an immense deal doing to it, of course, but I took a fancy to the place, and am putting it into thorough repair, introducing the electric light among other modern improvements; in fact, I am sparing no expense. Do you know anything about Harbledon Hall?"

"I used to do. Sir Eoland Shawe, the last tenant, is my brother," and the bald-headed gentleman spoke in a dry and uncommunicative manner. But a hint was not enough for Mr. Stackpoole.

"Then you are the very person to tell me about an absurd story I have heard it had something to do with a magic-lantern, I believe, some kind of scare the young people got up to pretend there were bogies in the house, and frighten their parents back to town, where they preferred to live. You see, I've heard all about it, and I only want it corroborating by a member of the family," and he laughed heartily, as though it were the best joke in the world. But the gentleman opposite him grew grave to severity, and said, "I am unable to understand your allusion to a magic-lantern performance which is supposed to have tried my brother's nerves, and absurd is the last word applicable to the circumstances under which Sir Roland was compelled to leave Harbledon Hall."

"Then I must have been misinformed in the matter," replied the undaunted Mr. Stackpoole, whose curiosity was now thoroughly aroused. "As I am about to live in the house, will you not tell me the real circumstances, that I may be able to contradict the foolish stories that one hears?"

"Why should it be necessary for you to contradict gossip on the subject? Sir Roland never mentions it. It is possible that some time you may learn for yourself why my brother left the house; then I think you will be satisfied that he acted wisely, and if not, I should be sorry to prejudice you against Harbledon Hall." And the gentlemen rose to join the ladies, and Mr. Stackpoole remained in a state of mystification., Evidently something had happened to drive Sir Roland Shawe and his family from Harbledon Hall with which neither old Judd nor the agent was acauainted. What could it be? For himself, so long as it was neither rats nor drains, he did not care; but with his wife it was different. If she had the least inkling that there was anything uncanny about the house, she would refuse to go into it at the eleventh hour, or, if she went, would make a point of seeing a ghost the very first dark night.

But she must hear no silly talk about it. Any ghosts that former inhabitants of the Hall had imagined they saw was when they went about the house starting at their own shadows by the dim light of oil-lamps. The electric light would put all that to rights. It was the best cure for such preposterous folly, and in its illumination Mr. Stackpoole felt that he should be more than a match for all the powers of darkness.

But shortly after meeting Sir Roland Shawe's brother an odd coincidence happened that drew his attention again to the subject of their conversation. Mrs. Stackpoole had written to her son at Malta telling him that his father had taken an old house in Surrey with which he had fallen in love, how beautifully he was fitting it up, that they expected to keep Christmas in it, and that it was at Harbledon Hall that they hoped to welcome him on his return to England. In reply Jack wrote, "So my father is again on the move. Well, this time I am glad he is taking you to a thoroughly accessible place, and not to Cornwall or Cumberland. But is the old house he has taken a fancy to not far from Mendleton? I suppose there can't be two Harbledon Halls in the county, but it is odd if it is the house of that name I have lately heard something about. There was a young civilian out here for his health he has gone to Egypt now and he told me that his uncle, a Sir Roland Smith, or some such name, had been fairly driven out of an old house in Surrey by ghosts. I'm sure he called it Harbledon Hall, and he said that his uncle was not in the least a nervous man, but it was more than he could stand, and he had to leave. I wish now that I had asked him all about it, but he was such a dull chap nothing he said interested me, so I lost the chance of learning particulars. Don't you be timid, dear mother. Let me tackle the bogies when I come home; I should enjoy nothing better."

Mrs. Stackpoole did not like this at all. It produced an eerie and creepy sensation, and her husband took care not to increase her discomfort by telling her of his conversation with Mr. Shawe.

"It is odd, my dear, very odd," he said in his most cheerful tones, "and we are obliged to confess that, somehow or other, someone or other received some sort of a fright at Harbledon Hall. Nothing can be more vague, and yet that is all that is known about it. A pity the whole silly business was not inquired into on the spot, for of course it would admit of a perfectly simple solution. Very likely one of the maids had supped rather more heavily than usual on cold pork, and in a paroxysm of indigestion walked in her sleep; someone saw her in her white nightgown, took her for a ghost, screamed, and got up a scare for it is always easier to cry out than to investigate. And there you have the whole history of a ghost story in a nutshell, my dear in a nutshell."

The workmen were punctually out of Harbledon Hall on the day agreed upon, and as punctually received their pay and their Christmas supper, and the house was ready for the reception of the new tenant, with the good wishes of all who had helped to prepare it for him. Mr. Stackpoole arranged that they should arrive after dark at Harbledon Hall, that he might surprise his wife with the electric light in every room and passage, and introduce her to her new home under its most cheerful and attractive aspect.

As they approached the house both Mrs. Stackpoole and her daughter exclaimed with delight, and Ella said it was too pretty to be real, it was like something on the stage. From every window of the house, from the basement to the garret, streamed the pure radiance of the electric light, undimmed by curtain or blind, sending shafts of light far into the surrounding darkness. From the porch the white light illumined the drive like a cold sunshine, and showed every pebble on the ground and every twig on the bare boughs.

"There, my dears," said Mr. Stackpoole triumphantly, as he led his wife and daughter into the brilliant hall; "this is how modern science drives away foolish fears of darkness by turning night into day. No one could be nervous or afraid of ghosts in a house lighted like this."

"No, indeed the thing would be impossible," replied Mrs. Stackpoole, her daughter, and son-in-law in confident chorus.

Christmas was kept with much festivity at Harbledon Hall, and it was impossible to say who was most delighted with the house the host or hostess, or the guests under its hospitable roof. Each was charmed with his own room, but Mrs. Stackpoole's morning-room was the general favourite, and afternoon-tea was frequently taken there in preference to the more stately drawing room. The grandchildren played in the empty rooms upstairs on rainy days, and every evening watched the miracle of lighting the house with the electric light with breathless interest. They regarded Grandpapa as a light-producing wizard, so that something of awe was mingled with their wildest frolics, and they did not dare to open the door of his own particular room, which was respectfully called the study, though its principal use was to smoke in, or to take a quiet nap before dinner.

It was the end of January, and the Stackpooles were daily congratulating themselves on their good fortune in meeting with a house so perfectly suited to all their requirements, when they wound up their New Year's festivities with a fancy ball. Several young people were staying in the house for the occasion who were to depart the day after the ball, leaving their host and hostess alone for the first time in their new house. Numbers of guests were coming from a distance, many of whom had accepted the invitation out of curiosity, as a dance afforded a good opportunity of spending a night under cheerful auspices in a house with the reputation of being haunted.

All their entertainments so far had been successful, but the last was to be the best, and the host and hostess threw their whole souls into the preparations to ensure its complete success. The room was charming, the floor perfect, the band that came from town the most renowned of the season. The costumes to be worn were of no special time or country, and the Stackpooles themselves set an example, of reckless catholicity in the matter, the hostess being dressed as Queen Elizabeth, and her husband as an Admiral of the Fleet of today, while Mrs. and Mr. Beaumont figured respectively as a Japanese lady and Spanish matador. By the time that the guests had arrived, clad in the garb of all ages and countries, the ball-room appeared to contain such a motley throng as the Day of Judgment alone could bring together. Here an ancient Greek danced with a Swedish peasant, and the Black Prince with a female captain of the Salvation Army, and there a clown and a nun waltzed gaily past Mahomet and a ballet-girl.

The electric light was a greater novelty then than it is now, and the guests were loud in their admiration of the fairy-palace appearance of the house as they approached, and of its brilliance within. Mr. Stackpoole was as delighted as a child with a new toy, and led his friends about showing them how by merely turning a button on the wall he could plunge a room in darkness or flood it with radiant light.

Dancing was kept up with great spirit till the small hours, and as the clock in the hall chimed a quarter-past three the old house resounded to the half sad and wholly romantic strains of a waltz by Waldteufel. The guests who came from a distance had begun to depart, and Mr. Beaumont stood in the porch, laughingly seeing Lady Jane Grey and Flora Macdonald into their carriage. Just then a maid gave a message to one of the footmen to Mrs. Beaumont, who sat fanning herself near the door of the ball-room. "If you please, ma'am, nurse says Master Harry is awake and crying with the music, and says he won't go to sleep till he sees you, ma'am."

"Tell nurse I will come directly," and, excusing herself to the lady who sat next to her, she slipped out of the room. In the hall she met her father as he was entering his study.

"I'm going to put this miserable encumbrance by," he said, smiling and nourishing the Admiral's cocked hat, which he had gallantly carried the whole evening to his great inconvenience.

"And I am on my way to the nursery to see little Harry," and Mrs. Beaumont ran upstairs, softly singing to the sweet music that floated from the ball-room. Mr. Stackpoole laid his hat on the table, and looked at the clock on the mantelpiece. "A quarter-past three! I'm tired, and the young people ought to be. Heighho! I'd rather give ten dinners than one dance," and he yawned profoundly, sank into a low chair by the fire, stretched his legs out before him, and closed his eyes. Sleep fell upon him instantly, and for several minutes he was lost in its depths, light and sound had ceased to exist for him, his brain was steeped in silent darkness.

Mr. Beaumont still stood in the porch; the servants had returned to the house, and he was alone. It was a mild winter's night. He flung a cloak over his matador's costume and stepped into the open air. "I sha'n't be missed for five minutes," he said to himself, "while I smoke a cigarette," and he walked briskly along a broad path some thirty yards from the house, from which he had a perfect view of the front of Harbledon Hall. And very pretty its cheerful brightness looked against the dark background of star-set sky. Brilliant rays of light shot from the undraped windows, and those that had the blinds drawn down showed the outline of objects in the room thrown upon them in shadow, as clearly as from a magic-lantern.

Involuntarily he raised his eyes to the window of Mrs. Stackpoole's sitting-room, and stood rooted to the spot. Two figures as clearly defined as silhouettes were visible on the pure square of the blind the shadows of an old man and a young man struggling together. From the shape of the heads Greorge Beaumont saw that they wore tie wigs, and there was the clearly cut shadow of the ruffles at the wrists, and the younger and taller man wore a large Steinkirk with richly-laced ends round his neck. At first he thought that they were guests dressed in the costume of the early Georgian period, though how they had gone upstairs into that room, or why there was a deadly struggle between them, he did not know. But wonder and speculation was swallowed up in terrified interest as he watched the course of the brief conflict. The elder and shorter man, who stooped considerably, appeared to be unarmed, and seized the younger man by the throat, when he shook himself free, stepped quickly back, drew his sword, and, plung-ing forward on his right foot, ran his opponent through the body. He staggered backward and fell out of sight below the level of the window, and there remained only the shadow of the younger man in clear profile on the blind. He stood for a minute looking downward, and George Beaumont had time to observe the finely-cut features of a total stranger. Then he saw that he wiped the blade of his sword, turned and walked away, and his shadow passed out of sight, leaving the win-dow-blind a blank, luminous square.

Indoors at the same time Mr. Stackpoole had been waked from his short sleep by a sound in his wife's sitting-room overhead, and he sprang to his feet with ev-ery faculty concentrated in listening. A noise as of chairs pushed back and upset on the polished floor, and a scuffling of feet as though two men were struggling together. Then a moment of silence, a loud stamp, and heavy fall that seemed to shake the ceiling, followed by deep groans. "Good Grod! What can be the mat-ter?" cried Mr. Stackpoole, and he rushed from the room into the hall. The front door stood open, though the inner glass doors were closed, and neither his son-in-law nor any servants were there. He stopped to call nobody, but ran upstairs to his wife's room just as his daughter came quickly down from the storey above with a white and terrified face. "Oh, Papa, someone has just frightened me so, but whoever he is he is in there! I saw him go into Mamma's room a few minutes ago, and I'm so glad you've come, for I dare not follow him!" and without ask-ing Ella of whom she was speaking, Mr. Stackpoole flung the door wide open and rushed into the room. No one was there. Not a chair or table displaced, and the electric light illuminating every corner of the room forbade the possibility of anyone being in hiding.

"It is the most extraordinary thing!" he exclaimed, wiping the perspiration of terror from his brow as he spoke; "I would not have your mother know of it for the world!"

"Have you seen him too?" said his daughter faintly.

"Seen whom, child? Seen what? No, I've seen nothing, but I've heard enough to last me my lifetime. God forbid that I should hear it again!" and he looked about the room and under the table, fairly stupefied with amazement.

"He passed me on the stairs just as I came out of the night nursery," said Mrs. Beaumont anxious to tell her experience without waiting to hear her father's. "A tall young man ran quickly by me dressed in a blue coat, with ruffles at the wrists and a great laced cravat, and a wig tied with a ribbon at the back. He car-ried a long thin sword in his hand. At first I thought it was Arthur Newton, who wore a powdered wig like his this evening, but I remembered his coat was black and he left early. When I saw his face it was a stranger's, and he looked cruel and passionate. I followed him till I saw him go into this room and shut the door after him."

"Then where the devil is he now?" said Mr. Stackpoole. "This is some miserable practical joke, but I'll get to the bottom of it and be even with them yet I'll get to the bottom of it!" and as he spoke the door that he had taken the precaution to close burst open, and his son-in-law entered in his matador's dress, pale and breathless, looking as if the bull had turned and given him chase.

"Oh, George, have you seen him too?" said his wife.

"Did you hear anything?" asked Mr. Stackpoole. "Sit down, man; you are trembling like a leaf!"

"There were two of them, an old man and a young man, in this room a minute ago! In God's name, who were they, and why did not you stop them before murder was done?" he said excitedly.

Mr. Stackpoole grew quiet and self-collected at the sight of his son-in-law's agitation. "Pull yourself together, George, and tell me what you mean. There is something up tonight that needs explaining."

"But where are they? They were in this room, and if you were with them you must have witnessed what happened, or if you only came upstairs just now you must have met the young man leaving the room. The old man will never stir again," and he lifted the tablecloth and looked under the table.

"How come you to speak confidently of who was in this room a few minutes ago, when you were downstairs all the while?" asked Mr. Stackpoole.

"I was smoking a cigarette in the garden after seeing the Westons off, walking on the broad path, when I looked up at Mamma's sitting-room window and saw the shadow of two men on the blind, shown up by the electric light as clear and sharp as in a magic-lantern. I saw their profiles perfectly, but I did not know their faces. They wore wigs tied behind, and ruffles at their wrists, and the younger, taller man, as I saw by his shadow, wore a laced Steinkirk round his neck. They struggled together, and the old man grasped the young man by the throat, but he tore himself free, drew his sword, and ran him through the body. He fell below the level of the window out of my sight, and the younger man stood for a minute, wiped his sword, then moved away, and left the blind a blank sheet of white."

"Good God! and I heard it all in my room below the struggle and the fall, and deep groans!" said Mr. Stackpoole.

"And I met the young man if it was anything human and he passed me on the stairs!" said his daughter, seizing her father by the arm. "Oh, Papa, Harbledon Hall is haunted; people were right about it! Do let us leave this dreadful place tomorrow!" And the concluding notes of the sad Waldteufel waltz sighed through the house as she spoke.

Mr. Stackpoole shook his head. "I don't see how that is to be done, for your mother must not be frightened. For heaven's sake try to look as if nothing had happened. We shall be missed downstairs; I'll go, and you two must manage to bid our guests good-night decently, and not to alarm those who remain till tomorrow. We must rouse no suspicions. George, fetch Ella a glass of champagne; it will do her good."

"Oh, don't leave me alone!" cried Mrs. Beaumont, like a frightened child.

"Then I'll send wine up for you both," said her father, "and mind you must follow me directly."

Mr. Stackpoole rejoined his guests, who had not missed him, and were in the midst of the last dance with as much freshness and enjoyment as if it had been the first in the evening. At length all the guests had departed except those composing the house party, and the ladies soon retired, leaving the gentlemen to have a smoke in the billiard-room.

"You don't look very well, Beaumont," said a young man dressed as a Tyrolean peasant, as he lit a cigar and looked up at his friend's pale face.

"It's nothing, only waltzing makes me giddy," and he mixed himself some brandy and soda.

One by one the guests bade good-night and left the room, till there only remained Mr. Stackpoole, his son-in-law, and Mr. Liston, a gentleman with very long legs, wearing tights to display them to advantage.

"Did your father-in-law know when he took Harbledon Hall that it was supposed to be haunted?" he said in a low voice to Mr. Beaumont. Mr. Stackpoole happened to hear the question, and replied to it himself.

"We heard some foolish gossip on the subject, for of course no place stands empty so long without legends being invented to account for the fact. But I am not the man to listen to vulgar chatter. I took the house, and have been highly delighted with it." And Mr. Beaumont could only admire his father-in-law's admirable self-possession.

"Just so, and the electric light is the true cure for the supposed supernatural. Of course you know how suddenly Sir Roland Shawe left the place?"

"Oh, yes, we've heard all about that," said Mr. Stackpoole, forcing a laugh.

"Do you know I doubt whether you have ever heard all about it; at least, if you have, you must be a cheerful sort of person if you can laugh at it," said Mr. Liston.

"Why, of course, the whole thing was a foolish practical joke. Something connected with a magic-lantern, if I remember rightly."

"Magic-lantern! I never even heard the word mentioned. No; if you care to hear the truth about it, I think I can tell it you. I've lived in the county all my life, and I know the story of Harbledon Hall by heart. I only wonder you don't. I should not tell you now if I thought it would make you nervous; but since you've put in the electric light and done up the house in such cheerful modern style the whole place is changed and anyone might enjoy living here."

"Let us hear the story," said Mr. Stackpoole abruptly.

"I see I've roused your curiosity. The story goes that some hundred and fifty years ago there lived in this house a certain father and son who hated one another like the devil, and it is needless to say that there was a woman in the case and a fortune at stake. The old man must have been an uncommonly bad lot, and he is said to have grossly insulted the young lady his son was about to marry, having in the first instance proposed to her himself and been refused. The two men had a deadly quarrel about it in this very house, and the upshot was that the son, mad with passion, ran his father through the heart and killed him on the spot. There, I sha'n't say anything more about it if it is too much for you," said Mr. Liston, struck by the white faces before him.

"Go on, go on," said Mr. Stackpoole.

"Well, one winter's night, now eight years ago, as Sir Roland Shawe was coming home late, walking across the garden, he looked up at the window of a room on the first floor where a light was burning, and he saw on the blind, in clear outline, the shadows of the old man and his son struggling together, and he saw the young man run his father through the body with his rapier."

"I cannot bear it! I cannot bear it!" said Greorge Beaumont, pale as death and looking ready to faint.

"You could but say that if you had seen the grim shadows yourself. It certainly is a horrid story, and though I can't say that I believe in ghosts myself, I can offer no explanations of the details I have given you. Sir Roland believed it, and he was a clear-headed, matter-of-fact sortof person. Other members of his family, too, saw and heard unaccountable things that night. One of his sons who was sitting up late for his father met the shadow of an evil-looking fellow dressed in a blue coat and wearing a powdered tie-wig, hurrying along an upper passage, carrying a naked rapier in his hand. And Lady Shawe was waked by a sound in the room next hers, which was the room where the shadows were seen on the blind a sound of struggling and upsetting of chairs, followed by a heavy fall and deep groans. Now, if only one person had thought that he had heard or seen unaccountable things, Sir Roland would have made the best of it and stayed on at Harbledon Hall; but, by Jove! when three rational beings are each an eye or ear witness it becomes intolerable! Whether you believe in ghosts or not, you can't put up with a thing like that!"

"By Heaven, you can't, that's true!" said Mr. Stackpoole, wiping his moist brow. "And now, Liston, that you have told me this, I'll tell you something in return. I and my family leave Harbledon Hall tomorrow for the precise reason that drove Sir Roland Shawe out of it eight years ago."

"Never!"

"As sure as I am alive we leave here tomorrow! I must find some reason for our sudden flight, but go we must, and I cannot have my wife alarmed."

"I would not spend another night in the house for the world!" said Beaumont.

"But, my dear Mr. Stackpoole, I hope that nothing that I have said leads you to make this extraordinary resolution. Your imagination is excited by what you have heard; there cannot possibly be any cause why you should leave this charming place that you have just fitted up to your own taste," said Mr. Listen soothingly.

"The story you have told us has only helped to explain what we already know. I tell you that this very night, not a couple of hours ago, in the blaze of the electric light and with the house full of company, Beaumont, my daughter, and myself have seen and heard the sights and sounds that drove Sir Roland Shawe out of Harbledon Hall; and we leave tomorrow or rather today, for it is nearly six o'clock now never to spend another night under this accursed roof!" and Mr. Stackpoole's voice shook as he spoke. "I have only to request," he added, "that you will treat this communication as strictly confidential, for neither Beaumont nor I shall care to speak or to be spoken to about what has occurred tonight."

Where was Mr. Stackpoole's intelligent curiosity on the subject of ghosts, and what had become of his courage? The one had been satisfied and the other daunted, and he had not the slightest desire to remain and investigate the mystery.

At late breakfast Mrs. Stackpoole was shocked by the appearance of her family. It would have been difficult to say wldch was most pale and haggard her husband, her daughter, or her son-in-law. They made the poor excuse that late hours did not suit them and that dancing knocked them up, and she told them that they looked like very young children who had been to their first pantomime the night before. When the last guest was gone Mrs. Stackpoole saw that there was something seriously disturbing her husband, and was at a loss to account for his changed humour.

"My dear, we will go up to town this afternoon with George and Ella," he said with quick decision.

"Impossible," replied his wife, calmly. "You, of course, can go if you like, but I really cannot."

"Oh, do come with us, Mamma! You know how much Papa wishes it," said her daughter.

"Yes, do come with us," urged her son-in-law with unwonted ardour; "it is so long since we met," forgetting that they had spent the last month together.

Mrs. Stackpoole laughed. "There is evidently some deep-laid plot among you three to hurry me off. Well, if you will be any the happier for my coming with you I'll do so, though it is most inconvenient to leave home in this sudden way," said the good-tempered lady.

And they travelled up to London that day, never to return to Harbledon Hall. Mr. Stackpoole so managed that his wife did not know his real reason for giving up the most charming house they had ever lived in. He preferred that she should attribute it to his restlessness and caprice, anything rather than that her nerves should be shaken by hearing the truth.

He consulted a fashionable physician, first giving him a hint that he wished to be ordered off to the South of France immediately, and the hint being taken, he told his long-suffering wife that Dr. Blank had recommended him to go abroad at once, and in two days they were en route for Marseilles. Mrs. Stackpoole was accustomed to her husband's impulsive, angular movements, so that it did not greatly disturb her; but when a week later he said that he had decided to give up Harbledon Hall, and to look for a place somewhere in the eastern counties which were as yet untrodden ground to him, she shed tears of present disappointment and prospective fatigue. When the much-enduring lady had dried her eyes and her husband had enumerated to her in detail every reason but the real one for which he was leaving their beautiful home, she said, "My dear, if I did not know better, I should be forced to believe that you too had seen the ghost that frightened Sir Roland Shawe out of Harbledon Hall eight years ago!"

NO. 5 BRANCH LINE: THE ENGINEER,
by Amelia Ann Blanford Edwards

His name, sir, was Matthew Price; mine is Benjamin Hardy. We were born within a few days of each other; bred up in the same village; taught at the same school. I cannot remember the time when we were not close friends. Even as boys, we never knew what it was to quarrel. We had not a thought, we had not a possession, that was not in common. We would have stood by each other, fearlessly, to the death. It was such a friendship as one reads about sometimes in books: fast and firm as the great Tors upon our native moorlands, true as the sun in the heavens.

The name of our village was Chadleigh. Lifted high above the pasture flats which stretched away at our feet like a measureless green lake and melted into mist on the furthest horizon, it nestled, a tiny stone-built hamlet, in a sheltered hollow about midway between the plain and the plateau. Above us, rising ridge beyond ridge, slope beyond slope, spread the mountainous moor-country, bare and bleak for the most part, with here and there a patch of cultivated field or hardy plantation, and crowned highest of all with masses of huge grey crag, abrupt, isolated, hoary, and older than the deluge. These were the Tors—Druids' Tor, King's Tor, Castle Tor, and the like; sacred places, as I have heard, in the ancient time, where crownings, burnings, human sacrifices, and all kinds of bloody heathen rites were performed. Bones, too, had been found there, and arrowheads, and ornaments of gold and glass. I had a vague awe of the Tors in those boyish days, and would not have gone near them after dark for the heaviest bribe.

I have said that we were born in the same village. He was the son of a small farmer, named William Price, and the eldest of a family of seven; I was the only child of Ephraim Hardy, the Chadleigh blacksmith—a well-known man in those parts, whose memory is not forgotten to this day. Just so far as a farmer is supposed to be a bigger man than a blacksmith, Mat's father might be said to have a better standing than mine; but William Price with his small holding and his seven boys, was, in fact, as poor as many a day-labourer; whilst, the blacksmith, well-to-do, bustling, popular, and open-handed, was a person of some importance in the place. All this, however, had nothing to do with Mat and myself. It never occurred to either of us that his jacket was out at elbows, or that our mutual funds came altogether from my pocket. It was enough for us that we sat on the same school-bench, conned our tasks from the same primer, fought each other's battles, screened each other's faults, fished, nutted, played truant, robbed orchards and birds' nests together, and spent every half-hour, authorised or stolen, in each other's society. It was a happy time; but it could not go on for ever. My father, being prosperous, resolved to put me forward in the world. I must know more, and do better, than himself. The forge was not good enough, the little world of Chadleigh not wide enough, for me. Thus it happened that I was still swinging the satchel when Mat was whistling at the plough, and that at last, when my future course was shaped out, we were separated, as it then seemed to us, for life. For, blacksmith's son as I was, furnace and forge, in some form or other, pleased me best, and I chose to be a working engineer. So my father by-and-by apprenticed me to a Birmingham iron-master; and, having bidden farewell to Mat, and Chadleigh, and the grey old Tors in the shadow of which I had spent all the days of my life, I turned my face northward, and went over into "the Black Country."

I am not going to dwell on this part of my story. How I worked out the term of my apprenticeship; how, when I had served my full time and become a skilled workman, I took Mat from the plough and brought him over to the Black Country, sharing with him lodging, wages, experience—all, in short, that I had to give; how he, naturally quick to learn and brimful of quiet energy, worked his way up a step at a time, and came by-and-by to be a "first hand" in his own department; how, during all these years of change, and trial, and effort, the old boyish affection never wavered or weakened, but went on, growing with our growth and strengthening with our strength—are facts which I need do no more than outline in this place.

About this time—it will be remembered that I speak of the days when Mat and I were on the bright side of thirty—it happened that our firm contracted to supply six first-class locomotives to run on the new line, then in process of construction, between Turin and Genoa. It was the first Italian order we had taken. We had had dealings with France, Holland, Belgium, Germany; but never with Italy. The connection, therefore, was new and valuable—all the more valuable because our Transalpine neighbours had but lately begun to lay down the iron roads, and would be safe to need more of our good English work as they went on. So the Birmingham firm set themselves to the contract with a will, lengthened our working hours, increased our wages, took on fresh hands, and determined, if energy and promptitude could do it, to place themselves at the head of the Italian labour-market, and stay there. They deserved and achieved success. The six locomotives were not only turned out to time, but were shipped, despatched, and delivered with a promptitude that fairly amazed our Piedmontese consignee. I was not a little proud, you may be sure, when I found myself appointed to superintend the transport of the engines. Being allowed a couple of assistants, I contrived that Mat should be one of them; and thus we enjoyed together the first great holiday of our lives.

It was a wonderful change for two Birmingham operatives fresh from the Black Country. The fairy city, with its crescent background of Alps; the port crowded with strange shipping; the marvellous blue sky and the bluer sea; the painted houses on the quays; the quaint cathedral, faced with black and white marble; the street of jewellers, like an Arabian Nights' bazaar; the street of palaces, with its Moorish courtyards, its fountains and orange-trees; the women veiled like brides; the galley-slaves chained two and two; the processions of priests and friars; the everlasting clangour of bells; the babble of a strange tongue; the singular lightness and brightness of the climate—made, altogether, such a combination of wonders that we wandered about, the first day, in a kind of bewildered dream, like children at a fair. Before that week was ended, being tempted by the beauty of the place and the liberality of the pay, we had agreed to take service with the Turin and Genoa Railway Company, and to turn our backs upon Birmingham for ever.

Then began a new life—a life so active and healthy, so steeped in fresh air and sunshine, that we sometimes marvelled how we could have endured the gloom of the Black Country. We were constantly up and down the line: now at Genoa, now at Turin, taking trial trips with the locomotives, and placing our old experiences at the service of our new employers.

In the meanwhile we made Genoa our headquarters, and hired a couple of rooms over a small shop in a by-street sloping down to the quays. Such a busy little street—so steep and winding that no vehicles could pass through it, and so narrow that the sky looked like a mere strip of deep-blue ribbon overhead! Every house in it, however, was a shop, where the goods encroached on the footway, or were piled about the door, or hung like tapestry from the balconies; and all day long, from dawn to dusk, an incessant stream of passers-by poured up and down between the port and the upper quarter of the city.

Our landlady was the widow of a silver-worker, and lived by the sale of fili-gree ornaments, cheap jewellery, combs, fans, and toys in ivory and jet. She had an only daughter named Gianetta, who served in the shop, and was simply the most beautiful woman I ever beheld. Looking back across this weary chasm of years, and bringing her image before me (as I can and do) with all the vividness of life, I am unable, even now, to detect a flaw in her beauty. I do not attempt to describe her. I do not believe there is a poet living who could find the words to do it; but I once saw a picture that was somewhat like her (not half so lovely, but still like her), and, for aught I know, that picture is still hanging where I last looked at it—upon the walls of the Louvre. It represented a woman with brown eyes and golden hair, looking over her shoulder into a circular mirror held by a bearded man in the background. In this man, as I then understood, the artist had painted his own portrait; in her, the portrait of the woman he loved. No picture that I ever saw was half so beautiful, and yet it was not worthy to be named in the same breath with Gianetta Coneglia.

You may be certain the widow's shop did not want for customers. All Genoa knew how fair a face was to be seen behind that dingy little counter; and Gi-anetta, flirt as she was, had more lovers than she cared to remember, even by name. Gentle and simple, rich and poor, from the red-capped sailor buying his ear-rings or his amulet, to the nobleman carelessly purchasing half the filigrees in the window, she treated them all alike—encouraged them, laughed at them, led them on and turned them off at her pleasure. She had no more heart than a marble statue; as Mat and I discovered by-and-by, to our bitter cost.

I cannot tell to this day how it came about, or what first led me to suspect how things were going with us both; but long before the waning of that autumn a coldness had sprung up between my friend and myself. It was nothing that could have been put into words. It was nothing that either of us could have explained or justified, to save his life. We lodged together, ate together, worked together, exactly as before; we even took our long evening's walk together, when the day's labour was ended; and except, perhaps, that we were more silent than of old, no mere looker-on could have detected a shadow of change. Yet there it was, silent and subtle, widening the gulf between us every day.

It was not his fault. He was too true and gentle-hearted to have willingly brought about such a state of things between us. Neither do I believe—fiery as my nature is—that it was mine. It was all hers—hers from first to last—the sin, and the shame, and the sorrow.

If she had shown a fair and open preference for either of us, no real harm could have come of it. I would have put any constraint upon myself, and, Heaven knows! have borne any suffering, to see Mat really happy. I know that he would have done the same, and more if he could, for me. But Gianetta cared not one sou for either. She never meant to choose between us. It gratified her vanity to divide us; it amused her to play with us. It would pass my power to tell how, by a thousand imperceptible shades of coquetry—by the lingering of a glance, the substitution of a word, the flitting of a smile—she contrived to turn our heads, and torture our hearts, and lead us on to love her. She deceived us both. She buoyed us both up with hope; she maddened us with jealousy; she crushed us with despair. For my part, when I seemed to wake to a sudden sense of the ruin that was about our path and I saw how the truest friendship that ever bound two lives together was drifting on to wreck and ruin, I asked myself whether any woman in the world was worth what Mat had been to me and I to him. But this was not often. I was readier to shut my eyes upon the truth than to face it; and so lived on, wilfully, in a dream.

Thus the autumn passed away, and winter came—the strange, treacherous Genoese winter, green with olive and ilex, brilliant with sunshine, and bitter with storm. Still, rivals at heart and friends on the surface, Mat and I lingered on in our lodging in the Vicolo Balba. Still Gianetta held us with her fatal wiles and her still more fatal beauty. At length there came a day when I felt I could bear the horrible misery and suspense of it no longer. The sun, I vowed, should not go down before I knew my sentence. She must choose between us. She must either take me or let me go. I was reckless. I was desperate. I was determined to know the worst, or the best. If the worst, I would at once turn my back upon Genoa, upon her, upon all the pursuits and purposes of my past life, and begin the world anew. This I told her, passionately and sternly, standing before her in the little parlour at the back of the shop, one bleak December morning.

"If it's Mat whom you care for most," I said, "tell me so in one word, and I will never trouble you again. He is better worth your love. I am jealous and exacting; he is as trusting and unselfish as a woman. Speak, Gianetta; am I to bid you good-bye for ever and ever, or am I to write home to my mother in England, bidding her pray to God to bless the woman who has promised to be my wife?"

"You plead your friend's cause well," she replied, haughtily. "Matteo ought to be grateful. This is more than he ever did for you."

"Give me my answer, for pity's sake," I exclaimed, "and let me go!"

"You are free to go or stay, Signor Inglese," she replied. "I am not your jailor."

"Do you bid me leave you?"

"*Beata Madre!* not I."

"Will you marry me, if I stay?"

She laughed aloud—such a merry, mocking, musical laugh, like a chime of silver bells!

"You ask too much," she said.

"Only what you have led me to hope these five or six months past!"

"That is just what Matteo says. How tiresome you both are!"

"O, Gianetta," I said, passionately, "be serious for one moment! I am a rough fellow, it is true—not half good enough or clever enough for you; but I love you with my whole heart, and an Emperor could do no more."

"I am glad of it," she replied; "I do not want you to love me less."

"Then you cannot wish to make me wretched! Will you promise me?"

"I promise nothing," said she, with another burst of laughter; "except that I will not marry Matteo!"

Except that she would not marry Matteo! Only that. Not a word of hope for myself. Nothing but my friend's condemnation. I might get comfort, and selfish triumph, and some sort of base assurance out of that, if I could. And so, to my shame, I did. I grasped at the vain encouragement, and, fool that I was! let her put me off again unanswered. From that day, I gave up all effort at self-control, and let myself drift blindly on—to destruction.

At length things became so bad between Mat and myself that it seemed as if an open rupture must be at hand. We avoided each other, scarcely exchanged a dozen sentences in a day, and fell away from all our old familiar habits. At this time—I shudder to remember it!—there were moments when I felt that I hated him.

Thus, with the trouble deepening and widening between us day by day, another month or five weeks went by; and February came; and, with February, the Carnival. They said in Genoa that it was a particularly dull carnival; and so it must have been; for, save a flag or two hung out in some of the principal streets, and a sort of festa look about the women, there were no special indications of the season. It was, I think, the second day when, having been on the line all the morning, I returned to Genoa at dusk, and, to my surprise, found Mat Price on the platform. He came up to me, and laid his hand on my arm.

"You are in late," he said. "I have been waiting for you three-quarters of an hour. Shall we dine together today?"

Impulsive as I am, this evidence of returning goodwill at once called up my better feelings.

"With all my heart, Mat," I replied; "shall we go to Gozzoli's?"

"No, no," he said, hurriedly. "Some quieter place—some place where we can talk. I have something to say to you."

I noticed now that he looked pale and agitated, and an uneasy sense of apprehension stole upon me. We decided on the "Pescatore," a little out-of-the-way trattoria, down near the Molo Vecchio. There, in a dingy salon, frequented chiefly by seamen, and redolent of tobacco, we ordered our simple dinner. Mat scarcely swallowed a morsel; but, calling presently for a bottle of Sicilian wine, drank eagerly.

"Well, Mat," I said, as the last dish was placed on the table, "what news have you?"

"Bad."

"I guessed that from your face."

"Bad for you—bad for me. Gianetta."

"What of Gianetta?"

He passed his hand nervously across his lips.

"Gianetta is false—worse than false," he said, in a hoarse voice. "She values an honest man's heart just as she values a flower for her hair—wears it for a day, then throws it aside for ever. She has cruelly wronged us both."

"In what way? Good Heavens, speak out!"

"In the worst way that a woman can wrong those who love her. She has sold herself to the Marchese Loredano."

The blood rushed to my head and face in a burning torrent. I could scarcely see, and dared not trust myself to speak.

"I saw her going towards the cathedral," he went on, hurriedly. "It was about three hours ago. I thought she might be going to confession, so I hung back and followed her at a distance. When she got inside, however, she went straight to the back of the pulpit, where this man was waiting for her. You remember him—an old man who used to haunt the shop a month or two back. Well, seeing how deep in conversation they were, and how they stood close under the pulpit with their backs towards the church, I fell into a passion of anger and went straight up the aisle, intending to say or do something: I scarcely knew what; but, at all events, to draw her arm through mine, and take her home. When I came within a few feet, however, and found only a big pillar between myself and them, I paused. They could not see me, nor I them; but I could hear their voices distinctly, and—and I listened."

"Well, and you heard—"

"The terms of a shameful bargain—beauty on the one side, gold on the other; so many thousand francs a year; a villa near Naples—pah! It makes me sick to repeat it."

And, with a shudder, he poured out another glass of wine and drank it at a draught.

"After that," he said, presently, "I made no effort to bring her away. The whole thing was so cold-blooded, so deliberate, so shameful, that I felt I had only to wipe her out of my memory, and leave her to her fate. I stole out of the cathedral, and walked about here by the sea for ever so long, trying to get my thoughts straight. Then I remembered you, Ben; and the recollection of how this wanton had come between us and broken up our lives drove me wild. So I went up to the station and waited for you. I felt you ought to know it all; and—and I thought, perhaps, that we might go back to England together."

"The Marchese Loredano!"

It was all that I could say; all that I could think. As Mat had just said of himself, I felt "like one stunned."

"There is one other thing I may as well tell you," he added, reluctantly, "if only to show you how false a woman can be. We—we were to have been married next month."

"We? Who? What do you mean?"

"I mean that we were to have been married—Gianetta and I."

A sudden storm of rage, of scorn, of incredulity, swept over me at this, and seemed to carry my senses away.

"You!" I cried. "Gianetta marry you! I don't believe it."

"I wish I had not believed it," he replied, looking up as if puzzled by my vehemence. "But she promised me; and I thought, when she promised it, she meant it."

"She told me, weeks ago, that she would never be your wife!"

His colour rose, his brow darkened; but when his answer came, it was as calm as the last.

"Indeed!" he said. "Then it is only one baseness more. She told me that she had refused you; and that was why we kept our engagement secret."

"Tell the truth, Mat Price," I said, well-nigh beside myself with suspicion. "Confess that every word of this is false! Confess that Gianetta will not listen to you, and that you are afraid I may succeed where you have failed. As perhaps I shall—as perhaps I shall, after all!"

"Are you mad?" he exclaimed. "What do you mean?"

"That I believe it's just a trick to get me away to England—that I don't credit a syllable of your story. You're a liar, and I hate you!"

He rose, and, laying one hand on the back of his chair, looked me sternly in the face.

"If you were not Benjamin Hardy," he said, deliberately, "I would thrash you within an inch of your life."

The words had no sooner passed his lips than I sprang at him. I have never been able distinctly to remember what followed. A curse—a blow—a struggle—a moment of blind fury—a cry—a confusion of tongues—a circle of strange faces. Then I see Mat lying back in the arms of a bystander; myself trembling and bewildered—the knife dropping from my grasp; blood upon the floor; blood upon my hands; blood upon his shirt. And then I hear those dreadful words:

"O, Ben, you have murdered me!"

He did not die—at least, not there and then. He was carried to the nearest hospital, and lay for some weeks between life and death. His case, they said, was difficult and dangerous. The knife had gone in just below the collar-bone, and pierced down into the lungs. He was not allowed to speak or turn—scarcely to breathe with freedom. He might not even lift his head to drink. I sat by him day and night all through that sorrowful time. I gave up my situation on the railway; I quitted my lodging in the Vicolo Balba; I tried to forget that such a woman as Gianetta Coneglia had ever drawn breath. I lived only for Mat; and he tried to live more, I believe, for my sake than his own. Thus, in the bitter silent hours of pain and penitence, when no hand but mine approached his lips or smoothed his pillow, the old friendship came back with even more than its old trust and faithfulness. He forgave me, fully and freely; and I would thankfully have given my life for him.

At length there came one bright spring morning, when, dismissed as convalescent, he tottered out through the hospital gates, leaning on my arm, and feeble as an infant. He was not cured; neither, as I then learned to my horror and anguish, was it possible that he ever could be cured. He might live, with care, for some years; but the lungs were injured beyond hope of remedy, and a strong or healthy man he could never be again. These, spoken aside to me, were the parting words of the chief physician, who advised me to take him further south without delay.

I took him to a little coast-town called Rocca, some thirty miles beyond Genoa—a sheltered lonely place along the Riviera, where the sea was even bluer than the sky, and the cliffs were green with strange tropical plants, cacti, and aloes, and Egyptian palms. Here we lodged in the house of a small tradesman; and Mat, to use his own words, "set to work at getting well in good earnest." But, alas! it was a work which no earnestness could forward. Day after day he went down to the beach, and sat for hours drinking the sea air and watching the sails that came and went in the offing. By-and-by he could go no further than the garden of the house in which we lived. A little later, and he spent his days on a couch beside the open window, waiting patiently for the end. Ay, for the end! It had come to that. He was fading fast, waning with the waning summer, and conscious that the Reaper was at hand. His whole aim now was to soften the agony of my remorse, and prepare me for what must shortly come.

"I would not live longer, if I could," he said, lying on his couch one summer evening and looking up to the stars. "If I had my choice at this moment, I would ask to go. I should like Gianetta to know that I forgave her."

"She shall know it," I said, trembling suddenly from head to foot.

He pressed my hand.

"And you'll write to father?"

"I will."

I had drawn a little back, that he might not see the tears raining down my cheeks; but he raised himself on his elbow, and looked round.

"Don't fret, Ben," he whispered; laid his head back wearily upon the pillow— and so died.

And this was the end of it. This was the end of all that made life life to me. I buried him there, in hearing of the wash of a strange sea on a strange shore. I stayed by the grave till the priest and the bystanders were gone. I saw the earth filled in to the last sod, and the gravedigger stamped it down with his feet. Then, and not till then, I felt that I had lost him for ever—the friend I had loved, and hated, and slain. Then, and not till then, I knew that all rest, and joy, and hope were over for me. From that moment my heart hardened within me, and my life was filled with loathing. Day and night, land and sea, labour and rest, food and sleep, were alike hateful to me. It was the curse of Cain, and that my brother had pardoned me made it lie none the lighter. Peace on earth was for me no more, and goodwill towards men was dead in my heart for ever. Remorse softens some natures; but it poisoned mine. I hated all mankind; but above all mankind I hated the woman who had come between us two, and ruined both our lives.

He had bidden me seek her out, and be the messenger of his forgiveness. I had sooner have gone down to the port of Genoa and taken upon me the serge cap and shotted chain of any galley-slave at his toil in the public works; but for all that I did my best to obey him. I went back, alone and on foot. I went back, in-tending to say to her, "Gianetta Coneglia, he forgave you; but God never will." But she was gone. The little shop was let to a fresh occupant; and the neighbours only knew that mother and daughter had left the place quite suddenly, and that Gianetta was supposed to be under the "protection" of the Marchese Loredano. How I made inquiries here and there—how I heard that they had gone to Naples —and how, being restless and reckless of my time, I worked my passage in a French steamer, and followed her—how, having found the sumptuous villa that was now hers, I learned that she had left there some ten days and gone to Paris, where the Marchese was ambassador for the Two Sicilies—how, working my passage back again to Marseilles, and thence, in part by the river and in part by the rail, I made my way to Paris—how, day after day, I paced the streets and the parks, watched at the ambassador's gates, followed his carriage, and at last, after weeks of waiting, discovered her address—how, having written to request an in-terview, her servants spurned me from her door and flung my letter in my face— how, looking up at her windows, I then, instead of forgiving, solemnly cursed her with the bitterest curses my tongue could devise—and how, this done, I shook the dust of Paris from my feet, and became a wanderer upon the face of the earth, are facts which I have now no space to tell.

The next six or eight years of my life were shifting and unsettled enough. A morose and restless man, I took employment here and there, as opportunity of-fered, turning my hand to many things, and caring little what I earned, so long as the work was hard and the change incessant. First of all I engaged myself as chief engineer in one of the French steamers plying between Marseilles and Constantinople. At Constantinople I changed to one of the Austrian Lloyd's boats, and worked for some time to and from Alexandria, Jaffa, and those parts After that, I fell in with a party of Mr. Layard's men at Cairo, and so went up the Nile and took a turn at the excavations of the mound of Nimroud. Then I became a working engineer on the new desert line between Alexandria and Suez; and by-and-by I worked my passage out to Bombay, and took service as an engine fitter on one of the great Indian railways. I stayed a long time in India; that is to say, I stayed nearly two years, which was a long time for me; and I might not even have left so soon, but for the war that was declared just then with Russia. That tempted me. For I loved danger and hardship as other men love safety and ease; and as for my life, I had sooner have parted from it than kept it, any day. So I came straight back to England; betook myself to Portsmouth, where my testimonials at once procured me the sort of berth I wanted. I went out to the Crimea in the engine-room of one of her Majesty's war steamers.

I served with the fleet, of course, while the war lasted; and when it was over, went wandering off again, rejoicing in my liberty. This time I went to Canada, and after working on a railway then in progress near the American frontier. I presently passed over into the States; journeyed from north to south; crossed the Rocky Mountains; tried a month or two of life in the gold country; and then, being seized with a sudden, aching, unaccountable longing to revisit that solitary grave so far away on the Italian coast, I turned my face once more towards Europe.

Poor little grave! I found it rank with weeds, the cross half shattered, the inscription half effaced. It was as if no one had loved him, or remembered him. I went back to the house in which we had lodged together. The same people were still living there, and made me kindly welcome. I stayed with them for some weeks. I weeded, and planted, and trimmed the grave with my own hands, and set up a fresh cross in pure white marble. It was the first season of rest that I had known since I laid him there; and when at last I shouldered my knapsack and set forth again to battle with the world, I promised myself that, God willing, I would creep back to Rocca, when my days drew near to ending, and be buried by his side.

From hence, being, perhaps, a little less inclined than formerly for very distant parts, and willing to keep within reach of that grave, I went no further than Mantua, where I engaged myself as an engine-driver on the line, then not long completed, between that city and Venice. Somehow, although I had been trained to the working engineering, I preferred in these days to earn my bread by driving. I liked the excitement of it, the sense of power, the rush of the air, the roar of the fire, the flitting of the landscape. Above all, I enjoyed to drive a night express. The worse the weather, the better it suited with my sullen temper. For I was as hard, and harder than ever. The years had done nothing to soften me. They had only confirmed all that was blackest and bitterest in my heart.

I continued pretty faithful to the Mantua line, and had been working on it steadily for more than seven months when that which I am now about to relate took place.

It was in the month of March. The weather had been unsettled for some days past, and the nights stormy; and at one point along the line, near Ponte di Brenta, the waters had risen and swept away some seventy yards of embankment. Since this accident, the trains had all been obliged to stop at a certain spot between Padua and Ponte di Brenta, and the passengers, with their luggage, had thence to be transported in all kinds of vehicles, by a circuitous country road, to the nearest station on the other side of the gap, where another train and engine awaited them. This, of course, caused great confusion and annoyance, put all our time-tables wrong, and subjected the public to a large amount of inconvenience. In the mean while an army of navvies was drafted to the spot, and worked day and night to repair the damage. At this time I was driving two through trains each day; namely, one from Mantua to Venice in the early morning, and a return train from Venice to Mantua in the afternoon—a tolerably full days' work, covering about one hundred and ninety miles of ground, and occupying between ten and eleven hours. I was therefore not best pleased when, on the third or fourth day after the accident, I was informed that, in addition to my regular allowance of work, I should that evening be required to drive a special train to Venice. This special train, consisting of an engine, a single carriage, and a break-van, was to leave the Mantua platform at eleven; at Padua the passengers were to alight and find post-chaises waiting to convey them to Ponte di Brenta; at Ponte di Brenta another engine, carriage, and break-van were to be in readiness, I was charged to accompany them throughout.

"Corpo di Bacco," said the clerk who gave me my orders, "you need not look so black, man. You are certain of a handsome gratuity. Do you know who goes with you?"

"Not I."

"Not you, indeed! Why, it's the Duca Loredano, the Neapolitan ambassador."

"Loredano!" I stammered. "What Loredano? There was a Marchese—"

"Certo. He was the Marchese Loredano some years ago; but he has come into his dukedom since then."

"He must be a very old man by this time."

"Yes, he is old; but what of that? He is as hale, and bright, and stately as ever. You have seen him before?"

"Yes," I said, turning away; "I have seen him—years ago."

"You have heard of his marriage?"

I shook my head.

The clerk chuckled, rubbed his hands, and shrugged his shoulders.

"An extraordinary affair," he said. "Made a tremendous esclandre at the time. He married his mistress—quite a common, vulgar girl—a Genoese—very handsome; but not received, of course. Nobody visits her."

"Married her!" I exclaimed. "Impossible."

"True, I assure you."

I put my hand to my head. I felt as if I had had a fall or a blow.

"Does she—does she go tonight?" I faltered.

"O dear, yes—goes everywhere with him—never lets him out of her sight. You'll see her—la bella Duchessa!"

With this my informant laughed, and rubbed his hands again, and went back to his office.

The day went by, I scarcely know how, except that my whole soul was in a tumult of rage and bitterness. I returned from my afternoon's work about 7.25, and at 10.30 I was once again at the station. I had examined the engine; given instructions to the Fochista, or stoker, about the fire; seen to the supply of oil; and got all in readiness, when, just as I was about to compare my watch with the clock in the ticket-office, a hand was laid upon my arm, and a voice in my ear said:

"Are you the engine-driver who is going on with this special train?"

I had never seen the speaker before. He was a small, dark man, muffled up about the throat, with blue glasses, a large black beard, and his hat drawn low upon his eyes.

"You are a poor man, I suppose," he said, in a quick, eager whisper, "and, like other poor men, would not object to be better off. Would you like to earn a couple of thousand florins?"

"In what way?"

"Hush! You are to stop at Padua, are you not, and to go on again at Ponte di Brenta?"

I nodded.

"Suppose you did nothing of the kind. Suppose, instead of turning off the steam, you jump off the engine, and let the train run on?"

"Impossible. There are seventy yards of embankment gone, and—"

"Basta! I know that. Save yourself, and let the train run on. It would be nothing but an accident."

I turned hot and cold; I trembled; my heart beat fast, and my breath failed.

"Why do you tempt me?" I faltered.

"For Italy's sake," he whispered; "for liberty's sake. I know you are no Italian; but, for all that, you may be a friend. This Loredano is one of his country's bitterest enemies. Stay, here are the two thousand florins."

I thrust his hand back fiercely.

"No—no," I said. "No blood-money. If I do it, I do it neither for Italy nor for money; but for vengeance."

"For vengeance!" he repeated.

At this moment the signal was given for backing up to the platform. I sprang to my place upon the engine without another word. When I again looked towards the spot where he had been standing, the stranger was gone.

I saw them take their places—Duke and Duchess, secretary and priest, valet and maid. I saw the station-master bow them into the carriage, and stand, bare-headed, beside the door. I could not distinguish their faces; the platform was too dusk, and the glare from the engine fire too strong; but I recognised her stately figure, and the poise of her head. Had I not been told who she was, I should have known her by those traits alone. Then the guard's whistle shrilled out, and the station-master made his last bow; I turned the steam on; and we started.

My blood was on fire. I no longer trembled or hesitated. I felt as if every nerve was iron, and every pulse instinct with deadly purpose. She was in my power, and I would be avenged. She should die—she, for whom I had stained my soul with my friend's blood! She should die, in the plenitude of her wealth and her beauty, and no power upon earth should save her!

The stations flew past. I put on more steam; I bade the fireman heap in the coke, and stir the blazing mass. I would have outstripped the wind, had it been possible. Faster and faster—hedges and trees, bridges, and stations, flashing past—villages no sooner seen than gone—telegraph wires twisting, and dipping, and twining themselves in one, with the awful swiftness of our pace! Faster and faster, till the fireman at my side looks white and scared, and refuses to add more fuel to the furnace. Faster and faster, till the wind rushes in our faces and drives the breath back upon our lips.

I would have scorned to save myself. I meant to die with the rest. Mad as I was—and I believe from my very soul that I was utterly mad for the time—I felt a passing pang of pity for the old man and his suite. I would have spared the poor fellow at my side, too, if I could; but the pace at which we were going made escape impossible.

Vicenza was passed—a mere confused vision of lights. Pojana flew by. At Padua, but nine miles distant, our passengers were to alight. I saw the fireman's face turned upon me in remonstrance; I saw his lips move, though I could not hear a word; I saw his expression change suddenly from remonstrance to a deadly terror, and then—merciful Heaven! then, for the first time, I saw that he and I were no longer alone upon the engine.

There was a third man—a third man standing on my right hand, as the fireman was standing on my left—a tall, stalwart man, with short curling hair, and a flat Scotch cap upon his head. As I fell back in the first shock of surprise, he stepped nearer; took my place at the engine, and turned the steam off. I opened my lips to speak to him; he turned his head slowly, and looked me in the face.

Matthew Price!

I uttered one long wild cry, flung my arms wildly up above my head, and fell as if I had been smitten with an axe.

I am prepared for the objections that may be made to my story. I expect, as a matter of course, to be told that this was an optical illusion, or that I was suffering from pressure on the brain, or even that I laboured under an attack of temporary insanity. I have heard all these arguments before, and, if I may be forgiven for saying so, I have no desire to hear them again. My own mind has been made up upon this subject for many a year. All that I can say—all that I know is—that Matthew Price came back from the dead, to save my soul and the lives of those whom I, in my guilty rage, would have hurried to destruction. I believe this as I believe in the mercy of Heaven and the forgiveness of repentant sinners.

THE SHADOW IN THE CORNER,
by Mary Elizabeth Braddon

Wildheath Grange stood a little way back from the road, with a barren stretch of heath behind it, and a few tall fir-trees, with straggling wind-tossed heads, for its only shelter. It was a lonely house on a lonely road, little better than a lane, leading across a desolate waste of sandy fields to the sea-shore; and it was a house that bore a bad name among the natives of the village of Holcroft, which was the nearest place where humanity might be found.

It was a good old house, nevertheless, substantially built in the days when there was no stint of stone and timber—a good old grey stone house with many gables, deep window-seats, and a wide staircase, long dark passages, hidden doors in queer corners, closets as large as some modern rooms, and cellars in which a company of soldiers might have lain perdu.

This spacious old mansion was given over to rats and mice, loneliness, echoes, and the occupation of three elderly people: Michael Bascom, whose forebears had been landowners of importance in the neighbourhood, and his two servants, Daniel Skegg and his wife, who had served the owner of that grim old house ever since he left the university, where he had lived fifteen years of his life —five as student, and ten as professor of natural science.

At three-and-thirty Michael Bascom had seemed a middle-aged man; at fifty-six he looked and moved and spoke like an old man. During that interval of twenty-three years he had lived alone in Wildheath Grange, and the country people told each other that the house had made him what he was. This was a fanciful and superstitious notion on their part, doubtless, yet it would not have been difficult to have traced a certain affinity between the dull grey building and the man who lived in it. Both seemed alike remote from the common cares and interests of humanity; both had an air of settled melancholy, engendered by perpetual solitude; both had the same faded complexion, the same look of slow decay.

Yet lonely as Michael Bascom's life was at Wildheath Grange, he would not on any account have altered its tenor. He had been glad to exchange the comparative seclusion of college rooms for the unbroken solitude of Wildheath. He was a fanatic in his love of scientific research, and his quiet days were filled to the brim with labours that seldom failed to interest and satisfy him. There were periods of depression, occasional moments of doubt, when the goal towards which he strove seemed unattainable, and his spirit fainted within him. Happily such times were rare with him. He had a dogged power of continuity which ought to have carried him to the highest pinnacle of achievement, and which perhaps might ultimately have won for him a grand name and a world-wide renown, but for a catastrophe which burdened the declining years of his harmless life with an unconquerable remorse.

One autumn morning—when he had lived just three-and-twenty years at Wildheath, and had only lately begun to perceive that his faithful butler and body servant, who was middle-aged when he first employed him, was actually getting old—Mr. Bascom's breakfast meditations over the latest treatise on the atomic theory were interrupted by an abrupt demand from that very Daniel Skegg. The man was accustomed to wait upon his master in the most absolute silence, and his sudden breaking out into speech was almost as startling as if the bust of Socrates above the bookcase had burst into human language.

"It's no use," said Daniel; "my missus must have a girl!"

"A what?" demanded Mr. Bascom, without taking his eyes from the line he had been reading.

"A girl—a girl to trot about and wash up, and help the old lady. She's getting weak on her legs, poor soul. We've none of us grown younger in the last twenty years."

"Twenty years!" echoed Michael Bascom scornfully. "What is twenty years in the formation of a strata—what even in the growth of an oak—the cooling of a volcano!"

"Not much, perhaps, but it's apt to tell upon the bones of a human being."

"The manganese staining to be seen upon some skulls would certainly indicate—" began the scientist dreamily.

"I wish my bones were only as free from rheumatics as they were twenty years ago," pursued Daniel testily; "and then, perhaps, I should make light of twenty years. Howsoever, the long and the short of it is, my missus must have a girl. She can't go on trotting up and down these everlasting passages, and standing in that stone scullery year after year, just as if she was a young woman. She must have a girl to help."

"Let her have twenty girls," said Mr. Bascom, going back to his book.

"What's the use of talking like that, sir. Twenty girls, indeed! We shall have rare work to get one."

"Because the neighbourhood is sparsely populated?" interrogated Mr. Bascom, still reading.

"No, sir. Because this house is known to be haunted."

Michael Bascom laid down his book, and turned a look of grave reproach upon his servant.

"Skegg," he said in a severe voice, "I thought you had lived long enough with me to be superior to any folly of that kind."

"I don't say that I believe in ghosts," answered Daniel with a semi-apologetic air; "but the country people do. There's not a mortal among 'em that will venture across our threshold after nightfall."

"Merely because Anthony Bascom, who led a wild life in London, and lost his money and land, came home here broken-hearted, and is supposed to have destroyed himself in this house—the only remnant of property that was left him out of a fine estate."

"Supposed to have destroyed himself!" cried Skegg; "why the fact is as well known as the death of Queen Elizabeth, or the great fire of London. Why, wasn't he buried at the cross-roads between here and Holcroft?"

"An idle tradition, for which you could produce no substantial proof," retorted Mr. Bascom.

"I don't know about proof; but the country people believe it as firmly as they believe their Gospel."

"If their faith in the Gospel was a little stronger they need not trouble themselves about Anthony Bascom."

"Well," grumbled Daniel, as he began to clear the table, "a girl of some kind we must get, but she'll have to be a foreigner, or a girl that's hard driven for a place."

When Daniel Skegg said a foreigner, he did not mean the native of some distant clime, but a girl who had not been born and bred at Holcroft. Daniel had been raised and reared in that insignificant hamlet, and, small and dull as it was, he considered the world beyond it only margin.

Michael Bascom was too deep in the atomic theory to give a second thought to the necessities of an old servant. Mrs. Skegg was an individual with whom he rarely came in contact. She lived for the most part in a gloomy region at the north end of the house, where she ruled over the solitude of a kitchen, that looked like a cathedral, and numerous offices of the sculler, larder, and pantry class, where she carried on a perpetual warfare with spiders and beetles, and wore her old life out in the labour of sweeping and scrubbing. She was a woman of severe aspect, dogmatic piety, and a bitter tongue. She was a good plain cook, and ministered diligently to her master's wants. He was not an epicure, but liked his life to be smooth and easy, and the equilibrium of his mental power would have been disturbed by a bad dinner.

He heard no more about the proposed addition to his household for a space of ten days, when Daniel Skegg again startled him amidst his studious repose by the abrupt announcement:

"I've got a girl!"

"Oh," said Michael Bascom; "have you?" and he went on with his book.

This time he was reading an essay on phosphorus and its functions in relation to the human brain.

"Yes," pursued Daniel in his usual grumbling tone; "she was a waif and stray, or I shouldn't have got her. If she'd been a native, she'd never have come to us."

"I hope she's respectable," said Michael.

"Respectable! That's the only fault she has, poor thing. She's too good for the place. She's never been in service before, but she says she's willing to work, and I daresay my old woman will be able to break her in. Her father was a small tradesman at Yarmouth. He died a month ago, and left this poor thing homeless. Mrs. Midge, at Holcroft, is her aunt, and she said to the girl, Come and stay with me till you get a place; and the girl has been staying with Mrs. Midge for the last three weeks, trying to hear of a place. When Mrs. Midge heard that my missus wanted a girl to help, she thought it would be the very thing for her niece Maria. Luckily Maria had heard nothing about this house, so the poor innocent dropped me a curtsey, and said she'd be thankful to come, and would do her best to learn her duty. She'd had an easy time of it with her father, who had educated her above her station, like a fool as he was," growled Daniel.

"By your own account I'm afraid you've made a bad bargain," said Michael. "You don't want a young lady to clean kettles and pans."

"If she was a young duchess, my old woman would make her work," retorted Skegg decisively.

"And pray where are you going to put this girl?" asked Mr. Bascom, rather irritably; "I can't have a strange young woman tramping up and down the passages

outside my room. You know what a wretched sleeper I am, Skegg. A mouse behind the wainscot is enough to wake me."

"I've thought of that," answered the butler, with his look of ineffable wisdom.
"I'm not going to put her on your floor. She's to sleep in the attics."

"Which room?"

"The big one at the north end of the house. That's the only ceiling that doesn't
let water. She might as well sleep in a shower-bath as in any of the other attics."

"The room at the north end," repeated Mr. Bascom thoughtfully; "isn't that
—?"

"Of course it is," snapped Skegg; "but she doesn't know anything about it."

* * * *

Mr. Bascom went back to his books and forgot all about the orphan from
Yarmouth, until one morning on entering his study he was startled by the appearance of a strange girl, in a neat black and white cotton gown, busy dusting the
volumes which were stacked in blocks upon his spacious writing-table—and doing it with such deft and careful hands that he had no inclination to be angry at
this unwonted liberty. Old Mrs. Skegg had religiously refrained from all such
dusting, on the plea that she did not wish to interfere with the master's ways.
One of the master's ways, therefore, had been to inhale a good deal of dust in the
course of his studies.

The girl was a slim little thing, with a pale and somewhat old-fashioned face,
flaxen hair, braided under a neat muslin cap, a very fair complexion, and light
blue eyes. They were the lightest blue eyes Michael Bascom had ever seen, but
there was a sweetness and gentleness in their expression which atoned for their
insipid colour.

"I hope you do not object to my dusting your books, sir," she said, dropping a
curtsey.

She spoke with a quaint precision which struck Michael Bascom as a pretty
thing in its way.

"No; I don't object to cleanliness, so long as my books and papers are not disturbed. If you take a volume off my desk, replace it on the spot you took it from.
That's all I ask."

"I will be very careful, sir."

"When did you come here?"

"Only this morning, sir."

The student seated himself at his desk, and the girl withdrew, drifting out of
the room as noiselessly as a flower blown across the threshold. Michael Bascom
looked after her curiously. He had seen very little of youthful womanhood in his
dry-as-dust career, and he wondered at this girl as at a creature of a species hitherto unknown to him. How fairly and delicately she was fashioned; what a
translucent skin; what soft and pleasing accents issued from those rose-tinted
lips. A pretty thing, assuredly, this kitchen wench! A pit that in all this busy
world there could be no better work found for her than the scouring of pots and
pans.

Absorbed in considerations about dry bones, Mr. Bascom thought no more of
the pale-faced handmaiden. He saw her no more about his rooms. Whatever
work she did there was done early in the morning, before the scholar's breakfast.

She had been a week in the house, when he met her one day in the hall. He was struck by the change in her appearance.

The girlish lips had lost their rose-bud hue; the pale blue eyes had a frightened look, and there were dark rings round them, as in one whose nights had been sleepless, or troubled by evil dreams.

Michael Bascom was so startled by an undefinable look in the girl's face that, reserved as he was by habit and nature, he expanded so far as to ask her what ailed her.

"There is something amiss, I am sure," he said. "What is it?"

"Nothing, sir," she faltered, looking still more scared at his question. "Indeed, it is nothing; or nothing worth troubling you about."

"Nonsense. Do you suppose, because I live among books, I have no sympathy with my fellow-creatures? Tell me what is wrong with you, child. You have been grieving about the father you have lately lost, I suppose."

"No, sir; it is not that. I shall never leave off being sorry for that. It is a grief which will last me all my life."

"What, there is something else then?" asked Michael impatiently. "I see; you are not happy here. Hard work does not suit you. I thought as much."

"Oh, sir, please don't think that," cried the girl, very earnestly. "Indeed, I am glad to work—glad to be in service; it is only—"

She faltered and broke down, the tears rolling slowly from her sorrowful eyes, despite her effort to keep them back.

"Only what?" cried Michael, growing angry. "The girl is full of secrets and mysteries. What do you mean, wench?"

"I—I know it is very foolish, sir; but I am afraid of the room where I sleep."

"Afraid! Why?"

"Shall I tell you the truth, sir? Will you promise not to be angry?"

"I will not be angry if you will only speak plainly; but you provoke me by these hesitations and suppressions."

"And please, sir, do not tell Mrs. Skegg that I have told you. She would scold me; or perhaps even send me away."

"Mrs. Skegg shall not scold you. Go on, child."

"You may not know the room where I sleep, sir; it is a large room at one end of the house, looking towards the sea. I can see the dark line of water from the window, and I wonder sometimes to think that it is the same ocean I used to see when I was a child at Yarmouth. It is very lonely, sir, at the top of the house. Mr. and Mrs. Skegg sleep in a little room near the kitchen, you know, sir, and I am quite alone on the top floor."

"Skegg told me you had been educated in advance of your position in life, Maria. I should have thought the first effect of a good education would have been to make you superior to any foolish fancies about empty rooms."

"Oh, pray, sir, do not think it is any fault in my education. Father took such pains with me; he spared no expense in giving me as good an education as a tradesman's daughter need wish for. And he was a religious man, sir. He did not believe"—here she paused, with a suppressed shudder—"in the spirits of the dead appearing to the living, since the days of miracles, when the ghost of Samuel appeared to Saul. He never put any foolish ideas into my head, sir. I hadn't a thought of fear when I first lay down to rest in the big lonely room upstairs."

"Well, what then?"

"But on the very first night," the girl went on breathlessly, "I felt weighed down in my sleep as if there were some heavy burden laid upon my chest. It was not a bad dream, but it was a sense of trouble that followed me all through my sleep; and just at daybreak—it begins to be light a little after six—I woke suddenly, with the cold perspiration pouring down my face, and knew that there was something dreadful in the room."

"What do you mean by something dreadful. Did you see anything?"

"Not much, sir; but it froze the blood in my veins, and I knew it was this that had been following me and weighing upon me all through my sleep. In the corner, between the fire-place and the wardrobe, I saw a shadow—a dim, shapeless shadow—"

"Produced by an angle of the wardrobe, I daresay."

"No, sir; I could see the shadow of the wardrobe, distinct and sharp, as if it had been painted on the wall. This shadow was in the corner—a strange, shapeless mass; or, if it had any shape at all, it seemed—"

"What?" asked Michael eagerly.

"The shape of a dead body hanging against the wall!"

Michael Bascom grew strangely pale, yet he affected utter incredulity.

"Poor child," he said kindly; "you have been fretting about your father until your nerves are in a weak state, and you are full of fancies. A shadow in the corner, indeed; why, at daybreak, every corner is full of shadows. My old coat, flung upon a chair, will make you as good a ghost as you need care to see."

"Oh, sir, I have tried to think it is my fancy. But I have had the same burden weighing me down every night. I have seen the same shadow every morning."

"But when broad daylight comes, can you not see what stuff your shadow is made of?"

"No, sir: the shadow goes before it is broad daylight."

"Of course, just like other shadows. Come, come, get these silly notions out of your head, or you will never do for the work-a-day world. I could easily speak to Mrs. Skegg, and make her give you another room, if I wanted to encourage you in your folly. But that would be about the worst thing I could do for you. Besides, she tells me that all the other rooms on that floor are damp; and, no doubt, if she shifted you into one of them, you would discover another shadow in another corner, and get rheumatism into the bargain. No, my good girl, you must try to prove yourself the better for a superior education."

"I will do my best, sir," Maria answered meekly, dropping a curtsey.

Maria went back to the kitchen sorely depressed. It was a dreary life she led at Wildheath Grange—dreary by day, awful by night; for the vague burden and the shapeless shadow, which seemed so slight a matter to the elderly scholar, were unspeakably terrible to her. Nobody had told her that the house was haunted, yet she walked about those echoing passages wrapped round with a cloud of fear. She had no pity from Daniel Skegg and his wife. Those two pious souls had made up their minds that the character of the house should be upheld, so far as Maria went. To her, as a foreigner, the Grange should be maintained to be an immaculate dwelling, tainted by no sulphurous blast from the under world. A willing, biddable girl had become a necessary element in the existence of Mrs. Skegg. That girl had been found, and that girl must be kept. Any fancies of a supernatural character must be put down with a high hand.

241

"Ghosts, indeed!" cried the amiable Skegg. "Read your Bible, Maria, and don't talk no more about ghosts."

"There are ghosts in the Bible," said Maria, with a shiver at the recollection of certain awful passages in the Scripture she knew so well.

"Ah, they was in their right place, or they wouldn't ha' been there," retorted Mrs. Skegg. "You ain't agoin' to pick holes in your Bible, I hope, Maria, at your time of life."

Maria sat down quietly in her corner by the kitchen fire, and turned over the leaves of her dead father's Bible till she came to the chapters they two had loved best and oftenest read together. He had been a simple-minded, straightforward man, the Yarmouth cabinet-maker—a man full of aspirations after good, innately refined, instinctively religious. He and his motherless girl had spent their lives alone together, in the neat little home which Maria had so soon learnt to cherish and beautify; and they had loved each other with an almost romantic love. They had had the same tastes, the same ideas. Very little had sufficed to make them happy. But inexorable death parted father and daughter, in one of those sharp, sudden partings which are like the shock of an earthquake—instantaneous ruin, desolation, and despair.

Maria's fragile form had bent before the tempest. She had lived through a trouble that might have crushed a stronger nature. Her deep religious convictions, and her belief that this cruel parting would not be for ever, had sustained her. She faced life, and its cares and duties, with a gentle patience which was the noblest form of courage.

Michael Bascom told himself that the servant-girl's foolish fancy about the room that had been given her was not a matter of serious consideration. Yet the idea dwelt in his mind unpleasantly, and disturbed him at his labours. The exact sciences require the complete power of a man's brain, his utmost attention; and on this particular evening Michael found that he was only giving his work a part of his attention. The girl's pale face, the girl's tremulous tones, thrust themselves into the foreground of his thoughts.

He closed his book with a fretful sigh, wheeled his large arm-chair round to the fire, and gave himself up to contemplation. To attempt study with so disturbed a mind was useless. It was a dull grey evening, early in November; the student's reading-lamp was lighted, but the shutters were not yet shut, nor the curtains drawn. He could see the leaden sky outside his windows, the fir-tree tops tossing in the angry wind. He could hear the wintry blast whistling amidst the gables, before it rushed off seaward with a savage howl that sounded like a war-whoop.

Michael Bascom shivered, and drew nearer the fire.

"It's childish, foolish nonsense," he said to himself, "yet it's strange she should have that fancy about the shadow, for they say Anthony Bascom destroyed himself in that room. I remember hearing it when I was a boy, from an old servant whose mother was housekeeper at the great house in Anthony's time. I never heard how he died, poor fellow—whether he poisoned himself, or shot himself, or cut his throat; but I've been told that was the room. Old Skegg has heard it too. I could see that by his manner when he told me the girl was to sleep there."

He sat for a long time, till the grey of evening outside his study windows changed to the black of night, and the war-whoop of the wind died away to a low complaining murmur. He sat looking into the fire, and letting his thoughts wander back to the past and the traditions he had heard in his boyhood.

That was a sad, foolish story of his great-uncle, Anthony Bascom: the pitiful story of a wasted fortune and a wasted life. A riotous collegiate career at Cambridge, a racing-stable at Newmarket, an imprudent marriage, a dissipated life in London, a runaway wife; an estate forfeited to Jew money-lenders, and then the fatal end.

Michael had often heard that dismal story: how, when Anthony Bascom's fair false wife had left him, when his credit was exhausted, and his friends had grown tired of him, and all was gone except Wildheath Grange, Anthony, the broken-down man of fashion, had come to that lonely house unexpectedly one night, and had ordered his bed to be got ready for him in the room where he used to sleep when he came to the place for the wild duck shooting, in his boyhood. His old blunderbuss was still hanging over the mantelpiece, where he had left it when he came into the property, and could afford to buy the newest thing in fowling-pieces. He had not been to Wildheath for fifteen years; nav, for a good many of those years he had almost forgotten that the drear; old house belonged to him.

The woman who had been housekeeper at Bascom Park, till house and lands had passed into the hands of the Jews, was at this time the sole occupant of Wildheath. She cooked some supper tor her master, and made him as comfortable as she could in the long untenanted dining-room; but she was distressed to find, when she cleared the table after he had gone upstairs to bed, that he had eaten hardly anything.

Next morning she got his breakfast ready in the same room, which she managed to make brighter and cheerier than it had looked overnight. Brooms, dusting-brushes, and a good fire did much to improve the aspect of things. But the morning wore on to noon, and the old housekeeper listened in vain for her master's footfall on the stairs. Noon waned to late afternoon. She had made no attempt to disturb him, thinking that he had worn himself out by a tedious journey on horseback, and that he was sleeping the sleep of exhaustion. But when the brief November day clouded with the first shadows of twilight, the old woman grew seriously alarmed, and went upstairs to her master's door, where she waited in vain for any reply to her repeated calls and knockings.

The door was locked on the inside, and the housekeeper was not strong enough to break it open. She rushed downstairs again full of fear, and ran bare-headed out into the lonely road. There was no habitation nearer than the turnpike on the old coach road, from which this side road branched off to the sea. There was scanty hope of a chance passer-by. The old woman ran along the road, hardly knowing whither she was going or what she was going to do, but with a vague idea that she must get somebody to help her.

Chance favoured her. A cart, laden with sea-weed, came lumbering slowly along from the level line of sands yonder where the land melted into water. A heavy lumbering farm-labourer walked beside the cart.

"For God's sake, come in and burst open my master's door!" she entreated, seizing the man by the arm. "He's lying dead, or in a fit, and I can't get to help him."

"All right, missus," answered the man, as if such an invitation were a matter of daily occurrence. "Whoa, Dobbin; stond still, horse, and be donged to thee."

Dobbin was glad enough to be brought to anchor on the patch of waste grass in front of the Grange garden. His master followed the housekeeper upstairs, and shattered the old-fashioned box-lock with one blow of his ponderous fist.

The old woman's worst fear was realised. Anthony Bascom was dead. But the mode and manner of his death Michael had never been able to learn. The housekeeper's daughter, who told him the story, was an old woman when he was a boy. She had only shaken her head, and looked unutterable things, when he questioned her too closely. She had never even admitted that the old squire had committed suicide. Yet the tradition of his self-destruction was rooted in the minds of the natives of Holcroft: and there was a settled belief that his ghost, at certain times and seasons, haunted Wildheath Grange.

Now Michael Bascom was a stern materialist. For him the universe with all its inhabitants, was a great machine, governed by inexorable laws. To such a man the idea of a ghost was simply absurd—as absurd as the assertion that two and two make five, or that a circle can be formed of a straight line. Yet he had a kind of dilettante interest in the idea of a mind which could believe in ghosts. The subject offered an amusing psychological study. This poor little pale girl, now, had evidently got some supernatural terror into her head, which could only be conquered by rational treatment.

"I know what I ought to do," Michael Bascom said to himself suddenly. "I'll occupy that room myself tonight, and demonstrate to this foolish girl that her notion about the shadow is nothing more than a silly fancy, bred of timidity and low spirits. An ounce of proof is better than a pound of argument. If I can prove to her that I have spent a night in the room, and seen no such shadow, she will understand what an idle thing superstition is."

Daniel came in presently to shut the shutters.

"Tell your wife to make up my bed in the room where Maria has been sleeping, and to put her into one of the rooms on the first floor for to-night, Skegg," said Mr. Bascom.

"Sir?"

Mr. Bascom repeated his order.

"That silly wench has been complaining to you about her room," Skegg exclaimed indignantly. "She doesn't deserve to be well fed and cared for in a comfortable home. She ought to go to the workhouse."

"Don't be angry with the poor girl, Skegg. She has taken a foolish fancy into her head, and I want to show her how silly she is," said Mr. Bascom.

"And you want to sleep in his—in that room yourself," said the butler.

"Precisely."

"Well," mused Skegg, "if he does walk—which I don't believe—he was your own flesh and blood; and I don't suppose he'll do you any hurt."

When Daniel Skegg went back to the kitchen he railed mercilessly at poor Maria, who sat pale and silent in her corner by the hearth, darning old Mrs. Skegg's grey worsted stockings, which were the roughest and harshest armour that ever human foot clothed itself withal. "Was there ever such a whimsical, fine, lady-like miss," demanded Daniel, "to come into a gentleman's house, and drive him out of his own bedroom to sleep in an attic, with her nonsenses and vagaries." If this was the result of being educated above one's station, Daniel declared that he was thankful he had never got so far in his schooling as to read words of two syllables without spelling. Education might be hanged for him, if this was all it led to.

"I am very sorry," faltered Maria, weeping silently over her work. "Indeed, Mr. Skegg, I made no complaint. My master questioned me, and I told him the truth. That was all."

"All!" exclaimed Mr. Skegg irately; "all, indeed! I should think it was enough."

Poor Maria held her peace. Her mind, fluttered by Daniel's unkindness, had wandered away from that bleak big kitchen to the lost home of the past—the snug little parlour where she and her father had sat beside the cosy hearth on such a night as this; she with her smart work-box and her plain sewing, he with the newspaper he loved to read; the petted cat purring on the rug, the kettle singing on the bright brass trivet, the tea-tray pleasantly suggestive of the most comfortable meal in the day.

Oh, those happy nights, that dear companionship! Were they really gone for ever, leaving nothing behind them but unkindness and servitude?

Michael Bascom retired later than usual that night. He was in the habit of sitting at his books long after every other lamp but his own had been extinguished. The Skeggs had subsided into silence and darkness in their drear ground-floor bed-chamber. Tonight his studies were of a peculiarly interesting kind, and belonged to the order of recreative reading rather than of hard work. He was deep in the history of that mysterious people who had their dwelling-place in the Swiss lakes, and was much exercised by certain speculations and theories about them.

The old eight-day clock on the stairs was striking two as Michael slowly ascended, candle in hand, to the hitherto unknown region of the attics. At the top of the staircase he found himself facing a dark narrow passage which led northwards, a passage that was in itself sufficient to strike terror to a superstitious mind, so black and uncanny did it look.

"Poor child," mused Mr. Bascom, thinking of Maria; "this attic floor is rather dreary, and for a young mind prone to fancies—"

He had opened the door of the north room by this time, and stood looking about him.

It was a large room, with a ceiling that sloped on one side, but was fairly lofty upon the other; an old-fashioned room, full of old-fashioned furniture—big, ponderous, clumsy—associated with a day that was gone and people that were dead. A walnut-wood wardrobe stared him in the face—a wardrobe with brass handles, which gleamed out of the darkness like diabolical eyes. There was a tall four-post bedstead, which had been cut down on one side to accommodate the slope of the ceiling, and which had a misshapen and deformed aspect in consequence. There was an old mahogany bureau, that smelt of secrets. There were some heavy old chairs with rush bottoms, mouldy with age, and much worn. There was a corner washstand, with a big basin and a small jug—the odds and ends of past years. Carpet there was none, save a narrow strip beside the bed.

"It is a dismal room," mused Michael, with the same touch of pity for Maria's weakness which he had felt on the landing just now.

To him it mattered nothing where he slept; but having let himself down to a lower level by his interest in the Swiss lake-people, he was in a manner humanised by the lightness of his evening's reading, and was even inclined to compassionate the weaknesses of a foolish girl.

He went to bed, determined to sleep his soundest. The bed was comfortable, well supplied with blankets, rather luxurious than otherwise, and the scholar had that agreeable sense of fatigue which promises profound and restful slumber.

He dropped off to sleep quickly, but woke with a start ten minutes afterwards. What was this consciousness of a burden of care that had awakened him—this sense of all-pervading trouble that weighed upon his spirits and oppressed his heart—this icy horror of some terrible crisis in life through which he must inevitably pass? To him these feelings were as novel as they were painful. His life had flowed on with smooth and sluggish tide, unbroken by so much as a ripple of sorrow. Yet to-night he felt all the pangs of unavailing remorse; the agonising memory of a life wasted; the stings of humiliation and disgrace, shame, ruin; a hideous death, which he had doomed himself to die by his own hand. These were the horrors that pressed him round and weighed him down as he lay in Anthony Bascom's room.

Yes, even he, the man who could recognise nothing in nature, or in nature's God, better or higher than an irresponsible and invariable machine governed by mechanical laws, was fain to admit that here he found himself face to face with a psychological mystery. This trouble, which came between him and sleep, was the trouble that had pursued Anthony Bascom on the last night of his life. So had the suicide felt as he lay in that lonely room, perhaps striving to rest his wearied brain with one last earthly sleep before he passed to the unknown intermediate land where all is darkness and slumber. And that troubled mind had haunted the room ever since. It was not the ghost of the man's body that returned to the spot where he had suffered and perished, but the ghost of his mind—his very self; no meaningless simulacrum of the clothes he were, and the figure that filled them.

Michael Bascom was not the man to abandon his high ground of sceptical philosophy without a struggle. He tried his hardest to conquer this oppression that weighed upon mind and sense. Again and again he succeeded in composing himself to sleep, but only to wake again and again to the same torturing thoughts, the same remorse, the same despair. So the night passed in unutterable weariness; for though he told himself that the trouble was not his trouble, that there was no reality in the burden, no reason for the remorse, these vivid fancies were as painful as realities, and took as strong a hold upon him.

The first streak of light crept in at the window—dim, and cold, and grey; then came twilight, and he looked at the corner between the wardrobe and the door.

Yes; there was the shadow: not the shadow of the wardrobe only—that was clear enough, but a vague and shapeless something which darkened the dull brown wall; so faint, so shadow, that he could form no conjecture as to its nature, or the thing it represented. He determined to watch this shadow till broad daylight; but the weariness of the night had exhausted him, and before the first dimness of dawn had passed away he had fallen fast asleep, and was tasting the blessed balm of undisturbed slumber. When he woke the winter sun was shining in at the lattice, and the room had lost its gloomy aspect. It looked old-fashioned, and grey, and brown, and shabby; but the depth of its gloom had fled with the shadows and the darkness of night.

Mr. Bascom rose refreshed by a sound sleep, which had lasted nearly three hours. He remembered the wretched feelings which had gone before that renovating slumber; but he recalled his strange sensations only to despise them, and he despised himself for having attached any importance to them.

"Indigestion very likely," he told himself; "or perhaps mere fancy, engendered of that foolish girl's story. The wisest of us is more under the dominion of imagination than he would care to confess. Well, Maria shall not sleep in this room any more. There is no particular reason why she should, and she shall not be made unhappy to please old Skegg and his wife."

When he had dressed himself in his usual leisurely way, Mr. Bascom walked up to the corner where he had seen or imagined the shadow, and examined the spot carefully.

At first sight he could discover nothing of a mysterious character. There was no door in the papered wall, no trace of a door that had been there in the past. There was no trap-door in the worm-eaten boards. There was no dark ineradicable stain to hint at murder. There was not the faintest suggestion of a secret or a mystery.

He looked up at the ceiling. That was sound enough, save for a dirty patch here and there where the rain had blistered it.

Yes; there was something—an insignificant thing, yet with a suggestion of grimness which startled him.

About a foot below the ceiling he saw a large iron hook projecting from the wall, just above the spot where he had seen the shadow of a vaguely defined form. He mounted on a chair the better to examine this hook, and to understand, if he could, the purpose for which it had been put there.

It was old and rusty. It must have been there for many years. Who could have placed it there, and why? It was not the kind of hook upon which one would hang a picture or one's garments. It was placed in an obscure corner. Had Anthony Bascom put it there on the night he died; or did he find it there ready for a fatal use?

"If I were a superstitious man," thought Michael, "I should be inclined to believe that Anthony Bascom hung himself from that rusty old hook."

"Sleep well, sir?" asked Daniel, as he waited upon his master at breakfast.

"Admirably," answered Michael, determined not to gratify the man's curiosity.

He had always resented the idea that Wildheath Grange was haunted.

"Oh, indeed, sir. You were so late that I fancied—"

"Late, yes! I slept so well that I overshot my usual hour for waking. But, by-the-way, Skegg, as that poor girl objects to the room, let her sleep somewhere else. It can't make any difference to us, and it may make some difference to her."

"Humph!" muttered Daniel in his grumpy way; "you didn't see anything queer up there, did you?"

"See anything? Of course not."

"Well, then, why should she see things? It's all her silly fiddle-faddle."

"Never mind, let her sleep in another room."

"There ain't another room on the top floor that's dry."

"Then let her sleep on the floor below. She creeps about quietly enough, poor little timid thing. She won't disturb me."

Daniel grunted, and his master understood the grunt to mean obedient assent; but here Mr. Bascom was unhappily mistaken. The proverbial obstinacy of the pig family is as nothing compared with the obstinacy of a cross-grained old man, whose narrow mind has never been illuminated by education. Daniel was beginning to feel jealous of his master's compassionate interest in the orphan girl. She was a sort of gentle clinging thing that might creep into an elderly bachelor's heart unawares, and make herself a comfortable nest there.

"We shall have fine carryings-on, and me and my old woman will be nowhere, if I don't put down my heel pretty strong upon this nonsense," Daniel muttered to himself, as he carried the breakfast-tray to the pantry.

Maria met him in the passage.

"Well, Mr. Skegg, what did my master say?" she asked breathlessly.

"Did he see anything strange in the room?"

"No, girl. What should he see? He said you were a fool."

"Nothing disturbed him? And he slept there peacefully?" faltered Maria.

"Never slept better in his life. Now don't you begin to feel ashamed of yourself?"

"Yes," she answered meekly; "I am ashamed of being so full of fancies. I will go back to my room tonight, Mr. Skegg, if you like, and I will never complain of it again."

"I hope you won't," snapped Skegg; "you've given us trouble enough already."

Maria sighed, and went about her work in saddest silence. The day wore slowly on, like all other days in that lifeless old house. The scholar sat in his study; Maria moved softly from room to room, sweeping and dusting in the cheerless solitude. The mid-day sun faded into the grey of afternoon, and evening came down like a blight upon the dull old house.

* * * *

Throughout that day Maria and her master never met. Anyone who had been so far interested in the girl as to observe her appearance would have seen that she was unusually pale, and that her eyes had a resolute look, as of one who was resolved to face a painful ordeal. She ate hardly anything all day. She was curiously silent. Skegg and his wife put down both these symptoms to temper.

"She won't eat and she won't talk," said Daniel to the partner of his joys. "That means sulkiness, and I never allowed sulkiness to master me when I was a young man, and you tried it on as a young woman, and I'm not going to be conquered by sulkiness in my old age."

Bed-time came, and Maria bade the Skeggs a civil good-night, and went up to her lonely garret without a murmur.

The next morning came, and Mrs. Skegg looked in vain for her patient handmaiden, when she wanted Maria's services in preparing the breakfast.

"The wench sleeps sound enough this morning," said the old woman. "Go and call her, Daniel. My poor legs can't stand them stairs."

"Your poor legs are getting uncommon useless," muttered Daniel testily, as he went to do his wife's behest.

He knocked at the door, and called Maria—once, twice, thrice, many times; but there was no reply. He tried the door, and found it locked. He shook the door violently, cold with fear.

Then he told himself that the girl had played him a trick. She had stolen away before daybreak, and left the door locked to frighten him. But, no; this could not be, for he could see the key in the lock when he knelt down and put his eye to the keyhole. The key prevented his seeing into the room.

"She's in there, laughing in her sleeve at me," he told himself; "but I'll soon be even with her."

There was a heavy bar on the staircase, which was intended to secure the shutters of the window that lighted the stairs. It was a detached bar, and always stood in a corner near the window, which it was but rarely employed to fasten. Daniel ran down to the landing, and seized upon this massive iron bar, and then ran back to the garret door.

One blow from the heavy bar shattered the old lock, which was the same lock the carter had broken with his strong fist seventy years before. The door flew open, and Daniel went into the attic which he had chosen for the stranger's bed-chamber.

Maria was hanging from the hook in the wall. She had contrived to cover her face decently with her handkerchief. She had hanged herself deliberately about an hour before Daniel found her, in the early grey of morning. The doctor, who was summoned from Holcroft, was able to declare the time at which she had slain herself, but there was no one who could say what sudden access of terror had impelled her to the desperate act, or under what slow torture of nervous apprehension her mind had given way. The coroner's jury returned the customary merciful verdict of "Temporary insanity."

The girl's melancholy fate darkened the rest of Michael Bascom's life. He fled from Wildheath Grange as from an accursed spot, and from the Skeggs as from the murderers of a harmless innocent girl. He ended his days at Oxford, where he found the society of congenial minds, and the books he loved. But the memory of Maria's sad face, and sadder death, was his abiding sorrow. Out of that deep shadow his soul was never lifted.

THE SECRET CHAMBER,
by Margaret Oliphant

Castle Gowrie is one of the most famous and interesting in all Scotland. It is a beautiful old house, to start with,—perfect in old feudal grandeur, with its clustered turrets and walls that could withstand an army,—its labyrinths, its hidden stairs, its long mysterious passages—passages that seem in many cases to lead to nothing, but of which no one can be too sure what they lead to. The front, with its fine gateway and flanking towers, is approached now by velvet lawns, and a peaceful, beautiful old avenue, with double rows of trees, like a cathedral; and the woods out of which these grey towers rise, look as soft and rich in foliage, if not so lofty in growth, as the groves of the South. But this softness of aspect is all new to the place,—that is, new within the century or two which count for but little in the history of a dwelling-place, some part of which, at least, has been standing since the days when the Saxon Athelings brought such share of the arts as belonged to them to solidify and regulate the original Celtic art which reared incised stones upon rude burial-places, and twined mystic knots on its crosses, before historic days. Even of this primitive decoration there are relics at Gowrie, where the twistings and twinings of Runic cords appear still on some bits of ancient wall, solid as rocks, and almost as everlasting. From these to the graceful French turrets, which recall many a grey chateau, what a long interval of years! But these are filled with stirring chronicles enough, besides the dim, not always decipherable records, which different developments of architecture have left on the old house. The Earls of Gowrie had been in the heat of every commotion that took place on or about the Highland line for more generations than any but a Celtic pen could record. Rebellions, revenges, insurrections, conspiracies, nothing in which blood was shed and lands lost, took place in Scotland, in which they had not had a share; and the annals of the house are very full, and not without many a stain. They had been a bold and vigorous race—with much evil in them, and some good; never insignificant, whatever else they might be. It could not be said, however, that they are remarkable nowadays. Since the first Stuart rising, known in Scotland as "the Fifteen," they have not done much that has been worth recording; but yet their family history has always been of an unusual kind. The Randolphs could not be called eccentric in themselves: on the contrary, when you knew them, they were at bottom a respectable race, full of all the country-gentleman virtues; and yet their public career, such as it was, had been marked by the strange leaps and jerks of vicissitude. You would have said an impulsive, fanciful family—now making a grasp at some visionary advantage, now rushing into some wild speculation, now making a sudden sally into public life— but soon falling back into mediocrity, not able apparently, even when the impulse was purely selfish and mercenary, to keep it up. But this would not have been at all a true conception of the family character; their actual virtues were not of the imaginative order, and their freaks were a mystery to their friends. Nevertheless these freaks were what the general world was most aware of in the Randolph race. The late Earl had been a representative peer of Scotland (they had no English title), and had made quite a wonderful start, and for a year or two had seemed about to attain a very eminent place in Scotch affairs; but his ambition was found to have made use of some very equivocal modes of gaining influence, and he dropped accordingly at once and for ever from the political firmament. This was quite a common circumstance in the family. An apparently brilliant beginning, a discovery of evil means adopted for ambitious ends, a sudden subsidence, and the curious conclusion at the end of everything that this schemer, this unscrupulous speculator or politician, was a dull, good man after all—unambitious, contented, full of domestic kindness and benevolence. This family peculiarity made the history of the Randolphs a very strange one, broken by the oddest interruptions, and with no consistency in it. There was another circumstance, however, which attracted still more the wonder and observation of the public. For one who can appreciate such a recondite matter as family character, there are hundreds who are interested in a family secret, and this the house of Randolph possessed in perfection. It was a mystery which piqued the imagination and excited the interest of the entire country. The story went, that somewhere hid amid the massive walls and tortuous passages there was a secret chamber in Gowrie Castle. Everybody knew of its existence; but save the earl, his heir, and one other person, not of the family, but filling a confidential post in their service, no mortal knew where this mysterious hiding-place was. There had been countless guesses made at it, and expedients of all kinds invented to find it out. Every visitor who ever entered the old gateway, nay, even passing travellers who saw the turrets from the road, searched keenly for some trace of this mysterious chamber. But all guesses and researches were equally in vain.

I was about to say that no ghost-story I ever heard of has been so steadily and long believed. But this would be a mistake, for nobody knew even with any certainty that there was a ghost connected with it. A secret chamber was nothing wonderful in so old a house. No doubt they exist in many such old houses, and are always curious and interesting—strange relics, more moving than any history, of the time when a man was not safe in his own house, and when it might be necessary to secure a refuge beyond the reach of spies or traitors at a moment's notice. Such a refuge was a necessity of life to a great medieval noble. The peculiarity about this secret chamber, however, was that some secret connected with the very existence of the family was always understood to be involved in it. It was not only the secret hiding-place for an emergency, a kind of historical possession presupposing the importance of his race, of which a man might be honestly proud; but there was something hidden in it of which assuredly the race could not be proud. It is wonderful how easily a family learns to pique itself upon any distinctive possession. A ghost is a sign of importance not to be despised; a haunted room is worth as much as a small farm to the complacency of the family that owns it. And no doubt the younger branches of the Gowrie family—the lightminded portion of the race—felt this, and were proud of their unfathomable secret, and felt a thrill of agreeable awe and piquant suggestion go through them, when they remembered the mysterious something which they did not know in their familiar home. That thrill ran through the entire circle of visitors, and children, and servants, when the Earl peremptorily forbade a projected improvement, or stopped a reckless exploration. They looked at each other with a pleasurable shiver. "Didyou hear?" they said. "He will not let Lady Gowrie have that closet she wants so much in that bit of wall. He sent the workmen about their business before they could touch it, though the wall is twenty feet thick if it is an inch; ah!" said the visitors, looking at each other; and this lively suggestion sent tinglings of excitement to their very finger-points; but even to his wife, mourning the commodious closet she had intended, the Earl made no explanations. For anything she knew, it might be there, next to her room, this mysterious lurking-place; and it may be supposed that this suggestion conveyed to Lady Gowrie's veins a thrill more keen and strange, perhaps too vivid to be pleasant. But she was not in the favoured or unfortunate number of those to whom the truth could be revealed.

I need not say what the different theories on the subject were. Some thought there had been a treacherous massacre there, and that the secret chamber was blocked by the skeletons of murdered guests,—a treachery no doubt covering the family with shame in its day, but so condoned by long softening of years as to have all the shame taken out of it. The Randolphs could not have felt their character affected by any such interesting historical record. They were not so morbidly sensitive. Some said, on the other hand, that Earl Robert, the wicked Earl, was shut up there in everlasting penance, playing cards with the devil for his soul. But it would have been too great a feather in the family cap to have thus got the devil, or even one of his angels, bottled up, as it were, and safely in hand, to make it possible that any lasting stigma could be connected with such a fact as this. What a thing it would be to know where to lay one's hand upon the Prince of Darkness, and prove him once for all, cloven foot and everything else, to the confusion of gainsayers!

So this was not to be received as a satisfactory solution, nor could any other be suggested which was more to the purpose. The popular mind gave it up, and yet never gave it up; and still everybody who visits Gowrie, be it as a guest, be it as a tourist, be it only as a gazer from a passing carriage, or from the flying railway train which just glimpses its turrets in the distance, daily and yearly spends a certain amount of curiosity, wonderment, and conjecture about the Secret Chamber—the most piquant and undiscoverable wonder which has endured unguessed and undeciphered to modern times.

This was how the matter stood when young John Randolph, Lord Lindores, came of age. He was a young man of great character and energy, not like the usual Randolph strain—for, as we have said, the type of character common in this romantically-situated family, notwithstanding the erratic incidents common to them, was that of dullness and honesty, especially in their early days. But young Lindores was not so. He was honest and honourable, but not dull. He had gone through almost a remarkable course at school and at the university—not perhaps in quite the ordinary way of scholarship, but enough to attract men's eyes to him. He had made more than one great speech at the Union. He was full of ambition, and force, and life, intending all sorts of great things, and meaning to make his position a stepping-stone to all that was excellent in public life. Not for him the countrygentleman existence which was congenial to his father. The idea of succeeding to the family honours and becoming a Scotch peer, either represented or representative, filled him with horror; and filial piety in his case was made warm by all the energy of personal hopes when he prayed that his father might live, if not for ever, yet longer than any Lord Gowrie had lived for the last century or two. He was as sure of his election for the county the next time there was a chance, as anybody can be certain of anything; and in the meantime he meant to travel, to go to America, to go no one could tell where, seeking for instruction and experience, as is the manner of high-spirited young men with parliamentary tendencies in the present day. In former times he would have gone "to the wars in the Hie Germanie," or on a crusade to the Holy Land; but the days of the crusaders and of the soldiers of fortune being over, Lindores followed the fashion of his time. He had made all his arrangements for his tour, which his father did not oppose. On the contrary, Lord Gowrie encouraged all those plans, though with an air of melancholy indulgence which his son could not understand. "It will do you good," he said, with a sigh. "Yes, yes, my boy; the best thing for you." This, no doubt, was true enough; but there was an implied feeling that the young man would require something to do him good—that he would want the soothing of change and the gratification of his wishes, as one might speak of a convalescent or the victim of some calamity. This tone puzzled Lindores, who, though he thought it a fine thing to travel and acquire information, was as scornful of the idea of being done good to as is natural to any fine young fellow fresh from Oxford and the triumphs of the Union. But he reflected that the old school had its own way of treating things, and was satisfied. All was settled accordingly for this journey, before he came home to go through the ceremonial performances of the coming of age, the dinner of the tenantry, the speeches, the congratulations, his father's banquet, his mother's ball. It was in summer, and the country was as gay as all the entertainments that were to be given in his honour. His friend who was going to accompany him on his tour, as he had accompanied him through a considerable portion of his life—Almeric Ffarrington, a young man of the same aspirations—came up to Scotland with him for these festivities. And as they rushed through the night on the Great Northern Railway, in the intervals of two naps, they had a scrap of conversation as to these birthday glories. "It will be a bore, but it will not last long," said Lindores. They were both of the opinion that anything that did not produce information or promote culture was a bore.

"But is there not a revelation to be made to you, among all the other things you have to go through?" said Ffarrington. "Have not you to be introduced to the secret chamber, and all that sort of thing? I should like to be of the party there, Lindores."

"Ah," said the heir, "I had forgotten that part of it," which, however, was not the case. "Indeed I don't know if I am to be told. Even family dogmas are shaken nowadays."

"Oh, I should insist on that," said Ffarrington, lightly. "It is not many who have the chance of paying such a visit—better than Home and all the mediums. I should insist upon that."

"I have no reason to suppose that it has any connection with Home or the mediums," said Lindores, slightly nettled. He was himself an *esprit fort*; but a mystery in one's own family is not like vulgar mysteries. He liked it to be respected.

"Oh, no offence," said his companion. "I have always thought that a railway train would be a great chance for the spirits. If one was to show suddenly in that vacant seat beside you, what a triumphant proof of their existence that would be! but they don't take advantage of their opportunities."

Lindores could not tell what it was that made him think at that moment of a portrait he had seen in a back room at the castle of old Earl Robert, the wicked Earl. It was a bad portrait—a daub—a copy made by an amateur of the genuine portrait, which, out of horror of Earl Robert and his wicked ways, had been removed by some intermediate lord from its place in the gallery. Lindores had never seen the original—nothing but this daub of a copy. Yet somehow this face occurred to him by some strange link of association—seemed to come into his eyes as his friend spoke. A slight shiver ran over him. It was strange. He made no reply to Ffarrington, but he set himself to think how it could be that the latent presence in his mind of some anticipation of this approaching disclosure, touched into life by his friend's suggestion, should have called out of his memory a momentary realisation of the acknowledged magician of the family. This sentence is full of long words; but unfortunately long words are required in such a case. And the process was very simple when you traced it out. It was the clearest case of unconscious cerebration. He shut his eyes by way of securing privacy while he thought it out; and being tired, and not at all alarmed by his unconscious cerebration, before he opened them again fell fast asleep.

And his birthday, which was the day following his arrival at Glenlyon, was a very busy day. He had not time to think of anything but the immediate occupations of the moment. Public and private greetings, congratulations, offerings, poured upon him. The Gowries were popular in this generation, which was far from being usual in the family. Lady Gowrie was kind and generous, with that kindness which comes from the heart, and which is the only kindness likely to impress the keen-sighted popular judgment; and Lord Gowrie had but little of the equivocal reputation of his predecessors. They could be splendid now and then on great occasions, though in general they were homely enough; all which the public likes. It was a bore, Lindores said; but yet the young man did not dislike the honours, and the adulation, and all the hearty speeches and good wishes. It is sweet to a young man to feel himself the centre of all hopes. It seemed very reasonable to him—very natural—that he should be so, and that the farmers should feel a pride of anticipation in thinking of his future speeches in Parliament. He promised to them with the sincerest good faith that he would not disappoint their expectations—that he would feel their interest in him an additional spur. What so natural as that interest and these expectations? He was almost solemnised by his own position—so young, looked up to by so many people—so many hopes depending on him; and yet it was quite natural. His father, however, was still more solemnised than Lindores—and this was strange, to say the least. His face grew graver and graver as the day went on, till it almost seemed as if he were dissatisfied with his son's popularity, or had some painful thought weighing on his mind. He was restless and eager for the termination of the dinner, and to get rid of his guests; and as soon as they were gone, showed an equal anxiety that his son should retire too. "Go to bed at once, as a favour to me," Lord Gowrie said. "You will have a great deal of fatigue—to-morrow."

"You need not be afraid for me, sir," said Lindores, half affronted; but he obeyed, being tired. He had not once thought of the secret to be disclosed to him, through all that long day. But when he woke suddenly with a start in the middle of the night, to find the candles all lighted in his room, and his father standing by his bedside, Lindores instantly thought of it, and in a moment felt that the leading event—the chief incident of all that had happened—was going to take place now.

II

Lord Gowrie was very grave, and very pale. He was standing with his hand on his son's shoulder to wake him; his dress was unchanged from the moment they had parted. And the sight of this formal costume was very bewildering to the young man as he started up in his bed. But next moment he seemed to know exactly how it was, and, more than that, to have known it all his life. Explanation seemed unnecessary. At any other moment, in any other place, a man would be startled to be suddenly woke up in the middle of the night. But Lindores had no such feeling; he did not even ask a question, but sprang up, and fixed his eyes, taking in all the strange circumstances, on his father's face.

"Get up, my boy," said Lord Gowrie, "and dress as quickly as you can; it is full time. I have lighted your candles, and your things are all ready. You have had a good long sleep."

Even now he did not ask, What is it? as under any other circumstances he would have done. He got up without a word, with an impulse of nervous speed and rapidity of movement such as only excitement can give, and dressed himself, his father helping him silently. It was a curious scene: the room gleaming with lights, the silence, the hurried toilet, the stillness of deep night all around. The house, though so full, and with the echoes of festivity but just over, was quiet as if there was not a creature within it—more quiet, indeed, for the stillness of vacancy is not half so impressive as the stillness of hushed and slumbering life.

Lord Gowrie went to the table when this first step was over, and poured out a glass of wine from a bottle which stood there,—a rich, golden-coloured, perfumy wine, which sent its scent through the room. "You will want all your strength," he said; "take this before you go. It is the famous Imperial Tokay; there is only a little left, and you will want all your strength."

Lindores took the wine; he had never drunk any like it before, and the peculiar fragrance remained in his mind, as perfumes so often do, with a whole world of association in them. His father's eyes dwelt upon him with a melancholy sympathy. "You are going to encounter the greatest trial of your life," he said; and taking the young man's hand into his, felt his pulse. "It is quick, but it is quite firm, and you have had a good long sleep." Then he did what it needs a great deal of pressure to induce an Englishman to do,—he kissed his son on the cheek. "God bless you!" he said, faltering. "Come, now, everything is ready, Lindores."

He took up in his hand a small lamp, which he had apparently brought with him, and led the way. By this time Lindores began to feel himself again, and to wake to the consciousness of all his own superiorities and enlightenments. The simple sense that he was one of the members of a family with a mystery, and that the moment of his personal encounter with this special power of darkness had come, had been the first thrilling, overwhelming thought. But now as he followed his father, Lindores began to remember that he himself was not altogether like other men; that there was that in him which would make it natural that he should throw some light, hitherto unthought of, upon this carefully-preserved darkness. What secret even there might be in it—secret of hereditary tendency, of psychic force, of mental conformation, or of some curious combination of circumstances at once more and less potent than these—it was for him to find out.

He gathered all his forces about him, reminded himself of modern enlightenment, and bade his nerves be steel to all vulgar horrors. He, too, felt his own
pulse as he followed his father. To spend the night perhaps amongst the skeletons
of that old-world massacre, and to repent the sins of his ancestors—to be brought
within the range of some optical illusion believed in hitherto by all the generations, and which, no doubt, was of a startling kind, or his father would not look
so serious,—any of these he felt himself quite strong to encounter. His heart and
spirit rose. A young man has but seldom the opportunity of distinguishing himself so early in his career; and his was such a chance as occurs to very few. No
doubt it was something that would be extremely trying to the nerves and imagination. He called up all his powers to vanquish both. And along with this call
upon himself to exertion, there was the less serious impulse of curiosity: he
would see at last what the Secret Chamber was, where it was, how it fitted into
the labyrinths of the old house. This he tried to put in its due place as a most interesting object. He said to himself that he would willingly have gone a long
journey at any time to be present at such an exploration; and there is no doubt
that in other circumstances a secret chamber, with probably some unthought-of
historical interest in it, would have been a very fascinating discovery. He tried
very hard to excite himself about this; but it was curious how fictitious he felt the
interest, and how conscious he was that it was an effort to feel any curiosity at all
on the subject. The fact was, that the Secret Chamber was entirely secondary—
thrown back, as all accessories are, by a more pressing interest. The overpower-
ing thought of what was in it drove aside all healthy, natural curiosity about itself.

It must not be supposed, however, that the father and son had a long way to
go to have time for all these thoughts. Thoughts travel at lightning speed, and
there was abundant leisure for this between the time they had left the door of
Lindores' room and gone down the corridor, no further off than to Lord Gowrie's
own chamber, naturally one of the chief rooms of the house. Nearly opposite
this, a few steps further on, was a little neglected room devoted to lumber, with
which Lindores had been familiar all his life. Why this nest of old rubbish, dust,
and cob-webs should be so near the bedroom of the head of the house had been a
matter of surprise to many people—to the guests who saw it while exploring, and
to each new servant in succession who planned an attack upon its ancient stores,
scandalised by finding it to have been neglected by their predecessors. All their
attempts to clear it out had, however, been resisted, nobody could tell how, or indeed thought it worth while to inquire. As for Lindores, he had been used to the
place from his childhood, and therefore accepted it as the most natural thing in
the world. He had been in and out a hundred times in his play. And it was here,
he remembered suddenly, that he had seen the bad picture of Earl Robert which
had so curiously come into his eyes on his journeying here, by a mental movement which he had identified at once as unconscious cerebration. The first feeling in his mind, as his father went to the open door of this lumberroom, was a
mixture of amusement and surprise. What was he going to pick up there? some
old pentacle, some amulet or scrap of antiquated magic to act as armour against
the evil one? But Lord Gowrie, going on and setting down the lamp on the table,
turned round upon his son with a face of agitation and pain which barred all further amusement: he grasped him by the hand, crushing it between his own. "Now
my boy, my dear son," he said, in tones that were scarcely audible. His counte-

nance was full of the dreary pain of a looker-on—one who has no share in the excitement of personal danger, but has the more terrible part of watching those who are in deadliest peril. He was a powerful man, and his large form shook with emotion; great beads of moisture stood upon his forehead. An old sword with a cross handle lay upon a dusty chair among other dusty and battered relics. "Take this with you," he said, in the same inaudible, breathless way—whether as a weapon, whether as a religious symbol, Lindores could not guess. The young man took it mechanically. His father pushed open a door which it seemed to him he had never seen before, and led him into another vaulted chamber. Here even the limited powers of speech Lord Gowrie had retained seemed to forsake him, and his voice became a mere hoarse murmur in his throat. For want of speech he pointed to another door in the further corner of this small vacant room, gave him to understand by a gesture that he was to knock there, and then went back into the lumber-room. The door into this was left open, and a faint glimmer of the lamp shed light into this little intermediate place—this debatable land between the seen and the unseen. In spite of himself, Lindores' heart began to beat. He made a breathless pause, feeling his head go round. He held the old sword in his hand, not knowing what it was. Then, summoning all his courage, he went forward and knocked at the closed door. His knock was not loud, but it seemed to echo all over the silent house. Would everybody hear and wake, and rush to see what had happened? This caprice of imagination seized upon him, ousting all the firmer thoughts, the steadfast calm of mind with which he ought to have encountered the mystery. Would they all rush in, in wild *déshabille*, in terror and dismay, before the door opened? How long it was of opening! He touched the panel with his hand again.—This time there was no delay. In a moment, as if thrown suddenly open by some one within, the door moved. It opened just wide enough to let him enter, stopping half-way as if some one invisible held it, wide enough for welcome, but no more. Lindores stepped across the threshold with a beating heart. What was he about to see? the skeletons of the murdered victims? a ghostly charnel-house full of bloody traces of crime? He seemed to be hurried and pushed in as he made that step. What was this world of mystery into which he was plunged—what was it he saw?

He saw—nothing—except what was agreeable enough to behold,—an antiquated room hung with tapestry, very old tapestry of rude design, its colours faded into softness and harmony; between its folds here and there a panel of carved wood, rude too in design, with traces of half-worn gilding; a table covered with strange instruments, parchments, chemical tubes, and curious machinery, all with a quaintness of form and dimness of material that spoke of age. A heavy old velvet cover, thick with embroidery faded almost out of all colour, was on the table; on the wall above it, something that looked like a very old Venetian mirror, the glass so dim and crusted that it scarcely reflected at all, on the floor an old soft Persian carpet, worn into a vague blending of all colours. This was all that he thought he saw. His heart, which had been thumping so loud as almost to choke him, stopped that tremendous upward and downward motion like a steam piston; and he grew calm. Perfectly still, dim, unoccupied: yet not so dim either; there was no apparent source of light, no windows, curtains of tapestry drawn everywhere—no lamp visible, no fire—and yet a kind of strange light which made everything quite clear. He looked round, trying to smile at his terrors, trying to say to himself that it was the most curious place he had ever seen—that he must show Ffarrington some of that tapestry—that he must really bring away a panel of that carving,—when he suddenly saw that the door was shut by which he had entered—nay, more than shut, undiscernible, covered like all the rest of the walls by that strange tapestry. At this his heart began to beat again in spite of him. He looked round once more, and woke up to more vivid being with a sudden start. Had his eyes been incapable of vision on his first entrance? Unoccupied? Who was that in the great chair?

It seemed to Lindores that he had seen neither the chair nor the man when he came in. There they were, however, solid and unmistakable; the chair carved like the panels, the man seated in front of the table. He looked at Lindores with a calm and open gaze, inspecting him. The young man's heart seemed in his throat fluttering like a bird, but he was brave, and his mind made one final effort to break this spell. He tried to speak, labouring with a voice that would not sound, and with lips too parched to form a word. "I see how it is," was what he wanted to say. It was Earl Robert's face that was looking at him; and startled as he was, he dragged forth his philosophy to support him. What could it be but optical delusions, unconscious cerebration, occult seizure by the impressed and struggling mind of this one countenance? But he could not hear himself speak any word as he stood convulsed, struggling with dry lips and choking voice.

The Appearance smiled, as if knowing his thoughts—not unkindly, not malignly—with a certain amusement mingled with scorn. Then he spoke, and the sound seemed to breathe through the room not like any voice that Lindores had ever heard, a kind of utterance of the place, like the rustle of the air or the ripple of the sea. "You will learn better tonight: this is no phantom of your brain; it is I."

"In God's name," cried the young man in his soul; he did not know whether the words ever got into the air or not, if there was any air;—"in God's name, who are you?"

The figure rose as if coming to him to reply; and Lindores, overcome by the apparent approach, struggled into utterance. A cry came from him—he heard it this time—and even in his extremity felt a pang the more to hear the terror in his own voice. But he did not flinch, he stood desperate, all his strength concentrated in the act; he neither turned nor recoiled. Vaguely gleaming through his mind came the thought that to be thus brought in contact with the unseen was the experiment to be most desired on earth, the final settlement of a hundred questions; but his faculties were not sufficiently under command to entertain it. He only stood firm, that was all.

And the figure did not approach him; after a moment it subsided back again into the chair—subsided, for no sound, not the faintest, accompanied its movements. It was the form of a man of middle age, the hair white, but the beard only crisped with grey, the features those of the picture—a familiar face, more or less like all the Randolphs, but with an air of domination and power altogether unlike that of the race. He was dressed in a long robe of dark colour, embroidered with strange lines and angles. There was nothing repellent or terrible in his air—nothing except the noiselessness, the calm, the absolute stillness, which was as much in the place as in him, to keep up the involuntary trembling of the beholder. His expression was full of dignity and thoughtfulness, and not malignant or unkind. He might have been the kindly patriarch of the house, watching over its fortunes in a seclusion that he had chosen. The pulses that had been beating in Lindores were stilled. What was his panic for? A gleam even of self-ridicule took posses-sion of him, to be standing there like an absurd hero of antiquated romance with the rusty, dusty sword—good for nothing, surely not adapted for use against this noble old magician—in his hand—

"You are right," said the voice, once more answering his thoughts; "what could you do with that sword against me, young Lindores? Put it by. Why should my children meet me like an enemy? You are my flesh and blood. Give me your hand."

A shiver ran through the young man's frame. The hand that was held out to him was large and shapely and white, with a straight line across the palm—a family token upon which the Randolphs prided themselves—a friendly hand; and the face smiled upon him, fixing him with those calm, profound, blue eyes. "Come," said the voice. The word seemed to fill the place, melting upon him from every corner, whispering round him with softest persuasion. He was lulled and calmed in spite of himself. Spirit or no spirit, why should not he accept this proferred courtesy? What harm could come of it? The chief thing that retained him was the dragging of the old sword, heavy and useless, which he held me-chanically, but which some internal feeling—he could not tell what—prevented him from putting down. Superstitition, was it?

"Yes, that is superstition," said his ancestor, serenely; "put it down and come."

"You know my thoughts," said Lindores; "I did not speak."

"Your mind spoke, and spoke justly. Put down that emblem of brute force and superstition together. Here it is the intelligence that is supreme. Come."

Lindores stood doubtful. He was calm; the power of thought was restored to him. If this benevolent venerable patriarch was all he seemed, why his father's terror? why the secrecy in which his being was involved? His own mind, though calm, did not seem to act in the usual way. Thoughts seemed to be driven across it as by a wind. One of these came to him suddenly now—

"How there looked him in the face,
An angel beautiful and bright,
And how he knew it was a fiend."

The words were not ended, when Earl Robert replied suddenly with impa-tience in his voice, "Fiends are of the fancy of men; like angels and other follies. I am your father. You know me; and you are mine, Lindores. I have power be-yond what you can understand; but I want flesh and blood to reign and to enjoy. Come, Lindores!"

He put out his other hand. The action, the look, were those of kindness, al-most of longing, and the face was familiar, the voice was that of the race. Super-natural! was it supernatural that this man should live here shut up for ages? and why? and how? Was there any explanation of it? The young man's brain began to reel. He could not tell which was real—the life he had left half an hour ago, or this. He tried to look round him, but could not; his eyes were caught by those other kindred eyes, which seemed to dilate and deepen as he looked at them, and drew him with a strange compulsion. He felt himself yielding, swaying towards the strange being who thus invited him. What might happen if he yielded? And he could not turn away, he could not tear himself from the fascination of those eyes. With a sudden strange impulse which was half despair and half a bewildering half-conscious desire to try one potency against another, he thrust forward the cross of the old sword between him and those appealing hands. "In the name of God!" he said.

Lindores never could tell whether it was that he himself grew faint, and that the dimness of swooning came into his eyes after this violence and strain of emotion, or if it was his spell that worked. But there was an instantaneous change. Everything swam around him for the moment, a giddiness and blindness seized him, and he saw nothing but the vague outlines of the room, empty as when he entered it. But gradually his consciousness came back, and he found himself standing on the same spot as before, clutching the old sword, and gradually, as though a dream, recognised the same figure emerging out of the mist which—was it solely in his own eyes?—had enveloped everything. But it was no longer in the same attitude. The hands which had been stretched out to him were busy now with some of the strange instruments on the table, moving about, now in the action of writing, now as if managing the keys of a telegraph. Lindores felt that his brain was all atwist and set wrong; but he was still a human being of his century. He thought of the telegraph with a keen thrill of curiosity in the midst of his reviving sensations. What communication was this which was going on before his eyes? The magician worked on. He had his face turned towards his victim, but his hands moved with unceasing activity. And Lindores, as he grew accustomed to the position, began to weary—to feel like a neglected suitor waiting for an audience. To be wound up to such a strain of feeling, then left to wait, was intolerable; impatience seized upon him. What circumstances can exist, however horrible, in which a human being will not feel impatience? He made a great many efforts to speak before he could succeed. It seemed to him that his body felt more fear than he did—that his muscles were contracted, his throat parched, his tongue refusing its office, although his mind was unaffected and undismayed. At last he found an utterance in spite of all resistance of his flesh and blood.

"Who are you?" he said hoarsely. "You that live here and oppress this house?"

The vision raised its eyes full upon him, with again that strange shadow of a smile, mocking yet not unkind. "Do you remember me," he said, "on your journey here?"

"That was—a delusion." The young man gasped for breath.

"More like that you are a delusion. You have lasted but one-and-twenty years, and I—for centuries."

"How? For centuries—and why? Answer me—are you man or demon?" cried Lindores, tearing the words as he felt out of his own throat. "Are you living or dead?"

The magician looked at him with the same intense gaze as before. "Be on my side, and you shall know everything, Lindores. I want one of my own race. Others I could have in plenty; but I want *you*. A Randolph, a Randolph! and *you*. Dead! do I seem dead? You shall have everything—more than dreams can give —if you will be on my side."

Can he give what he has not? was the thought that ran through the mind of Lindores. But he could not speak it. Something that choked and stifled him was in his throat.

"Can I give what I have not? I have everything—power, the one thing worth having; and you shall have more than power, for you are young—my son! Lindores!"

To argue was natural, and gave the young man strength. "Is this life," he said, "here? What is all your power worth—here? To sit for ages, and make a race unhappy?"

A momentary convulsion came across the still face. "You scorn me", he cried, with an appearance of emotion, "because you do not understand how I move the world. Power! 'Tis more than fancy can grasp. And you shall have it!" said the wizard, with what looked like a show of enthusiasm. He seemed to come nearer, to grow larger. He put forth his hand again, this time so close that it seemed impossible to escape. And a crowd of wishes seemed to rush upon the mind of Lindores. What harm to try if this might be true? To try what it meant—perhaps nothing, delusions, vain show, and then there could be no harm; or perhaps there was knowledge to be had, which was power. Try, try, try! the air buzzed about him. The room seemed full of voices urging him. His bodily frame rose into a tremendous whirl of excitement, his veins seemed to swell to bursting, his lips seemed to force a yes, in spite of him, quivering as they came apart. The hiss of the *s* seemed in his ears. He changed it into the name which was a spell too, and cried, "Help me, God!" not knowing why.

Then there came another pause—he felt as if he had been dropped from something that had held him, and had fallen, and was faint. The excitement had been more than he could bear. Once more everything swam around him, and he did not know where he was. Had he escaped altogether? was the first waking wonder of consciousness in his mind. But when he could think and see again, he was still in the same spot, surrounded by the old curtains and the carved panels—but alone. He felt, too, that he was able to move, but the strangest dual consciousness was in him throughout all the rest of his trial. His body felt to him as a frightened horse feels to a traveller at night—a thing separate from him, more frightened than he was—starting aside at every step, seeing more than its master. His limbs shook with fear and weakness, almost refusing to obey the action of his will, trembling under him with jerks aside when he compelled himself to move. The hair stood upright on his head—every finger trembled as with palsy—his lips, his eyelids, quivered with nervous agitation. But his mind was strong, stimulated to a desperate calm. He dragged himself round the room, he crossed the very spot where the magician had been—all was vacant, silent, clear. Had he vanquished the enemy? This thought came into his mind with an involuntary triumph. The old strain of feeling came back. Such efforts might be produced, perhaps, only by imagination, by excitement, by delusion—

Lindores looked up, by a sudden attraction he could not tell what: and the blood suddenly froze in his veins that had been so boiling and fermenting. Some one was looking at him from the old mirror on the wall. A face not human and life-like, like that of the inhabitant of this place, but ghostly and terrible, like one of the dead; and while he looked, a crowd of other faces came behind, all looking at him, some mournfully, some with a menace in their terrible eyes. The mirror did not change, but within its small dim space seemed to contain an innumerable company, crowded above and below, all with one gaze at him. His lips dropped apart with a gasp of horror. More and more and more! He was standing close by the table when this crowd came. Then all at once there was laid upon him a cold hand. He turned; close to his side, brushing him with his robe, holding him fast by the arm, sat Earl Robert in his great chair. A shriek came from the young man's lips. He seemed to hear it echoing away into unfathomable distance. The cold touch penetrated to his very soul.

"Do you try spells upon me, Lindores? That is a tool of the past. You shall have something better to work with. And are you so sure of whom you call upon? If there is such a one, why should He help you who never called on Him before?"

Lindores could not tell if these words were spoken; it was a communication rapid as the thoughts in the mind. And he felt as if something answered that was not all himself. He seemed to stand passive and hear the argument. "Does God reckon with a man in trouble, whether he has ever called to Him before? I call now" (now he felt it was himself that said): "go, evil spirit!—go, dead and cursed!—go, in the name of God!"

He felt himself flung violently against the wall. A faint laugh, stifled in the throat, and followed by a groan, rolled round the room; the old curtains seemed to open here and there, and flutter, as if with comings and goings. Lindores leaned with his back against the wall, and all his senses restored to him. He felt blood trickle down his neck; and in this contact once more with the physical, his body, in its madness of fright, grew manageable. For the first time he felt wholly master of himself. Though the magician was standing in his place, a great, majestic, appalling figure, he did not shrink. "Liar!" he cried, in a voice that rang and echoed as in natural air—"clinging to miserable life like a worm—like a reptile; promising all things, having nothing, but this den, unvisited by the light of day. Is this your power—your superiority to men who die? is it for this that you oppress a race, and make a house unhappy? I vow, in God's name, your reign is over! You and your secret shall last no more."

There was no reply. But Lindores felt his terrible ancestor's eyes getting once more that mesmeric mastery over him which had already almost overcome his powers. He must withdraw his own, or perish. He had a human horror of turning his back upon that watchful adversary: to face him seemed the only safety; but to face him was to be conquered. Slowly, with a pang indescribable, he tore himself from that gaze: it seemed to drag his eyes out of their sockets, his heart out of his bosom. Resolutely, with the daring of desperation, he turned round to the spot where he entered—the spot where no door was,—hearing already in anticipation the step after him—feeling the grip that would crush and smother his exhausted life—but too desperate to care.

III

How wonderful is the blue dawning of the new day before the sun! not rosy-fingered, like that Aurora of the Greeks who comes later with all her wealth; but still, dreamy, wonderful, stealing out of the unseen, abashed by the solemnity of the new birth. When anxious watchers see that first brightness come stealing upon the waiting skies, what mingled relief and renewal of misery is in it! another long day to toil through—yet another sad night over! Lord Gowrie sat among the dust and cobwebs, his lamp flaring idly into the blue morning. He had heard his son's human voice, though nothing more; and he expected to have him brought out by invisible hands, as had happened to himself, and left lying in long deathly swoon outside that mystic door. This was how it had happened to heir after heir, as told from father to son, one after another, as the secret came down. One or two bearers of the name Lindores had never recovered; most of them had been saddened and subdued for life. He remembered sadly the freshness of existence which had never come back to himself; the hopes that had never blossomed again; the assurance with which never more he had been able to go about the world. And now his son would be as himself—the glory gone out of his living—his ambitions, his aspirations wrecked. He had not been endowed as his boy was—he had been a plain, honest man, and nothing more; but experience and life had given him wisdom enough to smile by times at the coquetries of mind in which Lindores indulged. Were they all over now, those freaks of young intelligence, those enthusiasms of the soul? The curse of the house had come upon him—the magnetism of that strange presence, ever living, ever watchful, present in all the family history. His heart was sore for his son; and yet along with this there was a certain consolation to him in having henceforward a partner in the secret—some one to whom he could talk of it as he had not been able to talk since his own father died. Almost all the mental struggles which Gowrie had known had been connected with this mystery; and he had been obliged to hide them in his bosom—to conceal them even when they rent him in two. Now he had a partner in his trouble. This was what he was thinking as he sat through the night. How slowly the moments passed! He was not aware of the daylight coming in. After a while even thought got suspended in listening. Was not the time nearly over? He rose and began to pace about the encumbered space, which was but a step or two in extent. There was an old cupboard in the wall, in which there were restoratives—pungent essences and cordials, and fresh water which he had himself brought—everything was ready; presently the ghastly body of his boy, half dead, would be thrust forth into his care.

But this was not how it happened. While he waited, so intent that his whole frame seemed to be capable of hearing, he heard the closing of the door, boldly shut with a sound that rose in muffled echoes through the house, and Lindores himself appeared, ghastly indeed as a dead man, but walking upright and firmly, the lines of his face drawn, and his eyes staring. Lord Gowrie uttered a cry. He was more alarmed by this unexpected return than by the helpless prostration of the swoon which he had expected. He recoiled from his son as if he too had been a spirit. "Lindores!" he cried; was it Lindores, or some one else in his place? The boy seemed as if he did not see him. He went straight forward to where the water stood on the dusty table, and took a great draught, then turned to the door. "Lindores!" said his father, in miserable anxiety; "don't you know me?" Even then the young man only half looked at him, and put out a hand almost as cold as the hand that had clutched himself in the Secret Chamber; a faint smile came upon his face. "Don't stay here," he whispered; "come! come!"

Lord Gowrie drew his son's arm within his own, and felt the thrill through and through him of nerves strained beyond mortal strength. He could scarcely keep up with him as he stalked along the corridor to his room, stumbling as if he could not see, yet swift as an arrow. When they reached his room he turned and closed and locked the door, then laughed as he staggered to the bed. "That will not keep him out, will it?" he said.

"Lindores," said his father, "I expected to find you unconscious. I am almost more frightened to find you like this. I need not ask if you have seen him—"

"Oh, I have seen him. The old liar! Father, promise to expose him, to turn him out—promise to clear out that accursed old nest! It is our own fault. Why have we left such a place shut out from the eye of day? Isn't there something in the Bible about those who do evil hating the light?"

"Lindores! you don't often quote the Bible."

"No, I suppose not; but there is more truth in—many things than we thought."

"Lie down," said the anxious father. "Take some of this wine—try to sleep."

"Take it away; give me no more of that devil's drink. Talk to me—that's better. Did you go through it all the same, poor papa?—and hold me fast. You are warm—you are honest!" he cried. He put forth his hands over his father's, warming them with the contact. He put his cheek like a child against his father's arm. He gave a faint laugh, with the tears in his eyes. "Warm and honest," he repeated. "Kind flesh and blood! and did you go through it all the same?"

"My boy!" cried the father, feeling his heart glow and swell over the son who had been parted from him for years by that development of young manhood and ripening intellect which so often severs and loosens the ties of home. Lord Gowrie had felt that Lindores half despised his simple mind and duller imagination; but this childlike clinging overcame him, and tears stood in his eyes. "I fainted, I suppose. I never knew how it ended. They made what they liked of me. But you, my brave boy, you came out of your own will."

Lindores shivered. "I fled!" he said. "No honour in that. I had not courage to face him longer. I will tell you by-and-by. But I want to know about you."

What an ease it was to the father to speak! For years and years this had been shut up in his breast. It had made him lonely in the midst of his friends.

"Thank God," he said, "that I can speak to you, Lindores. Often and often I have been tempted to tell your mother. But why should I make her miserable? She knows there is something; she knows when I see him, but she knows no more."

"When you see him?" Lindores raised himself, with a return of his first ghastly look, in his bed. Then he raised his clenched fist wildly, and shook it in the air. "Vile devil, coward, deceiver!"

"Oh hush, hush, hush, Lindores! God help us! what troubles you may bring!"

"And God help me, whatever troubles I bring," said the young man. "I defy him, father. An accursed being like that must be less, not more powerful, than we are—with God to back us. Only stand by me: stand by me—"

"Hush, Lindores! You don't feel it yet—never to get out of hearing of him all your life! He will make you pay for it—if not now, after; when you remember he is there; whatever happens, knowing everything! But I hope it will not be so bad with you as with me, my poor boy. God help you indeed if it is, for you have more imagination and more mind. I am able to forget him sometimes when I am occupied—when in the hunting-field, going across country. But you are not a hunting man, my poor boy," said Lord Gowrie, with a curious mixture of a regret, which was less serious than the other. Then he lowered his voice. "Lindores, this is what has happened to me since the moment I gave him my hand."

"I did not give him my hand."

"You did not give him your hand? God bless you, my boy! You stood out?" he cried, with tears again rushing to his eyes; "and they say—they say—but I don't know if there is any truth in it." Lord Gowrie got up from his son's side, and walked up and down with excited steps. "If there should be truth in it! Many people think the whole thing is a fancy. If there should be truth in it, Lindores!"

"In what, father?"

264

"They say, if he is once resisted his power is broken—once refused. *You* could stand against him—you! Forgive me, my boy, as I hope God will forgive me, to have thought so little of His best gifts," cried Lord Gowrie, coming back with wet eyes; and stooping, he kissed his son's hand. "I thought you would be more shaken by being more mind than body," he said, humbly. "I thought if I could but have saved you from the trial; and *you* are the conqueror!"

"Am I the conqueror? I think all my bones are broken, father—out of their sockets," said the young man, in a low voice. "I think I shall go to sleep."

"Yes, rest, my boy. It is the best thing for you," said the father, though with a pang of momentary disappointment.

Lindores fell back upon the pillow. He was so pale that there were moments when the anxious watcher thought him not sleeping but dead. He put his hand out feebly, and grasped his father's hand. "Warm—honest," he said, with a feeble smile about his lips, and fell asleep.

The daylight was full in the room, breaking through shutters and curtains and mocking at the lamp that still flared on the table. It seemed an emblem of the disorders, mental and material, of this strange night; and, as such, it affected the plain imagination of Lord Gowrie, who would have fain got up to extinguish it, and whose mind returned again and again, in spite of him, to this symptom of disturbance. By-and-by, when Lindores' grasp relaxed, and he got his hand free, he got up from his son's bedside, and put out the lamp, putting it carefully out of the way. With equal care he put away the wine from the table, and gave the room its ordinary aspect, softly opening a window to let in the fresh air of the morning. The park lay fresh in the early sunshine, still, except for the twittering of the birds, refreshed with dews, and shining in that soft radiance of the morning which is over before mortal cares are stirring. Never, perhaps, had Gowrie looked out upon the beautiful world around his house without a thought of the weird existence which was going on so near to him, which had gone on for centuries, shut up out of sight of the sunshine. The Secret Chamber had been present with him since ever he saw it. He had never been able to get free of the spell of it. He had felt himself watched, surrounded, spied upon, day after day, since he was of the age of Lindores, and that was thirty years ago. He turned it all over in his mind, as he stood there and his son slept. It had been on his lips to tell it all to his boy, who had now come to inherit the enlightenment of his race. And it was a disappointment to him to have it all forced back again, and silence imposed upon him once more. Would he care to hear it when he woke? would he not rather, as Lord Gowrie remembered to have done himself, thrust the thought as far as he could away from him, and endeavour to forget for the moment—until the time came when he would not be permitted to forget? He had been like that himself, he recollected now. He had not wished to hear his own father's tale. "I remember," he said to himself; "I remember"—turning over everything in his mind—if Lindores might only be willing to hear the story when he woke! But then he himself had not been willing when he was Lindores, and he could understand his son, and could not blame him; but it would be a disappointment. He was thinking this when he heard Lindores' voice calling him. He went back hastily to his bedside. It was strange to see him in his evening dress with his worn face, in the fresh light of the morning, which poured in at every crevice. "Does my mother know?" said Lindores; "what will she think?"

"She knows something; she knows you have some trial to go through. Most likely she will be praying for us both; that's the way of women," said Lord Gowrie, with the tremulous tenderness which comes into a man's voice sometimes when he speaks of a good wife. "I'll go and ease her mind, and tell her all is well over—"

"Not yet. Tell me first," said the young man, putting his hand upon his father's arm.

What an ease it was! "I was not so good to my father," he thought to himself, with sudden penitence for the long-past, long-forgotten fault, which, indeed, he had never realised as a fault before. And then he told his son what had been the story of his life—how he had scarcely ever sat alone without feeling, from some corner of the room, from behind some curtain, those eyes upon him; and how, in the difficulties of his life, that secret inhabitant of the house had been present, sitting by him and advising him. "Whenever there has been anything to do: when there has been a question between two ways, all in a moment I have seen him by me: I feel when he is coming. It does not matter where I am—here or anywhere —as soon as ever there is a question of family business; and always he persuades me to the wrong way, Lindores. Sometimes I yield to him, how can I help it? He makes everything so clear; he makes wrong seem right. If I have done unjust things in my day—"

"You have not, father."

"I have: there were these Highland people I turned out. I did not mean to do it, Lindores; but he showed me that it would be better for the family. And my poor sister that married Tweedside and was wretched all her life. It was his doing, that marriage; he said she would be rich, and so she was, poor thing, poor thing! and died of it. And old Macalister's lease— Lindores, Lindores! when there is any business it makes my heart sick. I know he will come, and advise wrong, and tell me—something I will repent after."

"The thing to do is to decide beforehand, that, good or bad, you will not take his advice."

Lord Gowrie shivered. "I am not strong like you, or clever; I cannot resist. Sometimes I repent in time and don't do it; and then! But for your mother and you children, there is many a day I would not have given a farthing for my life."

"Father," said Lindores, springing from his bed. "two of us together can do many things. Give me your word to clear out this cursed den of darkness this very day."

"Lindores, hush, hush, for the sake of heaven!"

"I will not, for the sake of heaven! Throw it open—let everybody who likes see it—make an end of the secret—pull down everything, curtains, walls. What do you say?—sprinkle holy water? Are you laughing at me?"

"I did not speak," said Earl Gowrie, growing very pale, and grasping his son's arm with both his hands. "Hush, boy; do you think he does not hear?"

And then there was a low laugh close to them—so close that both shrank; a laugh no louder than a breath.

"Did you laugh—father?"

"No, Lindores." Lord Gowrie had his eyes fixed. He was as pale as the dead. He held his son tight for a moment; then his gaze and his grasp relaxed, and he fell back feebly in a chair.

"You see!" he said; "whatever we do it will be the same; we are under his power."

And then there ensued the blank pause with which baffled men confront a hopeless situation. But at that moment the first faint stirrings of the house—a window being opened, a bar undone, a movement of feet, and subdued voices—became audible in the stillness of the morning. Lord Gowrie roused himself at once. "We must not be found like this," he said; "we must not show how we have spent the night. It is over, thank God! and oh, my boy, forgive me! I am thankful there are two of us to bear it; it makes the burden lighter—though I ask your pardon humbly for saying so. I would have saved you if I could, Lindores."

"I don't wish to have been saved; but I will not bear it. I will end it," the young man said, with an oath out of which his emotion took all profanity. His father said, "Hush, hush." With a look of terror and pain, he left him; and yet there was a thrill of tender pride in his mind. How brave the boy was! even after he had been there. Could it be that this would all come to nothing, as every other attempt to resist had done before?

"I suppose you know all about it now, Lindores," said his friend Ffarrington, after breakfast; "luckily for us who are going over the house. What a glorious old place it is!"

"I don't think that Lindores enjoys the glorious old place today," said another of the guests under his breath. "How pale he is! He doesn't look as if he had slept."

"I will take you over every nook where I have ever been," said Lindores. He looked at his father with almost command in his eyes. "Come with me, all of you. We shall have no more secrets here."

"Are you mad?" said his father in his ear.

"Never mind," cried the young man. "Oh, trust me; I will do it with judgment. Is everybody ready?" There was an excitement about him that half frightened, half roused the party. They all rose, eager, yet doubtful. His mother came to him and took his arm.

"Lindores! you will do nothing to vex your father; don't make him unhappy. I don't know your secrets, you two; but look, he has enough to bear."

"I want you to know our secrets, mother. Why should we have secrets from you?"

"Why, indeed?" she said, with tears in her eyes. "But, Lindores, my dearest boy, don't make it worse for *him*."

"I give you my word, I will be wary," he said; and she left him to go to his father, who followed the party, with an anxious look upon his face.

"Are you coming, too?" he asked.

"I? No; I will not go: but trust him—trust the boy, John."

"He can do nothing; he will not be able to do anything," he said.

And thus the guests set out on their round—the son in advance, excited and tremulous, the father anxious and watchful behind. They began in the usual way, with the old state-rooms and picture-gallery; and in a short time the party had half forgotten that there was anything unusual in the inspection. When, however, they were half-way down the gallery, Lindores stopped short with an air of wonder. "You have had it put back then?" he said. He was standing in front of the vacant space where Earl Robert's portrait ought to have been. "What is it?" they all cried, crowding upon him, ready for any marvel. But as there was nothing to be seen, the strangers smiled among themselves. "Yes, to be sure, there is nothing so suggestive as a vacant place," said a lady who was of the party. "Whose portrait ought to be there, Lord Lindores?"

He looked at his father, who made a slight assenting gesture, then shook his head drearily.

"Who put it there?" Lindores said, in a whisper.

"It is not there; but you and I see it," said Lord Gowrie, with a sigh.

Then the strangers perceived that something had moved the father and the son, and, notwithstanding their eager curiosity, obeyed the dictates of politeness, and dispersed into groups looking at the other pictures. Lindores set his teeth and clenched his hands. Fury was growing upon him—not the awe that filled his father's mind. "We will leave the rest of this to another time," he cried, turning to the others, almost fiercely. "Come, I will show you something more striking now." He made no further pretence of going systematically over the house. He turned and went straight up-stairs, and along the corridor. "Are we going over the bedrooms?" some one said. Lindores led the way straight to the old lumber-room, a strange place for such a gay party. The ladies drew their dresses about them. There was not room for half of them. Those who could get in began to handle the strange things that lay about, touching them with dainty fingers, exclaiming how dusty they were. The window was half blocked up by old armour and rusty weapons; but this did not hinder the full summer daylight from penetrating in a flood of light. Lindores went in with fiery determination on his face. He went straight to the wall, as if he would go through, then paused with a blank gaze. "Where is the door?" he said.

"You are forgetting yourself," said Lord Gowrie, speaking over the heads of the others. "Lindores! you know very well there never was any door there; the wall is very thick; you can see by the depth of the window. There is no door there."

The young man felt it over with his hand. The wall was smooth, and covered with the dust of ages. With a groan he turned away. At this moment a suppressed laugh, low, yet distinct, sounded close by him. "You laughed?" he said, fiercely, to Ffarrington, striking his hand upon his shoulder.

"I—laughed! Nothing was farther from my thoughts," said his friend, who was curiously examining something that lay upon an old carved chair. "Look here! what a wonderful sword, cross-hilted! Is it an Andrea? What's the matter, Lindores?"

Lindores had seized it from his hands; he dashed it against the wall with a suppressed oath. The two or three people in the room stood aghast.

"Lindores!" his father said, in a tone of warning. The young man dropped the useless weapon with a groan. "Then God help us!" he said; "but I will find another way."

"There is a very interesting room close by," said Lord Gowrie, hastily—"this way! Lindores has been put out by—some changes that have been made without his knowledge," he said, calmly. "You must not mind him. He is disappointed. He is perhaps too much accustomed to have his own way."

But Lord Gowrie knew that no one believed him. He took them to the adjoining room, and told them some easy story of an apparition that was supposed to haunt it. "Have you ever seen it?" the guests said, pretending interest. "Not I; but we don't mind ghosts in this house," he answered, with a smile. And then they resumed their round of the old noble mystic house.

I cannot tell the reader what young Lindores has done to carry out his pledged word and redeem his family. It may not be known, perhaps, for another generation, and it will not be for me to write that concluding chapter: but when, in the ripeness of time, it can be narrated, no one will say that the mystery of Gowrie Castle has been a vulgar horror, though there are some who are disposed to think so now.

THE UPPER BERTH,
by F. Marion Crawford

Somebody asked for the cigars. We had talked long, and the conversation was beginning to languish; the tobacco smoke had got into the heavy curtains, the wine had got into those brains which were liable to become heavy, and it was already perfectly evident that, unless somebody did something to rouse our oppressed spirits, the meeting would soon come to its natural conclusion, and we, the guests, would speedily go home to bed, and most certainly to sleep. No one had said anything very remarkable; it may be that no one had anything very remarkable to say. Jones had given us every particular of his last hunting adventure in Yorkshire. Mr. Tompkins, of Boston, had explained at elaborate length those working principles, by the due and careful maintenance of which the Atchison, Topeka, and Santa Fé Railroad not only extended its territory, increased its departmental influence, and transported live stock without starving them to death before the day of actual delivery, but, also, had for years succeeded in deceiving those passengers who bought its tickets into the fallacious belief that the corporation aforesaid was really able to transport human life without destroying it. Signor Tombola had endeavoured to persuade us, by arguments which we took no trouble to oppose, that the unity of his country in no way resembled the average modern torpedo, carefully planned, constructed with all the skill of the greatest European arsenals, but, when constructed, destined to be directed by feeble hands into a region where it must undoubtedly explode, unseen, unfeared, and unheard, into the illimitable wastes of political chaos.

It is unnecessary to go into further details. The conversation had assumed proportions which would have bored Prometheus on his rock, which would have driven Tantalus to distraction, and which would have impelled Ixion to seek relaxation in the simple but instructive dialogues of Herr Ollendorff, rather than submit to the greater evil of listening to our talk. We had sat at table for hours; we were bored, we were tired, and nobody showed signs of moving.

Somebody called for cigars. We all instinctively looked towards the speaker. Brisbane was a man of five-and-thirty years of age, and remarkable for those gifts which chiefly attract the attention of men. He was a strong man. The external proportions of his figure presented nothing extraordinary to the common eye, though his size was above the average. He was a little over six feet in height, and moderately broad in the shoulder; he did not appear to be stout, but, on the other hand, he was certainly not thin; his small head was supported by a strong and sinewy neck; his broad muscular hands appeared to possess a peculiar skill in breaking walnuts without the assistance of the ordinary cracker, and, seeing him in profile, one could not help remarking the extraordinary breadth of his sleeves, and the unusual thickness of his chest. He was one of those men who are commonly spoken of among men as deceptive; that is to say, that though he looked exceedingly strong he was in reality very much stronger than he looked. Of his features I need say little. His head is small, his hair is thin, his eyes are blue, his nose is large, he has a small moustache, and a square jaw. Everybody knows Brisbane, and when he asked for a cigar everybody looked at him.

"It is a very singular thing," said Brisbane.

Everybody stopped talking. Brisbane's voice was not loud, but possessed a peculiar quality of penetrating general conversation, and cutting it like a knife. Everybody listened. Brisbane, perceiving that he had attracted their general attention, lit his cigar with great equanimity.

"It is very singular," he continued, "that thing about ghosts. People are always asking whether anybody has seen a ghost. I have."

"Bosh! What, you? You don't mean to say so, Brisbane? Well, for a man of his intelligence!"

A chorus of exclamations greeted Brisbane's remarkable statement. Everybody called for cigars, and Stubbs the butler suddenly appeared from the depths of nowhere with a fresh bottle of dry champagne. The situation was saved; Brisbane was going to tell a story.

I am an old sailor, said Brisbane, and as I have to cross the Atlantic pretty often, I have my favourites. Most men have their favourites. I have seen a man wait in a Broadway bar for three-quarters of an hour for a particular car which he liked. I believe the bar-keeper made at least one-third of his living by that man's preference. I have a habit of waiting for certain ships when I am obliged to cross that duck-pond. It may be a prejudice, but I was never cheated out of a good passage but once in my life. I remember it very well; it was a warm morning in June, and the Custom House officials, who were hanging about waiting for a steamer already on her way up from the Quarantine, presented a peculiarly hazy and thoughtful appearance. I had not much luggage—I never have. I mingled with the crowd of passengers, porters, and officious individuals in blue coats and brass buttons, who seemed to spring up like mushrooms from the deck of a moored steamer to obtrude their unnecessary services upon the independent passenger. I have often noticed with a certain interest the spontaneous evolution of these fellows. They are not there when you arrive; five minutes after the pilot has called "Go ahead!" they, or at least their blue coats and brass buttons, have disappeared from deck and gangway as completely as though they had been consigned to that locker which tradition unanimously ascribes to Davy Jones. But, at the moment of starting, they are there, clean-shaved, blue-coated, and ravenous for fees. I hastened on board. The *Kamtschatka* was one of my favourite ships. I say was, because she emphatically no longer is. I cannot conceive of any inducement which could entice me to make another voyage in her. Yes, I know what you are going to say. She is uncommonly clean in the run aft, she has enough bluffing off in the bows to keep her dry, and the lower berths are most of them double. She has a lot of advantages, but I won't cross in her again. Excuse the digression. I got on board. I hailed a steward, whose red nose and redder whiskers were equally familiar to me.

"One hundred and five, lower berth," said I, in the businesslike tone peculiar to men who think no more of crossing the Atlantic than taking a whisky cocktail at downtown Delmonico's.

The steward took my portmanteau, great coat, and rug. I shall never forget the expression of his face. Not that he turned pale. It is maintained by the most eminent divines that even miracles cannot change the course of nature. I have no hesitation in saying that he did not turn pale; but, from his expression, I judged that he was either about to shed tears, to sneeze, or to drop my portmanteau. As the latter contained two bottles of particularly fine old sherry presented to me for my voyage by my old friend Snigginson van Pickyns, I felt extremely nervous. But the steward did none of these things.

"Well, I'm damned!" said he in a low voice, and led the way.

I supposed my Hermes, as he led me to the lower regions, had had a little grog, but I said nothing, and followed him. One hundred and five was on the port side, well aft. There was nothing remarkable about the state-room. The lower berth, like most of those upon the *Kamtschatka*, was double. There was plenty of room; there was the usual washing apparatus, calculated to convey an idea of luxury to the mind of a North-American Indian; there were the usual inefficient racks of brown wood, in which it is more easy to hang a large-sized umbrella than the common tooth-brush of commerce. Upon the uninviting mattresses were carefully folded together those blankets which a great modern humorist has aptly compared to cold buckwheat cakes. The question of towels was left entirely to the imagination. The glass decanters were filled with a transparent liquid faintly tinged with brown, but from which an odor less faint, but not more pleasing, ascended to the nostrils, like a far-off sea-sick reminiscence of oily machinery. Sad-coloured curtains half-closed the upper berth. The hazy June daylight shed a faint illumination upon the desolate little scene. Ugh! how I hate that state-room!

The steward deposited my traps and looked at me, as though he wanted to get away—probably in search of more passengers and more fees. It is always a good plan to start in favour with those functionaries, and I accordingly gave him certain coins there and then.

"I'll try and make yer comfortable all I can," he remarked, as he put the coins in his pocket. Nevertheless, there was a doubtful intonation in his voice which surprised me. Possibly his scale of fees had gone up, and he was not satisfied; but on the whole I was inclined to think that, as he himself would have expressed it, he was "the better for a glass." I was wrong, however, and did the man injustice.

II.

Nothing especially worthy of mention occurred during that day. We left the pier punctually, and it was very pleasant to be fairly under way, for the weather was warm and sultry, and the motion of the steamer produced a refreshing breeze. Everybody knows what the first day at sea is like. People pace the decks and stare at each other, and occasionally meet acquaintances whom they did not know to be on board. There is the usual uncertainty as to whether the food will be good, bad, or indifferent, until the first two meals have put the matter beyond a doubt; there is the usual uncertainty about the weather, until the ship is fairly off Fire Island. The tables are crowded at first, and then suddenly thinned. Pale-faced people spring from their seats and precipitate themselves towards the door, and each old sailor breathes more freely as his sea-sick neighbour rushes from his side, leaving him plenty of elbow room and an unlimited command over the mustard.

One passage across the Atlantic is very much like another, and we who cross very often do not make the voyage for the sake of novelty. Whales and icebergs are indeed always objects of interest, but, after all, one whale is very much like another whale, and one rarely sees an iceberg at close quarters. To the majority of us the most delightful moment of the day on board an ocean steamer is when we have taken our last turn on deck, have smoked our last cigar, and having succeeded in tiring ourselves, feel at liberty to turn in with a clear conscience. On that first night of the voyage I felt particularly lazy, and went to bed in one hundred and five rather earlier than I usually do. As I turned in, I was amazed to see that I was to have a companion. A portmanteau, very like my own, lay in the opposite corner, and in the upper berth had been deposited a neatly folded rug with a stick and umbrella. I had hoped to be alone, and I was disappointed; but I wondered who my room-mate was to be, and I determined to have a look at him.

Before I had been long in bed he entered. He was, as far as I could see, a very tall man, very thin, very pale, with sandy hair and whiskers and colourless grey eyes. He had about him, I thought, an air of rather dubious fashion; the sort of man you might see in Wall Street, without being able precisely to say what he was doing there—the sort of man who frequents the Café Anglais, who always seems to be alone and who drinks champagne; you might meet him on a race-course, but he would never appear to be doing anything there either. A little over-dressed—a little odd. There are three or four of his kind on every ocean steamer. I made up my mind that I did not care to make his acquaintance, and I went to sleep saying to myself that I would study his habits in order to avoid him. If he rose early, I would rise late; if he went to bed late, I would go to bed early. I did not care to know him. If you once know people of that kind they are always turning up. Poor fellow! I need not have taken the trouble to come to so many decisions about him, for I never saw him again after that first night in one hundred and five.

I was sleeping soundly when I was suddenly waked by a loud noise. To judge from the sound, my room-mate must have sprung with a single leap from the upper berth to the floor. I heard him fumbling with the latch and bolt of the door, which opened almost immediately, and then I heard his footsteps as he ran at full speed down the passage, leaving the door open behind him. The ship was rolling a little, and I expected to hear him stumble or fall, but he ran as though he were running for his life. The door swung on its hinges with the motion of the vessel, and the sound annoyed me. I got up and shut it, and groped my way back to my berth in the darkness. I went to sleep again; but I have no idea how long I slept.

When I awoke it was still quite dark, but I felt a disagreeable sensation of cold, and it seemed to me that the air was damp. You know the peculiar smell of a cabin which has been wet with sea water. I covered myself up as well as I could and dozed off again, framing complaints to be made the next day, and selecting the most powerful epithets in the language. I could hear my room-mate turn over in the upper berth. He had probably returned while I was asleep. Once I thought I heard him groan, and I argued that he was sea-sick. That is particularly unpleasant when one is below. Nevertheless I dozed off and slept till early daylight.

The ship was rolling heavily, much more than on the previous evening, and the grey light which came in through the porthole changed in tint with every movement according as the angle of the vessel's side turned the glass seawards or skywards. It was very cold—unaccountably so for the month of June. I turned my head and looked at the porthole, and saw to my surprise that it was wide open and hooked back. I believe I swore audibly. Then I got up and shut it. As I turned back I glanced at the upper berth. The curtains were drawn close together; my companion had probably felt cold as well as I. It struck me that I had slept enough. The state-room was uncomfortable, though, strange to say, I could not smell the dampness which had annoyed me in the night. My room-mate was still asleep—excellent opportunity for avoiding him, so I dressed at once and went on deck. The day was warm and cloudy, with an oily smell on the water. It was seven o'clock as I came out—much later than I had imagined. I came across the doctor, who was taking his first sniff of the morning air. He was a young man from the West of Ireland—a tremendous fellow, with black hair and blue eyes, already inclined to be stout; he had a happy-go-lucky, healthy look about him which was rather attractive.

"Fine morning," I remarked, by way of introduction.

"Well," said he, eying me with an air of ready interest, "it's a fine morning and it's not a fine morning. I don't think it's much of a morning."

"Well, no—it is not so very fine," said I.

"It's just what I call fuggly weather," replied the doctor.

"It was very cold last night, I thought," I remarked. "However, when I looked about, I found that the porthole was wide open. I had not noticed it when I went to bed. And the state-room was damp, too."

"Damp!" said he. "Whereabouts are you?"

"One hundred and five—"

To my surprise the doctor started visibly, and stared at me.

"What is the matter?" I asked.

"Oh—nothing," he answered; "only everybody has complained of that state-room for the last three trips."

"I shall complain too," I said. "It has certainly not been properly aired. It is a shame!"

"I don't believe it can be helped," answered the doctor. "I believe there is something—well, it is not my business to frighten passengers."

"You need not be afraid of frightening me," I replied. "I can stand any amount of damp. If I should get a bad cold I will come to you."

I offered the doctor a cigar, which he took and examined very critically.

"It is not so much the damp," he remarked. "However, I dare say you will get on very well. Have you a room-mate?"

"Yes; a deuce of a fellow, who bolts out in the middle of the night and leaves the door open."

Again the doctor glanced curiously at me. Then he lit the cigar and looked grave.

"Did he come back?" he asked presently.

"Yes. I was asleep, but I waked up and heard him moving. Then I felt cold and went to sleep again. This morning I found the porthole open."

"Look here," said the doctor, quietly, "I don't care much for this ship. I don't care a rap for her reputation. I tell you what I will do. I have a good-sized place up here. I will share it with you, though I don't know you from Adam."

I was very much surprised at the proposition. I could not imagine why he should take such a sudden interest in my welfare. However, his manner as he spoke of the ship was peculiar.

"You are very good, doctor," I said. "But really, I believe even now the cabin could be aired, or cleaned out, or something. Why do you not care for the ship?"

"We are not superstitious in our profession, sir," replied the doctor. "But the sea makes people so. I don't want to prejudice you, and I don't want to frighten you, but if you will take my advice you will move in here. I would as soon see you overboard," he added, "as know that you or any other man was to sleep in one hundred and five."

"Good gracious! Why?" I asked.

"Just because on the last three trips the people who have slept there actually have gone overboard," he answered, gravely.

The intelligence was startling and exceedingly unpleasant, I confess. I looked hard at the doctor to see whether he was making game of me, but he looked perfectly serious. I thanked him warmly for his offer, but told him I intended to be the exception to the rule by which every one who slept in that particular state-room went overboard. He did not say much, but looked as grave as ever, and hinted that before we got across I should probably reconsider his proposal. In the course of time we went to breakfast, at which only an inconsiderable number of passengers assembled. I noticed that one or two of the officers who breakfasted with us looked grave. After breakfast I went into my state-room in order to get a book. The curtains of the upper berth were still closely drawn. Not a word was to be heard. My room-mate was probably still asleep.

As I came out I met the steward whose business it was to look after me. He whispered that the captain wanted to see me, and then scuttled away down the passage as if very anxious to avoid any questions. I went toward the captain's cabin, and found him waiting for me.

"Sir," said he, "I want to ask a favour of you."

I answered that I would do anything to oblige him.

"Your room-mate has disappeared," he said. "He is known to have turned in early last night. Did you notice anything extraordinary in his manner?"

The question coming, as it did, in exact confirmation of the fears the doctor had expressed half an hour earlier, staggered me.

"You don't mean to say he has gone overboard?" I asked.

"I fear he has," answered the captain.

"This is the most extraordinary thing—" I began.

"Why?" he asked.

"He is the fourth, then?" I explained. In answer to another question from the captain, I explained, without mentioning the doctor, that I had heard the story concerning one hundred and five. He seemed very much annoyed at hearing that I knew of it. I told him what had occurred in the night.

"What you say," he replied, "coincides almost exactly with what was told me by the room-mates of two of the other three. They bolt out of bed and run down the passage. Two of them were seen to go overboard by the watch; we stopped and lowered boats, but they were not found. Nobody, however, saw or heard the man who was lost last night—if he is really lost. The steward, who is a superstitious fellow, perhaps, and expected something to go wrong, went to look for him this morning, and found his berth empty, but his clothes lying about, just as he had left them. The steward was the only man on board who knew him by sight, and he has been searching everywhere for him. He has disappeared! Now, sir, I want to beg you not to mention the circumstance to any of the passengers; I don't want the ship to get a bad name, and nothing hangs about an ocean-goer like stories of suicides. You shall have your choice of any one of the officers' cabins you like, including my own, for the rest of the passage. Is that a fair bargain?"

"Very," said I; "and I am much obliged to you. But since I am alone, and have the state-room to myself, I would rather not move. If the steward will take out that unfortunate man's things, I would as leave stay where I am. I will not say anything about the matter, and I think I can promise you that I will not follow my room-mate."

The captain tried to dissuade me from my intention, but I preferred having a state-room alone to being the chum of any officer on board. I do not know whether I acted foolishly, but if I had taken his advice I should have had nothing more to tell. There would have remained the disagreeable coincidence of several suicides occurring among men who had slept in the same cabin, but that would have been all.

That was not the end of the matter, however, by any means. I obstinately made up my mind that I would not be disturbed by such tales, and I even went so far as to argue the question with the captain. There was something wrong about the state-room, I said. It was rather damp. The porthole had been left open last night. My room-mate might have been ill when he came on board, and he might have become delirious after he went to bed. He might even now be hiding somewhere on board, and might be found later. The place ought to be aired and the fastening of the port looked to. If the captain would give me leave, I would see that what I thought necessary were done immediately.

"Of course you have a right to stay where you are if you please," he replied, rather petulantly; "but I wish you would turn out and let me lock the place up, and be done with it."

I did not see it in the same light, and left the captain, after promising to be silent concerning the disappearance of my companion. The latter had had no acquaintances on board, and was not missed in the course of the day. Towards evening I met the doctor again, and he asked me whether I had changed my mind. I told him I had not.

"Then you will before long," he said, very gravely.

III.

We played whist in the evening, and I went to bed late. I will confess now that I felt a disagreeable sensation when I entered my state-room. I could not help thinking of the tall man I had seen on the previous night, who was now dead, drowned, tossing about in the long swell, two or three hundred miles astern. His face rose very distinctly before me as I undressed, and I even went so far as to draw back the curtains of the upper berth, as though to persuade myself that he was actually gone. I also bolted the door of the state-room. Suddenly I became aware that the porthole was open, and fastened back. This was more than I could stand. I hastily threw on my dressing-gown and went in search of Robert, the steward of my passage. I was very angry, I remember, and when I found him I dragged him roughly to the door of one hundred and five, and pushed him towards the open porthole.

"What the deuce do you mean, you scoundrel, by leaving that port open every night? Don't you know it is against the regulations? Don't you know that if the ship heeled and the water began to come in, ten men could not shut it? I will report you to the captain, you blackguard, for endangering the ship!"

I was exceedingly wroth. The man trembled and turned pale, and then began to shut the round glass plate with the heavy brass fittings.

"Why don't you answer me?" I said, roughly.

"If you please, sir," faltered Robert, "there's nobody on board as can keep this 'ere port shut at night. You can try it yourself, sir. I ain't a-going to stop hany longer on board o' this vessel, sir; I ain't, indeed. But if I was you, sir, I'd just clear out and go and sleep with the surgeon, or something, I would. Look 'ere, sir, is that fastened what you may call securely, or not, sir? Try it, sir, see if it will move a hinch."

I tried the port, and found it perfectly tight.

"Well, sir," continued Robert, triumphantly, "I wager my reputation as a A1 steward, that in 'arf an hour it will be open again; fastened back, too, sir, that's the horful thing—fastened back!"

I examined the great screw and the looped nut that ran on it.

"If I find it open in the night, Robert, I will give you a sovereign. It is not possible. You may go."

"Soverin' did you say, sir? Very good, sir. Thank ye, sir. Good night, sir. Pleasant reepose, sir, and all manner of hinchantin' dreams, sir."

Robert scuttled away, delighted at being released. Of course, I thought he was trying to account for his negligence by a silly story, intended to frighten me, and I disbelieved him. The consequence was that he got his sovereign, and I spent a very peculiarly unpleasant night.

I went to bed, and five minutes after I had rolled myself up in my blankets the inexorable Robert extinguished the light that burned steadily behind the ground-glass pane near the door. I lay quite still in the dark trying to go to sleep, but I soon found that impossible. It had been some satisfaction to be angry with the steward, and the diversion had banished that unpleasant sensation I had at first experienced when I thought of the drowned man who had been my chum; but I was no longer sleepy, and I lay awake for some time, occasionally glancing at the porthole, which I could just see from where I lay, and which, in the darkness, looked like a faintly-luminous soup-plate suspended in blackness. I believe I must have lain there for an hour, and, as I remember, I was just dozing into sleep when I was roused by a draught of cold air and by distinctly feeling the spray of the sea blown upon my face. I started to my feet, and not having allowed in the dark for the motion of the ship, I was instantly thrown violently across the state-room upon the couch which was placed beneath the porthole. I recovered myself immediately, however, and climbed upon my knees. The porthole was again wide open and fastened back!

Now these things are facts. I was wide awake when I got up, and I should certainly have been waked by the fall had I still been dozing. Moreover, I bruised my elbows and knees badly, and the bruises were there on the following morning to testify to the fact, if I myself had doubted it. The porthole was wide open and fastened back—a thing so unaccountable that I remember very well feeling astonishment rather than fear when I discovered it. I at once closed the plate again and screwed down the loop nut with all my strength. It was very dark in the state-room. I reflected that the port had certainly been opened within an hour after Robert had at first shut it in my presence, and I determined to watch it and see whether it would open again. Those brass fittings are very heavy and by no means easy to move; I could not believe that the clump had been turned by the shaking of the screw. I stood peering out through the thick glass at the alternate white and grey streaks of the sea that foamed beneath the ship's side. I must have remained there a quarter of an hour.

Suddenly, as I stood, I distinctly heard something moving behind me in one of the berths, and a moment afterwards, just as I turned instinctively to look—though I could, of course, see nothing in the darkness—I heard a very faint groan. I sprang across the state-room, and tore the curtains of the upper berth aside, thrusting in my hands to discover if there were any one there. There was some one.

I remember that the sensation as I put my hands forward was as though I were plunging them into the air of a damp cellar, and from behind the curtain came a gust of wind that smelled horribly of stagnant sea-water. I laid hold of something that had the shape of a man's arm, but was smooth, and wet, and icy cold. But suddenly, as I pulled, the creature sprang violently forward against me, a clammy, oozy mass, as it seemed to me, heavy and wet, yet endowed with a sort of supernatural strength. I reeled across the state-room, and in an instant the door opened and the thing rushed out. I had not had time to be frightened, and quickly recovering myself, I sprang through the door and gave chase at the top of my speed, but I was too late. Ten yards before me I could see—I am sure I saw it—a dark shadow moving in the dimly lighted passage, quickly as the shadow of a fast horse thrown before a dog-cart by the lamp on a dark night. But in a moment it had disappeared, and I found myself holding on to the polished rail that ran along the bulkhead where the passage turned towards the companion. My hair stood on end, and the cold perspiration rolled down my face. I am not ashamed of it in the least: I was very badly frightened.

Still I doubted my senses, and pulled myself together. It was absurd, I thought. The Welsh rare-bit I had eaten had disagreed with me. I had been in a nightmare. I made my way back to my state-room, and entered it with an effort. The whole place smelled of stagnant sea-water, as it had when I had waked on the previous evening. It required my utmost strength to go in and grope among my things for a box of wax lights. As I lighted a railway reading lantern which I always carry in case I want to read after the lamps are out, I perceived that the porthole was again open, and a sort of creeping horror began to take possession of me which I never felt before, nor wish to feel again. But I got a light and pro-ceeded to examine the upper berth, expecting to find it drenched with sea-water.

But I was disappointed. The bed had been slept in, and the smell of the sea was strong; but the bedding was as dry as a bone. I fancied that Robert had not had the courage to make the bed after the accident of the previous night—it had all been a hideous dream. I drew the curtains back as far as I could and examined the place very carefully. It was perfectly dry. But the porthole was open again. With a sort of dull bewilderment of horror, I closed it and screwed it down, and thrusting my heavy stick through the brass loop, wrenched it with all my might, till the thick metal began to bend under the pressure. Then I hooked my reading lantern into the red velvet at the head of the couch, and sat down to recover my senses if I could. I sat there all night, unable to think of rest—hardly able to think at all. But the porthole remained closed, and I did not believe it would now open again without the application of a considerable force.

The morning dawned at last, and I dressed myself slowly, thinking over all that had happened in the night. It was a beautiful day and I went on deck, glad to get out in the early, pure sunshine, and to smell the breeze from the blue water, so different from the noisome, stagnant odour from my state-room. Instinctively I turned aft, towards the surgeon's cabin. There he stood, with a pipe in his mouth, taking his morning airing precisely as on the preceding day.

"Good-morning," said he, quietly, but looking at me with evident curiosity.

"Doctor, you were quite right," said I. "There is something wrong about that place."

"I thought you would change your mind," he answered, rather triumphantly. "You have had a bad night, eh? Shall I make you a pick-me-up? I have a capital recipe."

"No, thanks," I cried. "But I would like to tell you what happened."

I then tried to explain as clearly as possible precisely what had occurred, not omitting to state that I had been scared as I had never been scared in my whole life before. I dwelt particularly on the phenomenon of the porthole, which was a fact to which I could testify, even if the rest had been an illusion. I had closed it twice in the night, and the second time I had actually bent the brass in wrenching it with my stick. I believe I insisted a good deal on this point.

"You seem to think I am likely to doubt the story," said the doctor, smiling at the detailed account of the state of the porthole. "I do not doubt it in the least. I renew my invitation to you. Bring your traps here, and take half my cabin."

"Come and take half of mine for one night," I said. "Help me to get at the bottom of this thing."

"You will get to the bottom of something else if you try," answered the doctor.

"What?" I asked.

"The bottom of the sea. I am going to leave the ship. It is not canny."

"Then you will not help me to find out—"

"Not I," said the doctor, quickly. "It is my business to keep my wits about me —not to go fiddling about with ghosts and things."

"Do you really believe it is a ghost?" I inquired, rather contemptuously. But as I spoke I remembered very well the horrible sensation of the supernatural which had got possession of me during the night. The doctor turned sharply on me—

"Have you any reasonable explanation of these things to offer?" he asked. "No; you have not. Well, you say you will find an explanation. I say that you won't, sir, simply because there is not any."

"But, my dear sir," I retorted, "do you, a man of science, mean to tell me that such things cannot be explained?"

"I do," he answered, stoutly. "And, if they could, I would not be concerned in the explanation."

I did not care to spend another night alone in the state-room, and yet I was obstinately determined to get at the root of the disturbances. I do not believe there are many men who would have slept there alone, after passing two such nights. But I made up my mind to try it, if I could not get any one to share a watch with me. The doctor was evidently not inclined for such an experiment. He said he was a surgeon, and that in case any accident occurred on board he must always be in readiness. He could not afford to have his nerves unsettled. Perhaps he was quite right, but I am inclined to think that his precaution was prompted by his inclination. On inquiry, he informed me that there was no one on board who would be likely to join me in my investigations, and after a little more conversation I left him. A little later I met the captain, and told him my story. I said that if no one would spend the night with me I would ask leave to have the light burning all night, and would try it alone.

"Look here," said he, "I will tell you what I will do. I will share your watch myself, and we will see what happens. It is my belief that we can find out between us. There may be some fellow skulking on board, who steals a passage by frightening the passengers. It is just possible that there may be something queer in the carpentering of that berth."

I suggested taking the ship's carpenter below and examining the place; but I was overjoyed at the captain's offer to spend the night with me. He accordingly sent for the workman and ordered him to do anything I required. We went below at once. I had all the bedding cleared out of the upper berth, and we examined the place thoroughly to see if there was a board loose anywhere, or a panel which could be opened or pushed aside. We tried the planks everywhere, tapped the flooring, unscrewed the fittings of the lower berth and took it to pieces—in short, there was not a square inch of the state-room which was not searched and tested. Everything was in perfect order, and we put everything back in its place. As we were finishing our work, Robert came to the door and looked in.

"Well, sir—find anything, sir?" he asked with a ghastly grin.

"You were right about the porthole, Robert," I said, and I gave him the promised sovereign. The carpenter did his work silently and skilfully, following my directions. When he had done he spoke.

"I'm a plain man, sir," he said. "But it's my belief you had better just turn out your things and let me run half a dozen four inch screws through the door of this cabin. There's no good never came o' this cabin yet, sir, and that's all about it. There's been four lives lost out o' here to my own remembrance, and that in four trips. Better give it up, sir—better give it up!"

"I will try it for one night more," I said.

"Better give it up, sir—better give it up! It's a precious bad job," repeated the workman, putting his tools in his bag and leaving the cabin.

But my spirits had risen considerably at the prospect of having the captain's company, and I made up my mind not to be prevented from going to the end of the strange business. I abstained from Welsh rare-bits and grog that evening, and did not even join in the customary game of whist. I wanted to be quite sure of my nerves, and my vanity made me anxious to make a good figure in the captain's eyes.

IV.

The captain was one of those splendidly tough and cheerful specimens of seafaring humanity whose combined courage, hardihood, and calmness in difficulty leads them naturally into high positions of trust. He was not the man to be led away by an idle tale, and the mere fact that he was willing to join me in the investigation was proof that he thought there was something seriously wrong, which could not be accounted for on ordinary theories, nor laughed down as a common superstition. To some extent, too, his reputation was at stake, as well as the reputation of the ship. It is no light thing to lose passengers overboard, and he knew it.

About ten o'clock that evening, as I was smoking a last cigar, he came up to me and drew me aside from the beat of the other passengers who were patrolling the deck in the warm darkness.

"This is a serious matter, Mr. Brisbane," he said. "We must make up our minds either way—to be disappointed or to have a pretty rough time of it. You see, I cannot afford to laugh at the affair, and I will ask you to sign your name to a statement of whatever occurs. If nothing happens to-night we will try it again to-morrow and next day. Are you ready?"

So we went below, and entered the state-room. As we went in I could see Robert the steward, who stood a little further down the passage, watching us, with his usual grin, as though certain that something dreadful was about to happen. The captain closed the door behind us and bolted it.

"Supposing we put your portmanteau before the door," he suggested. "One of us can sit on it. Nothing can get out then. Is the port screwed down?"

I found it as I had left it in the morning. Indeed, without using a lever, as I had done, no one could have opened it. I drew back the curtains of the upper berth so that I could see well into it. By the captain's advice I lighted my reading-lantern, and placed it so that it shone upon the white sheets above. He insisted upon sitting on the portmanteau, declaring that he wished to be able to swear that he had sat before the door.

Then he requested me to search the state-room thoroughly, an operation very soon accomplished, as it consisted merely in looking beneath the lower berth and under the couch below the porthole. The spaces were quite empty.

"It is impossible for any human being to get in," I said, "or for any human being to open the port."

"Very good," said the captain, calmly. "If we see anything now, it must be either imagination or something supernatural."

I sat down on the edge of the lower berth.

"The first time it happened," said the captain, crossing his legs and leaning back against the door, "was in March. The passenger who slept here, in the upper berth, turned out to have been a lunatic—at all events, he was known to have been a little touched, and he had taken his passage without the knowledge of his friends. He rushed out in the middle of the night, and threw himself overboard, before the officer who had the watch could stop him. We stopped and lowered a boat; it was a quiet night, just before that heavy weather came on; but we could not find him. Of course his suicide was afterwards accounted for on the ground of his insanity."

"I suppose that often happens?" I remarked, rather absently.

"Not often—no," said the captain; "never before in my experience, though I have heard of it happening on board of other ships. Well, as I was saying, that occurred in March. On the very next trip—What are you looking at?" he asked, stopping suddenly in his narration.

I believe I gave no answer. My eyes were riveted upon the porthole. It seemed to me that the brass loop-nut was beginning to turn very slowly upon the screw—so slowly, however, that I was not sure it moved at all. I watched it intently, fixing its position in my mind, and trying to ascertain whether it changed. Seeing where I was looking, the captain looked too.

"It moves!" he exclaimed, in a tone of conviction. "No, it does not," he added, after a minute.

"If it were the jarring of the screw," said I, "it would have opened during the day; but I found it this evening jammed tight as I left it this morning."

I rose and tried the nut. It was certainly loosened, for by an effort I could move it with my hands.

"The queer thing," said the captain, "is that the second man who was lost is supposed to have got through that very port. We had a terrible time over it. It was in the middle of the night, and the weather was very heavy; there was an alarm that one of the ports was open and the sea running in. I came below and found everything flooded, the water pouring in every time she rolled, and the whole port swinging from the top bolts—not the porthole in the middle. Well, we managed to shut it, but the water did some damage. Ever since that the place smells of sea-water from time to time. We supposed the passenger had thrown himself out, though the Lord only knows how he did it. The steward kept telling me that he could not keep anything shut here. Upon my word—I can smell it now, cannot you?" he inquired, sniffing the air suspiciously.

"Yes—distinctly," I said, and I shuddered as that same odour of stagnant sea-water grew stronger in the cabin. "Now, to smell like this, the place must be damp," I continued, "and yet when I examined it with the carpenter this morning everything was perfectly dry. It is most extraordinary—hallo!"

My reading-lantern, which had been placed in the upper berth, was suddenly extinguished. There was still a good deal of light from the pane of ground glass near the door, behind which loomed the regulation lamp. The ship rolled heavily, and the curtain of the upper berth swung far out into the state-room and back again. I rose quickly from my seat on the edge of the bed, and the captain at the same moment started to his feet with a loud cry of surprise. I had turned with the intention of taking down the lantern to examine it, when I heard his exclamation, and immediately afterwards his call for help. I sprang towards him. He was wrestling with all his might, with the brass loop of the port. It seemed to turn against his hands in spite of all his efforts. I caught up my cane, a heavy oak stick I always used to carry, and thrust it through the ring and bore on it with all my strength. But the strong wood snapped suddenly, and I fell upon the couch. When I rose again the port was wide open, and the captain was standing with his back against the door, pale to the lips.

"There is something in that berth!" he cried, in a strange voice, his eyes almost starting from his head. "Hold the door, while I look—it shall not escape us, whatever it is!"

But instead of taking his place, I sprang upon the lower bed, and seized something which lay in the upper berth.

It was something ghostly, horrible beyond words, and it moved in my grip. It was like the body of a man long drowned, and yet it moved, and had the strength of ten men living; but I gripped it with all my might—the slippery, oozy, horrible thing. The dead white eyes seemed to stare at me out of the dusk; the putrid odour of rank sea-water was about it, and its shiny hair hung in foul wet curls over its dead face. I wrestled with the dead thing; it thrust itself upon me and forced me back and nearly broke my arms; it wound its corpse's arms about my neck, the living death, and overpowered me, so that I, at last, cried aloud and fell, and left my hold.

As I fell the thing sprang across me, and seemed to throw itself upon the captain. When I last saw him on his feet his face was white and his lips set. It seemed to me that he struck a violent blow at the dead being, and then he, too, fell forward upon his face, with an inarticulate cry of horror.

The thing paused an instant, seeming to hover over his prostrate body, and I could have screamed again for very fright, but I had no voice left. The thing vanished suddenly, and it seemed to my disturbed senses that it made its exit through the open port, though how that was possible, considering the smallness of the aperture, is more than any one can tell. I lay a long time upon the floor, and the captain lay beside me. At last I partially recovered my senses and moved, and I instantly knew that my arm was broken—the small bone of the left forearm near the wrist.

I got upon my feet somehow, and with my remaining hand I tried to raise the captain. He groaned and moved, and at last came to himself. He was not hurt, but he seemed badly stunned.

* * * *

Well, do you want to hear any more? There is nothing more. That is the end of my story. The carpenter carried out his scheme of running half a dozen four-inch screws through the door of one hundred and five; and if ever you take a passage in the *Kamtschatka*, you may ask for a berth in that state-room. You will be told that it is engaged—yes—it is engaged by that dead thing.

I finished the trip in the surgeon's cabin. He doctored my broken arm, and advised me not to "fiddle about with ghosts and things" any more. The captain was very silent, and never sailed again in that ship, though it is still running. And I will not sail in her either. It was a very disagreeable experience, and I was very badly frightened, which is a thing I do not like. That is all. That is how I saw a ghost—if it was a ghost. It was dead, anyhow.

MR. GRAY'S STRANGE STORY,
by Louisa Murray

What may this mean....
So terribly to shake our dispositions
With thoughts beyond the reaches of our souls.
> —*Hamlet*, Act 1, Scene IV.

*

I am a minister of the Presbyterian Church of Canada, fifty years old, in sound health of body and mind. I have never had any belief in spiritualism, clairvoyance or any similar psychical delusions. My favourite studies at college were logic and mathematics, and no one who knew me could suspect me of belonging to that class of enthusiasts in which ghosts and other preternatural manifestations have their origin. Yet I have had one strange experience in my life which apparently contradicts all my theories of the universe and its laws, nor have I ever been able to explain it on any rational hypothesis. That there is some reasonable explanation I believe, and as there is no one living now, except myself, whom the facts concern, I have determined to give them to the world for the benefit of those who are interested in abnormal phenomena.

Twenty-five years ago I was minister of a newly built church, in a village on the shore of Lake Erie. The village had sprung up round the saw mills of Mason and Company, lately erected to turn the giant pines that grew on the sandy borders of the lake into lumber. When the pines were all worked up, the great saw mills and lumber yards sought another locality, and the village which had never had any individuality of its own dropped out of existence.

There was no manse, and I boarded in the house of the chief member of my congregation, Mr. Michael Forrest, who owned a fine farm of four hundred acres dose to the village.

The Red House Farm, as it was called from the colour of the paint Michael Forrest liberally bestowed on his buildings and fences, was in those days a pleasant place. There peace and plenty reigned, and everything within and without testified to good management, order and comfort.

My story opens in the parlour of the Red House, where, in the early afternoon of a splendid Indian summer day, a young man was writing at a desk placed under an open window that looked into a spacious verandah enclosed by cedar posts round which climbing plants were twined in picturesque profusion. This "best room" was never used by the family except on Sundays and festal occasions, and at other times was given up to the minister, the Rev. Gilbert Gray, who writes this narrative.

The hurry and bustle of dinner were over, the dinner things cleared away and the kitchen and dining-room made tidy. Mrs. Forrest was sitting in her rocking chair by the sunny kitchen window, and, her knitting in her lap, was taking her afternoon nap, her cat curled up at her feet. All was quiet in the house till light steps came tripping down stairs, and two pretty girls entered the verandah, sitting down on the high-backed bench of rustic work, each holding some bit of light needle-work in her hands. One was the only child of Farmer Forrest and his wife; the other a niece, brought up by Mrs. Forrest from infancy, and filling the place of a second daughter.

I have said they were two pretty girls, but Marjory Forrest was beautiful. She was a tall, graceful blonde, fair and pale, with rose-red lips, violet eyes, and hair the very colour of sun-light. She looked like the heroine of some happy love poem—happy, I say, for there was no hint of tragedy in her pure, serene face. Celia Morris had a Hebe-like face and form, with bright chestnut hair, merry brown eyes and a laughing mouth, showing two rows of pearly teeth. She was just eighteen; two years younger than Marjory.

They made a charming picture in their pretty print dresses, fresh and spotless, their bright heads bending over their work, and catching the changing lights and shades coming in through the autumn-tinted leaves. But the picture darkened and dissolved as a handsome young man stood in the open arch of the doorway. The girls smiled a welcome, and, taking off his hat, he stepped in and threw himself down on a pile of mats made of the husks of Indian corn. He was the son of the head of the great lumber firm of Mason and Company. His father was a hard-working, self-made man, but he prided himself on bringing up his son to be a gentleman. Not an idle gentleman, however, and he had lately sent the young man to the mills to gain some practical knowledge of business before admitting him to a junior partnership. As there had been many satisfactory dealings between Mr. Mason and Farmer Forrest, Leonard Mason was made welcome at the Red House, and speedily established himself on a friendly footing. His frank, un-affected manner, and freedom from what Mrs. Forrest called "city airs," pleased the farmer and his wife; his knowledge of music and light literature charmed Marjory and Celia. The young people were on the most familiar and friendly terms, but Leonard's attentions were so equally divided between them that if he had a preference only a very close observer could have discerned it.

To-day he did not respond as readily as usual to Celia's lively chatter, and he soon got up from his seat on the mats, and, placing himself against one of the posts, from which point of vantage he could better see Marjory's face, said, "I am going to Hamilton."

Marjory looked up with a startled glance. Celia laughed a quick little laugh as she asked, "not this very minute, are you?"

"I am going to-morrow; my father wants me."

"Well, I suppose you mean to come back again," said Celia lightly.

"Yes, but not for a week. Shall you miss me very much while I am away?"

"Why, of course; there won't be any one to sing 'Come into the garden, Maud.' Will there Marjory?"

"No, indeed," said Marjory.

"I wonder which of you will miss me most. If I knew, I would ask her to give me a lock of her hair to wear round my wrist as a keepsake."

Celia's eyes were fixed on Leonard with an eager questioning expression, but he was looking at Marjory, who kept her eyes steadily on her work, though a faint blush was stealing over her face.

"I'll tell you what we must do," said Leonard. "I'll get two long and two short lots, and you must both draw. Whoever draws two long lots loses a lock of her hair to 'I know'me.

"I know you won't refuse me," he continued pleadingly, "because there may be an accident to the train I am going on, and I may be killed, and then you'd be sorry for having been so unkind."

"What nonsense," cried Celia.

"Not at all," said Leonard, "wise men of old believed in the judgment of lots." And breaking off a slender vine-tendril he divided it into two long and two short lots, arranging them with some mysterious manipulations between his fingers. Then, kneeling on one knee, he held them to Marjory.

Slowly, with tremulous fingers and blushing cheeks, Marjory drew a long lot. Leonard seemed going to say something, but checking himself held out the lots to Celia. Celia did not blush; she grew deathly pale as she drew out her lot. It was a short one.

"I see you don't intend to lose, Miss Celia," said Leonard.

I think I hear now the wild, hysterical laugh with which she answered him. Then, I did not heed it.

"If you draw a short one this time," said Leonard, as he again held the lots to Marjory, "we shall have to try again," but as he spoke the second long lot was in her hand.

"Oh, kind fortune!" cried Leonard.

He tried to make Marjory look at him, but she would not meet his eyes. Still, those subtle signs that lovers learn to read the flickering flame on her cheek, the quivering of her lips and eyelids, who can say what—gave him courage. Snatching up her scissors, he held them over her head. "May I?" he asked beseechingly. With shy, timid grace she bent her fair head still lower; he felt the mute consent, and the next moment one long braid was severed from the rest and lying in his hand.

"Fasten it round my wrist with a true lover's knot," he whispered, softly touching her fingers with the braid. She took it at once, and as he pushed up his sleeve she wound it round his wrist, Leonard helping her to tie the mystic knot. Holding her hand, which did not try to escape, he drew her gently towards him and kissed the virgin lips that confidingly met his.

At that moment a shadow, as if from the wild flight of a bird, passed before the window at which I sat, and swift as an arrow from a bow Celia darted out of the verandah. Till then I had seen and heard all that passed in a sort of stupor, like that which sometimes takes possession of one who listens to his death sentence, though every word is indelibly written on the tablets of his memory. Unwittingly I had been playing the part of an eavesdropper. Now consciousness returned, and, like a man coming out of a trance, I got up and left the room and the house.

* * * *

I had walked fast and far before I returned to the Red House, and the moon, a brilliant hunter's moon, was flooding earth and heaven with light as I came in sight of the verandah. The inmates seemed all standing outside, among them a tall, finely-made young man, whom I at once recognized as Archie Jonson, farmer Forrest's nephew, generally supposed to be the heir to the Red House

Farm. A marriage between him and Celia had been planned by the farmer and his wife while the cousins were children. Archie had always been devoted to Celia, and she had been fond of him till he tried to win her for his wife. Then, either from coyness or coquetry, she became cold and unresponsive. His entreaties for an immediate marriage were indignantly refused, and the utmost concession she would make was that after she was one and twenty she might think about it. A quarrel ensued, and, deeply wounded, Archie left his home. He was passionately fond of the water, and being known as a brave and skilful sailor he found no difficulty in obtaining the place of mate on one of the best schooners on the lakes.

I was surprised at seeing him, as he was not expected home until after the close of navigation, but still more astonished when he came to meet me before I reached the house.

"Where's Celia?" he called out as he came near.

"Celia?" I exclaimed, with a sudden feeling of alarm, "Isn't she at home?"

"No; Marjory thought she went with you to the village."

"She hasn't been with me. I haven't seen her."

"My God!" he burst out passionately; "where can she be?"

"Perhaps she's hiding from you, for fun," I said.

"No; they had missed her before I got here."

The farmer was calling us to come on, and, as soon as we were near enough, he told us that shortly after dinner he had seen Celia running down the road to the bush. "But you see," he said, "I was so taken aback by Leonard coming to ask me for Marjory, that I forgot I had seen her till this minute."

"She must have gone to get maple leaves for her Christmas wreath," said Marjory.

"But what keeps her so late?" said Mrs. Forrest.

"Why, you needn't be scared about her," said the farmer; "there's nothing to harm her. There hasn't been a bear or a wolf, or even a rattlesnake, seen in these woods for forty years; nor no such vermin as tramps, neither."

"There's that swamp," rejoined his wife; "she's always hunting for some sort of weeds in it, and I often think she'll fall in and get drowned."

"She couldn't be drowned if she didn't walk into the middle of it on purpose," said the farmer. "But where's Archie going?"

"To bring home Celia," Archie called back, as he walked off at a pace that soon took him out of sight.

"I'm sure I'm glad he's gone after her," said Mrs. Forrest. "She might have hurt her foot on a stub or a stone, and not be able to walk."

I suggested that Leonard and I had better follow Archie, and Leonard said he was going to make the same proposal.

"Archie won't want you," said the farmer. "If Celia has hurt herself, he can carry her home as easy as a baby; and like the job, too, I guess."

"Oh, let them go, father!" said Marjory. "You see how anxious mother is, and so am I."

"All right, let them go if they like," said the farmer; adding in an irritable tone, that showed he was himself getting uneasy, "women are always making a fuss about nothing."

The moon was at the full, and the sky without a cloud. Every cluster of golden rod and purple aster along the fences, every stick and stone on the road were as dearly seen as at noonday. Leonard and I hurried on filled with an unspoken dread. The road was at first in a straight line, but on coming to a piece of marshy land it turned away to the bush; a path from this turning led to the swamp, a few yards distant.

These swamps are often places of surpassing beauty. There every species of wild fowl make their nests and rear their young broods, and the brilliant flowers and luxuriant leaves of all kinds of water plants form lovely aquatic gardens, richly coloured with ever-varying tints from April to December, and always the delight of an artist's eye. Round the edges of the swamp the water is usually shallow enough for the hunters to wade through in pursuit of their game, but in the centre it is often dangerously deep, and only to be crossed in a skiff or canoe.

Where the road divided, Leonard would have kept a straight course to the bush, but a terrible fear dragged me in the other direction. "No; come this way!" I cried, and he turned and followed me in silence. Faster and faster we hurried on till we reached the swamp. There a heart-rending sight met our eyes. Archie Jonson was struggling through the beds of water-lilies, reeds and rushes that obstructed his way, clasping Celia in his arms. Her long hair fell down dank and dripping, her arms hung stiff and lifeless, her face gleamed ghastly white under the strong moonlight. She was dead! "Drowned! drowned!"

As he ran towards him, Archie laid her on a grassy mound. Her limbs were not distorted and her face was composed, except that her eyes were wide open as if in startled surprise. "You are a doctor as well as a minister," Archie said to me, hoarsely; "see if there is any life left."

There was none. She had been dead for hours. As I said so, Archie sprung up from his kneeling attitude beside Celia, and turned to Leonard with a deadly rage and hatred in his eyes.

"This is your doing," he said.

"Mine!" exclaimed Leonard. "Are you mad?"

"I am not mad. There is Celia, the girl I loved better than my life, lying dead before my eyes, and you are her murderer!"

"Good Heavens!" cried Leonard, "What do you mean?"

"The shock has been too much for him," I said. "Archie, my poor fellow, you don't know what you are saying."

"I know very well what I am saying. he—that man there—fooled Celia, poor little innocent child, with his fine flattering manners till she thought he was making love to her, and when she found out he had only been play-acting with her, she couldn't bear it. It made her crazy, and she came down to the swamp and drowned herself. Oh, my God, she drowned herself. But it was he made her do it."

"I never made love to Celia in my life," said Leonard. "I loved Marjory from the first hour I saw her."

"Oh, I dare say. You were only playing with Celia, but she thought you were in earnest. Listen to me, minister," he continued, controlling his passion with wonderful self-command; "I had a warning, but I was a blind idiot and did not take it. Three nights ago, I dreamed that I saw Celia standing on a bank sloping down to a big piece of water, and a man was standing beside her, and while I was looking on in a stupid kind of wonder, I saw she was slipping down towards the water and not able to stop herself, and she held out her hand to the man and cried to him to help her, but he turned right round and went up the bank. Then I woke,

288

and the dream seemed so real it made me feel queer; but I never had any belief in dreams, and when I got up and went out into the daylight, I laughed at myself for being frightened at a night-mare and thought no more about it. But the next night the dream came again; and this time I saw Celia throw herself into the water; and the man stood on the bank and looked on. Then I knew the dream was sent to warn me of some danger to Celia, though I couldn't tell what it meant, and I came home as quick as I could. And the first person I saw was the man I had seen in my dream—the man I am looking at now, and I heard he was going to marry Marjory; and Celia could not be found. Then when aunt Forrest mentioned the swamp, the meaning of the dream came to me like a flash, and I made for the swamp, but I had come too late—too late to save her, but not too late to revenge her wrongs."

I attempted to reason with him as well as I could, and tried to show him how wicked and absurd it was to let a dream—a nightmare, as he had himself called it —put such wild fancies into his head.

"And you cannot know that she drowned herself; it may have been an accident," I said.

"It was no accident; she drowned herself in her madness. When I got to the swamp I saw a bit of ribbon hanging on the reeds, and I went on till I came to the deep water; there I found her. She had not sunk very far down because her skirt had caught on a stake that stood up there, and I got her out easily enough. But she was dead; and you, Leonard Mason, will have to answer to me for her death."

"I tell you I am innocent of her death as you are!"

"Can you swear it?" cried Archie. "Can you swear it while she lies there before your eyes?"

"I can, I never had any love for Celia, and I never tried to make her think I had. I swear it before the God that hears me!"

As Leonard uttered this oath, Archie kept his eyes fixed on him with piercing intensity; but Leonard met the searching gaze without flinching.

"If you have sworn to a lie," Archie said, "your sin will find you out, and you will have to answer to me for what you have done when you least expect it."

Then he wheeled round, and going to his dead sweet-heart, took her in his arms. "Go before me, minister," he said—"go before me, and tell them *what* is coming."

He would not allow me to help him, so Leonard and I walked on before, and Archie followed with his piteous burden. He was a tall powerful young man, besides being under such a strong excitement as gives threefold strength to every nerve, and he carried poor Celia's death-weight, as if she had been a living child.

But I can write no more of that night of grief and anguish. When the dismal morning came, Archie had gone.

* * * *

Three days after her death Celia was laid in the village graveyard; a peaceful spot away from all noise or traffic, on the side of a gentle hill within site of the Red House. No one but Archie Jonson, Leonard Mason and myself ever suspected the manner of her death. It was naturally supposed that while gathering flowers in the swamp she had fallen into some hidden pool from which the water plants that covered it would prevent her escape.

Archie was not at her funeral, nor had he returned to the farm, but, two days after she was buried, he wrote to Mrs. Forrest telling her that he had rejoined his vessel, the *White Bird*, which was going up Lake Superior with a cargo, the last trip she intended to make that season. The letter made no mention of Celia and was very brief, but it was calmly and coherently written, and the Forrests hoped he intended to come home when the schooner was laid up. But this gleam of light was soon lost in deeper darkness. In the middle of November a letter from the owners of the *White Bird* came to Michael Forrest, informing him that the vessel with all her crew had been lost on Lake Superior in one of those sudden storms which, after a long period of fine weather in the fall, sometimes break over the lakes. Her figure head, on which her name and that of the firm to which she belonged were carved, had been found floating, and recognized by another vessel, confirming the fears for her fate that had been felt. The bodies of the crew were never found, for the ice-cold depths of Lake Superior never give up their dead.

The winter passed slowly and sadly at the Red House, but with the spring came the promise of new hope and joy. Mr. Mason had built a pretty house for Leonard and his bride near the Mills, of which Leonard was to be chief manager. They were to be married in May, and the month famous for its caprice wore its fairest aspect that year. The sorrows which Marjory had gone through seemed only to have deepened the tender sweetness of her delicate beauty, and purified the happiness that illumined her lovely eyes. Leonard, as handsome and charming as ever, had grown more manly and thoughtful, and, if possible, was more in love with Marjory than ever. The old people gained new life from Marjory's happy prospects, and if I had not known what depths of regret sad remembrance can lie silent and secret in the human heart I might have thought that Celia and Archie were forgotten.

The wedding day came in warm and bright, and as full of opening buds and blossoms as if it had been expressly made for the occasion. The ceremony was to take place in the Red House parlour at six o'clock in the evening. The supper was to follow immediately. The bride and bride-groom were then to be driven to the nearest station to meet the train for Hamilton where they were to stay a few days and then go on to Niagara Falls to spend the remainder of their honeymoon there.

It was a busy day at the Red House. Two or three young girls from the village came to help in the pleasant task of putting all the rooms in festal array, and in preparing the dainties liberally provided for the wedding feast.

As the time for the ceremony drew near, the day's excitement rose higher and higher. The bridesmaids were dressing the bride, Mrs. Forrest and two favourite assistants were setting out the supper table. The farmer had taken most of the guests to see his new peach orchard. Two young men, one a cousin of Leonard's who had come from Hamilton to be the best man, were chatting and laughing through an open window with two pretty girls who were decorating the wedding cake with dainty little flags bearing embroidered mottos placed among loves and doves and other appropriate devices in sugar. Leonard and I were standing in the doorway of the verandah, and the eager bridegroom was looking at his watch.

"It only wants twelve minutes to six," he said, "I hope Marjory is ready."

"Your watch is too fast," I said, laughing. "Mine wants fully a quarter."

As I spoke a boy employed to do "chores" came round the barnyard and said, "There's a man wants to see Mr. Leonard Mason."

"A man—what man?" asked Leonard impatiently.

"Dun know. He says he must see you for a minute."

"Oh, hang it!" said Leonard. "Well, I suppose I can give him a minute," and he stepped out of the verandah. Then, looking back at me, he exclaimed, "I hope the day is not going to change."

It was already changing. Grey clouds coming up from the lake were creeping over the sun. An icy wind followed them, chilling me to the bone, and I heard a distant peal of thunder. Farmer Forrest came hurrying his guests into the verandah. "Is all ready, minister?" he enquired. "Where's Leonard?"

"He went to the yard to speak to a man that wanted to see him," I answered.

"Well, we'd best go into the parlour now, and receive the bride and bridegroom in state," said the farmer leading the way.

As Leonard did not come at once, I went to meet him, wondering at his delay. The clouds were growing darker; there was a sharp gleam of lightning, and the thunder that followed showed it was nearer. The storm was certainly coming up, but it might be only a shower.

I looked all round the horizon, and while I was noting the darkening clouds, two men going up the road to the graveyard came into my view; a gleam of the fading sunlight making them distinctly visible. The one in front was more than commonly tall, and led the way with swift, vigorous strides. He was dressed in what seemed a sailor's rough jacket and trousers, and a sailor's glazed hat with floating ribbons. His companion followed him with curiously unequal steps, as if dragged by some invisible chain. It was easy to recognize in this last Leonard in his new wedding suit; and as I gazed the conviction flashed upon me that the man in front was Archie Jonson. After all, then, Archie had not been drowned when the *White Bird* was lost. But by what strange power had he compelled Leonard to leave his waiting bride and follow him to the graveyard?

Such an extraordinary proceeding was both mysterious and alarming, and might be dangerous for Leonard; and on the impulse of the moment I followed them as fast as I could. I was a rapid walker, but they had a start of some minutes, and I could not overtake them.

When I entered the graveyard the whole sky was wrapped in a black pall except a little space above the plot of ground, bordered with periwinkles, in which Celia's grave lay. The white stone at the head of the grave and the figures of two men beside it stood vividly out under that clear space, while the black cloud came swiftly on as if to swallow them up. The tall man had his hand on the gravestone, his face was turned towards me and I could see every feature. It was Archie Jonson's face, lividly pale; or it might have been the shadow of the thunder cloud that made it appear so. Leonard's back was towards me, and he confronted Archie—if Archie it was—in a fixed and moveless attitude. I saw them distinctly for a moment; the next the black cloud that seemed almost to touch the ground covered them, and all was hidden from eyes. Then a bolt of blue flame with a red light in its centre shot from the cloud, and an awful crash seemed to rend the heavens. A blinding torrent of rain succeeded, but it ceased in a minute or two; the cloud passed on, and the sun, now near its setting, shone clear in the western sky. Anxiously I looked round for Leonard and his mysterious companion. Leonard was lying stretched on Celia's grave; Archie, or his avenging ghost, or whatever had assumed his likeness, had disappeared.

Going up to Leonard, I found him dead; killed by the lightning I supposed, though I saw no sign of its having touched him. As I was still stooping over, half stunned by the shock, his cousin and two or three other young men came round me. They had heard a confused account of our having gone to the graveyard, and while others were looking for us in the barns and out-houses, they had come to see if it could be true. We made a rough litter of pine boughs on which we laid poor Leonard, the young men carrying the bier while I walked before, wondering how it would be possible for me to tell the awful tidings it was my hard fate to bring.

But it was not left to me. Marjory, who had been waiting and watching in an agony of terror at Leonard's absence, had seen the ominous procession coming down the hill, and before anyone could prevent her she was flying madly to meet it. Desperately I tried to stop her, but she broke away from me, saw her lover's dead body lying on the bier, and fell at the feet of the bearers in a death-like swoon; her dainty wedding dress and fair hair wreathed with flowers, lying in the muddy pools the thunder-rain had made.

It was long before she could be brought back to life, and then her mind was gone. She remembered nothing of the past, she had no recognition of the present; she knew no more, not even her mother; she never spoke, and did not seem conscious of anything said to her. She lingered a few days in this state, and then died so quietly that the watchers did not know when she passed away.

The poor old people did not long survive the wreck of all their earthly hopes. The Red House farm was sold, and Michael Forrest's property was divided among relations he had never known.

Leonard Mason's death was, of course, attributed to lightning. The "chore" boy's description of the man with whom Leonard had gone to the grave was so fanciful, and so mixed with improbable incidents, that his tale was not credited by anyone. From some dreamy, incoherent utterances of Mrs. Forrest's, it was afterwards believed that Leonard had gone to the graveyard at Marjory's desire to lay a wreath of flowers on Celia's grave; and when the conjecture was added that the unknown man must have been an express messenger from Hamilton, bringing the wreath that had delayed by some mistake, the mystery was supposed to be explained. As for the strange things connected with this tragedy that had come to my knowledge, I kept them hidden in my breast.

I have never seen or heard anything of Archie Jonson since his inexplicable appearance on that fatal day; and I have been informed that it was absolutely impossible the best sailor that ever lived could have escaped in such a storm as that in which the *White Bird*, with her crew, foundered.

www.ingramcontent.com/pod-product-compliance
Lightning Source LLC
Chambersburg PA
CBHW020602260626
47157CB00003B/829